Praise for the novels of Karen Marie Moning

ICED

"Moning returns to the heady world of her Fever series, and the results are addictive and consistently surprising. . . . The best elements of Moning's sensual, shadowy epic are still here, from the sensual and enigmatic Fae to the super-alpha heroes and the breathless pace of their escalating conflicts. At its heart is a heroine whose development is likely to become the stuff of legends as this unforgettable, haunting series continues to evolve."
—*RT Book Reviews*, four stars

"This is one of my favorite 2012 reads. . . . It's engaging, hilarious, amazing and Dani is going to be one heck of a woman."
—*USA Today*

"A gripping story that combines excellent storytelling with believable characters that are rendered both superhuman and superbly human, with emotional fragility and psychological vulnerability in an unstable world fraught with danger . . . Fast-paced, with nonstop action set in a fascinating urban fantasy world of Dublin under siege, this is a smart, bold and textured success."
—*Kirkus Reviews*

"Moning is a master storyteller. I don't know how she does it, but she begs me to get on my knees and pay worship to the woman who has brought me the best, most labyrinthine stories and characters I've ever had the

privilege to get to know. She weaves brilliantly, unapologetically, and without exception, and she has threaded the needle into me and I've been pulled, over and over, into her tapestry, and I don't think I'm ever getting out. *Iced* is no exception."
—*The Bawdy Book Blog,* five stars

"Moning has taken a beloved series and made it better. . . . [She] has a way of bringing the reader into the story with her imaginative writing style and characters that are colorful and entertaining. . . . Please give *Iced* a try, you will become a Dani fan just like I did."
—*Night Owl Paranormal,* Top Pick

"An exciting opening of a new Fever saga . . . Readers will enjoy that the prime Fever cast plays major roles and the introduction of two new unique dangerous Fae who widen the mythos."
—*Genre Go Round Reviews*

"[Moning] has always managed to give me everything I want in a book. . . . *Iced* will not disappoint."
—*Open Book Society*

"We get edge of your seat action and danger. We get the promise of so much more to come. All in all, this is an excellent start to Dani's trilogy."
—*Scandalicious Book Reviews*

"Of course, I ended up loving this book. Just like I love everything [Moning] writes."
—*Fiction Vixen Book Reviews*

SHADOWFEVER

The #1 *New York Times, Wall Street Journal,* and *Publishers Weekly* bestseller

"Moning has taken her heroine—and her readers—on a turbulent, emotionally devastating and truly unforgettable ride! Enormous kudos!"
—*RT Book Reviews,* Top Pick and Gold Medal

"Epic is the word that first came to my mind after I read the words 'The End' and closed the book on what was an amazing journey. I don't think I've ever read a more satisfying final book in a series. I can't even count how many times I was taken by surprise, shocked, blindsided and thrilled. I was left emotionally spent and completely happy with the many unexpected paths this story took."
—*Fiction Vixen Book Reviews*

"A simple review can never adequately describe *Shadowfever,* words on a page being spectacularly poor substitutes for the strength of feeling and broad emotional spectrum captured between its covers. Ms. Moning is more than a storyteller, her characters far more tangible than fictional beings could ever be thought to be, and she has created a world of infinite complexity that openly challenges us, dares us to experience it and remain only a passive observer, and then yanks us in with a shocking brute strength as it subjects us to the sharpest of pains sparsely interspersed with the warmest of joys. Enter into this final piece of the puzzle with a first-aid kit at the ready, as Ms. Moning is a master at inflicting wounds designed to injure but not kill, and she subjects both her characters and us to numerous events that leave indelible marks on the soft flesh of our hearts.

Despite the pain, we revel in the emotional injuries, honored to be privy to a book capable of having such a remarkable effect."
—*Supernatural Snark*

"*Shadowfever* delivers an outstanding conclusion to a fabulous series."
—*Night Owl Paranormal,* Top Pick

"*Shadowfever* did not end the Fever series world with a whimper. It definitely was a bang. A big, wet and fulfilling bang. Take that however you feel is necessary."
—*Parajunkee's View*

"Ms. Moning, much like Mac, takes her story and runs with it, balls to the wall, 550 pages to its uncompromising and satisfying conclusion."
—*Fresh Fiction*

"*Shadowfever* is an explosion of mystery, action, passion, lust, love and magic. As I read this last book in the series I experienced surprise and wonder, shock and horror, sorrow and grief, hope and joy, and, in the end, satisfaction; I couldn't have hoped for more."
—*Beyond Her Book*

"I cried, I laughed, I screamed, I cursed, I dropped my Kindle due to astonishment, and I'm sure that I repeated that cycle several times throughout the book. I had this perfect way of how things would come together, and none of it happened the way I had it planned in my head. What KMM did was so beyond anything I could have divined, it made the book that much more awesome in my eyes. So, I'm sure as you may have guessed, I give this five stars. I would give it five hundred if I could. It was just that perfect for me."

—*The Romance Reviews*

"This series is exactly what an epic fantasy should be. An adventure. In every way."

—*Penelope's Romance Reviews*

"*Shadowfever* surpassed every expectation I had. For as many theories as I have discussed, I was completely shocked at most of the outcomes. There was not a single aspect I was disappointed in. My favorite part is that Barrons and Mac stay so true to their characters. Barrons doesn't change, or yield to Mac. And I think KMM does an excellent job with keeping him so consistent. He stays broody, and possessive, and mysterious. An excellent end to my favorite series. This book gets an A++++++ from me. Thank you Karen Marie Moning for this extraordinary series."

—*Smexy Books*

"I was in shock at how perfectly Karen was able to write this. She is an absolute genius."

—*Yummy Men and Kickass Chicks*

"This book was everything I expected, wanted, needed, craved . . . and so much more."

—*Candace's Book Blog*

"I can't remember the last time I'd had so much fun watching a story unwind."

—*My Vamp Fiction*

DARKFEVER

"A wonderful dark fantasy . . . give yourself a treat and read outside the box."
—CHARLAINE HARRIS

"Moning's newest foray contains suspense and plenty of setup. It's a compelling world filled with mystery and vivid characters, and this, combined with the hint of sparks between Jericho and Mac, will stoke reader's fervor for *Bloodfever,* the next installment."
—*Publishers Weekly*

"*Darkfever* is masterfully rendered, a dark and sexy fantasy featuring a Buffy of the Fae, with a sly sense of humor and maturity of handling that's a delight to read."
—*BookPage*

"Moning launches a remarkable new series that's exotic and treacherous. . . . Clear off space on your keeper shelf—this sharp series looks to be amazing!"
—*RT Book Reviews*

"A seductive mix of Celtic mythology and dark, sexy danger."
—*Chicago Tribune*

BLOODFEVER

"I loved this book from the first page. . . . More. I want more."

—LINDA HOWARD

"Moning's delectable Mac is breathlessly appealing, and the wild perils she must endure are peppered with endless conundrums. The results are addictively dark, erotic, and even shocking."

—*Publishers Weekly*

"Spiced with a subtle yet delightfully sharp sense of humor, *Bloodfever* is a delectably dark and scary addition to Karen Marie Moning's Fever series."

—*Chicago Tribune*

"Moning brilliantly works the dark sides of man and Fae for all they are worth."

—*Booklist*

FAEFEVER

"Erotic shocks await Mac in Dublin's vast Dark Zone, setting up Feverish . . . expectations for the next installment."
—*Publishers Weekly*

"Ending in what can only be described as a monumental cliffhanger, the newest installment of this supernatural saga will have you panting for the next. Breathtaking!"
—*RT Book Reviews*

"A gift of epic proportions to paranormal romance fans."
—*Penelope's Romance Reviews*

"An exciting read, with wonderfully described fight scenes and sizzling scenes with the Fae princes."
—*Night Owl Romance*

DREAMFEVER

"Freaking fabulous! So utterly wonderful that you really must read this series, if you're not already."
—*Literary Escapism*

"This book is absolutely riveting. By far, the most fascinating book I have read this year."
—*Penelope's Romance Reviews*

"Mac's evolution from typical twenty-something to unrelenting warrior has been shocking, graphic and painful. Moning pulls no punches as she sets Mac on this ghastly path!"
—*RT Book Reviews*

"This series should come with a warning on it. Because it's about as addictive as any illegal drug and will take over your life until the next book is finished!"
—*Book Chick City*

"Brutal, deep and leaving us with heaps and heaps of questions, *Dreamfever* is an undeniably great urban fantasy."
—*Vampire Book Club*

BY KAREN MARIE MONING

FEVER NOVELS
Iced

THE FEVER SERIES
Darkfever
Bloodfever
Faefever
Dreamfever
Shadowfever

GRAPHIC NOVEL
Fever Moon

NOVELLA
Into the Dreaming

THE HIGHLANDER SERIES
Beyond the Highland Mist • *To Tame a Highland Warrior*
The Highlander's Touch • *Kiss of the Highlander*
The Dark Highlander • *The Immortal Highlander*
Spell of the Highlander

ICED

ICED

A Fever Novel

KAREN MARIE MONING

DELL
NEW YORK

2013 Dell Mass Market Edition

Copyright © 2012 by Karen Marie Moning, LLC
Excerpt from *Burned* by Karen Marie Moning copyright © 2014 by Karen Marie Moning, LLC

Published in the United States by Dell, an imprint of Random House, a division of Random House LLC, a Penguin Random House Company, New York.

DELL and the HOUSE colophon are registered trademarks of Random House LLC.

Originally published in hardcover in the United States by Dell, an imprint of Random House, a division of Random House LLC, in 2012.

This book contains an excerpt from the forthcoming book *Burned* by Karen Marie Moning. This excerpt has been set for this edition only and may not reflect the final content of the forthcoming edition.

ISBN 978-0-440-24641-1
eBook ISBN 978-0-440-33980-9

Cover design: Eileen Carey
Cover illustration: © Les and Dave Jacobs/cultura/Corbis (man)

Printed in the United States of America

www.bantamdell.com

9 8 7 6 5 4 3 2 1

Dell mass market edition: March 2014

For the love of it

Part 1

_____

Music is the stuff of the cosmos.
Imagine a world without melody of any
kind. No birds singing. No crickets
chirping. No tectonic plates shifting. It
really is all about the fat lady singing.
If she stops—

—*The Book of Rain*

PROLOGUE

Dublin, you had me at "Hello"

Imagine a world that doesn't know its own rules. No cell phones. No Internet. No stock market. No money. No legal system. A third of the world's population wiped out in a single night and the count rising by millions every day. The human race is an endangered species.

A long time ago the Fae destroyed their world and decided to take ours. History says they moved in on us between 10,000 and 6,000 B.C., but historians get a lot wrong. Jericho Barrons says they've been here since the dawn of time. He should know, because I'm pretty sure he has, too.

For a long time there was a wall between our worlds. With the exception of a few cracks, it was a solid barricade, especially the prison that held the Unseelie.

That barricade is gone now and the prison walls are dust.

All of the Fae are free: the deadly Dark Court and the imperious Light Court, who are every bit as deadly, just prettier. A Fae is a Fae. Never trust one. We're being hunted by voracious monsters that are nearly impossible to kill. Their favorite food? People.

As if that's not bad enough, there are fragments of

Faery reality drifting around that swallow up anything in their path. They're tricky to spot; you can drive right into one, if you're not careful. The night the walls fell, Faery itself was fractured. Some say even the inimical Hall of All Days was changed, and opened new portals onto our world. The drifting is the part that really gets me. You can go to sleep in your own bed and wake up in a completely different reality. If you're lucky, the climate won't kill you instantly and the inhabitants won't eat you. If you're really really lucky, you'll find your way home. Eventually. If you're superlucky, time will pass at a normal rate while you're gone. Nobody's that lucky. Folks vanish all the time. They just disappear and are never seen again.

Then there are the amorphous Shades that lurk in the dark and consume every living thing in their path, right down to the nutrients in the soil. When they're done, all that's left is dirt that an earthworm couldn't live in—not that they leave those either. It's a minefield outside that door. Walk lightly. Your parents' rules don't apply. *Do* be afraid of the dark. And if you're thinking there might be a monster under your bed or in your closet, there probably is. Get up and check.

Welcome to Planet Earth.

This is our world now—one that doesn't know its own rules. And when you've got a world that doesn't know its own rules, everything dark and nasty that was once held in check comes slithering out of the cracks to try to take a shot at whatever it wants. It's a free-for-all. We're back to being cavemen. Might is right. Possession is nine-tenths of the law. The bigger and badder you are, the better your odds of surviving. Get a gun or learn to run. Fast. Preferably both.

Welcome to Dublin, AWC—After the Wall Crash—where we're all fighting for possession of what's left of the planet.

The Fae have no king, no queen, no one in charge. Two psychotic, immortal Unseelie princes battle for dominion over both races. Humans have no government. Even if we did, I doubt we'd listen to them. It's complete chaos.

I'm Dani "Mega" O'Malley.

I'm fourteen.

The year was just officially declared 1 AWC, and the streets of Dublin are my home. It's a war zone out there. No two days are alike.

And there's no place else I'd rather be.

ONE

"Ding-dong! The witch is dead": subtitled Rowena who?

"I say we take Mac's suggestion and pump the room full of concrete," Val says.

I wince. Just hearing her name makes my stomach hurt. Me and Mac used to be two peas in the Mega pod, close as sisters. She'd kill me in a heartbeat now.

Well, she'd try.

I'm faster.

"Exactly how do you expect us to get concrete trucks down into the catacombs beneath the abbey?" Kat demands. "To say nothing of how much it would take to seal that chamber. It's three times the size of Inspector Jayne's training green, with a ceiling as high as any cathedral!"

I shift position, tucking my knees up, careful to be real quiet. My legs are cramped from sitting with them crossed beneath me. I'm in the cafeteria at the abbey, high up on a beam in the ceiling rafters where nobody can see me, munching a Snickers bar and eavesdropping. It's one of my favorite perches for scoping out the details. I'm a good climber, fast and agile. Since I'm still just a kid in most people's opinions, folks rarely let me in on the scoop. No worries there. I became a pro at letting myself in years ago.

"What are you suggesting we do, then, Kat?" Margery says. "Leave the most powerful Unseelie prince ever created frozen in a little ice cube beneath our home? That's crazy!" The cafeteria is full of *sidhe*-seers. Most of them murmur agreement but they're like that. Whoever's talking loudest at the moment is the person they agree with. Sheep. Half the time I'm spying, it's all I can do not to jump down there, waggle my ass and say *Baaaa,* see if any of them catch my drift.

I've been at the abbey most of the night, waiting for people to wake up and wander in for breakfast, impatient for those who've been up all night like me to tell everyone else the news and start discussing it. I don't need as much sleep as other people, but when I do finally crash, I'm as good as dead. It's dangerous to lose consciousness as hard as I do, so I'm always careful about where I sleep—behind a lot of locked doors, with booby traps in place. I know how to take care of myself. I've been on my own since I was eight.

"It's hardly an ice cube," Kat says. "The Unseelie King himself imprisoned Cruce. You saw the bars shoot up from the floor around him."

I've got no family. When my mom was killed, Ro made me move into the abbey with the other *sidhe*-seers—those of us who can see the Fae, and could even before the walls fell. Some of us have unique gifts, too. We used to think of ourselves in terms of us and them, humans and Fae, until we learned that the Unseelie King tampered with us way back, mixing his blood with the bloodlines of six ancient Irish houses. Some say we're tainted, that we have the enemy within. I say anything that makes you stronger, duh, makes you stronger.

"The alarm's not set," Margery counters. "And none of us can figure out how to arm the grid that keeps people from getting in. Worse, we can't even get the door closed. Mac tried for hours."

I don't puke the bite of chocolate and peanuts I'm trying to swallow but it's close. I got to get over my reaction to her name. Every time I hear it, I see the look on her face when she learned the truth about me.

Feck that! I knew what would happen if she found out I killed her sister. Got no business being mopey about it. If you know what's coming and don't do anything to stop it, you got no right to act all surprised and pissy when the crap hits the fan. Rule #1 in the Universe: the crap always hits the fan. It's the nature of crap. It's a fan magnet.

"She said it won't respond to her," Margery says. "She thinks the king did something to it. Barrons and his men tried to muscle it closed, but no luck. It's stuck open."

"Just anyone can wander in," says Colleen. "We found the Meehan twins standing down there this morning, hands around the bars, staring up at him like he was some kind of angel!"

"And what were *you* doing down there this morning?" Kat says to Colleen. Colleen looks away.

Tainted blood or not, I've got no complaints about being a *sidhe*-seer. I got the best gifts of all. None of the other *sidhe*-seers know how to deal with me. I'm superfast, superstrong, have superhearing, supersmell, and wicked sharp eyesight. I don't know if I taste better or not. Since I can't taste with anyone else's tongue, I guess I'll never know. The superfast part is the best. I can whiz through a room without people even seeing me. If they feel the breeze of me passing, they usually blame it on an open window. I open windows everywhere I go. It's my camo. If you walk into a room with a lot of open windows, look sharp at breezes that seem contrary to what's coming in from the outside.

"That's because he *looks* like an angel," Tara says.

"Tara Lynn, don't you go there for even a second,"

Kat says sharply. "Cruce would have destroyed us all if he'd thought he had something to gain by it, and that was *before* he read the Book and absorbed its power. Now, he *is* the *Sinsar Dubh*—the darkest, most twisted magic of the Fae race. Have you forgotten what it did to Barb? Don't you remember how many people the Book massacred when it *didn't* have a body? Now it has one. And it's beneath our abbey. And you think it looks like an angel? That it's pretty? Have you lost your mind?"

I wasn't beneath the catacombs last night so I didn't get to see what happened with my own eyes. I'd been keeping a distance from that person whose name I'm not saying. I heard what happened, though. It's all anyone's talking about.

Dude, V'lane is Cruce!

He isn't even Seelie. He's the worst of all the Unseelie princes.

I can hardly believe it. I had the wickedest crush on him! I thought he was the one who was going to save us all, fighting the good fight, on the human side of the war. Turns out he *was* war—literally, as in the Four Horsemen of the Apocalypse's War, riding alongside his three Unseelie prince brothers: Death, Pestilence, and Famine. Sure enough our myths were right. When they rode our world again everything went straight to hell. Nobody even knew he was alive. Cruce was supposed to have been killed three-quarters of a million years ago. Instead he was masquerading as V'lane all that time, disguising himself with glamour, infiltrating the Seelie court, manipulating events, orchestrating the prime opportunity to take what he wanted—dominion over both races.

Fae have patience like beaches have sand. 'Course, I guess patient is easy to be when you live, like, for-fecking-ever.

I also heard he was one of the four who raped M— that person whose name I'm not thinking—that day at the church when the Lord Master turned the princes loose on her.

And I'd told him I was going to give him my virginity one day! He'd brought me chocolates, been all flirty-flirty!

V'lane is Cruce. *Dude*. Sometimes that's all you can say.

Tara holds Kat's glare defiantly. "That doesn't mean I want to set him free. I'm just saying he's beautiful. Nobody can argue with that. He has wings like an angel."

He *is* beautiful. And we have big, big problems. I went down to the catacombs last night, the instant everyone finally cleared out. I made my way through the underground maze until I found the chamber that once held the *Sinsar Dubh*. And still holds it—just in another skin.

V'lane doesn't look like V'lane anymore. He's sealed in the center of a block of ice, surrounded by a cage of glowing bars. His head is back, his eyes are iridescent fire, he's roaring, and his enormous black-velvet wings are spread wide. Brilliant tattoos snake beneath skin that shimmers like gold dust. And he's naked. If I hadn't seen other penises in movies, I'd be worried about losing my virginity.

"Black wings, Tara," Kat says. "As in black magic, as in 'deadly.' He was dangerous before. He's a thousand times worse now. The King never should have let him read the whole Book. He should have stopped him."

"Mac said the King didn't want to leave the *Sinsar Dubh* split up," says Colleen. "He was worried we wouldn't be able to keep it locked down in two places."

I dig around in a pocket of the backpack I always got over a shoulder—you never know what you might need when, and I'm always on the go—and pull out another Snickers bar. There's that fecking name again. Eating soothes the bruise I'm getting from repeated sucker-punches to my belly.

"We couldn't keep it locked down when it was in only one place," Kat says.

"Because Rowena *let* it out," Val says.

I learned that part of the story earlier this morning, listening to *sidhe*-seers talking in the showers. When the *Sinsar Dubh* took possession of Rowena last night, that person I'm not naming killed her. But not before Ro bragged about how she set the *Sinsar Dubh* free. And still, some folks are talking about having a service for the old bat! I say the Grand Mistress of the *sidhe*-sheep is dead. Hoo-fecking-rah! Break out the cake and party hats!

"It weakened Rowena," Kat says.

Rowena was *born* weak. Power-hungry witch.

"Maybe Cruce will weaken us," Kat says.

I plaster a sigh around a bite of candy bar and swallow it. The new temporary leader of the abbey and interim Grand Mistress of *sidhe*-seers around the world just made a big mistake. I learned a thing or two from that unnamed person when we used to hang together. *Sidhe*-sheep need a firm hand. Not firm like Ro's, which was bullying, belittling, and tyrannical, but firm in a way that doesn't make the herd stampede. Fear and doubt are major stampeders. Kat should have said something like what a good thing it was they were all so much stronger than Rowena. Even a kid can see what's going on in the room down there. The *sidhe*-seers are afraid. Rowena is dead. Dublin is a riot-ravaged mess filled with monsters. One of the good guys turned out to be the bad guy. Their lives changed too quickly in too many ways for them to deal with. They're easy targets to be swayed by the most persuasive, strongest leader, and that means Kat needs to become one, fast.

Before somebody a lot less capable and kind does.

Somebody like Margery, who's even now watching the crowd through narrowed eyes, like she's got a thermometer up its butt, taking its temperature. She's a year older than Kat, and was part of Ro's inner circle when the old witch was alive. She's not going to put up with a changing of the guard that doesn't include her. She'll make trouble every chance she gets. I hope Kat knows how treacherous she can be. Anyone that was ever close to Ro for longer than like—one second—has something seriously scary about her. I know. I was closest to her of all. *Sidhe*-sheep politics. Dude, I hate them. They tangle you up like sticky spiderwebs. I love living on my own!

Still, I miss the abbey every now and then. Especially when I think about them baking cookies and stuff. Hearing voices in the background when you doze is nice. Knowing even if you are misunderstood, you aren't totally alone in the world isn't the worst thing.

Kat's right: the *Sinsar Dubh* we used to have locked up and magicked down beneath our abbey is nothing compared to what we've got under our floorboards now.

The problem is it doesn't look like the *Sinsar Dubh* anymore.

All of the darkest magic and power of the Fae race is no longer trapped between the covers of a book. It's in the body of a Fae prince in all his naked, winged glory. And if you've never seen a Fae prince before, that's one jaw-dropping, eye-popping, mind-scrambling amount of glory.

It's only a matter of time before somebody sets him free.

Kat hasn't even made her way around to the killer-critical fact yet: lots of people know he's down there now, crammed to the gills with every last bit of the deadly magic of the Fae race.

I know people. I've seen all the shapes and sizes they come in. Somebody's going to be stupid enough to believe they can control him. Somebody's going to find a way through that ice.

Jericho Barrons is only one of a lot of different folks that hunted the *Sinsar Dubh* for thousands of years. None of them ever knew where it was. If they had, they'd have descended on our abbey back in the dark ages when a rough-piled, round stone tower was all that concealed the entrance to our underground city. And they would have pulled it, stone from stone, into rubble, until they got what they came for.

Now a whole bunch of humans and Fae know exactly where the most powerful weapon ever created is being stored.

Folks talk.

Soon the whole world is going to know it's here.

I snort, imagining hordes descending on us, rioting, raging, brandishing weapons. Stupid *sidhe*-sheep too busy squabbling about the best way to fight back, to get around to fighting back. I sigh.

Kat glances up.

I stop breathing, hug my knees tight to my chest and stay perfectly still.

After a moment Kat shakes her head and goes back to the conversation.

I sigh again but softer.

She just made her second mistake.

Confronted by something she couldn't explain, she pretended it wasn't there. Dude, ostrich much?

Oh, yeah. Just a matter of time.

I wait a few minutes for things to get heated again, take advantage of the commotion and freeze-frame out.

I love moving the way I do.

I can't imagine life any other way.

Whenever something is bugging me, all I need to do is

zoom around the city, spy on all the slo-mo Joes trudging through, and I instantly feel a million times better.

I've got the coolest gig in the world.

I'm a superhero.

Until recently, I was the only one I knew of.

According to my mom, I didn't make the normal toddler transition from crawling to walking. I went from lolling on my back, counting pudgy toes and cooing happily while she changed my diapers (I've never seen any reason to cry when someone is cleaning poop off you), to what she initially thought was teleporting. One second I was on the living room floor, the next I'd vanished. She was afraid the Fae had taken me—they used to do that to *sidhe*-seers if they discovered them—until she heard me rummaging around in the pantry trying to get a jar of baby food open. It was creamed corn. I remember. I still love creamed corn. Not much fuel-power there though. I burn through the punch of sugar-energy in no time.

I never got to go to school.

You don't want to know how she kept me from leaving the house. There aren't many options with a kid who can move faster than you can blink. And none of them are PC.

I'm not the only superhero in Dublin anymore, which annoys the feckity-feck out of me, but I'm slowly coming around to seeing it might be a good thing.

I was getting complacent. And that turns into sloppy if you're not careful. Bored, too. It's not much fun always being the best and fastest. A little competition keeps you on your toes, makes you try harder, live larger.

I'm all about that: living large.

I want to go out in a blaze of glory while I'm young. I don't want to break piece by piece, lose my mind and die wrinkly and old. Given the current state of our world,

I'm not sure any of us have to worry about that anymore.

Top on my list of dudes to beat are Jericho Barrons and his men. Like me, they're superfast and superstrong. Much as I hate to admit it—they're faster. But I'm working on it.

Barrons can pluck me right out of thin air (dude, why isn't it thick air? The things people say!) while I'm freeze-framing, which is what I call the way I get around. I start at point A, lock down a mental snapshot of everything around me, hit the gas, and in a blink I'm at point B. It's only got a couple of downsides. One, I'm constantly bruised from running into things at top speed because some of the things I lock down on my mental grid aren't stationary, like people and animals and Fae. Two, freeze-framing requires a ton of food for fuel. I have to eat constantly. It's a pain in the butt collecting and carrying that much food. If I don't eat enough, I get limp and wobbly. It's pathetic. I'm a gas tank that's either full or empty. There's no half tank with me. You know those movies where folks wear rounds of ammo on their body? I wear protein bars and Snickers.

At least once a night I whiz over to Chester's, Dublin's underground hot spot for partying and scoring whatever your fantasy is and angling for a shot at immortality, owned and operated by Barrons's go-to dude Ryodan, and I start killing every Fae hanging around outside it. It usually takes all of five seconds for his men to show up, but I can do a lot in five seconds.

Chester's is a safe-zone. Killing Fae is prohibited there, no matter what they do. And they do some sick stuff.

Killing humans, however, isn't prohibited at Chester's. That's a major issue with me, so I keep giving Ryodan grief and I'm not about to stop.

One of these nights I'm going to be faster than him, faster than all of them.

Then I'm going to slay every Fae in Chester's.

Second on my list of competition are the Fae I hunt. Some of them *can* teleport. They call it "sifting." I don't understand the physics of it. I just know it's faster than freeze-framing. Which would worry me more if I didn't have the Sword of Light, one of two weapons that can exterminate their immortal asses, so they leave me alone for the most part. She-who-isn't-getting-named has the other weapon, the Spear.

My stomach hurts again. As I peel open a protein bar, I decide to start thinking of her as "That Person," abbreviated to TP. Then maybe my mind will slide over thoughts of "TP" without hitching and kicking me in the stomach.

Last are the Unseelie princes. There used to be four. Cruce is out of the picture for now. Two are at large, in Dublin, no longer under the Lord Master's rule, which makes them way more dangerous than they used to be. They've begun fighting with each other and are striking out on their own. There's major trouble coming from those two. Not only can they sift, just looking at them makes you weep blood. And if you have sex with them . . . well don't! Enough said. Already cults are forming around them. Sheep are always looking for a new shepherd when the terrain gets rocky.

I don't test myself against the princes. I keep my distance. I sleep with my sword in my hand. I shower with it. I never let anyone else touch it. I love my sword. It's my best friend.

I killed the other Unseelie prince. I'm the only person who ever has. Dani Mega O'Malley slayed an Unseelie prince! Gotta love it. Only problem is, now the two that are left have a wicked hate-on for me. I'm hoping they'll be too busy fighting with each other to come after me.

My life consists mainly of watching my city. Keeping tabs on all that's changing. I love knowing the details, spreading the important news around. I don't know what Dublin would do without me.

I run a newspaper called *The Dani Daily* that I put out three times a week. Sometimes I'll do a special edition if something big comes up. I collect messages at what's left of the General Post Office, from folks who are having problems with tough-to-kill Fae. I like to swoop in and save the day! I take my beat seriously, like Inspector Jayne and the Guardians who patrol the streets at night. Dublin needs me. I'm not about to let her down.

I just published my first book, *Dani Does Dublin: the ABCs of the AWC*. Dancer helps me print and distribute it. The reviews have been great. Only problem is, whenever I learn new stuff, which is like constantly, I have to put out a revised edition. I'm on the fifth already.

Some of the folks I help are real basket cases, afraid of their own shadow. I can tell just by looking at them they won't survive long. It makes me sad but I do all I can.

I decide to pop over to the General Post Office now, see if anybody left notes for me.

I polish off my protein bar in two gulps and pocket the wrapper. Don't know why I can't bring myself to litter, considering the streets are covered with debris from the riot the night Dublin fell, but adding to it feels wrong.

I narrow my eyes, look down the street far as I can see, plot each obstacle on my mental grid until it all snaps into place: abandoned cars with open doors just waiting to slam me if I'm off by an inch, streetlamps ripped from the pavement with chunks of concrete attached at the base and strips of metal sticking out that are going to kill my shins if I'm not careful, tables flung through pub windows blocking the sidewalks. You get the idea.

I take a deep breath and give in, set that *sidhe*-seer place in my head free and slide into a different way of being. Ro used to try to get me to explain it to her, like maybe she could figure out how to do it if she tried hard enough. The best I can come up with is this: it's like picking your whole self up mentally and shoving it sideways, till suddenly you're . . . just something else. I shift Dani-gears, I guess. The rush is megaintense and, well . . . I can't imagine life without it because there's no such thing as life without it.

I do it now, shift hard and fast, and then I'm whole and free and perfect. Wind in my hair! Freeze-framing! Can't even feel my feet, because I got wings on them! I scrunch up my face in concentration and push harder, faster, every nanosecond is going to count if I'm going to beat—

I slam into a wall.

Where the feck did *that* come from?

How could I have missed it on my grid?

My whole face is numb and I can't see. The impact snaps me out of freeze-framing and sends me into a blind stumble. When I finally get my balance, I'm still not able to focus. I hit the wall so hard it temporarily blinded me. My face is going to be black and blue for days, eyes swollen to slits. How embarrassing! I hate walking around with all my mistakes on my face, right there for anybody to see!

I waste precious seconds trying to recover and all I can think is: good thing it was a wall, not an enemy. I'm a sitting duck right now and it's my own fault. I know better than to lead with my head when I'm freeze-framing. You can kill yourself that way. The body can take a much harder impact than the face. You'll drive your nose up into your brain, if you're not careful.

"Sloppy, Mega," I mutter. I still can't see. I wipe my bloody nose on my sleeve and reach out to feel what I hit.

"That's my dick," Ryodan says.

I snatch my hand away. "Gah!" I choke out. I can feel my face again—because, like, it's going up in flames. What kind of universe makes me reach out at exactly that fecking level to feel what I think is a wall and puts my hand on a penis?

Then I remember this is Ryodan and scowl. "You did that on purpose!" I accuse. "You saw my hand go out and you stepped right into it!"

"I'd do that why, kid?"

Ryodan has the most infuriating way of asking questions without the proper inflection at the end. His voice doesn't rise at all. I don't know why it annoys me so much. It just does. "To embarrass me and make me feel stupid! Always angling for the advantage, aren't you?" Ryodan makes me totally crazy. I can't stand him!

"Sloppy is an understatement," Ryodan says. "I could have killed you. Pull your head out, kid. Watch where you're going."

My vision is finally starting to clear. "I. Was. Watching," I say pissily. "You stepped into my way."

I look up at him. Dude is tall. The only streetlamp that works is smack behind his head, casting his face in shadow, but that's the way he likes it. I swear he stages every place he goes in order to keep the light at his back for some reason. He's wearing that faint half smile he usually has on, as if he's perpetually amused by us lesser mortals.

"I am *not* a lesser mortal," I say testily.

"Didn't say you were. In fact, it's precisely because you're not lesser that you're on my radar."

"Well, get me off it."

"Can't."

I get a sinking feeling. Not too long ago Ryodan tracked me down where I was hanging out up on top of my favorite water tower and told me he had a job for me. I refused, of course. Since then I've been telling myself he filled whatever vacancy he had with someone else.

I don't want to fall in with Ryodan and his men. I get the feeling you don't ever get to fall back out. You just keep falling.

Of course, that doesn't stop me from snooping around Chester's. You have to know your competition, know what they're up to. Dude wants something from me, I want to know what. Last week I found a back way into his club that I bet nobody but me and his men know about. I think they thought it was so well hidden they didn't need to bother protecting it. Did I ever see some things! My face gets hot again, remembering.

"I've been waiting for you to report for work, Dani. You must have encountered a problem I don't know about."

Report for work, my ass. I don't answer to anyone. The way he says that last part makes it sound like he's been keeping major tabs on me and knows every problem I have and don't have. "I'll say this one more time. Never going to happen."

"You don't understand. I'm not giving you a choice."

"You don't understand. I'm taking it. You're not the boss of me."

"You better hope I am, kid, because you're a risk in my city. And there are only two ways I deal with uncontrolled variables. One of them is to offer you a job."

The look he gives me makes it clear I don't want to know what the second option is. I wipe more blood from my nose and puff myself up. "Thought it was Barrons's city," I say.

He ignores my jibe. "A risk I won't take. You're too fast, too strong, and too stupid."

"There's nothing stupid about me. I *am* fast and strong, though." I preen. "Best of the best. Dani Mega

O'Malley. That's what they call me. The Mega. Nobody's got nothing on me."

"Sure they do. Wisdom. Common sense. The ability to differentiate between a battle worth fighting and the posturing of adolescent hormones."

Gah! I don't posture! I don't have to! I'm the real thing, one hundred percent superhero! Ryodan knows just how to get under my skin but I'm not giving him the satisfaction of showing it. "Hormones don't interfere with my thought processes," I say coolly. "And as fecking *if* my 'adolescent hormones' are any different than yours. Talk about the pot calling the kettle black." After my clandestine visit last week, I know a thing or two about Ryodan.

"You're human. Hormones will undermine you at every turn. And you're way too young to know shit about me."

"I'm not too young to know anything. I know you and the other dudes are all sex all the time. I saw those women you keep—" I clamp my mouth shut.

"You saw."

"Nothing. Didn't see nothing." I don't slip often. At least I didn't used to. But things are weird lately. My mood changes like a chameleon in a kaleidoscope. I get touchy and end up saying things I shouldn't. Especially when someone keeps calling me "kid" and ordering me around. I'm unpredictable, even to myself. It bites.

"You've been on level four." His eyes are scary. Then again, this is Ryodan. His eyes are scary a lot.

"What's level four?" I say innocently, but he's not buying it for a minute. Level four is like something out of a porn movie. I know. I was watching a lot of them until recently, until somebody who doesn't give one little tiny ounce of crap about me read me the riot act, like TP cared. It's stupid to think just because somebody yells at you like they worry about how you're growing up and who you're becoming that they care about you.

He smiles. I hate it when he smiles. "Kid, you're flirting with death."

"You'll have to catch me first."

We both know it's empty bravado. He can.

He locks gazes with me. I refuse to look away even though it feels like he's sifting through my retinal records, reviewing everything I've seen. Long seconds pass. I notch up my chin, shove a hand in my jeans pocket and cock my hip. Jaunty, flippant, bored, my body says. 'Case he's not getting the message from the look on my face.

"I felt a breeze in the private part of my club last week," he says finally. "Somebody passing by fast. I thought it had to be Fade not wanting to be seen for some reason, but it wasn't. It was you. Not cool, Dani. Way not cool. Am I speaking your language well enough to penetrate that rock-hard, suicidal, adolescent head of yours."

I roll my eyes. "Gah, old dude, please don't try to talk like me. My ears'll fall off!" I flash him a cocky, hundred-megawatt grin. "It's not my fault you can't focus on me when I pass. And what's with all this adolescent bunk? I know how old I am. *You* the one needs reminding? Is that why you keep throwing it at me like some kind of insult? It isn't, you know. Fourteen is on top of the world."

The next thing I know he's in my space, swallowing it up. Barely leaving me room to be. I'm not about to stick around for it.

I freeze-frame around him.

Or I try to.

I crash, full frontal into him, smacking my forehead on his chin. Not hard either. Freeze-framing into him should have split my head again, not tickled like a stumble.

I slam it into Mega-reverse.

I succeed in backpedaling a pansy foot or two. I don't even make it out of arm's reach.

What the feck?

I'm so discombobulated by failure that I just stand there like an idiot. Until this precise moment, I wasn't even sure I knew how to *spell* the F-word, much less do it. Fail, with a big fat F. Me.

He grabs my shoulders and starts pulling me to him. I don't know what he thinks he's doing but I'm not getting anywhere *near* close to Ryodan. I explode into a Dani-grenade, all fists and teeth, and ten kinds of you-don't-want-to-hold-me-when-the-pin-is-out.

At least I try to.

I noodle off one limp punch before I stop myself so I won't telegraph any more catastrophic news to a dude that doesn't miss a trick and won't hesitate to use any weakness against me.

What the feck is wrong with me?

Did slamming into him do something to me? Like break me?

Superspeed—gone.

Superstrength—gone.

I'm as weak as a Joe and . . . ew! Stuck in Ryodan's arms. Close. Like we're about to slow dance, or get all kissy.

"Dude, you *like* me or something? Get off me!"

He looks down at me. I can see the mind working behind his eyes. I don't like Ryodan's mind working when he's looking at me.

"Fight, kid."

I tilt my nose up at a defiant angle, jut my jaw at my best "feck you" slant. "Maybe I don't feel like it. You said there's no point. You keep telling me how large and in-charge you are."

"Never stopped you before."

"Maybe I don't want to break a nail," I toss out all nonchalant-like, to cover up that I just tried fighting. *And* fleeing. And for the first time in, well—*ever*— I'm . . . norm—

The word sticks like a hard, spiky burr in the back of my throat. I can't cough it up. I can't swallow it.

It's okay. I don't need to be able to say it. It's not true. It never will be.

I've never been that word. It's not part of my reality. I probably just forgot to eat enough. I take a hasty mental tally of my fuel consumption over the past few hours: eleven protein bars, three cans of tuna, five cans black beans, seven Snickers. Okay, so my menu's coming up a little light, but not enough to drain my gas tank. I step on the freeze-frame pedal again.

I still don't move. Motionless is me. That and way freaked out.

He's holding my hand, looking at my short nails that TP painted black the night she found out the truth about me. I don't know why I haven't taken it off yet. It chips like crazy in no time with all the fighting I do.

"You don't have nails to break. Try again."

"Let go of my hand."

"Make me."

Before I can snap off a pithy, brilliant reply, my head is back, my spine is arched like a bow, and Ryodan's face is in my neck.

He bites me.

The fecker *bites* me!

Right on the neck!

Fangs bracket my jugular. I feel them, sharp and deep, sinking into me. It hurts.

Ryodan *does* have fangs! I didn't imagine what I

thought I saw on the rooftop the other night when he was telling me he had a job for me!

"What the feck you doing? You a vamp or something? You turning me?" I'm horrified. I'm . . . intrigued. How much stronger might I get? Are vampires real? Fairies are. I suppose that flings the closet door wide open. Everything's going to be springing out now. Does TP know about this? Is Barrons a vampire? What's going on here? Dude, my world just got so much more interesting!

Suddenly I'm staggering for footing, resisting nothing and looking like a drunken pinwheel doing it. It pisses me off, Ryodan making me look clumsy in front of him. I wipe a smear of blood from my neck and glare at it. When was the last time somebody spilled my blood? Like never. Sure, I bang myself up. But nobody else does. Not anymore.

Bleeding? Clumsy? Slow? Who *am* I?

"I know your taste now, kid. I know your scent like I know my own. You will never be able to pass me again without me knowing it's you. And if I ever catch you on the lower levels of Chester's . . . or anywhere in my club for that matter . . . "

I jerk my glare from my hand to his face.

He smiles at me. There's blood on his teeth.

Fact: it's just wrong to be smiled at by someone who has your blood on his teeth. It offends to the bone. Where were his fangs? Did he *have* fangs? Natural or cosmetic implants? You never know with folks these days. They didn't retract with a smoothly audible *snick* like on TV or I would have heard it. I have superhearing. Well, sometimes I do. Like when I also have superspeed and superstrength. Which used to be all the time. Until exactly now.

" . . . don't let me . . . "

His gaze does that unnerving flickery thing it does

sometimes. I think it's because he looks me up and down so quick that I can't focus on his eyes changing directions, I just see a kind of ocular shiver. I wonder if I can do it, too, superspeed a single part of me, like maybe tap a finger hyperfast. I need to practice. Assuming I can superspeed again at *all*. What the feck is wrong with me? Did I stall? How could I stall? I don't stall!

" . . . unless you're working for me and there at my direction. That's the deal." He's cold. Ice cold. And I know without him even saying what the second option is: die. Work for me or die. It pisses me off big-time.

"Are you giving me an ultimatum? Because that is so not cool." I don't emote disdain. I *become* disdain. I flash him number seventeen of my thirty-five Looks of Death. Grown-ups! They see a teenager with a little more stuff going on than they know what to do with, so they try to lock them down, box them up, make them feel bad just for being what they are. Like I can even help it. Dancer's right, adults are afraid of the kids they're raising.

"If growing up means turning out like you," I say, "I'm never doing it. I know who I am and I like it. I'm not changing for anybody."

"One day, kid, you'll be willing to mortgage your fucking soul for somebody."

"I don't think you should say 'fucking' around me. In case you forgot, I'm only fourteen. And news flash, dude, I've got no soul. There aren't any banks. And there isn't any currency. Ergo. Never. Going. To. Happen."

"I'm not sure you could be any more full of yourself."

I cut him a smug look. "I'm willing to try."

Ryodan laughs. The instant he does, I flash back to what I saw on level four the other night. He was laughing then, too. The look on the woman's face and the noise she was making when he did that thing he was doing— Gah! Old dude! Gross! What's wrong with me?

He's looking at me hard.

It makes me want to blink out of existence.

Ryodan looks at people different than anybody else I know. Like he has X-ray vision or something and knows exactly what's happening inside people's skulls.

"No mystery there, kid. If you live long enough, you do know what they're thinking," he says. "Humans are predictable, cut from patterns. Few evolve beyond them."

Huh? He did *not* just answer my thought. No fecking way.

"I know your secret, Dani."

"Got no secrets."

"Despite all the swaggering you do, you don't want anybody to see you. Not really see you. Invisa-girl. That's who you want to be. I wonder why."

I flip him off with both hands and freeze-frame with everything I've got.

It works this time! Fecking-A, it's good to be me! Wind in my hair! Mega on the move! Leaps tall buildings in a single bound!

Well, maybe that last part's a little exaggeration, but still . . .

Zooooooooom! I freeze-frame through the streets of Dublin.

When I slam into the next wall, it knocks me out cold.

TWO

"Ice ice baby"

Since I sleep like the dead, I come to hard. It doesn't matter whether I've fallen asleep or been knocked out. I'm always broody at first because I can't shake off slumber as fast as most folks. My dreams get tangled up with the real world and it takes a while for them to melt away, like icicles dripping off gutters in the morning sun.

Not this time.

I come up from unconsciousness like a live wire: flat on my back one second, the next on all fours, then I've got my sword at Ryodan's throat.

He knocks it away. It flies out of my hand and crashes into the wall of his office.

I lunge after it and crash into the wall myself, but who cares? My sword's in my hand again. I spine up to the wall, blade straight out in front of me, never taking my eyes off him, waiting for him to try to take it from me again. It's going through his heart if he does.

"We can do this all day if you like," he says.

"You knocked me out," I say through clenched teeth. I'm spitting mad, my face is throbbing and my teeth hurt. It's a wonder I have any left.

"Correction. I got in your way. You knocked yourself out. I told you to watch where you're going."

"You're faster than me. That means you're supposed to yield right of way."

"Like we're cars. Cute. I don't yield. Ever." He hooks a foot around a chair and kicks it toward me. "Sit."

"Feck you."

"I'm stronger than you, faster than you, and lack the human emotion that drives you. That makes me your worst nightmare. Sit. Or I'll make you sit."

"I can think of a couple worse," I mutter.

"You want to play games. I don't think you'll like mine."

I think it over. I'm worried because of earlier, when I stalled. What if it happens again and he figures it out? I'm double worried because he knocked me out cold, mid freeze-frame. It's obvious I can't escape if he doesn't want to let me go. I'm in Chester's, on his turf, with all his men in the vicinity. Even if Barrons is around, he's not going to help me. I'm pretty sure TP has him hating me now.

I take stock of the room. I've never been in his office before. LED screens serve as cove moldings, lining the entire perimeter of the ceiling, flashing from one zone to the next. From here Ryodan watches everything. I'm in the guts of his club.

"How'd I get here?" There's one possible answer. I'm just trying to buy more time to orient myself. Gingerly I touch my nose, feel the tip. It's alarmingly bulbous and squishy.

"I carried you."

It makes me so mad I almost can't breathe. He knocked me out, picked me up like a sack of potatoes, toted me through the streets of Dublin and hauled me through the middle of all the skeevy folks and fairies that hang at

Chester's, probably with everybody staring at me and smirking. I haven't been helpless for a long time.

Fact: he could do it again if he felt like it. Over and over. This dude standing in front of me could chain me down worse than anything my mom or Ro ever did to me.

I decide the wisest thing is to humor him until he lets me leave. Then I'll eat everything I can get my hands on, test myself, make sure I'm working right, hole up somewhere safe and lie low for a while. I'll spend my time in hiding, working on getting faster and stronger, so I never have to put up with a moment like this again. I thought these kinds of days were gone for good.

I sit.

He doesn't look all smug like I would have. He gives me . . . like a look of approval or something.

"Don't need your approval," I say irritably. "Don't need anybody's."

"Stay that way."

I scowl at him. I don't get Ryodan at all. "Why am I here? Why'd you bring me to Chester's? Get to the point. I got stuff to do. Busy schedule, you know. I'm in demand."

I look around. The office is made of solid glass, walls, ceiling, and floor. Nobody can see in, but you can see out. It's freaky walking on a glass floor. Like the bottom's dropping out of your world with every step you take. Even sitting, you feel a kind of vertigo.

I look down. There are acres of dance floor beneath me. The club has multiple tiers, maybe a hundred sub-clubs on split levels, each with its own theme. Seelie, Unseelie, and humans hang together and strike who knows what kind of deals. Here in post-wall Dublin, anything you want can be had at Chester's, for a price. For a second I forget he's there, fascinated by watching it all between my high-top sneakers. I could sit here for days, study stuff, get smarter. Itemize every caste of Fae, spread the word around the city, what they are, how they can be defeated, or at least escaped from or restrained until I can get there to kill them with my sword. That's a big part of the reason I've been so determined to get inside Chester's. How can I protect my city if I can't warn everyone about all its dangers? I got a job to do. I need all the intel I can get.

There's a Seelie male on the dance floor, blond and beautiful like V'lane was before he dropped his glamour and revealed himself as an Unseelie. In the next subclub over is a lower caste of dark Fae that I've never seen before, shiny wet and segmented, with— *Ew!* The many segments are coming apart and scurrying off into a hundred different directions like roaches! I hate roaches. They begin to disappear up people's pants legs. I pick my feet up off the floor and sit cross-legged on the chair.

"You watch everything."

It's not a question so I don't answer. I look at him, fold my arms and wait.

There's that smile again.

I poke out my lower lip defiantly. "What am I? Like a walking joke to you? Why do you always smile when you look at me?"

"You'll figure it out." He moves to his desk, opens a drawer, pulls out a sheet of paper and hands it to me. "Complete and sign this."

I take it and look at it. It's a job application. I give him a look. "Dude. Post-apocalyptic world. Who does job applications anymore?"

"I do."

I squint at it, then him. "What are you paying me?" I angle.

"Dude. Post-apocalyptic world. Who does money anymore."

I snicker. First sign of any sense of humor he's shown.

Then I remember where I am and why. I wad it up and throw it at him. It bounces off his chest.

"You're wasting time, kid. The sooner you do what I tell you, the sooner you can get out of here." He goes to his desk, gets another and hands it to me with a pen.

I relax. He plans to let me leave. Maybe even soon.

I skim the application. It has the usual blanks: name, address, date of birth, education, prior job history, places for signature and date. Fanciest application I've ever seen, with the name CHESTER'S worked into an ornate border that frames the page.

Everybody clings to something when the world melts down. I suppose Ryodan likes having his business details all squared up, no matter the chaos at his door. It's not like it'll kill me to fill out the stupid thing, agree to do whatever he wants, then get the feck out of here and go into deep hiding. I sigh. Hiding. Me. I pine for the days when I was the only superhero in town.

"If I fill this out, you'll let me leave?"

He inclines his head.

"But I have to do some kind of job for you?"

He inclines his head again.

"If I do that job, are we through? For good? Just one job, right?" I have to make this convincing or he'll figure out I plan to disappear.

Once more he gives me that imperial nod that's hardly a nod, like he's stooping to acknowledge my puny existence.

I don't ask him what the job is because I have no intention of ever doing it. I'm never going to be anyone's solution to folks' problems again. I crossed lines for Ro. Big lines. Deep lines. She's dead. I'm free. Life starts now. I study him. He's perfect stillness, with the light behind his face as usual, features in shadow.

Cats get still like him. Before they pounce.

Something's going on here, bigger than I'm seeing.

My face hurts. My eyes are puffy and the left one's trying to swell shut. "You got any ice?" I need to buy time to figure out what's going on. Plus, if he leaves for ice I can snoop through his office.

He gives me a look I've seen men do before, especially to women: chin down, looking up from beneath his brows, with a faintly mocking smile. There's something in that look I don't get but the challenge is unmistakable. "Come here," he says. "I'll heal you." He's sitting behind his desk, watching me. Still, so still. It's like he's not even breathing.

I look at him. I don't know what to make of him. Part of me wants to get up, go around that desk and find out what he's talking about. "You could do that? Make my bruises and cuts go away?" I'm always beat up and my muscles are constantly strained from overuse. Sometimes I burn through my shoes and scrape the skin right off my feet. It gets old.

"I can make you feel better than you've ever felt in your life."

"How?"

"There are some secrets, Dani O'Malley, that you learn only by participating."

I consider that. "So. You got any ice?"

He laughs and presses a button on his desk. "Fade. Ice. Now."

"Gotcha, boss."

A few minutes later I'm sitting with an ice pack on half my face, squinting around it to fill out Ryodan's stupid application. I'm almost done and ready to sign when I get the strangest feeling in my hand, the one holding the page.

It's my left hand, my sword hand, the one that turned black a little while ago, the night I stabbed a Hunter through the heart and killed it. Or rather, the night I *thought* I killed a Hunter. Truth is, I'm not actually sure

I did but I'm not about to print a retraction. The public needs to believe in certain things. When I went back to take pictures of it for *The Dani Daily* to show folks it was gone, completely. Not a trace remained. Not a single drop of black blood anywhere. Barrons says they can't be killed. After the incident I thought I was going to lose my hand. My veins turned black and my whole hand went cold as a block of ice. I had to wear a glove for days. Told the *sidhe*-sheep I got poison sumac. Rare around these parts but there used to be some. Don't know if the Shades ate it all. Wonder if they did, if they got itchy bellies inside.

Now it's all tingly and weird. I study it, wondering what might go wrong with me next. Maybe stabbing the Hunter did something to me. Maybe that's why I stalled. Maybe there are worse things on the horizon.

That is so not me! Optimism is me. Tomorrow's my day. You never know what grand adventures wait around the next corner!

"Kid, you going to sit there all day daydreaming, or sign the fucking thing."

That's when I see it. I'm so stunned my mouth opens, and hangs there catching flies for a minute.

I almost signed it!

He must have been sitting over there, laughing his butt off inside, congratulating himself.

My head snaps up. "So, what exactly does the spell in the border of this thing do?" I've never seen anything like it. And I've seen a lot of spells. Ro was a pro at them. Some really nasty ones. Now that I'm seeing it, I can't believe I missed it. Cleverly tucked into the ornate black border are shimmering shapes and symbols, slithering, in constant motion. One of them is trying to crawl off the page and onto my lap.

I wad it up and throw it at him. "Nice try. *Not.*"

"Ah, well. It was possible you would sign. It was the simplest solution."

He's completely unperturbed. I wonder, does anything shake him up, make him lose his cool, get hot about something, scream and yell? I can't see it. I think Ryodan glides through life in the same coolly amused mood all the time. "What would it have done to me if I'd signed it?" I ask. Curiosity. I have it in spades. Mom swore it was going to be the death of me. Something's got to be. There are worse things.

"Some secrets—"

"Yeah, yeah, blah-blah, participating and all that bunk. Got it."

"Good."

"Didn't want to know anyway."

"Yes you did. You can't stand not knowing things."

"So, what now?" We're at an impasse, him and me. I suspect his "application" was really a contract. A binding contract, the kind that knits up your soul and tucks it in someone else's pocket. I heard of them but never believed they were real. If anybody had a way to sew up a soul in a business deal, it would be Ryodan. Jericho Barrons is an animal. Pure lawless beast. Not so Ryodan. Dude's a machine.

"Congratulations, kid," he says. "You passed my first test. You may just get the job yet."

I sigh. "This is going to be a long day, isn't it? You serve lunch around here? And I'm going to need more ice."

A door I didn't even know was there in the glass wall of his office opens, revealing a glass elevator.

Chester's is way bigger than I thought. As we ride the elevator down, I'm riveted by the view.

And a little worried.

That he's letting me see so much means that whether I signed his stupid application or not, he thinks he has me buttoned up.

Ryodan's glass office isn't the only place he can watch things. It's the tip of the iceberg, and, dude, I do mean iceberg, as in megatons of stuff hidden beneath the surface. The central club part of Chester's—the interior half, a dozen levels the public sees—is barely a tenth of it. That main part where everybody hangs out and dances and makes deals with the devil is constructed inside a much larger structure. Ryodan and his dudes live *behind* the walls of that club in what's beginning to look like a vast underground city, from where I am. All the walls are two-way glass. They can go to any level, by elevator or catwalk, and watch anything that's happening at any time. Serious thought went into designing this place. There's no way they built it all since the walls fell last Halloween. I wonder how long it's all been here, beneath the polished, glitzy, glamorous Chester's that used to exist, hot spot for movie stars and models and the über-rich. I wonder if, like our abbey, their underground world has been beneath a changing exterior for millennia.

I couldn't be more impressed. It's so brilliant I'm jealous. This is snooping elevated to a whole new techno-nerd level of expertise.

"Like what you see, kid."

I pick at my cuticles, pretending to be bored.

The elevator stops and the doors swish open. I figure we must be at least half a mile beneath Dublin.

First thing that hits me is the cold. I pull my coat tighter but it doesn't do a lot of good. Love the look of leather. Hate the insulation of it.

Second thing that hits me is the quiet. In most parts of Chester's you can hear faint strains of some kind of music or conversation, 24/7. At least some kind of white noise. This level is still as death.

Third thing is how dark it is.

Ryodan is waiting for me outside the elevator.

"Can you actually see out there?" Does he have another superpower on me? I see good in the dark, but not in pitch-black.

He nods.

I hate Ryodan. "Well, I can't. So, turn on some fecking lights. Besides, Shades much?"

"They don't bother me."

The Shades don't bother him. Shades eat everything. They don't discriminate. "Bully for you. They bother me. Lights. Pronto."

"The lights aren't working down here."

Before I can dig one out, he removes a flashlight from his pocket and hands it to me. Coolest one I ever seen, shaped like a bullet. It's tiny, sleek, silver, and when I turn it on lights up the hallway beyond the elevator like the sun came out.

"Dude," I say reverently, "you got the best toys."

"Off the elevator, kid. We've got work to do."

I follow him, my breath frosting the air.

I used to think there were only six levels in Chester's. Now I know there are at least twenty; I counted on the way down. The level we're on holds three very different subclubs. I glimpse things through the open doors of clubs that no fourteen-year-old should see. But then, that's been the story of my life.

The cold is getting worse the farther down the hall we go, as we make for a pair of tall doors. It slices through my long coat, cutting into my skin. I shiver and my teeth start to chatter.

Ryodan glances at me. "How cold can you get before you die."

Blunt and to the point. That's Ryodan for you. "Dunno. I'll tell you when I think I'm pushing it."

"But colder than most humans."

As usual with him, it's not a question, but I nod anyway. I can take more of everything than most humans.

Still, by the time we stop outside the pair of closed doors at the end of the hall, I'm hurting. I've been stamping my feet with every step for fifty yards. I begin to jog in place, to keep the blood from icing in my veins. My throat and lungs burn with each breath I take. I can feel the cold pressing at the other side of those doors like a presence. I look at Ryodan. His face is frosted. When he raises a brow, ice shatters and hits the floor.

I shake my head. "Can't." No way I'm going in there.

"I think you can."

"Dude, I'm awesome. I'm even All That sometimes. But I have limits. Think my heart's getting sludgy."

Next thing I know his hand is on my chest like he's feeling me up.

"Get off me!" I say, but he's manacled his other hand around my wrist. I shake my head and slant my face away like I can't even stand to look at him. I can't stop him. Not with words or actions. I may as well let him do it, and get it over with.

"You're strong enough." He drops his hand.

"Am not." It's been a rough morning. Sometimes I like to test myself. Now isn't one of them. Not after my earlier stutter.

"You'll survive."

I look up at him. Weird thing is, as mad as he makes me, as unpredictable as he is, I believe him. If Ryodan thinks I can take it, who am I to argue? Like he's infallible or something. Figures I'd put more faith in the devil than any god.

"But you'll have to do it at your top speed."

"Do what?"

"You'll see." The double doors are tall and ornately carved. They look heavy. When he touches the knob and pushes the door open, his fingers are instantly encased in ice. When he takes his hand away, chunks of frozen skin are left on the handle. "Don't stop once you're in there. Not even for a second. Your heart will last only as long as you're moving. Stop and you're dead."

He could figure all that out from a palm on my chest? "And I'm going to go in there *why*?" I can't see a single reason to take such a risk. I like living. I like it a lot.

"Kid, Batman needs Robin."

Dude. I go all soft and melty inside and swallow a dreamy sigh. Robin to his Batman! Superhero partners. There are lots of versions where Robin gets way stronger. He could have had me at hello if he'd said that first. "You don't want me to work for you. You want a superhero *partner*. That's a whole different story. Why didn't you just *say* so?"

He steps into the room and I hate to admit it but I'm awed that he can do it. I couldn't and I know it. The blast of killing cold coming through the open door makes me want to cry from the sheer pain of it, makes me want to turn and run the other way as fast as I can, but he just pushes forward into it. He doesn't move fluid, as usual. It's like he's shoving himself into concrete, by sheer force of will. I wonder why he doesn't go fast, the way he's telling me to.

That he can do it at all provokes me. Am I going to be a chicken? Let myself be outdone? This is Ryodan. If I'm ever going to be able to beat him, I have to take risks.

"What am I looking for?" I say through chattering teeth, psyching myself up to freeze-frame. I *really* don't want to go in there.

"Anything and everything. Absorb all details. Look

for any clue. I need to know who did this to the patrons of my club. I guarantee protection. I deliver it. If word of this gets out . . . "

He doesn't finish the sentence. He doesn't have to. It can't get out. Chester's has to be safe ground with no exceptions or he'll lose business. And Ryodan isn't one of those men who will ever tolerate losing anything that's his, for any reason. "You want me to play detective for you."

He looks back at me. His face is coated with ice. It cracks at the seam of his lips when he speaks. "Yes."

I can't help but ask. "Why me?"

"Because you see everything. You aren't afraid to do what it takes and not breathe a word of it to anyone."

"Talking like you know a thing or two about me."

"I know everything about you."

The chill I get from those quietly delivered words is almost worse than what's coming out of the club. I know people. Ryodan doesn't talk big. Doesn't blow smoke up other people's tushes or bluff. He can't know everything. No fecking way he knows everything. "Quit talking. I need to concentrate if you want me to put both my superbody and my superbrain to work at the same time. That's a whole lot of Mega-nitude."

He laughs, I think. The sound is flat and tinkles like ice in his throat.

I shine my flashlight into the darkened club. A hundred or so humans are frozen, mid-gyration, mid-sex, mid-dying, mixed in with a caste of Unseelie I've only seen a time or two: the caste that served as the Lord Master's imperial guard. The room is decorated in tribute to their rank, all red and black, with frosted red velvet drapes and ice-dusted black velvet chaises, red leather sofas and padded racks and lots of chains on every piece of furniture. Leather straps. Sharp blades.

There are puddles of black ice on the floor. Human blood.

Torture. Murder. People slaughtered.

It sinks in and I just stare a second, trying to get a grip on my temper. "You let this happen. You *let* people be killed by those monsters!"

"They come here of their own volition. The line into my club last night wrapped around two city blocks."

"They're confused! Their whole world just melted down!"

"You sound like Mac. This isn't new, kid. The weak have always been food for the strong."

Her name is a kick in my stomach. "Yeah, well Mom taught me not to play with my food before I ate it. Dude, you're a fecking psychopath."

"Careful, Dani. You've got a glass house of your own."

"I got no place like Chester's."

"It's a famous quote."

"Not too famous if I don't know it."

"People who live in glass houses shouldn't throw stones. Maybe you want to talk about your mother."

I look away. I'll pocket my stones for a little while. At least until I know for sure exactly what he knows about me.

I turn my attention back to the room and my tension melts away, replaced by an anticipatory thrill. I love mysteries. Way to test my brain! Dancer and me do logic puzzles. He beats me sometimes. Dancer's the only person I've ever met that I think might be smarter than me. What's with this place? What happened? "You got cameras in here?" I say.

"They stopped working while everything was still normal."

As if anything was ever "normal" in this torture chamber. Now it's even weirder.

Each person and Fae in the room is frozen solid, silent, white, iced figurines. Twin plumes of diamond-ice crystals extend from many of their nostrils; exhales frozen. Unlike Cruce, who is contained inside a solid block of ice, these folks look like they somehow got frozen right where they stood. I wonder if I pinged one of the Fae it would shatter.

"You think it was the Unseelie King did this?"

"No reason I can see," Ryodan says. "He's not the kind to waste time on small stuff. Hurry up, kid. Standing in here is no picnic."

"Why are you?"

"I take nothing for granted."

He means he thinks it's possible one of them isn't completely frozen. "You're watching my back."

"I watch all my employees' backs."

"Partner," I correct, and I don't even like that. I was flattered when he called me Robin to his Batman, but I'm over it already. This is who he is: someone who runs a place where humans get killed for the amusement of the Fae.

I save them. He damns them. That's a gulf between us no bridge will ever span. I'll look into this. But not for him. For humans. Sides have to be taken. I know which one I'm on.

I go all cool inside, thinking about how many folks in Dublin need a little help to survive, and just like that I'm perfect and on fire and free, and I slip sideways into freeze-framing like gliding into a dream.

Moving like I do makes seeing things a little difficult. That's why I stood at the door, looking in so long, collecting observations from a distance. Even freeze-framing, the chill causes intense pain in every bone in my body. As I whiz past him I say, "What's the temp in here?" planning to get the answer on my way back around.

"No thermometer can take it," he says by my ear, and I realize he's freeze-framing, too. He's right beside me. "Don't touch anything. It's too cold to risk."

I circle a Fae guard at top speed. Around and around, looking for clues. If the Unseelie King did this, why would he choose here? Why ice his own guards?

"Is this the only cl-club that g-got iced?" I stutter with cold.

"Yes."

"Wh-When?" I stamp my foot in hyperspeed, pissed that I'm stuttering. Doesn't matter that it's from the cold, it makes me sound pansy. Next thing you know, I'll lisp.

"Eight days ago."

A few days after Ryodan cornered me on my water tower. I cock my head. I just heard a sound in a completely frozen room. I whiz back to where I was when I heard it and go in tight circles, listening hard.

Silence.

"D-Did you hear th-th-that?" I manage to spit out. My face is going numb and it's getting harder to move my lips. I circle a human woman, frozen mid-coitus. It's not hoarfrost that turned her white. She's covered with hard rime, the kind of ice that builds up on a cold foggy night. Over it all is a layer of clear ice a good inch thick.

"Yes." Ryodan flashes past me. Warily, we circle the room on opposite ends, watching everything real careful-like.

It's hard to listen good when you got so much wind in your ears from moving like we do. Ryodan and I have been practically shouting at each other the whole time we've been talking. "Like a high–p-p-pitched whine," I say. I'm not going to be able to stay in the room much longer. There it was again! Where was it coming from? I whiz though the subclub faster and faster. Ryodan and I do figure eights between the frozen figurines, trying to isolate it.

"You f-feel that?" I ask. Something's happening . . . I feel a vibration, like the floor has the tremors, like everything is . . . *changing*.

"Fuck!" Ryodan explodes. Then his hands are on my waist, and he's tossing me over his shoulder like that stupid sack of potatoes again, and moving faster than I've ever managed to move in my whole life.

That's when they begin to pop, going off like firecrackers. Fae and humans explode, filling the air with icy, flesh-colored shrapnel.

One after the next, they blow violently, and with each new explosion, the next one blows harder. The furniture is popping now, too. Sofas erupt into icy splinters of wood and rock-hard chunks of stuffing. Racks get blasted into smithereens of metal shards. It sounds like a thousand machine guns going off.

A pair of knives whiz by, chased by a dozen ice picks.

I bury my nose in Ryodan's back. My face has taken enough of a beating for the day. I'm not in the mood for anything sharp in it. Something slams me in the back of my head and I wrap my arms around my skull. I hate being over his shoulder but he's faster than me. I tense, pelleted by chunks, waiting for one of those nasty-looking blades or picks to sink into me.

We're halfway down the hall, almost to the elevator. The other two clubs have begun blowing up, too. I hear an enormous, deep, rumbling sound and realize the floor is cracking beneath us.

Chunks of ceiling begin to fall.

At the elevator, Ryodan flings me from his shoulder into the compartment in one smooth motion.

I explode right back out. "Fecking thing is going to blow and you want me *on* it?"

"It'll last long enough to get you out of here."

"Bull-fecking-*crikey*! I give you fifty-percent odds I'll make it!"

"I'll take them."

I'm in the air, over his shoulder, slammed back into the elevator again. The whole ceiling of the hallway is coming down now, crown moldings, drywall, steel girders. He'll be crushed. Not that I care. "What about you?"

His smile is fanged. Creeps me out. "What, kid, you care?"

He slams the doors closed with his bare hands and I swear he gives the thing a push from below.

I shoot up into Chester's.

THREE

_____

"When the cat's away . . ."

Under normal circumstances I'd have snooped through Ryodan's office, but my day hadn't been normal and I was in a pissy mood.

Two things were on my mind: get as far away from Ryodan as possible while he was busy dying (hopefully), and kill as many Fae inside Chester's as I could on my way out.

The club "proper" was unprotected. Hoo-fecking-rah.

His dudes had whizzed past me so fast my hair shot straight up in the air five, six, seven times, minus Barrons, who doesn't much leave TP's side. No doubt they were heading down to the iced level, to save their boss. Keep him from being crushed. With any luck, the whole club would collapse into a pile of rubble and kill them all.

Somehow I doubted it.

They were like Barrons. I wasn't even sure they *could* be killed. If so, it was probably only by a single weapon, hidden inside an invisible box, on an invisible planet, with an atmosphere that would burn up any living thing instantly, like a gazillion light-years away.

But I knew a few things that *could* be killed.

And my sword hand has a permanent itch.

Slaying Unseelie gives me a rush that's almost as intense as freeze-framing. The only thing missing is TP at my back, but I know if I ever have TP at my back again, she'll be trying to shove a spear through my heart.

Supercharged on adrenaline and anger, I slice and dice my way through the subclub that bugs me the most: the one where the waitresses dress like school kids, in short, pleated plaid skirts and white socks, and crisp white blouses with starched collar points.

Kids. They're the worst victims of the fall. There are so many of them hiding in the streets, with no clue how to survive.

At Chester's, grown women are dressing like kids to trade favors for pieces of Unseelie flesh, the latest drug on the market. It has epic healing powers, and temporarily gives humans extra strength and stamina. I hear it makes sex really intense, too. The things people are willing to do for a quick high—eat pieces of our enemies' flesh! Makes me want to knock heads together.

So I do.

I get a few good elbow jabs in on the waitresses, too. Half of them are those stupid See-You-in-Faery chicks who chirp the stupid phrase at each other every time they part, like going to Faery is something to aspire to instead of something to avoid like ten variations of the black plague.

They should be out in the streets, helping us fight and rebuild our world. Instead they're in here, consorting with the enemy, selling themselves for a shot at immortality. I don't buy that bunk. I think the Unseelie made that part up—that if you eat enough Unseelie flesh, eventually you become immortal, too, and you can hang with them in Faery all social-like.

I slay every last one of the Fae in the kiddie subclub, ignoring the waitresses screaming at me to stop. Some people just don't know what's good for them.

There's black blood on my hands, goop in my hair, and my eyes are so swollen from my earlier collisions that I can barely see, but I don't need to see much. I've got a homing device where Fae are concerned. I sense Unseelie. I slay.

I feel a big bad one behind me, worse than any of the ones I've killed so far, oozing all kinds of power. Sword back, poised for the killing blow, I whirl and bring my blade slashing down—

And miss!

The Unseelie ducks, rolls, and springs lightly to his feet half a dozen tables away. He flips his long black hair over a muscled, tattooed shoulder and hisses at me.

I lunge after him without even thinking and am about to slam into him when I realize what he is.

I change direction mid-lunge and scramble back, feet pedaling air. Feck, feck, feck, one of the Unseelie princes found me!

This is a battle I'm not up to today! I wasn't expecting this because I never heard of any of the princes strolling into Chester's!

I crash into a table, fall over backward, roll onto all fours and launch myself away. I'm about to find out if I can freeze-frame faster than it can sift. I rip open a power bar, shove half of it in my mouth and start shifting gears when the Unseelie prince says, "Lass, what the bloody hell are you doing? Have you taken a look around?"

I'm seeing through slits from all the swelling in my face, and my vision is a little dim, but I scan the place quick-like. All activity in the club has stopped. Fae and humans are lined up at balconies, staring at me from every level.

I tune in to what they're saying.

"Crazy. The kid's nuts."

"Somebody needs to put that bitch down."

"I'm not going near her. Did you see her move? Do you see what she's holding?"

"The Sword of Light," a Fae says icily. "*Our* sword."

"Take it from her!"

"How dare she?"

"Kill her now."

"I bet I can sift faster than she can slay," one growls.

I toss my hair from my eyes, on all fours, every muscle tense, waiting. We'll sure as feck find out.

"Who permitted that . . . that revolting . . . human . . . *thing* in here? Where is our host? This is neutral ground!"

"He swore an oath to us. He has failed us!"

I can't help but smirk. Assuming Ryodan survives the collapse, he's going to be seriously pissed. I just accomplished exactly what he'd tried to "hire" me to prevent. Ruined his rep. The whole club now knows Ryodan can't guarantee safety at Chester's. It'll be all over Dublin within an hour. I might as well print up a special edition of *The Dani Daily,* broadcasting it. Good. If fewer folks come to Chester's, fewer folks will die.

I glance back at the dude I initially thought was an Unseelie prince. The moment he'd spoken, I'd relaxed. Now that I'm slo-mo again, I see the differences.

I almost killed a human. Well, a human that's in the process of becoming something else. If he hadn't spoken up, I still might not be sure who he was, but I've never heard a Fae call anybody "lass." I don't think they'd stoop to it, not even to fake someone out.

It's the Scot who crashed my water tower party the same night Ryodan did.

They'd faced off with each other, all bristling hostility, giving me time to escape. It had seemed he was there either to help me or to feck with Ryodan. Whichever—that makes him good for me.

This dude has problems as big as mine, maybe bigger. I consider him. He doesn't like Ryodan. And he's got some serious mojo. I can feel it shivering in the air around him. He could be a valuable ace in my hidey-hole. If he can be trusted.

"You're a MacKeltar, right?"

"Christian," he says.

"Aren't your uncles some kind of warlocks or something? They helped hunt the *Sinsar Dubh*."

"Druids, lass. Not warlocks."

"Can you fight?"

He gives me a mocking look. "I don't need to. I can walk you out of here without lifting a finger."

Big talk. I decide to let him try.

He flanks me and we head for the door. Between what he looks like and my sword, every last occupant of Chester's draws back as we pass. I can't help but swagger a little.

Hisses, jeers, threats follows us.

But no one makes a move.

I could get used to this. Who needs TP? I got what looks like an Unseelie prince at my side and nobody, but nobody—not even the Unseelie—mess with their princes. Oh, yeah, this guy's going to be a major plus in my column. I take a sidewise glance at him.

If I can get past that he looks like the most terrifying of all the Unseelie.

Beyond him I catch a glimpse of myself in a mirror. Between the bruises, swollen eyes, cuts, and blood of all colors, I'm not looking so hot myself.

Sword up, I squint through puffy eyelids and memorize faces on the way out.

Out in the streets, in the thick of battle, sometimes you have to make hard choices. Sometimes you can't save everyone.

Humans that hang at Chester's are never going to be at the top of my list.

FOUR

"I want a girl with a mind like a diamond"

I'm attracted to her.

    She's fourteen. And I'm attracted to her.

I'm eight years older than she is. Eleven if you count the three years I spent trying to escape the Fae Silvers. Eight or eleven: what's the difference? It makes me one seriously fucked-up Highlander.

Or whatever the hell I am.

She's a bloody mess, literally. Covered with guts and gore from killing, her nose is crusted with dried blood, she's bruised, and she's going to have two fierce black eyes before nightfall. It's too late for ice to knock down the swelling.

And she's on fire.

Light shines out of her delicate, battered face, blazes in her green eyes. She's got a head of curly red hair that falls halfway down her back. Everything about her is brilliant and intense. She's aware and invested in the world in ways most adults never get around to being. I know. I was once, too. Back when I thought hearing the truth in everyone's lies was my biggest problem. She does everything one hundred and ten percent, with all her heart.

That's what gets me.

Attraction isn't always about sex. Sometimes it's about something far subtler, and far bigger.

I watched her fight.

And something stirred inside me that I thought was dead.

Not my dick. That's working great. Better than ever. Always hard. Always ready.

What stirred was like gentle rain on a warm summer day. Sweet. Tender. Something I used to be. With my clan. With my nieces and nephews.

She reminds me of my Highlands—to which I can never return.

I know exactly what she's going to be one day. Bloody hell is she ever.

Worth. Waiting. For.

Too bad I won't be here anymore.

Take her now.

"Fourteen," I growl. I've gotten good at arguing with the voice inside my head. I get a lot of practice. An Unseelie prince wouldn't give a second thought about her age. An Unseelie prince would see only that she has the right parts, and temper to spare. The bigger the fight, the better the feast.

"Why the feck does everybody keep saying that like it's some kind of insult? Like, maybe I managed to forget for a minute?" she says crossly. "Geez! I've never seen so many people obsessed with my age!"

Dani bristling is something to see. I smile.

She takes a wary step away from me. "Dude, you planning to eat me or something?"

My smile vanishes. I look away.

I wear a mask. A face that isn't mine.

I used to have what women called a killer smile.

Now I have a killer's smile.

"'Cause, like Ryodan already bit me once today. I'm not in the mood for any more teeth in me anywhere."

Ryodan bit her? One more reason to kill him. I look back at her, my face void of all expression. There's no point in trying to look reassuring. This face can't pull it off. "No biting. I promise."

She squints at me suspiciously. "Dude, what are you? Unseelie or human? What happened to you?"

"Mac happened to me." She flinches when I say it, and I wonder why. I blame Jericho Barrons, too. If I survive what I'm turning into, I'll kill them both. Hate ripples through me, dense and black and suffocating. If not for them, I'd still be me. Then again, if Mac hadn't done what she'd done, I wouldn't be here at all. Then again, if Barrons hadn't done what he'd done, or rather failed to do, what Mac did might not have turned me into this. Barrons didn't check my tattoos before we performed a dangerous Druid ritual, then he abandoned me in the Silvers to die. When Mac found me in the Silvers, she fed me Unseelie to keep me alive. It's impossible to decide which one of them I blame the most. So I blame both and I'm getting happier about that every day.

I saw Mac a few nights ago, across the club at Chester's, looking blond and beautiful and happy. I want to take all that shiny-happy-blondness, twist it into a garrote, and strangle her with it. Hear her beg, and kill her anyway, love every minute of it.

Later that night, I'd stared at myself in the mirror for a long time. Arm bent behind my head, scratching my back with a knife—it itches all the time now—relishing the slide of warm blood on my skin as it ran down my spine into my jeans. I used to hate blood. Now I could bathe in it. Mother's milk.

"Yeah, she does that," Dani agrees with a sigh. "She happened to me, too."

"What did she do to you?"

"It's more like what she *will* do to me if she catches me," she says. "Don't want to talk about it. You?"

"Don't want to talk about it."

"Better things to talk about anyway. So, what were you doing at Chester's?"

Good question. I have no bloody clue. I think the sheer number of Unseelie gathered calls to something in my blood. I don't know why I go half the places I go anymore. Sometimes I don't even remember the hours leading up to it. I just become aware that I'm someplace new with no memory of when I decided to go or how I got there. "I wanted a beer. Not many choices left in Dublin anymore."

"No shit," she agrees. "Not just for beer, for everything. Which side are you on?" she says bluntly. "Human or Fae?"

It's a good question. I don't have a good answer.

I can't tell her I don't discriminate. I despise everyone. Well, almost. There's this fourteen-year-old redhead with a mind like a diamond. "If you're asking if I've got your back, lass, I do."

She narrows her eyes and peers at me. We're standing outside Chester's in a pool of light. The sky is so overcast it looks like dusk at three in the afternoon. I get a sudden image of us from above: slim, delicate-faced young girl in a long black leather coat, hands on her hips, staring up at a Highlander-going-Unseelie prince. The image is painful. I should be a good-looking twenty-two-year-old college student with a killer smile and a bright future ahead of me. We'd plot and plan and fight the good fight together. That version of me would watch out for her. Make sure nobody does to her what the voice in my head tells me the first Unseelie that catches her without her sword is going to do. What a part of me wants to do, too. Fury fills me. At them. At me. At everything. "You never take that sword off your body, right?"

She backs up a step, hands going to her ears. "Dude, my hearing works great. You don't need to yell."

I didn't know I was. But a lot of things come out differently than I mean them to now. "Sorry. I'm just saying, you *do* realize what will happen to you if one of the Unseelie catches you. Right?"

"Never going to happen," she says smugly.

"With that attitude, it will. Fear is healthy. Fear is good. It keeps you on your toes."

"Really? 'Cause I think it's a waste of time. Bet you don't fear nothing," she says admiringly.

Every time I look in the mirror. "Sure I do. That you'll get sloppy and slip up and one of them will grab you. Snuff you out."

She tilts her head, eyes narrowed on my face. Not many people look me full in the face anymore. Not for long anyway. "Maybe you aren't all Unseelie prince yet. Maybe we can, like, work out some kind of arrangement."

"What do you have in mind?"

"I want to shut down Chester's. Torch it. Exterminate it."

"Why?"

She cuts me a look of scorn and disbelief. "You saw it in there! They're fecking monsters! They hate humans. They use them and eat them and kill them. And Ryodan and his men let them!"

"Say we do close down the place, say we burn it to the ground. They'll just find another place to go."

"No they won't," she insists. "They'll pull their heads out. They'll smell the coffee percolating and see we saved them!"

A rush of emotion, cloyingly sweet as funeral lilies, floods me, swells my tongue with a taste both familiar and sickening. She's tough, smart, capable, a stone-cold killer when she needs to be.

And she's so bloody naïve.

"They're at Chester's because they *want* to be at Chester's. Make no mistake about that, lass."

"No. Fecking. Way."

"Yes fecking way."

"They're confused!"

"They know exactly what they're doing."

"I thought you were different but you're not! You're just like Ryodan! Just like everyone. Ready to write them all off. You don't see that some people need saving."

"You don't see that most people are beyond saving."

"Nobody's beyond saving! Nobody! Ever!"

"Dani." I say her name tenderly, savoring the pain she makes me feel.

I turn and walk away. There's nothing for me here.

"So, that's it, then?" she yells after me. "You won't help me fight either? Gah! Sheep! You're all big fat fecking sheep waggling big fat fecking sheep asses!"

She's too young. Too innocent.

Too human. For what I'm becoming.

FIVE

"Our house is a very very very fine house"

"Hungry?" Dancer says as I bang in the door and throw my backpack and MacHalo on the couch.

"Starving."

"Cool. Went shopping today."

Me and Dancer love to go "shopping," aka looting. When I was a kid, I used to dream that I got forgotten inside a department store after it closed with nobody around, which meant I could have anything I wanted.

That's the world now. If you're tough enough to brave the streets, and got balls enough to go into the dark stores, anything you can carry out is yours. First thing I did when the walls went down was hit a sporting goods store and cram a duffel bag full of high-top sneakers. I burn through them quick.

"Found some canned fruit," he says.

"Dude!" It's getting harder to find. Plenty of the ick-stuff on the shelves. "Peaches?" I say hopefully.

"Those weird little oranges."

"Mandarin." Not my favorite but better than nothing.

"Found some ice cream toppings, too."

My mouth instantly waters.

One of the things I miss most is milk and all the things

it made possible. A while back, a couple of counties to the west, some folks had three milk cows that the Shades didn't get, but then other people tried to steal them and they all shot each other. And the cows. I never did get that part of it. Why shoot the cows? All that milk and butter and ice cream re-*moo*-ved from our world forever! I snicker, cracking myself up. Then I see the table and the spread of food and it cracks me up more. "You expecting an army?"

"Of one. I know how you eat."

And he's fascinated by it. Sometimes he just sits and watches me. Used to freak me out but not so much anymore.

I decimate the feast, then we sack out on the couch and watch movies. Dancer's got everything wired for power, with the quietest generators I've ever seen. He's smart. He survived the fall without a single superpower, no family, and no friends. He's seventeen and all alone in the world. Well, technically he has family but they're somewhere in Australia. With splinters of Faery reality slicing everything up, no planes flying and nobody about to take a boat out, they may as well be dead.

If they aren't.

Nearly half the world is. I know he thinks they're dead. We don't talk about it. I know it from the things he doesn't say.

Dancer was in Dublin checking out Trinity College's Physics Department, trying to decide where he wanted to go to grad school when the walls fell, leaving him cut off and alone. Homeschooled by multiple tutors and smarter than anybody I ever met, he finished college six months ago, speaks four languages fluently and can read three or four more. His folks are humanitarians, über-rich from old money. His dad is or was some kind of ambassador, his mom a doctor who spent her time organizing free medical care for third world countries.

Dancer grew up all over the world. I have a hard time wrapping my brain around his kind of family. I can't believe how well he adapted. He impresses me.

I watch him sometimes when he's not watching me. He catches me now.

"Thinking how hot I am, Mega?" he teases.

I roll my eyes. That kind of stuff isn't between us. We just hang together.

"Speaking of hot . . . "

I roll my eyes bigger, because if he's finally about to say something about how much prettier I am since the Gray Woman took my looks then gave me back a little extra, I'm out of here. He's been cool so far about not commenting. I like it that way. Dancer's . . . well, Dancer. He's my safety zone. There's no pressure here. It's just two kids in a fecked-up world.

" . . . try some hot water. Mega, you're a mess. I got the shower working again. Go take one."

"It's just a little blood—"

"It's a bucket. Maybe two."

"—and a few bruises."

"You look like you got hit by a truck. And you smell."

"I do not," I say indignantly. "I would know. I have supersmell."

He looks at me hard. "Mega, I think you have guts in your hair."

I reach up, dismayed. I thought I got them all out on the way over. I root around in my curls and pull out a long slimy piece.

I stare at it, revolted, thinking how maybe I should cut my hair really short or start wearing a ball cap all the time, then I look at him and he's looking at me like he's going to toss his cookies, then all the sudden we both start cracking up.

We laugh so hard we can't breathe. We're on the floor, holding our sides.

Guts in my hair. What kind of world am I living in? Even though I was always different, and saw things other people didn't see, I never thought I'd be sitting on a sofa, in a virtual bomb shelter underground, with security cams and trapdoors and booby traps all around us, hanging with a seventeen-year-old (hot!) genius who makes sure I eat more than protein and candy bars (he says I'm not getting the right vitamins and minerals for proper bone health) *and* knows how to get a shower running in post-wall Dublin.

He plays a mean game of chess, too.

He pauses the movie when I head for the shower. I grab a change of clothes on the way in.

This is Dancer's place, not mine. But he keeps things stocked for me in case I come by. Like me, he's got lots of other digs, too. You have to keep moving in this city to increase your odds of survival, and set things real careful when you leave, so you know if somebody's invaded your turf while you were gone. It's a dog-eat-dog world. People kill each other over milk.

The hot water lasts four glorious minutes. I scrub my hair, wrap it in a towel and study my face in the steamed-up mirror. Bruises are me. I know the progression: black turns purple, purple goes green, then you get all jaundiced-looking for a while. I look past the bruises. I lock eyes with my reflection and don't look away. The day you look away you start to lose yourself. I'm never going to lose myself. You are what you are. Deal with it or change.

I toss the towel, finger-comb my hair, tug on jeans, a tee, and consider a pair of combat boots. Dancer picked them out for me. Said I won't burn through the soles as fast. I decide to give them a try.

I grab another bowl of puny orange slices on the way back to the sofa, pop open a jar of marshmallow cream and slather it on, then coat it all with hard-shell choco-late.

Dancer and me get down to business. He starts the movie again while I get out the game board. He kicked my butt at Go Bang for hours the last time I dropped in, but I'm feeling lucky tonight. I even magnanimously ac-cept a restricted second move when I win the flip for opening play.

I do something I haven't done in a long time. I let my guard down. I'm drunk on fruit and marshmallow cream and the thrill of winning at Go Bang. I was up all night last night, and my day was long and eventful.

Besides, Dancer's got killer booby traps around his place, almost as good as mine.

I push my backpack out of the way and fall asleep on his couch, fist under my cheek, sword in my hand.

I don't know what wakes me but something does and I lift my head a few inches, slit my eyes and peer around.

Big, scary-looking men surround me.

I blink, trying to clear my vision. It's hard to do when my eyes are even more swollen than they were when I went to sleep.

Dimly I realize I'm the focal point of a circle of ma-chine guns.

I shoot up to sitting and I'm just about to freeze-frame when a hand slams me back into the couch so hard the wood frame cracks behind my shoulder blades.

I lunge up, and get slammed right back down again.

One of the men laughs. "Kid doesn't know when to stay down."

"She'll learn."

"Bet your ass she will. *If* he lets her live."

"He sure as fuck shouldn't. Not after what she did."

"Dani, Dani, Dani."

I flinch. I've never heard anyone say my name so gently. It creeps me all kinds of out.

He's towering over me, arms crossed over his chest, scarred forearms dark against the rolled-up sleeves of a crisp white shirt. Heavy silver cuffs glint at both wrists. The light is smack behind his head, as usual.

"You didn't really think I'd let you get away with it," Ryodan says.

SIX

"I will break these chains that bind me"

"Hurt's a funny thing," Ryodan says.

I say nothing. It's taking all my energy to stand, despite the chains holding me. I'm somewhere in Chester's, in a room with stone walls. I feel the distant beat of rhythmic bass behind me, in the soles of my feet. If I didn't have supersenses, I wouldn't be able to pick it up at all. Because it's so faint, I know I'm far beneath the public part of the club, probably at the bottom. That means the lower levels didn't get as badly damaged in the explosion yesterday as I hoped.

They put a bag over my head when they brought me in. Wherever I am, they didn't want me to be able to find my way back. It's a logical deduction that they plan to let me live. You don't bag the head of somebody who's never going to see anything again. A single low-watt lamp illuminates the room behind him—or fails to. There's barely enough light to see him standing a dozen feet away.

"Some people fall apart when they get hurt," he says. "Puddle into apathy and despair and never recover. They wait all their lives for someone to come along and rescue them." He moves in that strangely fluid way—not freeze-framing but not walking like a Joe either—a ripple of muscle and cascade of wind. Then he's standing in front of me. "But others . . . well, they don't go from hurt to pain. They flash from insult to fury. They raze everything in sight, which usually succeeds in obliterating the very thing that hurt them. However, it causes collateral damage."

I hang my head so he can't see the fire in my eyes. "Dude. Bored. If I'd ever been hurt, I'd give a shit. But I haven't."

He pushes the hair out of my face with both his hands, sliding his palms over my cheeks. It takes all I've got to conceal a shiver. He forces my chin up. I flash him my best hundred-Megawatt smile.

We lock eyes. I'm not looking away first.

"It didn't hurt you when your mother left you in a cage like a dog, and forgot you for days while she was off with one of her endless string of boyfriends."

"You've got a seriously wild imagination."

He grabs a handful of my hair close to the scalp and uses it to keep me from looking away, as if I fecking planned to. When he reaches into one of my coat pockets and pulls out a Snickers bar, my mouth waters. I fought him and his men so hard back at Dancer's place that I'm drained. I pretend my spine is a broomstick so I don't sag into the chains holding me to the wall. Pretending is a game I'm good at.

He rips it open with his teeth. I smell chocolate and my stomach hurts.

"How many times did you curl in that cage, chained by a collar around your neck, waiting, wondering if she was going to remember you this time. Wondering what would kill you first: hunger or dehydration. What was it—five days she left you sometimes. No food or water. You slept in your own—"

"You want to shut up now."

"When you were eight, she died while you were locked up. Rowena didn't find you for a week."

That's the story. I don't say anything. There's nothing to say. Things got real simple in that cage. There are only two things to worry about in life: either you're free or you're not. If you're free, there's nothing to worry about. If you're not, you kick the shit out of everything around you until you are.

"Sometimes her boyfriends played with you."

Not that way. Never that way. I'm a virgin and I take it seriously. I'm going to lose it in a really epic way someday, when I'm ready. I'm all about gathering up some fan-fecking-tastic experiences to compensate for the crappy ones I had as a kid. That's why I wanted to give it to V'lane or maybe Barrons when I was old enough. Someone stellar. I want it to be with someone who will make it a night to remember.

"Are we like swapping philosophies, Ryodan? 'Cause if so, here's one of mine. Feck you. Past is past."

"It carves you."

"Vanishes. Means nothing," I say.

"You can never outrun it."

"I can outrun the wind."

"The wound you refuse to dress is one that will never heal. You gush lifeblood and never even know why. It will make you weak at a critical moment when you need to be strong."

"I get it, all right? You're going to torture me to death by talking. Kill me now. Get it over with. But use something quick and clean. Like a chain saw. Maybe a grenade."

He touches my cheek. "Dani."

"Is that pity, Ryodan? 'Cause I don't need it. Thought you were tougher than that."

His thumb brushes my mouth and he gives me a look I don't understand. I head-butt his hand away.

"You think you're going to chain me to a wall then stand here and tell me why it's okay that I am the way I am? That because of all the crap folks put me through when I was young it's all right that I turned out like this? Dude, I don't have a problem with how I turned out. I like me."

"Rowena made you kill your first human when you were nine years old."

How the feck does he *know* this stuff? She made it a game. Told me she wanted to know if I could whiz in and dump extra milk in Maggie's cereal bowl without her seeing me. Of course I could. Maggie died, sitting there at the breakfast table. Ro told me it was a coincidence, that she was old and had a heart attack. When I was eleven, I found out the truth. Ro hated Maggie because she'd been rallying *sidhe*-seers to elect a new Grand Mistress. I found the old witch's journals. She chronicled everything she did, like she thought one day she'd be immortalized and people would want to read her private memoirs. I have all those journals now, tucked away in a safe place. I'd poisoned Maggie that day with the "milk" I'd added to her bowl. I'd done a lot of other things, too, that I hadn't understood.

"Significant words there: Rowena made me. I got over it a long time ago."

"Funny, your speech is changing, kid. Getting all grown-up-like."

"Dude," I add.

"You're going to be a tough one to crack."

"Let me give you a clue: substitute the word 'impossible' for 'tough.'"

He peels the wrapper back from the Snickers. Offers me a bite.

I turn my head away. I won't eat like a chained-up animal.

"When we find your little boyfriend, you'll change your mind."

My guts unknot and I almost slump into the chains with relief but I lock my knees so I can't. He said "when" we find, which means they haven't. I don't telegraph unless I slip. I was afraid they had Dancer. He must have left while I was sleeping. He keeps odd hours, goes off sometimes until he feels like coming back. I can't always find him when I want to. Sometimes I don't see him for days. It's good to know he's safe somewhere. They didn't get him. They only got me. I can handle this kind of stuff. I cut my teeth on it. Dancer . . . well, until the walls fell, he lived a charmed life. I never want him to have to deal with these men.

"He isn't my boyfriend."

"How long will you make me keep you here, Dani?"

"Until you figure out it isn't going to do you any good."

He smiles faintly and turns away. At the door, he pauses and puts his hand on the light switch like he's giving me a choice. As if all I have to do is give him a look that says "Please don't leave me in the dark" and he won't.

I flip him off big and showy, with both hands chained over my head.

He leaves me without my sword, in the dark.

I don't worry.

I know Ryodan. If anyone is going to kill me, it'll be him. That means he's got this place protected from Shades and Fae or he'd never have left me here.

I'm hungry and tired. I close my eyes and play an old game with myself, one I learned young.

I pretend I have a giant, cushy pillow in my stomach, filling it up softly, absorbing the acid that boils from extreme hunger. I pretend that I'm stretched out in a downy soft bed in a perfectly safe place where nobody can hurt me.

Hanging by manacles around my wrists, I sleep.

"What did you *think* was going to happen, Dani?" Mac says.

I squint my eyes open a slit and groan. TP is here, standing right in front of me.

I do a quick scan. I don't see her spear but I know it's on her somewhere. She doesn't go anyplace without it.

"Not fair," I say. "You can't kill me while I'm chained up. Dude, you have to at least give me a fighting chance. Unchain me." I won't fight her. But I will run. I can out-run TP till the end of days.

"I don't understand, Dani," she says. "You had to know when you killed all those Fae in front of thousands of witnesses that it would put you on the shit-list of every person and Fae with any power in this city, with Ryodan and his men first in line. Were you *trying* to become Dublin's most wanted?"

"Not like you weren't for a while, and you survived."

"I had Barrons at my back. You pissed off your potential version of Barrons."

I'm deliberately obtuse. "Christian MacKeltar? He's not pissed at me."

"Ryodan."

"Ryodan isn't Barrons and never will be!"

"Agreed. But he could have your back, if you'd let him. Instead, you not only blatantly antagonized him, you put him in a position where he has to punish you. You defied him in front of the entire city. *Dani, Dani.*"

"Who the feck's side are you on? And why aren't you trying to kill me?"

"I don't need to. You've got the whole city lined up waiting to do that. *Dani! Dani!*"

"They have to catch me first. Why do you keep saying my name like that?"

"*Wake up*. You're caught," TP says. "I know you're not stupid. What are you doing? *Dani! Dani!*"

"Same thing you always did. Taking a stand. Not backing down. Even if I don't have all the answers and can't predict how I'll get out of this one, I *will* get out of this one."

I'm still waiting for a spear through my gut. Instead TP smiles and says, "Hold on to that thought."

"Wake *up*, Dani!"

My face stings like somebody slapped me. I squint my eyes open when I thought they already were.

Jo's standing in front of me. My cheek stings. I'd rub it but I'm chained.

"Where did TP go?" I say, confused.

"What?" Jo says.

I lick my lips, or try to. My mouth is so dry my tongue doesn't make any difference. My lower lip is split and crusted with dried blood. The base of my skull hurts. I must have banged myself a good one passing out, or got hit in the back of my head when I was fighting Ryodan's men.

"I'm sorry I hit you but I was afraid you were . . . oh, Dani! What did he do to you? He beat you! Then I hit you, too!" She looks like she might cry. She touches my face gently and I flinch.

"Get off me!"

"I'm going to kill him," she whispers, and something in the softly spoken words surprises me. Like she's turning all bloodthirsty, becoming like me.

I try to figure out if TP was the dream or Jo is, or they both are. I have the weirdest dreams sometimes. As if TP would actually bother trying to give me advice. I should have known it was a dream instantly by the fact that she wasn't killing me.

"I ran into him," I tell her. "As in collided. Twice. That's why my face is so beat up." Well, it's most of the reason.

"Are you *defending* Ryodan? Look what he's done to you! Dani, has he brainwashed you? Are you getting Stockholm syndrome?"

"What the feck's Stockholm got to do with any of this? Ain't that some city in Sweden?"

She wraps her arms around me and gets all in my space. It's awkward with my hands chained above my head and my ankles shackled to the floor. She sort of hugs me and I can't get her off me because I'm stuck.

"Dude!" I give a whole body shrug, trying to dislodge her. She's tenacious, lopping all over me. "What are you doing?"

When she pulls back I see she's crying. I must look pretty bad.

"Why did you do it?" She sniffs and wipes her nose with the back of her hand. "We talked and talked about it, and can't figure it out. You didn't just wave a red flag at a bull. You sauntered right up to it, punched it in the face then tried to dance on its horns. Dani, what were you thinking?"

I sigh. People ask the stupidest questions. Sometimes you *don't* think. You just do. Some moments are too golden to pass up. You play—you pay. I've always been okay with that.

I peer at her suspiciously. Jo can't be here. Not in the guts of Chester's. "You're not real," I say.

She feels my forehead. "You're running a fever."

I know. I'm dripping sweat and freezing cold. I always get a fever if I get dangerously hungry. It's another fecking weakness. So many superstrengths. So many limits. I don't let folks know about them. "Must have caught a cold," I tell her. I have food stuffed in every pocket, but with my hands chained above my head I can't get to one bite of it.

"Get a protein bar out of my pocket and feed it to me." If this is really happening, I'll get strong again and my body temp will drop back to normal. If this is a dream, at least I'll get to dream the taste of food. I've got nothing to lose and everything to gain. "I don't suppose you've seen a key to these manacles lying around somewhere convenient?" I say with no hope. Ryodan's not sloppy.

Four protein bars later I know I'm not dreaming. My head is still throbbing but starting to clear. TP wasn't real.

But Jo is.

She tells me word spread everywhere that I'd single-handedly taken on a bunch of Fae in Chester's then sauntered out all cocky-like with an Unseelie prince. Margery insisted the Unseelie prince had killed me, and managed to convince a lot of *sidhe*-sheep to write me off, taking up right where Rowena left off, smearing my name.

Kat had seen things differently. She'd done some investigating before making her decision. According to onlookers, the "prince" who'd walked me out hadn't been wearing a torque. The Unseelie princes have silver torques around their necks that glow like they're radioactive. The necklace seems to be part of them, inseparable like their tattoos and wings. That told Kat all she needed to know: if the prince wasn't wearing a torque, it had to be Christian who'd escorted me out.

I'm not sure how she made the next deductive leap, but I'm glad she did. She sent a group of girls to Chester's to search for me, believing Ryodan had gone after me and captured me.

I'm amazed by how speedily she acted. Maybe Kat's

going to do all right by the *sidhe*-seers. "How did she figure out I was missing so quickly?"

"You've been gone for three days, Dani."

I'm stunned. I've been chained down here for three days? No wonder I'm starving.

"How the feck did you find me? I figured I was like, buried in the dungeon of Chester's or something."

"You are. I saw Ryodan get off an elevator hidden in the wall outside the retroclub. The door didn't close all the way and I slipped in when nobody was looking."

I close my eyes and sigh.

There were three mistakes in that sentence. (1) Ryodan doesn't get seen if he doesn't want to. (2) The doors around this place don't stay slightly open. (3) Nobody slips into them without being noticed.

The only way Jo saw Ryodan get off an elevator was if he let her.

Which means he hadn't been able to find my "little boyfriend" over the past three days. But he'd sure found somebody else to use against me.

On the insides of my eyelids I see Jo chained, beaten.

Ryodan hadn't even had to leave his club. He just sat back and waited for whoever showed up first, looking for me.

I open my eyes. "Get out of here, Jo," I say. "Now."

"Neither of you are going anywhere," Ryodan says as he steps from the shadows.

SEVEN

"I fall to pieces"

I'm absurdly easy to break if you know the right buttons to push.

If you've read any comics, you know superheroes have a critical vulnerability: the society they protect.

Jo's part of my society. Fact is, any *sidhe*-sheep chained up next to me would have me singing a new tune. Well, maybe not Margery.

Actually, probably even her, too.

The hard thing for me is knowing I can take more than everyone else. Like that stupid bunny that used to be in commercials all the time, I take a licking and keep on kicking. And punching. And breathing.

Not true other folks. They die so easily.

Besides, I'm not afraid of the big sleep. I figure it's just another adventure.

I try to talk Ryodan out of chaining Jo up.

He doesn't listen to me.

Jo goes ballistic when he grabs her. Screaming and yelling and kicking. I'm kind of impressed by how hard she fights.

I think watching Dublin get destroyed on Halloween, seeing our friend Barb get taken by the *Sinsar Dubh* and ridden as a machine-gun-toting bitch to massacre so many of us, plus living in a world where you have to shake your shoes out before you put them on to make sure you don't get eaten by a Shade faster than you can say "Aw, shit" is messing with Jo's head.

She used to be like Kat, all even-tempered and cautious with decisions, didn't have a sharp word for anyone.

"I'm going to kill you, you bastard, you won't get away with this!" she's shouting. "Let me go! Get your hands off me, you son of a bitch!"

Ryodan chains her next to me. She struggles but it's like watching a fly batting at a window, trying to get outside. You know it's never going to work.

I give her a look. "Got any more bright ideas, Jo? Try bringing a few babies for him to torture next time."

She gives her chains a violent jerk. We're bolted to a stone wall.

"Good luck with that." If I couldn't break them with my superstrength, she's got a snowball's chance in hell. I think he has the metal spelled. I think he has everything spelled. I want to know where he learns his spells so I can sign up for a crash course. If I've been down here three days, I should be, well, messier than I am. How did he keep me unconscious for three days? Put me in some kind of suspended animation? I seriously have to pee.

"I was trying to help," she says.

"You should have just taken a baseball bat to my head. Put me out of my misery." I could have held out down here forever until she went and served herself up to Ryodan as a weapon.

Ryodan stands in front of us, legs apart, arms folded over his chest. He's a big dude. I wonder if Jo knows he has fangs. I wonder what he is. I wonder why she's staring at him like that. She hates him.

I trash my pointless wonderings and cut to the chase.

Procrastinating is number three on my Stupid List. You still end up exactly where you didn't want to be, doing exactly what you didn't want to do, with the only difference being that you lost all that time in between, during which you could have been doing something fun. Even worse, you probably stayed in a stressed-out, crappy mood the whole time you were avoiding it. If you know something is inevitable, do it and get it over with. Move on. Life is short.

If he tortures Jo, I'll cave.

I know it.

He knows it.

Ergo, torturing her is a great big fat waste of time. His. Mine. Hers.

"What do you want from me, Ryodan?" I say.

"It's decision time, Dani."

"Deaf much? I said. What do you want from me?"

"You owe me compensation."

"Dude, the bush is ready. Why you still beating around it?"

"I've lived a long time, kid, and I've never heard anyone mutilate the English language quite like you."

"How long is that?" Jo says.

I yawn, big and dramatic. "Still beating. And me all bush-like." I give an all-body, bushy bristle.

His eyes narrow on me like he's thinking. Like maybe he hasn't decided exactly what he wants from me yet. That worries me. It should be real simple: he wants me to work for him. I know he's not as bright as I am, so I help him out.

"I'll look into your little ice mystery, Ryodan. I'll put it at the top of my priority list. Unchain us already."

"It's not that simple anymore. You complicated the fuck out of things when you decided to defy me publicly. Nobody does that and lives."

"Breathing here," I say.

"Do you have to keep saying 'fuck' around her? She's barely thirteen," Jo says.

"Fourteen," I correct irritably.

"My men want you dead. They're pushing for a dramatic execution, in the club. They say it's the only way to appease the patrons of Chester's."

"I always wanted to go out in a big way," I say. "Maybe we could do some fireworks, huh? I think there are some left up at that old petrol station on O'Clare."

"Nobody's executing anyone," Jo says. "She's a child."

"I'm not a fecking child. I don't think I was even born that way."

"I told them I believe you can be useful," Ryodan says. "That I can control you."

I bristle and rattle my chains. Nobody controls me. Not anymore.

"They say you'll never answer to anyone. Not even Barrons is on my side."

No doubt because TP was telling Barrons to tell Ryodan to kill me. Or let her do it.

"It's eight against one," he says.

"It's eight against two," Jo says. "If you count her sister *sidhe*-seers—and you'd better—it's eight against thousands."

"Your numbers have been severely diminished," Ryodan says.

"Worldwide, we're over twenty thousand."

"I didn't know that," I say to Jo. "Why didn't I know that?" To Ryodan, I say, "Dude, kill me or free me."

"If you kill her," Jo says, "you'll incur the wrath of every *sidhe*-seer in the world. They'll hunt you. Dani's a legend among us. We won't lose her."

"If I decide to kill her," Ryodan says, "no one will ever know what happened to either of you."

I blink, mentally replaying what Jo said again and

again, but I can't hear it enough. "Really? I'm a legend? Like, around the whole world they know of me? Say it again!" I preen. I had no idea. There might be a little swagger left in my body after all. I cock a jaunty hip.

"Let her go," Jo says to Ryodan, "and I'll stay in her place."

"The feck you'll stay!" I explode.

"You're offering to stay here. Chained up. With me. In exchange for her." A smile plays at his lips.

"As long as you have me as a hostage, she'll behave."

"The feck you'll stay!" I say again since nobody reacted like they were supposed to, like, by obeying me. Or paying any attention to me at all.

"I haven't forgotten what you did to my cell phone, *sidhe*-seer," Ryodan says.

"You were taking pictures on our property. It's private," Jo says.

"You're on my property. It's private."

"I'm not taking pictures. I came to take back something that's ours. Something you had no right to take."

"I'm not a something. Or a child," I say.

"She had no right to kill the patrons of my club. She'd been warned. Repeatedly."

"And you know how well she listens. You shouldn't have brought her into your club and left her alone with a sword. Could you possibly be that stupid?"

"Dudes, quit talking about me like I'm not here!"

"*Sidhe*-seer, tread lightly," he says to Jo, and his voice goes real soft. Soft from Ryodan is never good.

"Let me stay in her place. She's just a kid."

"I'm *not* a kid! And she's not fecking staying here. Nobody's staying here! Except maybe me!"

"You do understand what it would mean," he says to Jo, like I'm not even having a violent, noisy fight with a wall and four chains. "If she makes a single misstep, you're dead."

I feel the blood drain from my face. I *always* misstep. Misstep is my middle name, right after Mega. I can't *not* misstep. I have feet.

"I understand."

"She doesn't mean it!" I shout. "She doesn't even know what she's talking about! She doesn't have any clue what you dudes are really like. Besides, I don't really even care about her at all. You can kill her. So, you may as well let her go."

"Shut up, Dani," Jo says.

"You'll have to sign an employment application," Ryodan tells Jo.

"Don't sign it, Jo! He's got some kind of spell on it."

"Am I being held hostage or applying for a job?" Jo says.

"I'm short a few waitresses. Some of them were—" Ryodan gives me a look. "—collateral damage the other day."

"I didn't kill any humans."

"Two of them had enough Unseelie in them that apparently you couldn't tell the difference," Ryodan says.

I killed humans? How much Unseelie had they eaten?

"You want me to be a *waitress*?" Jo says, horrified, like it's a fate worse than death. "I tried to wait tables in high school. I can't. I drop plates. I spill drinks. I'm a researcher. A linguist. I live in my head. I don't wait tables."

"Conveniently, I have two applications handy." Ryodan withdraws a folded packet of papers from his pocket.

"Why two? I ain't waiting tables," I say belligerently.

"I have to serve *Fae*? As in take orders and *fill* them? And bring things to their tables?" Jo can't seem to wrap her brain around it. Like she'd rather stay chained to the wall than wait tables.

"And my men. Occasionally, I imagine, even me. With

a smile." He looks her up and down, slo-mo. "You'll look good in the uniform. Do we have a deal." In typical Ryodan fashion, his voice doesn't rise at the end of the question. He knows they have a deal. He can read Jo like a book with see-through covers.

My chains rattle as I test them with everything I've got. He is *not* putting Jo to work in the kiddie subclub. She's got the kind of face that's so delicate and pretty that she can wear really short hair like she does and look totally hot. Even those stupid glasses she wears when she reads just make her look good because they make her bones seem even more dainty. She has something ethereal. She is *not* wearing a short plaid skirt, tight white blouse, socks, and baby doll heels. She will *not* be waiting on him and his men! Chester's will swallow her up like a tasty morsel and spit out blood and gristle.

"No, Jo," I say flatly. "Don't you dare."

"We have a deal," Jo says.

He unchains Jo, hands her the "application" and a pen.

She flattens it out on the wall and signs it without even reading it.

He folds it up and hands it back to her. "Take the elevator back up the way you came. Lor is waiting for you there. He'll get you a uniform. You start tonight. You have a single priority—make my patrons happy."

"Lor is waiting for me," Jo says. She pushes a hand through her short dark hair and gives him a look that kind of surprises me, it's got so much balls in it. "I thought you said your men expected you to kill us."

"If you don't hand him the signed application, he will. I suggest you make sure he sees it the instant you get off the elevator."

"What about Dani?"

"She'll be up soon."

"She comes with me now," Jo says.

"Never. Tell. Me. What. To. Do." Ryodan's talking soft again, and I don't know about Jo but it gives me a shiver when he speaks like that.

"Get out of here, you stupid fecking *sidhe*-sheep!" I say. "I'll be fine. I'd have been finer if you'd never showed up!" He owns her now. He's got some kind of spell on her. It pisses me off so bad I'm shaking.

After Jo leaves, Ryodan glides toward me in that weird fluid way he has. He didn't move that way in front of Jo. He walked all slow-mo when she was here.

I see the glint of a silver knife in his hand.

"Dude, no need to cut me. I'll sign the fecking application. Just give me a pen." I have to get out of here. I have to save Jo. She put herself on the line for me. I can't stand it.

"Kid, when will you learn."

"You'd be amazed the things I know."

"You might be able to thrash your way out of a spider-web, but thrashing in quicksand doesn't work. The harder you fight, the more ground you lose. Struggling merely expedites your inevitable defeat."

"Never been defeated. Never will be."

"Rowena was a spiderweb." He touches my cheek with the hand holding the knife. The silver glints an inch from my eye. "Do you know what I am."

"A great big pain in my ass."

"Quicksand. And you're dancing on it."

"Dude, what's with the knife?"

"I'm not interested in ink anymore. You're going to sign my contract in blood."

"Thought you said it was an application," I say pissily.

"It is, Dani. To a very exclusive club. What's Mine."

"Ain't nobody's."

"Sign."

"You can't make me."

"Or Jo dies. Slowly and painfully."

"Dude, why are you still talking? Unchain me and give me the fecking contract already."

There's a guillotine above my neck. I hear it swishing as it slices through the air. There's a name carved into the shiny blade: JO. I see it in my periphery with every step I take. It's going to make me nuts.

After I sign his fecking contract—I got a paper towel in my fist because my palm's still bleeding where he cut me—he lets me go. Just like that. Unchains my other arm and legs, offers to heal me, to which I say a great big kiss-my-booty, then escorts me to the elevator and tells me to go wherever my current version of home is.

I expect him to tell me I have to move into Chester's so he can watch my every move, like Barrons did with M—TP.

I expect him to go all control-freak on me.

I don't expect him to give me my sword back and send me on my way with a casual reminder to show up for "work" tomorrow at eight P.M. He says there's something else he wants me to see.

I hate this.

He's not reeling off one thousand and one Ryodan commandments like I thought he would.

He's giving me all kinds of rope to hang myself with. I tie knots with rope. And I move really fast. It's inevitable I'll get tangled up in all that rope somehow, with a loop or two around my neck.

How am I going to get Jo out of this?

Four of his big scarred dudes are waiting for me when I get off the elevator. I glance warily around for Barrons and TP as I wave my contract big and noisy at Ryodan's men so they don't give me any grief before they take it from me to put it wherever it is Ryodan plans to keep it and I'm going to have to eventually steal it back from. I'm out of protein bars and not in the mood for a pissing contest. Fortunately, TP is nowhere to be seen.

I hit the bathroom under heavy guard. What do they think I'll do? Blow the place up? I can't. I don't have my backpack. No MacHalo either. They didn't bring it when they nabbed me at Dancer's. I'd look out a window but there aren't any in the club. My bones tell me it's night. I don't take chances with Shades. I refuse to die so stupidly. "I need flashlights," I say, blowing out of the bathroom.

One of the dudes grunts and walks away. The rest of them escort me through the subclubs. I get stared at by every Fae we pass. There's murder in their eyes.

Something weird happens to me on the way out.

Freeze-framing feels like picking myself up mentally and shifting sideways into a different way of being, and I like it.

Now, as I walk out and see all the pissed-off faces, human and Fae, a completely different part of me gets picked up and shifted sideways without me even trying—in fact, I'm pretty sure I'm resisting—and I don't like it one bit, because all the sudden I'm seeing my world with what feels like totally different eyeballs.

I don't like these eyeballs. They see things wrong.

The Fae hate me. A lot of the humans do, too.

Ryodan's men want me dead and I have no idea why he's keeping me alive.

TP—oh, feck it—Mac, the best friend I ever had, *Mac*—who made me a birthday cake and hung with me and treated me cool, and sold a piece of her soul to the Gray Woman to save me, hates me, too. She wants to kill me because I killed her sister on Rowena's orders before I ever even knew Mac existed.

Jo's life dangles on a thread held by my completely unreliable hands.

And I have a thought that I've never had in my entire fourteen years of life (and I've had a lot of thoughts!), and it's a little muffled (probably because I'd rather not hear it) and it goes something like this:

Geez, Dani, what the feck have you done?

I've always been a speedboat blasting across the whitecaps, thriving on sensation, wind in my hair, salt spray on my face, having the time of my life. Never looking back. Never seeing what happens around or behind me.

These new eyeballs see my wake. They see what I leave behind when I've passed.

Boats capsized. People flailing in the waves.

People I care about. I'm not talking about Dublin, my city that I always keep cool and impersonal with no real face. These people have faces.

We pass Jo. She's already dressed and at her new post, paired with another waitress, being trained. She *does* look good in the uniform. She gives me a look as I pass, part exasperation, part plea to behave. Her trainer stares daggers at me. I wonder if the waitresses I killed were her friends.

"They shouldn't have eaten so much Unseelie," I mutter in my defense.

I try to shift back to the way I was before I got off the elevator, back to Dani "the Mega" who doesn't give a crap.

Nothing happens.

I try it again.

Still feeling the breeze from that guillotine.

One of Ryodan's dudes, Lor, hands me a flashlight. "Gee," I say, "thanks. A whole flashlight against a city of Shades."

"They moved on. Mostly."

I roll my eyes. "'Mostly' might be okay with you

'cause, like, they don't eat whatever you dudes are. Why is that?"

Lor doesn't answer me, but I didn't expect him to.

The second we reach the door, I freeze-frame.

I can outrun anything.

Even myself.

EIGHT

"And I'm hungry like the wolf"

I click on a flashlight and head for the nearest store I know of that still has Snickers on the shelves so I can replenish my supplies. I have a bottomless stomach and it hurts from hunger. That's a feeling I take pains to avoid. Especially when my head's still throbbing so bad. I'd put ice on it, but if I've been out for three days, it's too late. Ice only works if you use it right away. I root through my hair, find the swollen, bruised patch at my nape that's causing so much pain, and sigh, wondering what I hit and when. Some folks think since I'm always banged up I'm a glutton for pain. I'm not. It's just the way my life is.

Like I thought, it's night, so the streets are pretty much deserted. Folks do their "shopping" during the day. Those that do hunt at night, do just that—hunt. They come out in packs, armed to the gills, and go after any Unseelie they can find.

A lot of the night-hunters have a death wish. They don't know how to live in the world the way it is now, so they take crazy risks. I end up bailing out vigilantes left and right. Sometimes they run into Jayne, and before anybody can say, "Don't shoot, we're human," there's casualties. Everybody's got jumpy trigger fingers.

Things sure have changed since the walls fell last October. Seven months ago the streets were easy. Hit the night, kill some Fae, then kill some more. The Unseelie were simple to take by surprise because they had such a low opinion of humans. They didn't see us as a serious threat.

They do now.

They're on guard, more dangerous, harder to trap, and impossible to kill unless you're me or Mac or a Shade. Shades are cannibals. Life is life. They don't discriminate. We have humans fighting Fae, humans fighting humans, Fae fighting each other, and all of us trying to get rid of the Shades.

I slow to a Joe-walk, running out of steam. I need food fast. I already ate everything I had stuffed in my pockets. Three days of starvation does a number on me. Swinging my sword around my wrist (it took me months to perfect that move—and it is *smooooth*!), I duck into a convenience store with broken-out windows, shelves spilled sideways, cash register open and overturned. I can't see why anybody would bother stealing money. It doesn't get you anything. People's eyes are finally open, money's as worthless as it always really was. Used to amaze me when I was little how everybody passed around pieces of paper that they all agreed to pretend meant the same thing when everybody knew it didn't mean anything. It was the first adult conspiracy I became aware of. Made me think maybe no adults should ever be the boss of me. I'm the smartest person I know. Except maybe for Dancer. Not bragging. It's a real pain in the ass a lot of the time.

"Buying" nowadays operates on something solid and real: the barter system. Ryodan has the bartenders and waitresses at Chester's coached to take certain items he either wants for himself or can turn around for something else he wants. If you have a big item he's interested in, he'll give you a line of credit. I hear he gets favors from the Fae in exchange for making them a place where they can prey on humans. Though I hate Jo working at Chester's, in a way I'm glad because I'll get more inside scoop now. Figure out what motivates Ryodan, what his weaknesses are. Dude's got to have some chink in his armor. Everybody's got their kryptonite.

I circle a pile of clothes and husks (fecking Shades, I hate them!) and head for my candy rack.

It's empty.

Not a single Snickers.

Not a single anything for that matter.

I head down the cracker aisle.

The shelves are bare.

My stomach growls. Pissily. My knees aren't wobbling yet but they're close.

I turn my flashlight to wide beam and sweep it around the store.

The place has been cleaned out.

I'd blow out a melodramatic sigh but it's an expenditure of energy I suddenly can't afford. I'm no longer swinging my sword or bouncing from foot to foot the way I do a lot. I'm not moving a hair I don't have to. My life just got harder. When you're a supercar like me, you either need a huge gas tank, which I don't have at five feet two and three-quarters first thing in the morning, or you need to live in a city with a lot of gas stations.

My gas stations are drying up.

It's okay. I saw this coming. Dancer did, too. I squirreled away stashes of food, water, and medical supplies in lots of hidey-holes around Dublin months ago. Me and Dancer have been building on those reserves in our spare time over the past few weeks. He doesn't know where all my hideouts are, and I don't know where he keeps all his stuff. That way if somebody tries to torture one of us to tell, we can't totally wipe each other out. I tried to tell the *sidhe*-sheep to do it, but they thought I was crazy. They said that with more than half the population gone there was plenty of stuff in the stores to last a good long while. I said somebody was going to try to monopolize food distribution. Dude, barter system— food and water are the premium. They said everyone was too busy trying to survive. I said that wouldn't last long and didn't they read *A Canticle for Leibowitz,* see how things trend? They said what did *A Canticle for Leibowitz* have to do with food? And I said should I start calling you *sidhe*-simpletons instead of *sidhe*-sheep? Do I have to spell out everything? Can't we metaphor some things?

I hate always being right, I mutter in my head. Talking takes breath and breathing takes gas I don't have.

I Joe-walk out of the store and nearly have a fecking heart attack when I see the Unseelie prince standing there, half in the shadows. The half-out part of him is splashed with moonlight, but the moon doesn't glow the same way it used to before the Fae came. It's rarely the same color from night to night. Tonight it has a silvery purple luminosity, making half of him a black silhouette, the other half lavender-metallic. He's tattooed and beautiful and eerie and exotic, and gets my heart thumping in a way that has nothing to do with fear.

My sword flashes up. My blade is long and alabaster. I lock my elbow so my arm doesn't wobble.

"Easy, lass."

"Fecking *stop* sneaking *up* on me like that!" How can I not hear him? Him and Ryodan can both get the jump on me. It makes me crazy. I have superhearing. My hearing is so good that I can hear air displacement when other people move, for feck's sake. Nobody sneaks up on me. Both of them managed to do it that night on the water tower, and Christian just did it again. Got within five feet of me without me even knowing it.

"Sword. Lower."

"Why should I do that?" He's turning erotic, like the other UPs. My used-to-be best friend Mac calls them death-by-sex Fae because they can kill with sex. And that's the best-case scenario. Worst case? They turn you Pri-ya like they did Mac. They leave you alive, totally addicted to sex, insatiable and out of your mind. The other UPs corralled me once, kept me between them, and did things to me I don't like to think about. I don't want sex to be that way. Like you're some kind of helpless animal. I've had helpless animal up to my eyebrows already in my life. What Christian is throwing off isn't a tenth of what the other UPs have, but it's bad.

"I'll never hurt you, lass."

"Says the Unseelie prince." But I lower my sword, prop it against my leg. I wasn't sure how much longer I was going to be able to hold it up anyway.

The muscles in his face ripple, like they're competing to shape an expression, and rage is looking like the victor, and I get the feeling calling him an Unseelie prince might just have been a tiny error of judgment on my part. Been making a few of those lately.

"Say my name, lass."

I cover my ears and look at him like what the feck? His voice just came out as big as a house.

"Say my fucking name!" Thunder rolls in the sky. I wrap my arms around my head to mute his voice. Times like this, I hate my superhearing. I look up. There's no storm moving in. It's him. Influencing the weather, just like Fae royalty. I look back down. A veneer of ice coats the sidewalk around him, a shimmer of crystals dusts his black boots and frosts halfway up his jeans.

"Christian," I say.

He inhales sharp, like something hurts in him somewhere just from me saying his name, and closes his eyes. His face ripples, goes smooth like Silly Putty just out of the egg then ripples again. I wonder if I touched it, I could mold it into shape, maybe stamp some funnies from the comic section of the newspaper on it. Cracking myself up again!

"Say it again, lass."

If it keeps him from turning all UP on me, fine. "Christian. Christian. Christian."

He smiles faintly. I think. Feck if I can figure out what's going on with his face. No more than I can figure out how he keeps sneaking up—

"Holy flour chunks!" It dawns on me. "You can *sift*! You really are turning total UP. Like with all the superpowers. Dude! What else are you getting?"

If it was a smile, it just disappeared. He doesn't look as happy as I'd be if I was getting all that juice. I bet *his* fuel tank doesn't run out of gas. I'm so jealous I could spit. But that, too, would require energy.

He moves forward, steps from the shadows, and I see he's carrying a box under his arm.

"I'm going to kill Ryodan," he says.

I unwrap my arms from around my head. We're doing normal conversational tones again. I tuck the sword beneath my coat.

"Good luck with that. You figure out how to, you let me know, okay?"

"Here, take this." He shoves the box at me.

I fumble for it, clumsy from hunger. It's slippery with a coating of ice. I catch it as it hits the ground. Sloppy! I recognize the color and shape now that it's in my hands, and light up like a Christmas tree. "Christian!" I beam. I'll say his name however many times he wants. I'll crow it from the top of water towers. What the feck, I'll compose a jaunty ditty for him and sing it as I whiz around Dublin!

He just handed me a whole box of Snickers! I rip open

a wrapper, break the half-frozen bar in half and cram it in my mouth sideways.

When I toss my hair out of my face and look up to thank him around a mouthful, he's gone.

Three candy bars later what just happened sinks in.

I sit on the curb, stow the candy bars away in my pockets and pack, and say, "Aw, bugger."

Christian knew how bad I needed food. He watches me. I wonder why. I wonder how often. I wonder if he's out there right now, looking at me from somewhere and I don't even know it. Dude, I got an Unseelie prince spying on me. Great.

Tank full again, I swing by Dublin Castle. Three days was a long time to be out of commission. I got a job to do. A beat to walk. A superhero's work is never done. Between patrolling my city, printing and distributing the *Daily,* slaying Unseelie, keeping an eye on Jo and the other *sidhe*-seers—and now working for Ryodan all night every night—there aren't going to be enough hours in the day!

"Where the bloody hell have you been?" Inspector Jayne says the instant he sees me. "I've got Unseelie spilling out of every cage. We agreed that you would come by three times a week and slay them with the sword—and that's barely enough as it is. I haven't seen you in five days! Five bloody days! If you won't take your responsibilities seriously, my men will relieve you of that weapon."

He stares at the pucker of leather, where my sword's tucked beneath a long coat that brushes the laces of my high-top sneakers. It's May and almost too warm to be wearing my favorite black leather. Soon I'm going to have to sling the sword over my back and deal with everybody staring at it, coveting it. At least now lots of folks don't know I have it. Then again my rep *is* starting to precede me. Jo said I was a legend!

"You just try that, dude." I swagger onto the training green, between him and his men. A few dozen of them are in full armor, sweating up a stink-storm. Supersmell is a pain in the butt sometimes. He's been working them hard. I wonder what's with that. It's night. He usually has his men out hunting at night, patrolling, keeping the streets safe.

We glare at each other.

He softens. He always does. He has a hard time looking at me and staying mad. He sees his own kids in my face. Jayne's got a supersoft spot for children. He and his wife have been taking in orphans left and right. I don't know how he feeds them all. But Jayne's no dummy. I suspect he's got stores stashed away, too. Till tonight, it seemed like most of us were playing by the same rules. Take a lot—but leave some.

No rules anymore. Somebody's cleaning the shelves. That's just not civilized.

"Damn it all to hell, Dani, I was worried about you!"

"Get over it, Jayne. I take care of myself just fine. Always have."

He gets that look in his eyes that always makes me uncomfortable, like he's about to put a fatherly arm around me or wipe a smudge of blood off my cheek. I shudder. My sword hand's itching and I'm all about scratching it. "I'm here now. Quit wasting time. Which Unseelie you want dead first?"

"Do you know why we're not out hunting tonight?"

I don't like being cued to speak so I just look at him.

"No room in the cages. Go make me all of it. And don't leave until you have."

He glances again at the pucker of sword under my coat then does something he does a lot. He looks at his men, and looks back at me again, all cool and speculative-like. He's not seeing a kid when he does it. He's seeing an obstacle.

I know Jayne real well. He doesn't even know he does it.

He's wondering if they could take my sword. Wondering if he'd let his men kill me to get it. If I told him that, he'd deny it to the end of days. He thinks he really cares about me, and on a level he does. He thinks he'd like to take me home to his wife and make me part of their family, give me the kind of life he's pretty sure I didn't have.

But there's four feet of a shiny metal problem between us, and it's four feet of immense power. And it changes everything. I'm not a kid. I'm what stands between him and something he wants for all the right reasons. And he isn't so sure he wouldn't do something very wrong for all the right reasons.

My sword and Mac's spear are the only two weapons that can kill Fae. That makes them hands-down the hottest Big Ticket items in—not just Dublin—but the world. A part of Jayne is like Barrons. He wants to kill Fae— and I have the weapon he needs to do it. He can't help himself. He's a leader. And a good one. Every time he sees me, he will instinctively assess whether he thinks he can take it from me. And one day he might make a move.

I don't hold it against him.

I'd do the same.

I see when he decides it's not a risk worth taking because he's still not sure I won't kill some of his men, maybe even him. I keep those doubts in his mind. The subconscious part where all this stuff takes place.

He says something nice to me, but I don't absorb it. Jayne's a good man, good as they come. It doesn't make him any less dangerous. Some folks think I'm a little psychic along with my other superpowers. I'm not. I just see the ways folks telegraph. Pick up on tiny clues other folks don't, like the way their muscles tense in their fingers when they look at my sword like they're imagining how it would feel to hold it, or how their gaze darts to the side when they say they're glad it's *my* responsibility not theirs. Funny thing to me is how their conscious and subconscious seem to be so split, like they aren't talking to each other at all. Like competing feelings can't possibly coexist inside you. Dude, they do all the time. I'm an emotional Ping-Pong ball between paddles: one day I can't wait to have sex, the next I think semen's the grossest thing in the world. Monday I'm crazy about Dancer, Tuesday I hate him for mattering to me. I just go with it, focus on whichever feeling I have most often and try to keep my mouth shut when it's the other. But most folks got Id and Ego living on different floors in their head's house, in different rooms, and they've locked all the doors between them, and nailed sheets of plywood over that, because they think they're, like, sworn enemies that can't hang together.

Ro thought the whole subconscious/conscious issue had something to do with why I am the way I am. She said I have the neurological condition synesthesia out the ass, with all kinds of cross regions of my brain talking to each other. Old witch was always psychoanalyzing me (as in she was the psycho and I was being analyzed). She said my Id and Ego are best buds, they don't just live on the same floor, they share a bed.

I'm cool with that. Frees up space for other stuff.

I take off, tune out, and do what I do best.

Kill.

NINE

*And it all goes boom, chicka boom,
boom-boom, chicka boom*

"What is this place?" I ask Ryodan.

"You got lots of places around the city, kid."

I don't say "Yes." Lately, everybody seems to know everything about me anyway. And he doesn't say, "Well, I do, too." When Ryodan wastes words, he does it in the worst possible way. He gets all philosophical. Yawn the feck out of me. There's observation of fact that keeps you alive like understanding Jayne, and there's philosophizing. Way different things. The former is my gig.

We're standing on a concrete loading dock, outside commercial doors at an industrial warehouse on the north side of Dublin. Ryodan drove us here in a military Humvee. It's parked behind us, barely visible in the night, black on black, wheels and everything, with black windows. It's something I would've driven. If I'd found one. But I didn't. It's pure badass. And I thought Barrons's cars were cool.

I begin my investigation. There are no lights on around the building. "Dude, got Shade protection?"

"Don't need it. Nothing alive inside."

"What about the folks that come and go?"

"Only during daylight."

"Dude. Night. I'm here."

He looks at me, looks at my head, and his lips twitch like he's trying not to bust out laughing. "You don't need that . . . whatever the fuck it is."

"Ain't dying by Shade. It's a MacHalo." First thing I did this morning was swing by Dancer's and grab my stuff.

The MacHalo is a brilliant invention. In Dublin alone it's saved thousands of lives. It's named after my used-to-be best friend Mac, the person who invented the bike helmet covered with LED lights, front, sides, rear. I added a few brackets to mine for better coverage in fast-mo. (Though I've always wondered if I could fast-mo through a Shade even without it.) It's the ultimate in Shade protection. I heard they're going gangbusters around the world. Everybody in Dublin's got one. For a while there I was making and delivering them to survivors every day. Some folks say the Shades have left Dublin. Moved on for greener pastures. But Shades are sneaky and it only takes one to kill you instantly. I'm not taking any chances.

"What does this place have in common with your club?" I say.

He gives me a look that says, "Dude, if I knew that do you think I'd have enlisted your puny help?"

I snicker.

"Something funny here."

"You. All prickly and pissed 'cause there's something you don't know. Got to call on the megaservices of the Mega."

"Ever occur to you I'm using you for reasons your inferior human brain can't begin to understand."

It's another of his questions that doesn't sound like a question. It's such an irritating tactic, I wish I'd thought of it myself. Now if I start doing it, I'll look like a copy-cat. Of course it had occurred to me that he had ulterior motives. Everyone does. Now I'm the one feeling all prickly and pissy. I go into observation mode, ruffle my feathers back down into a duck-coat so I'm more likely to quack up than get pissy. Humor is a girl's best friend. The world's a funny place.

I estimate the double doors of the warehouse at thirty feet, with an entrance nearly twice as wide if you slide back all four panels of the doors. The corrugated metal is throwing off such intense cold that my breath freezes a few puffs from my face and hangs in the air like small frosty clouds. When I punch one, it tinkles to the ground in a dusting of ice and my mind attaches a pattern to a pattern: I see the dusting of ice up Christian's jeans. I consider it for a moment then decide no way. Fae royalty can minorly affect the weather around them. Key word there is "minorly." This is major stuff. And Christian's not even full-blooded Fae.

The doors are coated with clear ice. I reach for my sword.

Ryodan's front is against my back, and his hand is on my hand on the sword hilt before I even process that he moved. I go totally still, don't even breathe. He's touching me. I don't think when he gets this close to me. I just turn on static in my head real loud and focus on trying to get away as fast as possible. Riding in a car with him sucked. Closed compartment. Electrified sardine can. Rolling down the windows hadn't helped a bit. This is a gazillion times worse.

"Dude." I pump up the volume on my static station.

"What are you doing, Dani?"

His face feels real close to my neck. If he bites me again, I'm going to kick his ass. "I was thinking about poking the ice, seeing how thick it is."

"Two and one-sixteenth inches."

"Get off me."

"Get off your sword. Or I won't continue to let you keep it."

Fecker can take my sword away like Jayne never could. Like only the UPs can. One more reason I can't stand Ryodan. "Can't get off my sword till you get your hand off mine. Pressure much?" I say testily.

We both sort of let go at the same time. I glare at him, or where I think he is, but he's not there. I find him twenty feet away, near a small, normal-size door. He opens it. His face instantly frosts. "Ready?" he says.

"You don't move that way in front of Jo."

"What I do with Jo is none of your business."

"You better not be doing nothing with Jo. I'm staying in line like a good little soldier." And fecking-A does it ever chafe. Report to work at eight P.M. Gah. Report. Like I don't have plans of my own. Like I didn't spend hours hunting for Dancer and I'm not two *Dani Dailies* behind and haven't spent most of my fecking day working on one, after whizzing out to the abbey to make sure Jo's okay. She had some seriously sick scoop for me about the new, segmented Unseelie, but other than that she hadn't wanted to talk much. I think she's pretty upset with me. Nothing new there. If there weren't any *sidhe*-sheep upset with me, I wouldn't know who I was, or if the Earth was still orbiting the sun. "I'm behaving. She's safe. You just leave her alone."

He smiles faintly. "Or what, kid."

"You know something, dude, if you don't put a question mark at the end of your questions, I'm not answering them anymore. It's rude."

He laughs. I hate it when he laughs. It tries to put me right back on the porno level of Chester's and that just grosses me out, so I do the static-thing in my head again.

I freeze-frame past him so fast his hair blows straight up. I make sure to go through a pile of dust, and give it a little extra twist with my heel as I whiz by so it shoots straight up his nose (a trick I perfected at the abbey!).

He sneezes. Just like a real person. I'm half surprised to find he actually breathes.

The cold slams into me like a brick wall and for a second I can't inhale.

Then I feel him at my back, an inch from my figurative rear tire like he's drafting off my freeze-frame. It sets my teeth on edge. Makes my temper hot and breathing is easy again.

Like the first scenario he showed me, a frozen hush fills the space like those mornings in fresh, new-fallen snow when no one else is awake and the world is stiller than you ever thought it could be until you take that first step that squeaks in the drift. I always wanted to have a wicked snowball fight with somebody on mornings like those but nobody else has ever been able to keep up. Lobbing snowballs at folks is like picking tin cans off a fence with a BB gun.

I flash through the warehouse, checking it all out, fascinated in spite of being ordered here and bossed around. I love a good puzzle. What's freezing these places and why?

A few dozen Unseelie are iced in the entry bay.

Ryodan has lower-caste grunts working for him. There are lots of Rhino-boys iced in mid-action. Like the subclub in Chester's, the place is killingly cold. It makes my heart feel dull and tight. I don't stop moving, won't stop moving for anything.

Rhino-boys are frozen loading and unloading pallets and crates, gray skin coated white, shellacked by a clear layer of ice. Whatever happened to them happened fast. They had no warning. Their frosted expressions are completely normal.

Well . . . as normal as Unseelie ever look. I think.

I whiz around two beefy ones, studying their bumpy rhino faces, gashed mouths bared on tusks, analyzing that thought.

It occurs to me that maybe their expressions aren't normal. I'm basing my assumptions on what I know of humans, of how our faces react. Christian is proof that I can't do that. I can't even figure out when Christian is smiling.

Logic demands I eliminate my assumption that the Rhino-boys had no warning. Can a Rhino-boy look terrified? I don't know. Perhaps they show fear by something so small and weirdly Fae as a tiny rainbow-hued glint in their beady little eyes, and the white frost is concealing it. I've never noticed what their faces look like when I kill them. I'm usually too busy looking at the next one I plan to stab. I'm suddenly looking forward to finding one tonight and performing a test. Any excuse to kill an Unseelie is an awesome one.

What would do something like this?

And why?

It has to be a Fae because I just can't see a human managing to build a freeze-ray gun that works on this scale only to go vigilante.

Then again . . . . I can't eliminate that possibility either.

So far, both places I've seen iced are exactly the kind of places I would ice myself. If I had such a wicked cool weapon.

Most folks wouldn't believe that someone who can move like me, fight and hear like me, could exist. Ergo, I can't rule out the possibility that someone else might be so smart they figured out how to build a massive freeze-ray gun that's capable of reducing the temperature of places to the frigidity of objects in space. Given enough time, I think Dancer could manage it. He's that smart!

Bugger. I have facts and no connections. I can deduce nothing. Yet.

Suddenly I see past the frozen figures.

The warehouse is packed full of boxes, crates, and pallets, piled everywhere. There's a pile of iced electronic stuff that looks like audio equipment of some kind. I guess maybe for the club. Crates are stacked to the ceiling, and more stuff was being brought in when whatever happened did.

I make one crystal clear deduction: Ryodan's the dude emptying the stores! Preying on humans just like the Unseelie. Stealing our ability to survive so he can sell it back to us at whatever cost he decides to demand.

It's all iced. Every bit of it.

I wonder if any of the edible stuff can be thawed and saved. People are going to die because he's such a greedy pig.

I'm so pissed that I smash open a crate as I go whizzing by. "Oops," I say, all innocent and accident-like. Wood splinters, two-by-fours go flying in all directions.

Automatic weapons explode from the wreckage and skid across the iced floor, where they smash into frozen Unseelie who shatter like little glass goblins.

Okay, so that crate had guns in it. It just means I kicked open the wrong crate. I'm so sure he's the prick stockpiling the food that I kick another, not even pretending it was by accident this time. More guns.

I go on a smashing rampage. Each time I smash a box or crate open that holds ammo or guns, I get madder. Figures he'd hide the food from me before he brought me here. I'm about to kick open my fifth crate when Ryodan suddenly has me hanging in midair by the collar of my coat, manhandles me into potato-sack-girl over his shoulder again, superspeeds me out the door, slams me into a telephone pole and says, "What the fuck is wrong with you?" at the precise moment the whole building blows up.

* * *

"Dude, are you arming these places to blow?" I say on the way back to Chester's. "Is this another of your stupid tests? I have to solve your little mystery in the whopping three seconds I get to study it before the scene gets blown to smithereens?" The whole building had exploded outward, for a city block. We'd barely freeze-framed from the shrapnel zone in time.

"I lost a great deal of personal property in both explosions. I sacrifice nothing that is mine from which I might profit."

"Which translates into as long as I'm useful, since you think I'm yours, I'm not going to get the—" I drag a finger across my neck.

"Kid, you might just annoy me into killing you."

"Right back at you, boss."

He smiles and I feel myself starting to smile back and it pisses me off so I look out the window and get real intent on what scenery I can make out in the pinkish moonlight, which isn't much because the Shades took everything worth looking at out here. Got three hidey-holes down this way and a big stash. Didn't know Ryodan was holing up here, too. I'll vacate this district as soon as I get time to relocate.

"Observations," he says.

"Four imperial Unseelie guards were the only commonality I was able to isolate endemic to both scenes." They'd been standing, armed, at the dock doors, overseeing the delivery.

He gives me a sidewise look. "Wow. That was, like, a whole sentence. With nouns and verbs and connective tissue. Endemic. Fancy word."

"Sloppy, dude. Should have omitted the connective tissue part."

"Nothing else."

I give him a look. I hate his statement-questions. I'm not answering them anymore.

He laughs. "Nothing *else*." His voice rises on *else* about one one-hundredth of a note higher than the word "nothing," a concession only someone like me with superhearing would ever be able to pick up. Still, it's a concession. From Ryodan. Rarer than water in the desert.

"The ice was layered the same. Maybe hoarfrost. Definitely hard rime. Clear ice on top of it all. The hard rime's weird. White ice comes from fog freezing. What's fog doing inside both these buildings?"

"How did the place blow?"

I think back. It happened so fast and we were outside, and he was blocking my view, and I was more focused on getting him off me than anything else. I hate to, but I admit, "I can draw no conclusions, circumstances being what they were."

He looks sidewise at me again.

"Talking like you, dude, thinking it might get all this stupid fecking stuff over with sooner. Communication is hard enough when everybody's trying."

"Isn't that the truth. Give me your hand."

"No."

"Now."

There's no way I'm giving him my hand.

He says something soft in a language I don't understand. My arm jerks up. I watch in horror as my hand passes to his side of the Humvee, palm up.

He drops a Snickers in it, murmurs something, and my hand is my own again. I wonder when, how, and why my fecking appetite became everyone else's business.

"Eat."

I think about throwing the candy bar back in his face or out the window. I refuse to let my fingers close around it.

But I sure could use it.

He brakes, comes to a stop in the middle of the road, turns toward me, grabs the collar of my coat, pulls me across the expanse between our seats and leans in. Locks eyes. We're maybe eight inches apart, and I think the only reason my nose ain't touching his is because one of the brackets on my MacHalo is just about touching his forehead. My butt's no longer touching the seat.

I've never seen such clear eyes as Ryodan's got. Most folks are crammed full of emotions, with lines around them like battle scars. I can tell by looking at grown-ups if they've spent their years laughing or crying or resenting the whole world. I hear moms say to their kids when they make faces, "Careful, your face will stick like that." And it really does. By middle age most folks wear whatever they felt the most in their lives smack on their kisser for all the world to see. Dude, so many of them should be embarrassed! It's why I laugh so much. If my face is going to stick, I'm going to like looking at it.

Looking at Ryodan is like staring the devil in the face. It's obvious what he's felt the most—nothing. Ruthless. Cold dude.

"I won't ever hurt you unless you make me, Dani."

"You being the one who gets to decide what constitutes the definition of 'make.' Big fat lot of wiggle room in there."

"I don't need wiggle room."

"Because you annihilate."

"Another of those fancy words."

"Dude. What did you just do to me?"

"Gave you what you needed but were too stubborn to take." He closes my fingers around the candy bar with his. I can't shake him off fast enough. "Eat, Dani."

He drops me back into my seat, puts the Humvee in gear again and takes off.

I munch the candy bar despite the sour taste in my mouth, thinking how I used to be invisible.

"Superheroes are never invisible," he says. "They're just deluded."

Turning my head toward the buildings flashing by, I screw up my face and stick out my tongue.

He laughs. "Sideview mirror, kid. And careful. Your face'll stick like that."

I head out into the streets with boxes of freshly printed dailies (I love the smell of new ink!) in a battered grocery cart the minute my time is my own again. I can run with a cart and slap my papers up on poles faster than I can do it on my crotch rocket. My bike's for pleasure, for pure downtime, when I got nothing else weighing down on me, like always saving the world. I don't get to ride it much.

Ryodan's reminder that I'm to report to work every single night at eight P.M. on the dot is still ringing in my ears, making me nuts. What the feck can he possibly have to torture me with every night? Is he icing these stupid scenarios himself just for an excuse to mess with me?

I head west and begin my usual route. It's a little after midnight. It shouldn't take me more than a couple hours, then I'll start hunting for Dancer again. I'm getting a little worried about him. Most times he goes somewhere else without telling me, he's only gone a few days. I don't know all his haunts any more than he knows all mine but I'll keep checking those I do.

I've got certain posts and poles and benches that folks frequent, like regular newspaper stands, waiting for my latest updates. Folks have probably been a little worried with my paper being late and all. I've got important info to share tonight.

I glance down at my rag, proud of it. The ink is crisp and clean, and it looks real professional.

The Dani Daily

May 21, 1 AWC

New Unseelie Caste!
Update your DDD Manual!

BROUGHT TO YOU EXCLUSIVELY BY *TDD*
YOUR ONLY SOURCE FOR THE LATEST NEWS
IN & AROUND DUBLIN!

Dudes, I discovered a brand new kind of Unseelie hanging at Chester's!

Calling this one Papa Roach, and I don't mean the band! Take notes: it's three to four feet tall, with a shiny brownish-purplish segmented body, six arms, two legs, and the smallest head you ever saw, like the size of a walnut, with little fish-egg eyes. It can break down into segments that are the size of roaches that crawl inside your clothes, and get under your skin—LITERALLY!

If you see this thing coming, run like heck because I haven't figured out a way to kill it yet. You want to carry a can of hair spray or fill a spray bottle with gas and *always* have some matches on you (I got a blowtorch myself). That way if you get cornered, you can spray them and set them on fire. It doesn't kill them but it sure keeps them busy while you run.

I'll keep you posted, Dublin!
Dani out!

I don't tell them the worst part is what Jo told me this morning—that some of the waitresses at Chester's *encourage* the bugs to get under their skin. I don't want to give them any ideas. This Unseelie has a specialty: it feeds on human fat. Presto—tiny waist! Hello bug—goodbye cellulite! Don't like those dimpled thighs? Bug up. The walls haven't been down long enough for folks to get dystopian-thin, and with the amped-up sexuality of so much Fae royalty walking around dangling the promise of potential immortality, the focus on fashion and beauty has never been more extreme.

Jo told me that a couple of the waitresses are real proud to have one. It's becoming a status symbol or something, like hair extensions or boob jobs. Jo said the waitresses claim they don't kill humans, they just eat their fat, and they can hardly feel them in their skin at all.

I think that's bull. I think they hitch a ride because they're getting more from humans than fat. I think they experience everything their "host" experiences: pleasure, pain, whatever. The Unseelie are bugging us and we let them. They invade our bodies and gather intel from the inside, then report back to Papa, who probably reports back to the Unseelie princes, the better to prey on us. What do these idiot waitresses think? That the bug will eventually return to its own body and leave them all pretty and thin, no harm no foul?

Dude, it's an Unseelie! There's always a catch.

I zip around the corner to my first pole, grocery cart rattling.

When I see one of my papers from last week still hanging up, gleaming pinkish-white in the rosy moonlight, it surprises me. Folks always take them down, and take them home, wherever that is. Darn few get left behind.

As I get closer, I realize it's not my paper.

What the feck? What's on my pole? Folks know to leave me notes at the General Post Office.

I slip into fast-mo, get nose-to-nose with it.

I'm so flabbergasted my jaw about hits the pavement.

The Dublin Daily

May 20, I AWC

**YOUR *ONLY* SOURCE FOR *CREDIBLE* NEWS IN
AND AROUND NEW DUBLIN
BROUGHT TO YOU BY *WECARE*
WE BRING YOU ALL THE NEWS THAT MATTERS.
WE WILL HELP YOU SURVIVE!
*WECARE***

"Gah, dudes! Plagiarize much?" I pluck the offending matter from my pole and almost drop the thing, my eyeballs are so freaked out. "*The Dublin Daily* not *The Dani Daily*? Like, maybe they could have an original thought? Holy mimicking monkeys, they aped my intro! Hardly even changed any fecking words!"

I scan it, quick-like.

Don't be fooled by IMITATION dailies. *The Dublin Daily* is the ONLY daily you'll ever need. We can help you TURN YOUR POWER AND WATER BACK ON!!!

Join us now!

Unlike IMITATION dailies, WeCARE delivers all the important news direct to your door, no matter how difficult your "door" is to reach.

DON'T subject yourself to terrible threats in the streets in order to read OVERINFLATED JUVENILE BOASTS that advise you to indulge in DANGEROUS fireworks and battles!

WeCARE will come to YOU.
WeCARE will fight your battles FOR YOU.
WeCARE will keep you safe and IN THE LIGHT.
Who cares about you? WE do.
WeCARE.

"Buh!" It's all I can come up with. "Buh!" I say again. I can't even stand to keep reading. I ball it up and crush it into a tiny hard wad. Finally I manage, "Imitation?" I'm so perturbed I can't even cuss. I can barely talk. "Overinflated? Who's *writing* this drivel?"

I been keeping Dublin safe and in the light since last October! Months of delivering food and supplies to folks too scared to leave their hidey-holes. Months of fighting monsters, of finding and collecting little kids that got orphaned on Halloween when their folks were out celebrating and never came home because they got devoured by Shades or some other Unseelie. Months of rounding up people and taking them to Inspector Jayne so they could learn to fight.

Nobody else ever bothered to step forward and help folks survive.

Now this?

I'm getting dissed by some paper that's pretending *I'm* the pretender?

"There is some serious ass-kicking going to happen," I mutter. As soon as I find out who the feck We-the-feck-Care is.

I spend the next few hours whizzing around my city, tearing the stupid things off my posts and putting up *The Dani Daily.*

They used my posts. Couldn't even find their own places to put them up.

Reaching out to MY market by taking MY posts. Stupid fecking copycats. I'm so mad, I'm steaming. If anybody was watching from above, all they'd see is a blur of motion leaving two plumes of pure pissed-offedness trailing out of my ears.

I figure tomorrow's got to be a better day.

Lately, it seems all I ever figure is wrong.

TEN

"Cat scratch fever"

Four nights he's come to me, murmuring my name.

Kat, he says and he makes of that one syllable an exquisite melody with which not even the divine orchestral choir of all the angels in heaven could compete.

He chimes my name in the language of the Unseelie and it makes my ears ring until my mind is emptied of all thought, until my eyes are incapable of beholding any vision other than him. He is so beautiful that merely looking at him makes me weep, and when I brush tears from my cheeks, my hands come away tainted red by blood.

He wakes me but doesn't wake me.

He takes me to a place that is so perfect and serene and free of worry that I want to stay there forever.

Kat, he says, *my name is Cruce. Not V'lane. I was so weary of wearing his golden shining face. He was never half the Fae I am. I have you in the Dreaming, is it not beautiful? Do you not feel divine here with me? You need not fear me. I am not what I seem.*

I am in danger.

Terrible danger.

And I cannot tell a soul because they are all looking to me to lead, to be strong and show them the way.

I am their hope.

I am afraid "their hope" will soon be beyond all hope. They judged Rowena so harshly! They have no idea what she faced. God knows how many years she withstood similar torment before she succumbed! Who knows what caliber of person she was before the *Sinsar Dubh* tampered with her mind. Did it happen to her every night like it does to me? Did the darkness beneath our stone fortress beeline straight for her head, her heart, her bed, the moment she lay down and tried to relinquish for a few stolen hours the heavy mantle of rule?

I cannot help but wonder if this hasn't been going on for millennia. If the Unseelie King knew when he interred his deadly alter ego beneath our sacred ground and charged us with guarding it then infused our blood with his own to make us strong—or is it that very kiss of evil in our veins that makes us weak?—how much hell on earth he was going to cause. How many women's lives he would ruin. How many humans would one day die.

I wonder if thousands of times before me a woman stepped into the position I occupy, assumed leadership of our Order, and was instantly subjected to the harshest test of will imaginable: besieged by the insidious seduction of the *Sinsar Dubh*.

Take me, free me, be invincible, save the world.

Oh, the siren song of power. Even I who care nothing for power am not immune.

I do not believe it was ever quiet down there. Not for a moment!

I do not believe any Grand Mistress was ever spared.

Remarkable we kept it hidden so long!

He came to me that first night the Unseelie King imprisoned him beneath our home. I slept, and while I was vulnerable, he came to me in my dreams. He has come to me each night since.

I tried sleeping pills. They only drugged me, rendering me more vulnerable to the pleasures of temptation.

He shows himself to me, in all his glory. He shows me how much more beautiful Cruce is and always was. V'lane was a pale imitation of the real thing. Cruce is black and white and brilliant and hard and strong and perfect. He wraps velvet wings around me and makes me feel things I've never imagined.

I agree with Margery.

I want that chamber pumped full of concrete or lead or iron, or anything that might bar the path between him and me.

I do not know a tenth of the spells Rowena knew. And still she failed.

I can't even get the door closed!

The night the Book was laid to rest, I left the chamber celebratory, with my heart feeling lighter than it had in a long time. The *Sinsar Dubh* was finally off the streets, and although the method of confinement was not all I'd hoped, I'd envisioned a reprieve. A time of rest and rebuilding, precious, necessary time to come to terms with the many changes in our lives, the endless killing, time to grieve the loss of our many sisters.

It was not to be.

He comes to me with his promises and his lies, with his beauty and unchained desires, and he says that I am all that he needs. He says I and I alone can rule at his side and that my special gift of emotional empathy makes me the only woman capable of ever truly understanding him to the deepest degree, on that rare and uncompromising level of emotional bonding an Unseelie prince must have, or will go mad without. He says I am his only possible mate and he has waited an eternity to have me.

He claims he is being wrongly accused, and we are all being tricked. He says he is *not* the *Sinsar Dubh*. He claims the moment he was imprisoned in his block of ice, the king took it all back.

He says we are being played by a clever, cunning, mad ruler who cares nothing for his children, who never has, who loves only his concubine, and once he had her in his arms again, reclaimed the power of the *Sinsar Dubh*, too. He says the concubine still isn't fully Fae, and the king retrieved his spells so he might resume his work, that it was all sleight of hand in the chamber that night.

He tells me he was made out to look like the villain again so we wouldn't search too hard for the Unseelie King, so we would worry instead about containing the only prince capable of stopping him when he decides our world is expendable, which Cruce assures me the king will one day do—and not too far in the future.

He tells me I must be humanity's savior. When I am ready, he will show me the way to free him. He says that only I am strong enough, levelheaded enough, to see the truth when it stands before me, wise enough to make the hard decisions.

He speaks with a forked tongue and I know it!

And I am *still* losing the battle.

I wake in the morning smelling of him. Tasting him in my mouth, feeling his tongue on my skin. Filled with him, as no man has ever filled me: body, mind, soul. He makes love to me and I resist but somehow I'm not resisting. In my dreams I say no but do it anyway and love each exquisite, soul-charring moment of it. I wake up coming over and over again from my invisible lover. Shuddering with heat.

And need.

And shame.

My sisters count on me. I am their leader.

How will I survive this? How do I stop him from coming to me? There must be spells to block him, wards, runes to place around my bed! Maybe I should leave the abbey, now, before it's too late. Can I leave my sisters? *Dare* I leave my sisters? If I don't leave right now, will I ever again have the strength of will to go, or will I find myself down there one night, trembling hands on the bars, willing to do anything it takes to set Cruce free?

How many died the night Rowena let the *Sinsar Dubh* out, how many murders weighed on her conscience? Did she even have a conscience left by then or had it been corrupted completely?

Who will step up if I leave?

There's no guarantee the next woman will be any stronger than me, or more capable of resisting his seduction. How long would Margery last, in the face of such temptation? How cruel might she become with the power of the *Sinsar Dubh* blackening her heart?

God help me, I must stay.

I must win this silent, invisible war, with no one the wiser.

God help me.

ELEVEN

"Trouble ahead, trouble behind"

"There you are," Jo says as I saunter past the kiddie subclub. "It's almost eight-thirty. I thought you were supposed to be here at eight." She's got on makeup. She never wears makeup. And she did something sparkly on her eyelids and between her boobs. It makes me mad. I don't know why she changed. She was just fine the way she was.

The words "supposed to be here" chafe me raw. They're insult heaped on injury. I had a crappy day. It's already taking every ounce of my self-control to hide how much it kills me to see Jo waitressing, wearing a short kicky skirt, serving Fae. But I choke it down because if I let an ounce of it show, who knows what Ryodan might do? The dude's as predictable as an Interdimensional Fairy Pothole, those pieces of fractured Fae reality drifting around that you never know what's inside of till you're ass-deep in alligators.

"Mac's looking for you," she says.

I rubberneck wildly, trying to search every subclub in Chester's at once. "She here?"

"What?" Jo looks at me blankly, and I realize I must have spoken in fast-mo. That happens sometimes when

I get agitated. I start to vibrate, and I think all other people hear is the high-pitched whine of a mosquito.

"Is she here?" I slow down for a sec to talk then speed up the rubbernecking.

"No. She left with Barrons half an hour ago. You're going to give yourself whiplash if you don't slow down your head, Dani. It's creepy when you do that. You just missed each other. If you'd been on time, you wouldn't have. What's wrong? You just went as white as a sheet."

If I'd been on time.

Did Mac come here looking for me? Was she hunting me? Does she know I'm supposed to show up for "work" at eight?

I feel woozy. I need to get the blood back in my head. Sometimes I think my heart and veins go into fast-mo without the rest of me, prepping my body for flight or fight, sending all the juice to my sword hand or my feet, and away from my brain. It's the only thing that explains how stupid I go when I get mad or worried. But then, guys work the same way with their dicks, and they can't fast-mo, so maybe it's just a human design flaw. Intense feeling? Ha! Instant brain death.

"Where the fuck is my drink, bitch? You want a piece of me or what?" an Unseelie at a nearby table growls. It means it, literally.

"Tell me you're not eating Unseelie," I say.

"Ew! Never!" Jo says like she can't believe I asked.

"Did you get highlights in your hair?"

She touches it, with a self-conscious smile. "A few."

"You never have highlights. And you don't wear makeup."

"Sometimes I do."

"Like, not once in the whole time I've known you. And I ain't never seen you with sparkly stuff on your boobs."

She starts to say something then shakes her head.

"You dressing up for these creeps?"

"Bitch, I said where's my drink?"

I look at the Unseelie. It's looking Jo up and down, licking thin, nasty lips like she's its next meal. Way too personal-like.

An Unseelie just called Jo a bitch. Pressure builds behind my sternum. My hand goes to the hilt of my sword. Before I can close a finger around it, I'm hemmed in by a mountain range of men with attitudes as big as avalanches. Being in the middle of four of Ryodan's dudes is sort of like standing on a glacier while being gently electrocuted. Never felt anything like it, except from the dude himself, and Barrons.

"That Unseelie called Jo a bitch," I say. Clearly, the Unseelie deserves to die.

"Boss says if you kill a Fae in his protected area, the waitress dies in front of you, real slow," Lor says. "Then we kill you. We'll never remind you of this again. We'll never intervene again. It's on your head, kid. Control your temper or you'll kill her. *You*. We're merely the weapon by which she'll die. And we're inventive as fuck when it comes to slow killing."

Jo's eyes are huge. She sees their faces. Knows how moody I am.

I sigh and let go of my sword. "Wow, dude, I've never heard you string so many complete sentences all together in, like, ever. You're downright loquacious tonight." Brute force is Lor's usual way of dealing with things. His idea of seduction is capture-and-abduct. You don't want to catch this dude's eye. You end up in his bed whether you want to or not. I give him a baleful glare. He's telling me to control myself, and the only way I see to do that inside Chester's is maybe beat myself over the head with a riot baton a few times and knock myself out.

"Bitch, I said where the fuck is my drink?"

Temper nearly pops my skull. My brain empties. My sword hand swells, full of blood and eagerness.

Jo gives me a look and turns away.

Then she goes to play fetch and deliver to an Unseelie. Who isn't respecting her. I'm never going to survive this.

But she has to.

So I have to.

I turn away, shoulder through the dudes, making sure to pop Lor a good one with an elbow as I go.

He snarls.

I bat my lashes at him.

He says, "Kid, you need to grow your ass up in a hurry."

"Funny. I think everybody else needs to grow their ass down."

"Like a horse, honey, somebody's going to break you."

"Never. Going. To. Happen."

I'm bored off my gourd, sitting in Ryodan's office. I thought we were going to go out investigating, hunt for clues about what's icing these places. So far the only commonality I see is Ryodan. Both places that got iced were his, like someone's targeting him and the dregs of the society I protect: Fae and Fae-loving humans. It occurs to me if enough of his places get iced, and word gets around, folks will start avoiding Chester's. The club could die from lack of patrons. "One can always hope," I say pissily. Ryodan doesn't even acknowledge that I've spoken. I shift in my chair and glare at the top of his head.

He's doing paperwork.

He's been doing paperwork for over an hour. What kind of paperwork can possibly need to be done in this kind of fecked-up world?

He didn't say anything when I walked in, so I didn't say anything.

We've been sitting here in total silence for one hour, seven minutes, and thirty-two seconds.

I tap a pen on the edge of his desk.

I'm not about to say the first word.

"So, why the feck am I here again?" I say.

"Because I told you to be," he says, without raising his head from whatever stupid thing he's working on.

"Are you going to make me do your filing next? Am I Robin to your Batman, or some stupid temp assistant here to help you sharpen pencils? Don't we have better things to do, like solve a mystery? Do you *want* more of your places to get iced? We just hanging around waiting for it to happen?"

"Robin and a stupid temp assistant would have been on time."

I sit up straight from my bored slump, tapping faster. "*That's* what this is all about? You're punishing me because I was late?"

"Bright girl. Stop tapping that pen. You're driving me bugfuck."

I tap faster. He's driving me bugfuck, too. "So, like if I'm on time next time, I won't have to sit here and watch you do stupid stuff I can't believe you even do?"

Half the pen—the part not in my fist—is suddenly plastic powder. I blink at it.

I didn't see him move, he crushed the pen so fast. Now I see little crumbles of blue plastic on the blade of his hand, ink smeared on the paper he's working on. I sit up even straighter. I have a lot to compete with if I'm ever going to be as fast as him.

"I do what I do, Dani, because the mundane makes the world go around. Whoever controls the daily grind controls everyone else's reality."

"*That's* why you're stealing all the food?"

"Ah, that's why you had your crate-smashing fit. No. I hoard weapons. Someone else is stockpiling food. That's too mundane even for me. I arm the swarm, feed the greed. Someone else is getting ready to starve them."

I give him an admiring look in spite of myself. "You know it's been going on." He's known for longer than I have.

"Someone started clearing the stores a while back. Where've you been?"

"Like, chained in somebody's dungeon. Dude, can we *please* go do something before I die of boredom? We got a mystery to solve!"

He looks at me. How did I ever think his face was impassive? It says whole sentences.

I roll my eyes. "You've got to be kidding me."

He inclines his head, waiting.

"You're actually going to make me say it?"

He folds his arms over his chest.

I nearly choke on my tongue trying to get it out. But I'll do anything to not have to sit in this office all night. Watching the Unseelie between my high-tops is getting old. I've taken mental notes out the wazoo. My young body needs to see some action. There's a live wire inside me, sizzling beneath my skin. If I don't discharge, I'll die. Bring on the night! There's stuff happening out there and I'm stuck in here!

"I'll. Be. On. Time. Next time."

"Good. Next time you won't have to sit in my office all night."

I shoot up from the chair. "Awesome, let's go!"

He pushes me back down. "But tonight you screwed up. So, tonight you do."

Seven hours later it occurs to me that Lor might be right. I might be breakable. Seven hours of boredom and I'm a puddle of willingness, ready to do virtually anything guaranteed to result in a change of scenery. Chains I can deal with. Boredom, no way. My brain gets ahead of my feet and I don't like to think about where I'm going. I just go.

At six A.M. on the dot Ryodan looks up and says, "Tonight at eight, Dani."

I glare murder at him and head for the door. It doesn't open. I glare at it. A whole night wasted. More seconds ticking by as I wait for my jailer to set me free.

There aren't many crimes in my book. Not many sins either.

But top on both of those lists is killing time. Have fun with it, make something cool, play video games, work hard if you feel like it, but *do* something. Killed time is an abortion, life that never gets lived, gone, just gone. A cage and a collar killed way too much of mine.

Just when I'm about to blow, he does something and the door retracts into the smooth glass wall.

As I storm out I hear him say, "You wasted my time, Dani. I wasted yours."

I whirl on him, fists at my waist. "That's bullshit! It wasn't even proportionate!"

"It rarely will be."

"Thirty little fecking minutes cost me nine and a half hours?"

"The way you treat me is the way I will treat you. Since I'm bigger and older, I imagine it will always be worse."

"Oh, *now* you get all proportionate. If you're going to be as much of a dickhead as you are big and old, dude, that's some serious dickheadedness. That's not fair. You can't be totally disproportionate one minute and then all quid pro quo the next."

"I can be anything I want."

"Oh, whose fecking comic book *is* this?" I explode. "That's *my* line."

He laughs and his face changes. All the sudden he doesn't look so old. He looks happy. Free. Totally different. I see lines around his eyes from laughing that I never noticed before. My mind flashes straight back to level four and I see him behind that woman again and he groans like he did that night, then he laughs, and I feel almost sick to my stomach remembering. I don't know what's wrong with me. I wish I'd never fecking gone down to level four! I stand there and gape at him.

The door slides shut in my face.

"You're early."

I give him a mutinous look. Of course he thinks my being early is about him. It's not. Mac was at Chester's last night at eight. I think she's hunting me. Since I can't be late to avoid her, I have to be early. "Watch broke. Thought I was on time."

"You don't wear a watch."

"See? I knew I had a problem. I'll just dash out and get one. Be back tomorrow. On time." Jewelry gets caught on things in battle. The only concession I make is a bracelet Dancer gave me that I wear snug on my arm. Besides, without him around, giving orders, I might actually make some progress in the investigation.

"Don't even think about it."

I drop into a chair in his office, dangle a leg over the side. "What are we doing tonight," I say just like him. No inflection at the end.

"Ah, Dani, if only you took instruction in all things so well."

"You'd be bored."

"So would you. There are three other iced places in Dublin."

"Three!" I sit up straight in my chair. "Are they all yours?"

"Local places. Unrelated to me in any way."

Bugger, there goes my theory about him being the target, along with my hope that Chester's might die a slow death. "Casualties?"

"About fifty between the three."

"Humans or Fae?"

"Humans."

"*All* humans?"

He nods.

I let out a low whistle. Fifty more people dead. The human race just keeps getting hammered with blow after blow. "Then why do you care? It didn't happen on your turf. Nothing of yours was damaged or destroyed."

"I have other reasons for wanting it stopped."

"Like what? You move fast like me. You can outrun anything. You can steal more stuff to replace what got iced. So what's the deal?" What motives does a dude like him have?

"The walls between our realms were destroyed on Halloween. Since then things have changed. Human laws of physics are no longer laws, they're wishful thinking. It's possible parts of Faery are manifesting spontaneously, bleeding through into our reality. It's possible it's happening randomly, instantly, and without warning. I didn't see surprise on anyone's face at either of my properties. Put the big picture together, even for people who can move like you and me."

I snap up straight to full attention, both feet on the floor, not liking that at all. "You mean if it happened in the place I was standing, I'd be alive one second, dead the next. I wouldn't even know it. I'd just be gone!" My hands fist. I'm so freaked I want to fight something right now.

"Exactly. Instant death. No warning. No awareness. I don't know about you, but that offends the fuck out of me."

No blaze of glory, no epic battle! I'd die a totally meaningless death. Worse, I wouldn't even get to experience it. How much would that suck, to go through my whole life waiting to die, and then not even know it happened? I think Death is like the final stage of a video game. And if what Ryodan is saying is true, and I get iced, I'll never reach that final stage. I'll get wiped right out of existence on the second-to-last level. I want to *play* that last level when it's time. I want to taste it all, even the dying.

I'm suddenly one hundred and ten percent invested in solving this mystery. Fifty more folks dead coupled with the possibility of a completely meaningless death is powerful motivation. You don't get a big write-up in the history books unless you go out in a big way. I crunch thoughts and regurgitate them. "Well, first of all, the humans in your subclub were a little preoccupied with things like getting tortured and dying so it's understandable if they didn't notice that they were about to die in some other unexpected and surprising way, and second, I can't say for certain what surprise looks like on an Unseelie's face but I got a great idea: I'll go downstairs and kill a few right now and we'll collect some empirical data." I don't bother to mention I already hunted and killed half a dozen different kinds this morning after I left but I still couldn't decide what their expressions meant. Their faces just don't work like ours.

When he doesn't bother to dignify my dig with a response, I say, "*Three* new places?" What if the "bleeding through" starts to speed up? There could be dozens of iced spots soon. Assuming that's what's happening, how the feck are we going to stop it?

"All iced last night within a few hours of each other. Two of them have already exploded."

I shoot to my feet. "Dude, we got to get to the third, before it goes, too!"

TWELVE

"Life is a highway, I wanna ride it all night long"

I slo-mo-Joe it across Halfpenny Bridge.

We didn't learn a single new thing at the latest ice sculpture. Like the others, it blew shortly after we arrived. I freeze-framed out of there through flesh-colored shrapnel I pretended *wasn't* parts of fingers and faces I'd failed to save.

The new places that got iced have nothing in common that I can see. There were two of those small underground pubs that've been springing up all over the city, and a fitness center where three people were frozen doing yoga in the middle of a bunch of crystal bowls. How weird is that? People doing yoga in times like these!

So far I've got an underground club at Chester's, a warehouse on the outskirts of the city, two inner-city small pubs, and a fitness center. Humans, Unseelie, and Imperial guards all at some places but not others, so whatever's happening doesn't appear to be targeting a certain person like Ryodan or group of victims. It's looking more like a random, spontaneous event with each scene I see.

I'm trudging, which I don't usually do, because I'm thinking hard and when I'm thinking hard plus freeze-framing I run into things a lot. My bruises are fading and sometimes I try to be my normal-colored self for like a whole day. I'm too wired for sleep. I get like that sometimes and can't do anything about it but ride it out. I need something to do or I'm going to drive myself nuts.

I find Dancer in his favorite corner penthouse on the south side of the river Liffey. The two outer walls are solid floor-to-ceiling windows that look out over the streets. When I get there, he's stretched out on a rug in the sunshine with his shirt off, eyes closed, glasses on the floor beside him.

Dancer's going to be a big guy one day, if he ever gains weight. Last time we measured ourselves, he was fourteen inches taller than me, lanky and lean. He forgets to eat. His hair is dark with some wave and he never cuts it until it gets in his way, then he asks me to trim it. It's soft. I like it to his chin as it is now, falling away from his face. When he wears his glasses, which is pretty much every minute he's awake because he's so nearsighted (he hates them and before the walls fell he was going to get Lasik), he looks like a hunky geek. I'd never tell him that! I like his hands. His feet are ginormous! His eyes aren't green or blue, they're aqua, like they're Fae-brushed. He's got better eyelashes than me.

When I see him I don't say, "Dude, where you been, I was starting to worry," because me and Dancer don't do that to each other. He survived the walls going down all by himself. So did I. And I don't say, "What happened the night Ryodan showed up and took me, where'd you disappear to?" It doesn't matter. We're here now. It's like somehow we know in our guts that it'll never be too long, the other is always going to walk through the door one day, eventually.

He props up on an elbow when the door closes. He knows it's me because I had to disarm ten booby traps before I got to the door. Nobody else could make it through one of his gauntlets without tripping some alarm. Well, except for Ryodan, who seems to be the exception to every fecking rule.

My heart squinches a little when I look at him. I never had siblings but I think he's like a brother to me. I can never wait to see him again, tell him all the ideas I've been thinking, the things I've seen, and get his take on it all. Sometimes when we see each other we can't stop talking for hours and hours and we get so excited we start to stumble over our words trying to say it all so fast. I consider telling him about the iced scenes and the mystery I'm looking into but I don't want Dancer to be any bigger on Ryodan's radar than he already is. That Ryodan even knows he exists makes me nuts. I want Dancer safe. And I know him. If he got the tiniest hint of a big mystery like this, he'd start poking into all kinds of places that could get him killed. It doesn't matter how über-impressed I am with how smart he is. Ryodan's *worse* than walls falling or the world melting down. You don't survive if he doesn't want you to.

"Mega, I've been thinking—"

"Stop the presses! Do I need to put out a special edition of *The Dani Daily*?"

"Might."

He grins and I grin back. Dancer thinking has stellar results. You wouldn't believe the bombs he can build. We blow up things sometimes just for fun. You know, things that need to be blown up anyway like places where a lot of Shades used to hide that maybe they would return to one day like birds along a migration route, if it was still there.

"You got me wondering about Papa Roach's babies," he says.

"Yeah?" I stretch out in the sun next to him, prop up on an elbow, too, facing him. I love being able to see his eyes without his glasses in the way. It's a rare treat.

"Do you know how long they can stay separate from a body, either Papa or human?"

"Dunno. Dancer, I finally found *Scream 4*. Want to watch it tonight?"

"Watched it last night," he says absently, running a hand through his hair, making it stand up funny in a totally hot way, and I can tell by the way his eyes are unfocused that he's lost in thought and not aware of stuff around him. He gets that way a lot.

"You watched it without me?" I'm hurt. Me and Dancer love horror flicks. We gorge on them because they make us laugh. They have a way of putting the world in perspective. We'd been hunting for *Scream 4* for a while, planning to watch it. Dancer doesn't usually watch movies alone, least not that I know of.

"But I'll watch it again. It was cool."

"Cool." I still feel hurt, even though there's no reason for it. He's watching it with me tonight. So what if he saw it last night, too? And so what if he saw it with someone else? I don't care about stuff like that. What happens when I'm not around ain't got nothing to do with me. "What about Papa Roach?"

"Blowing them up doesn't work. Torching them is no good either. But what if we keep them from returning to a body? Any body. Human or their own. Wouldn't that solve the problem? Our goal is to keep them from getting inside more people. They're immortal, and your time is too important to waste running around after thousands of them with your sword. So, I started thinking what about a tough, impossible-to-escape spray-plastic? Encase them and keep them from being able to reattach to anything. I've been working on a formula. Once it's done, we can fill those small fertilizer tanks we swiped from the hardware store and test it out. I already rigged up a couple of sprayers to fit."

So, that's where he'd been. And when he got done working last night he watched a movie to chill. No big.

"I've got something that sets hard at a quarter-inch thick. I'm still trying to get it to gel to the perfect degree of solidity. I think I've figured out a way to add iron to the mix without making it too rigid. How do the segments attach to Papa? Tentacles? Suckers? How do they get under human skin? Can you catch me a couple to test it on?"

"You're the Shit, you know that," I say.

"No, *you're* the Shit," he says and grins, and we say it back and forth a couple of times. He thinks I'm the Shit because I can actually catch them. I was born with my gifts. Dancer is always thinking, trying to find ways to do things better. Surviving the fall with no special powers and no friends wows the feck out of me.

We relax on the floor because sunshine in Dublin is rare, and we talk about anything and everything except things like where I was when he was wherever he was. I don't tell him I was in a dungeon for almost four days and he doesn't ask. I like that about him. Friends don't build cages for each other.

We watch the sun move across the sky, and sometimes he gets up to get me things to eat. He tells me he's been checking stores and nearly every single one has been wiped clean. I have to stop myself three times from almost spilling the beans about the iced stuff I've been seeing.

When it's getting near seven o'clock, I start getting antsy and it makes me mad because I don't want to have to leave but somebody else is pulling my strings and I've got to go. I have to get to Chester's early enough to avoid Mac but not so early Ryodan gets all cocky about it.

I sigh.

"Something worrying you, Mega?" Dancer says.

"Just got to go take care of some things."

"I thought we were going to watch a movie. I found a whole box of Skittles at the airport. And jerky. The hot stuff."

I smack myself in the forehead. Skittles, jerky, and a movie. What was I thinking, saying hey, let's watch a movie tonight. My nights don't belong to me anymore. Somebody else owns them. That's not just a bitter pill to swallow. For someone like me it's a suicide tooth. It's irrelevant that I *want* to go work on the ice mystery and keep more innocent folks from dying. I can't handle that Ryodan gets to dictate when, how, and where I do it. It almost makes me not want to work on it at all. I hate being controlled.

I can't not go to Chester's because I don't know what Ryodan will do to Jo if I don't show, and there's no way I'm running the risk of finding out. I don't know if he'd hunt me down here, smash up the TV and DVD player, and take Dancer and put him in his dungeon. I never know what that dude will do next.

But I'm crystal clear about one thing he's doing.

Ruining my life.

I bang into Ryodan's office. "I been in enough cages in my life," I say. I got worked up on the way over, talking to myself in my head about the unfairness of it all.

He glances up from his paperwork.

"Paperwork! Holy replicating reams! Is that all you ever do? It's no wonder you want me coming around so much. Got to liven up your boring life with the super-excitement of the Mega." I'm so mad, I'm vibrating and the papers on his desk flutter in the breeze. When I get really mad, I cause a kind of air displacement that does on a tiny scale what the Fae do on a massive scale, except I can't affect the temperature. I do it sometimes to freak people out, get them off balance. It used to bug the crap out of Ro.

He catches a paper before it flies off the desk. "Something wrong."

How does he *do* that? Say questions without them sounding like questions at all? I been practicing and it's not easy. Vocal cords want to go up at the end of an interrogatory. I been trying to reprogram myself. Not because I plan to start acting like him (at least not around him) but because I think it's good to test yourself, override compulsion. Learn more self-control.

My hair's flying around my head in a cloud, getting in my eyes. I shove it back with both hands, wishing me and Dancer were eating jerky and hanging cool. "Yeah! Like, I might just have a life! Like I might just have plans for things that conflict with your stupid report-to-work-every-night-at-eight rule! Nobody else has to work every single night! Maybe I could get a couple of nights off to do something *I* want to do. Is that too fecking much to ask?"

"You have a date."

Another nonquestion, but the word "date" in the same thought with Dancer makes me say, "Huh?"

Ryodan stands and dwarfs me. I live in a world of people who are taller than me, but Jo says she thinks I'm going to grow more. I measure myself a lot. I don't want to be stuck at five foot two and three-quarters forever.

"You mentioned plans. You didn't say what they were."

"None of your fecking business."

"Everything is my business."

"Not my personal life. That's why they call it personal."

"This is about your little boyfriend."

"Don't talk about him. Don't even think about him.

And he's not little. Stop calling him little. One day he's going to be bigger than you. You just wait and see."

"This isn't the time to play house and get clumsy with a kid that doesn't know what to do with his own dick."

He just made me think about Dancer's dick. The thought is so uncomfortable I start bouncing from foot to foot. "Who said anything about dicks? I just want to watch a movie tonight!"

"Which one."

"How could that possibly *matter*?"

He gives me a look.

"*Scream 4*. Happy?"

"Wasn't very good."

"Dancer said it was," I say crossly. Has everybody seen it but me?

"Shows what he knows."

"You got a problem with Dancer?"

"Yes. He's the reason you're in a shit mood tonight and I have to put up with it. So fix the shit mood or I'll fix Dancer."

My hand goes to the hilt of my sword. "Don't you even think about trying to take anything from me that's mine."

"Don't make me."

His fangs just slid out. I shake my head and whistle. "Dude, what are you?"

He looks at me long and hard and I see something in his eyes that I almost get but don't. It's a look that I feel like I should know but just can't make sense of. There's more of a breeze in the small, closed office than I usually manage to generate, and I realize he's vibrating, too— and he makes wind, too. I'm beyond annoyed. Is there anything I can do that he can't do? When I look down through the glass floor, I see that everyone beneath us is moving slo-mo. We're both freeze-framing. I didn't realize I'd shifted all the way up.

He drops back into slo-mo first.

It takes me a sec longer to get ahold of my temper. When I manage to shift down, I flop into a chair and sling a leg over the side. I speak belligerence in every language known to man. Sign language is my native tongue.

Ryodan is like the ocean. He is what he is. And he's not about to change. There's no point in fighting the tide. It ebbs. It flows. You ride it. He's got me by the short hairs and he's not about to let go.

"So, what are we doing tonight? *Boss*." I put all my aggravation into the last word.

There's that look again. Mystery to me. Sometimes I can read him like a book, other times the only things I see on his face are two eyes, a nose, and a mouth.

I roll my eyes. "What?"

"Something's come up. I was going to tell you." He goes back to his paperwork, dismissing me. "You can go."

I sit up straight. "Really? You mean it?"

"Get out of my office, kid. Go watch your movie."

I can't get to the door fast enough. I yank it open.

"But watch out for icy spots. I hear they're deadly."

I pause on the threshold, getting mad all over again. I had a happy feeling for all of one stinking second before he went and squashed it. "You just had to say that. You can't help yourself, can you? You think the only thing to do with a parade is rain on it. Some people know to enjoy the parade because, dude, the rain always comes back."

"The wise man ensures his survival before enjoying it. The fool dies enjoying it."

Skittles, jerky, and Dancer are calling my name. I rip open a candy bar, bouncing from foot to foot. "But what if the wise man never gets *around* to the enjoying part?" I got a lot of unlived experiences waiting for me.

Sometimes I want to be just what I am. Fourteen and free.

"Perhaps the wise man knows being alive *is* the enjoying part."

"Have more places gotten iced since last night?" I should have kept my mouth shut. I shouldn't have asked. Responsibility adds weight and years to my shoulders when he nods.

He rubs salt in the wound. "But maybe you'll get lucky, watching a movie with your little boyfriend, and nothing will happen. Bright side of it is, if something does, you'll never know."

'Cause I'd like, be dead instantly. Bright side, my ass. Ryodan knows just how to push my buttons.

I roll my eyes, close the door and sit back down. I'll be fourteen later. Like probably next year. When I'm fifteen.

Without looking up, he says, "I said get out of here, kid."

"Cancel your plans, dude. Folks are dying. We've got work to do."

This one takes the cake, way out on the south side of Dublin, where things get rural.

Behind a shack that's barely managing to stay upright, with a swayback porch and a roof that looks like a really old person's mouth without dentures in, a man, a woman, and a little boy are frozen, doing laundry the old-fashioned way that Ro used to wash her Grand Mistress robes. She said it kept her humble. There wasn't a humble bone in that porky old witch's body, not even a nice hair anywhere.

The man's hands are iced to an antique washboard and he has some weird kind of metal thing iced on his shoulders like part of a frame that holds your head still if you broke your neck. The child is frozen, banging a spoon against the bottom of a battered pot. I don't let myself look at the kid long. It slays me when they die. He never even got to have a life. The woman got iced while she was lifting a shirt from a bucket of soapy water. I stand at the edge of the lawn, shivering, absorbing as many details as I can from a distance, getting ready to freeze-frame in. If this scene behaves anything like the others, it's going to explode soon.

"How did you even hear of this one?" The pubs I understand, even the fitness center because it was in Dublin and Ryodan knows everything that goes on in the city. But these are farmers doing laundry out in the country.

"I hear everything."

"Yeah, but how?"

"That was supposed to terminate your line of questioning."

"Dude, news flash. 'Supposed to' never works with me."

"Observations."

"They knew it was coming, whatever it was." Which makes me feel a whole lot better. I can stop worrying about dying with no warning. Although the boy was looking down at the pot he was holding, the grown-ups' mouths were open, their faces contorted. "They saw it and screamed. But why didn't they run? Why didn't she drop the shirt she was washing? It doesn't make sense. Does it freeze them mildly before it totally ices them? Could they have a small reaction but not be able to fully move? Did it sneak up on the other folks at the other scenes from behind?"

"I need answers, kid, not questions."

I puff out a breath. It gets foggy but doesn't ice. "It's not as cold as the other scenes."

"It's older. It's thawing."

"How do you know that?"

"There's a drop of condensation on the end of the man's nose that's about to fall."

I squint. "I don't see no stinking drop. You can't see that far that clearly." I have supereyes and I can't see it.

"Jealous, kid." He lets the last word rise that one-hundredth of a note that he does sometimes when he's humoring me. There's a smile in his voice. It pisses me off more.

"There is no fecking way you can see a drop of water from here!"

"There's another sliding down between the woman's breasts. Just above the mole on her left one."

"Dude, you can't outsee me by that much!"

"I can out-everything you." He gives me a look that I usually see in the mirror.

Just like that I'm in a total snit. "Then I guess you don't need me, and I'm wasting my time." I turn around and stomp back to the Humvee. But before I make it five steps, he's in my way, looming over me, arms crossed, looking at me weird. "Not in the mood, Ryodan. Get out of my way!"

"Being needed is toxic."

"It's good to be needed. Means you're important."

"It means there's an imbalance of power. There was no shortage of life-suckers before the walls fell. You're not responsible for the world just because you're more capable."

"'Course I am. That's what more capable folks do."

"You could ask me to teach you."

"Huh?" This night is getting weird in a hurry. "Teach me like you're teaching a class or something? What are you going to call it: 'You Too Can Be a Sociopath 101'?"

"It would be more like a graduate-level class."

I start to snicker. His sense of humor sneaks up on you. Then I remember who's talking and bite it off.

"You want to be faster, stronger, smarter. Ask me to teach you."

"I ain't asking you for nothing. And you might be faster and stronger. For now. No way you're smarter."

"Your choice. But turn around because you're not leaving. It's night, and you know what that means."

"Like, it's dark?"

"You're with me until dawn."

"Why dawn? You a vamp or a zombie or something that can't stand the light?"

He freeze-frames away, moves in on the scene. "I like sex for breakfast, kid. I eat early and often."

There I am thinking normal thoughts about iced people and how much he bugs me, then he slams me in the eyeballs with sex for breakfast stuff, and just like that my hormones do that crazy thing they do sometimes, where they start slapping up pictures all over the inside of my head and each one is more embarrassing than the last. And I can't close my internal eyes because they don't really exist and hormones are more stubborn and unpredictable than even me.

I wish I'd never watched porn movies or seen Ryodan "eating breakfast" because then the pictures wouldn't be so vivid and hard to get rid of.

But there he is, in graphic detail because I know exactly what he looks like naked, I saw him. I know how his body moves. He's got a lot of muscle. Scars, too. I know that when he has sex he laughs like the world is a perfect place. And when he did that, my hands curled into fists because I thought about touching his face like maybe I could catch joy in my hands and hold it. I had all kinds of fecking strange and stupid thoughts standing there on level four. I could so kick the shit out of myself for watching. I don't get hormones. I don't understand why the horny little buggers would even notice an old dude like him.

"You coming."

I shake myself mentally, pick up and shift sideways. Nothing happens.

"You've got to be kidding me," I mutter.

"Kid, why are you still standing there." He's freeze-framing around the frozen trio. "It could blow any second."

I don't move, thinking how much I hope it will, so he won't figure out I've lost my superpowers again.

"I have to, uh, use the, uh—" I gesture to the woods behind me. "Need a little privacy. Be right back."

Just like I hoped, while I'm in the shrubbery, pretending to pee, the laundry people blow.

The ride back to Dublin is a long and silent one.

THIRTEEN

"The very worst part of you is me"

I'm on the roof of a building, across the street from the pile of concrete, twisted metal, and broken glass that once was Chester's. The club is deep underground now. Usually there's a line for blocks, but it's four in the morning and everyone who wanted to be inside got inside about an hour ago. I guess that means enough people died to open up additional standing room because I didn't see anyone come out.

A black Humvee pulls up.

It's what I've been waiting for.

I used to hate being up high, which is ironic, considering I'm a Highlander. Or I was.

I'm getting used to heights. The view's better. You see more and you might as well be invisible. People don't look up much, not even in times like these, when they should because you never know what's in the sky above you, getting ready to feed on you, maybe a Hunter, or a Shade. Or me.

I watch her get out of the Humvee. She's bouncing from foot to foot between steps, moving sideways and forward at the same time, eating a candy bar. I've never seen anyone with so much energy. Her hair is auburn fire in the moonlight. Her skin is luminous. She has

sweet young curves and long legs. Her features are bone
china fine, and expressions rush across her skin like my
new Unseelie tattoos rush beneath mine.

But it's the heart of the girl that gets me.

He's big and towers over her. Hard face. Hard body.
Hard walk. They look so wrong together. They're talking. She keeps looking up at him like he gets on her last
nerve. Good. Her hand hovers near the hilt of her sword
and I know what she's thinking. She despises Chester's.
She can barely stand to be in the same place with Fae
without killing them. She hates them. All of them.

It's a category that will soon include me.

The owner of Chester's looks up.

I'm deep in shadows on the roof, throwing a light
glamour, a new power I've been testing, trying to make
my face more palatable to her.

I focus on projecting a general blanket of night and
emptiness so he can't see me.

His gaze stops right where I am and he gets a smug-ass
look on his face, but that's his look most of the time. I've
nearly decided that while he might sense a disturbance
in the night up here, he can't actually see me when he
inclines his head in that arrogant, imperial way so characteristic of the dickhead.

Rage washes over me, thick and intense and smother-
ing, and for a few seconds I drift in a black place where
everything's icy and wasted and evil and I *like* it. I'm
glad I'm going Unseelie prince. I say bring on the power.

I say let there be war.

I throw back my head and slide a mane of hair over
my shoulders. Cutting it doesn't do a bloody thing. I
sleep, I wake up, it's there again. I turn my face up to the
moon and inhale greedily. I want to drop to all fours and
bay like a wild thing drunk on being hungry and strong,
a beast that could fuck for days without cease if I could
only find something that could take it as hard and long

as I can give it. I want to chime to the moon in Unseelie, and hear it chime back. I can smell death in the city, everywhere, and it's intoxicating. I can smell need and sex and hunger and it's so bloody sweet—humanity ripe for the plucking and playing and eating! I shift my dick in my jeans. It's painfully hard. And the Earth is round.

I look back down, my eyes narrow. My boots are crusted with ice. The roof has gone white in a circle of snow and glittering ice in a fifteen-foot radius around me. I lope lightly along the edge of the roof, crunching snow, following as they go around back. This is going to be so much easier when I don't have to use my feet.

He isn't what he's pretending to be with her.

I watch him all the time. I'm going to be there when he stops pretending. I'm going to be her bulletproof vest, her shield, her fallen fucking angel whether she wants one or not. He's pretending he's almost human. He's no more human than me. He's pretending to be nice, like he's safe to be around, like he doesn't have fangs for a reason. He's pretending the term the "Gavel Effect" wasn't coined about him, meaning you're fine with him. Right up until you're not.

Right up until you're dead.

The devil in a businessman's suit, he bides his time, gathers information, processes it, and when he makes a decision, the gavel falls and everyone that pissed him off or offended him or just breathed wrong dies.

She won't be given a stay of execution. No one gets one. The only things that matter to him are others of his kind.

She thinks he's not an animal like Barrons. That he's more civilized. She's right, he is more polished. But it only makes him more dangerous. With Barrons you *expect* to get fucked up royally. With Ryodan you don't see it coming.

He's treating her like she's fourteen and he's a normal

adult, acting like he's taken her under his wing. Like he needs her detecting skills, same as Barrons did to Mac, and she's falling for it, same as Mac. He's lining up his dominoes, so they fall more easily when he feels like pushing them over, conserving energy so he doesn't have to hunt her when he's ready to kill her.

A bastard like him has one use for women. And she's not old enough. Yet. I can't decide which would be worse, if he killed her before she was old enough or waited and made her one of his endless string of women.

She's not that kind of girl, the endless string type. You get a shot at something like her once in a lifetime. And if you screw it up there's a special place in hell for you.

She breaks away from him suddenly and stomps off ahead. She's pissed. I smile.

I pull out my knife, twist my arm over my shoulder and scratch my back with it. Blood trickles. I sigh with relief, but it doesn't last long. Sleeping is a real bitch. My back itches all the time and human drugs don't work on me. I twist to get a better scratch.

My blade hits bone with a dull clunk. I saw at it with the serrated tip of the blade but can't get the angle right. I don't have any friends that are glad to see me, nobody to lend a helping hand. I tried to get Dad to cut them out of my back. He said they're attached to my spine and it would kill me. I don't believe that. Nothing kills me. They itch. I want them gone almost as much as I'm beginning to want them.

Fucking wings.

Funny how things work out. Dani killed an Unseelie prince to save Mac, and I end up turning into the replacement for the prince Dani killed. But it's not the lass's fault. It's Mac's. For needing saving. Later, for forcing me to eat something I would never have eaten if I'd been in my right mind.

I wonder if my wings will get as big as Cruce's. I wonder what it would feel like to fly the night sky with him and the other two. I see a vision in my head sometimes of the four of us, swooping down over the city, black wings beating air, filling the sky, owning the world. I can hear the sound we make as the four of us chime deep in our bodies. There's a special, bloodcurdling song the Unseelie princes sing, sometimes it plays in my head while I sleep. The call to the Wild Hunt burns in my blood.

I back up to the corner of a small brick building on the roof that houses heat pumps, lean against it and drag my back from side to side across the edge, scratching, watching as they move toward a metal door in the ground.

He catches up with her and they walk together again.

She glides through the night. He punches into it, a boxing glove with razor blades for knuckles. When she passes, the world is a better place. He leaves bloody footprints in a graveyard of bones.

He lifts the door, light blazes up from a hole in the ground, and she descends, my angel, into a sordid hell.

He squats at the edge and watches her go and, for a split second, I see an unguarded expression on his face.

It chills even a creature as cold as me.

I know that look. I've seen it on my own face.

Then the son of a bitch looks up at me and, this time, there's no question in my mind that he sees me. He looks straight at me and inclines his head with a mocking smile. I return it coolly. My nod says, "Yes, yes, I see you, too. Be very careful."

I can't decide if what he just let me see was real—or another of his games. They don't call him the master of manipulation for nothing. Barrons breaks heads. Ryodan turns them inside out. Barrons fucks you up. Ryodan makes you fuck yourself up. He pushes buttons and rearranges things according to his own private, coolly sociopathic plan.

I liked it better when I thought he was going to kill her.

I stop scratching.

I want those wings. They'll make the fight that's coming easier.

He's a walking dead man.

If he wasn't serious about what he just showed me, and he's gaming me, he gamed the wrong Unseelie prince. I'll kill him long before he gets around to killing her. I know how men like him work. I'm becoming one.

If he *was* serious about what he just showed me, he showed it to the wrong Unseelie prince. Because what he showed me is that he sees the same things in her I do.

He knows she's worth waiting for.

And when it's time, he intends to be the one. That's why he's keeping her close. To those of us who live forever, a few years isn't long to wait.

Not for something worth waiting for. Not for a once-in-a-lifetime girl.

A few years are a mere blink of an eye to men like us, for whom women crush sweetly like rotting pumpkins after Halloween. Sex isn't easy for me anymore. I'm always holding back. Human women are breakable.

Not this one.

He sees her like I do: at seventeen, twenty, thirty. Superimposed over the fourteen-year-old, he sees the woman she'll become.

And he's staking his claim.

Over my. Dead. Fucking. Body.

And I can't die.

But I know one of his kind that recently did, and I know how. I hear there's a Hunter up there in the night sky that likes Unseelie royalty.

Soon I'll have the wings to find him.

* * *

My superpowers come back three blocks from Chester's. I know because I've been trying to tap a finger in hyperspeed on my thigh the whole way back. Finally did it. I still haven't managed to make only my eyes move like Ryodan but I've been practicing and can get certain parts of my body to speed up for short amounts of time. Only problem is, the place where the part connects to my body gets a little sore, like I stressed out the muscles where the slow-mo and fast-mo parts are having a kind of what-the-feck-are-we-doing-here battle with each other.

But it's not like I could sit in the Humvee with the dude, who would love to know sometimes I'm helpless, and practice trying to freeze-frame my whole body. If he stopped sudden, I could go shooting straight through the windshield and then I'd be all cut up for days on top of my usual bruises.

I look at him, irritated. "Why are *you* never bruised?" What is he? Like the exception to everything? And if so, where do I apply?

"Participating and all that bunk," he says. In other words, I don't get to know because I'm not in whatever his inner circle is. Fine. Don't want to be there anyway.

"You got some kind of magic salve, dude? Because it's only fair to share stuff like that."

He pulls up to the curb out front of Chester's. I hop out of the Humvee the second he parks and instantly start bouncing from foot to foot, sideways, in between steps forward, to make sure I'm working right again. No way I'd go inside Chester's with no superpowers. I whip out a candy bar, devour it then munch three more in quick succession, stockpiling energy. "Aren't we done for the night? What else have you got for me to do?" I just spent an hour in an electrified sardine can with Ryodan, after losing my powers. He saturates confined spaces, like he's got ten people's stuff crammed into his body. He's pissed at me for not inspecting the scene before it blew. I'm pissed at me, too, but it wasn't like I had any choice. Without superpowers, I'm not getting anywhere near one of those scenes. It was a sucky drive. I want some time alone, or time with Dancer. He recharges me. Hanging with him is simple and pretty much perfect.

He doesn't answer me and I look at him. He's staring up at the roof of a building across the street and he's got an amused, smug look on his face. I search the shadows of the roofline but I can't figure out what he's checking out. There's nothing up there. "Dude, you listening to me? Hello? Do you even know I'm here?"

He continues looking at the roof like he's seeing something I can't see. Like that stupid drop of condensation I'm still not sure I believe was there.

"I always know you're there, Dani. I tasted your blood. I feel you all the time."

Okay, that's disturbing.

"You mean like when I'm around," I clarify for him.

"How do you think I found you at your little boyfriend's place."

"You need to look at him harder if you think he's little."

"And so breakable."

"Stop talking about him. He's none of your business. Just what are you saying? That you could find me, like, anywhere, anytime?" There's a right answer and wrong answer to that question.

"Yes."

That was the wrong answer. I get so mad I'm breathless. "Bull. Liar."

He laughs and looks at me. "Want to play hide-and-seek, little girl?" He purrs it in a voice I've never heard him use before, and he actually makes it a question.

His fangs are out.

"Dude, you are one weird . . . whatever you are." I'm nearly at a loss for words.

He laughs again and I can't even stand to look at him so I charge off to the door in the ground that is the new entrance to Chester's.

He holds the door up for me. I sigh gustily as I descend the ladder. I hate Ryodan.

So I'm walking across the dance floor, cutting a beeline straight for the stairs to head up to Ryodan's office to do whatever it is he wants me to do, when I see *her*.

She's moving across the main dance floor with Jericho Barrons behind her, and it looks like they're heading for one of the subclubs, though I can't figure out why. Mac doesn't like it here any more than I do.

I freeze.

I hate seeing her. I hate not knowing what's going on in her life. I hate what I've done. Can't change it, though, so no point in feeling it.

Ryodan slams into my back, knocking me forward into the crowd. "Walk much?" I say testily as I careen off of a hulking Rhino-boy that gnashes yellowed tusks at me.

As usual, he doesn't miss a trick. His gaze does that ocular-shiver thing all over my face. "I thought you and Mac were friends."

"We are friends," I lie.

"Then go say hi."

Shit, I hate how much he notices. "We might have had a tiny tiff."

"Tiny, my ass."

"Quit nosing into my business."

"Learn not to wear it on your face, kid. Except in private, with me and no one else. You need some serious training. Telegraph like that, it's only a matter of time before somebody hoists you on your own entrails."

"Dude, who *uses* words like entrails? Or hoists?"

"Tell me what happened."

I fist my hands at my waist. "It's none of your business and that's the beginning and end of it. Some things you can horn into. Some things you can't. Stay the fuck out of it."

He looks at me weird. "You said fuck. Not feck."

"That's all you got from what I just said?"

"You want privacy on this. I'll give it to you. See how easy that was. If you want something, ask me for it. You'll find I can be a generous man. When you treat me right. If you ever figure out what that is."

He moves past me and heads for his office.

I can't help myself, I look back at Mac. I grin and kick myself inside for doing it but there was a time when I loved waking up every day in Dublin, different than I do now, because I knew *she* was there at Barrons Books & Baubles and we were going to go do something cool that day and then she baked me a birthday cake and picked me out presents and we watched movies and we fought back-to-back and I ain't never had anything like that before and sometimes I feel like a homeless dog out in the rain and thunder and I'm muddy and cold and I'm staring in the window at the pretty collie sleeping on a doggie bed close to the fire, and there's a name on the bowl that's next to her, and I wonder what it would be like to—

"Gah! Get over yourself, wussy-girl." I got big-dog teeth and a big-dog bite and I know the rules: you stay inside, you get collared and spayed. I pick myself up and start to freeze-frame after Ryodan when a commotion in

Mac's general direction makes me stop, stay in slow-mo and glance back.

There's a new type of Unseelie in Chester's tonight and they're something out of a horror flick. They look like anorexic wraiths that might drift around graveyards, breaking open coffins and feeding on rotting corpses. They're draped in black cloaks with hoods so you can't see their faces, and they don't walk, they hover and glide just above the floor. I glimpse a flash of bone at the sleeves. In their hoods I catch a quick hint of pale, bloodless skin and something black. There are twenty or so of them in the subclub Mac and Barrons are just entering. They make me think of carrion crow that sense the coming of a storm and perch in treetops everywhere, waiting for the destruction to begin so they can swoop down on the dying and tear flesh from bone with sharp beaks. I'm suddenly certain they don't have normal mouths. And equally certain I'd rather never see what they do have.

They turn toward Mac like they're a single unit or something, which is totally creepy, and begin making a chittering noise that sets every nerve in my body on edge. There are no snakes in Ireland. Not because St. Patrick banished them like folks like to tell, but because of the island and climate issues. When I was a kid I was fascinated by snakes because I'd never seen one. I took a holiday after Mom died and Ro freed me, before she started controlling me, too, and went to a bunch of museums and zoos. I saw a rattlesnake. When it moved its tail, it had the same effect on me as these hooded Unseelie when they chitter. The dry, dusty rattle elicited some kind of atavistic response in me and got me thinking maybe genetic memory really does exist and certain sounds just make you want to run like hell.

What are they? How come I've never seen them before? What's their unique prey? How do they feed? How can they be killed? Better yet, why are they all peeling away from Mac like she has the Unseelie version of the bubonic plague?

There are too many people on the dance floors between us. I can't get a good view. I slide sideways into fast-mo, blow past Lor and Fade guarding the stairs at the bottom, making sure I catch Lor a good one with an elbow and snicker when he grunts, then stop at the top of the stairs and look down. Much better view.

The wraiths are chittering even louder, gliding back from Mac and Barrons, but it's Mac all those dark hoods are turned toward.

"Interesting," Ryodan says close to my ear. "You have to wonder why they can't get out of her way fast enough. I've never seen them do that before." Ryodan doesn't like Mac. He never has. She got between him and his best boy-bud.

I give him a look. "I'll tell you a secret, Ryodan. You mess with her, Barrons'll kill you." I drag a finger across my neck. "Just like that. You aren't all that. Barrons'll stomp your ass, hands down."

He smiles faintly. "I'll be damned. You have a crush on Barrons."

"I do not have a crush—"

"You do, too. It's all over your face. Anybody could see it."

"Sometimes, boss, you're just wrong."

"I'm never wrong. You might as well take out a billboard. 'Dani O'Malley thinks Jericho Barrons is hot.' My offer to teach you is still open. Save you from future embarrassment. If I can see it on your face, he can, too."

"He never figured it out before," I grumble, then realize I just admitted it. Ryodan has a tricky way of wording things that makes you say things you didn't mean to say. "Maybe I'll ask Barrons to teach me," I mutter, and turn away from the stairs, heading for his office. I run smack into his chest. "Dude, move. Trying to get some-where here."

"No one but me is ever going to teach you, Dani."

He touches me before I see it coming, has his hand under my chin, turning my face up. My shiver is instant and uncontrollable.

"That's non-negotiable. You signed a contract with me that grants exclusivity. You won't like it if you try to break it."

I glare at him, wondering what the heck I actually signed. Kind of hoping I never find out.

"What are we doing here? Pansy talk or work? You got something else for me to do or not?" I glance over my shoulder one more time as I push past him. Barrons is standing in front of Mac like a shield, and I allow myself a quick flash of a smile. Ryodan is right, I need to learn to hide what I'm feeling. She's safe. She'll always be safe with Barrons in the picture. I never have to worry about Mac. Just about what she might do to me one day. I'd rather worry about that than Mac, so essentially all is right with my world.

FOURTEEN

"Knock, knock, knockin' on heaven's door"

It turns out Ryodan didn't have diddly-squat for me to do. There were no other iced scenes to visit so he made me hang around his office with him.

I wanted to go back out and examine the debris of the warehouse scene that exploded the other night, pick through it more thoroughly for clues (thinking I could move my hidey-holes at the same time), but he told me to study all the folks and Fae through the glass floor and see if I thought any of them might be responsible for what was happening.

I said, dude, you said you think it's happening spontaneously, like some part of Faery is bleeding through. Now you want me checking out individuals like they might be doing it. Which one is it?

He said both and went back to his paperwork. I don't think he feels the same sense of urgency I do, since it's only been humans getting iced lately and none of them on his turf. If he doesn't start showing me some investigative action, I'll be forced to work on it on my own time, and I don't know how to squeeze everything in, plus sleep every few days or so.

Mac left pretty quick. She seemed to get real nervous about what was happening with the ZEWs. That's Zombie Eating Wraiths for short, because that's what they look like. They had dirt and cobwebs on their cloaks, clues to where they hole up. I relaxed once she was gone. Then I got tense again having to watch Jo down there in the kiddie subclub, showing off so much leg to the Unseelie, and there's no question they were liking it. I'd like to have legs like Jo some day, all curvy and smooth-skinned and pretty.

No bruises!

She kept looking up at Ryodan's office with a weird look on her face, all longing-like, like she must have known I was up there. I didn't know she missed me so much! It made me feel bad for not spending more time with her. Sometimes she'd look real hard at the stairs like she was hoping maybe I'd come down.

I watched, sword hand itching all the while, because there were so many things in the club preying on humans that needed killing. By dawn I was a seething knot of repressed, homicidal *sidhe*-seer thoughts, and not one bit wiser about who or what was behind the icings.

Two good things came from the hours I sat there till he finally let me leave. I learned about four new types of Unseelie and I composed my next *Dani Daily*. I plan to clean it up a little visually, make it even more professional-like before printing.

Now, sitting up on my favorite water tower perch, I read through my handwritten copy one more time, proofing it before I go to press.

The Dani Daily

May 24, 1 AWC

**Brought to you exclusively
by DANI MEGA O'MALLEY aka
I Give a Rat's Ass
and unlike IMITATION newcomers
I always have been
YOUR ONLY CREDIBLE SOURCE FOR THE
LATEST NEWS IN & AROUND DUBLIN!**

Who's been bringing you the facts about what's what ever since the walls fell? Me.

Who searched you out and brought food and news to your hidey-holes when you were too afraid to leave them? Me. Who carried messages, hunted for missing family members, and brought them home to you if they were alive? Dani Mega O'Malley.

Who dug through the rubble for wallets and IDs, and gave you back their things so you could grieve? It wasn't some fly-by-night organization that got most of their whole first paper's "news" out of being snarky about me. That's not news. That's slander. I give you facts you can use.

Who's been killing your enemies and teaching you how to fight for the past seven months? Who rounded up the children and took them to safety? Don't forget what you know is true just because somebody else suddenly pops up, imitating MY paper, making crazy fecked-up claims. I haven't seen any power or water running yet that isn't generator-powered, and, folks, I can hook that up for you.

I Care
Always will, Dublin.
Dani out!

I don't do rebuttals and I ain't got no love letters in me, so this'll have to do. Once I print and post it, I'm going to hole up and sleep like the dead for ten hours. Been up two or three days now. I always forget until I'm about to keel over.

I've been sitting on my water tower, looking down over the city, watching the sun come up. The air is clean like it never was before the walls fell. It's foggy but not smoggy like it used to be. I love living in a harbor town. Once, when I was nine, I stowed away on a fishing boat. They couldn't get rid of me until the end of the day because they needed the full day's catch. They finally ended up letting me ride up front, wind in my hair, salt spray in my face. The docks have always fascinated me with big ships coming and going places, tales of adventure and excitement stuck to their hulls like barnacles! Now they just sit, dead in the water like so much else. I've got a cool hidey-hole on one of them. I decide I ain't been there in a while and I'll catch some z's there later.

The sky is platinum, the sea slate, and the river Liffey is sliding down through the city, metallic. Fog spills silver lace over it all. Takes my fecking breath away!

I could admire it for hours but I got a job to do.

People got short memories. They get fear-blind and easily dazzled. Especially during times of war when the world starts looking so dark and gritty that shiny things start looking shinier. I got to keep reminding them of the things they know are true.

Me and Dublin, we're peas in the Mega pod. This is my city and my paper and I don't give up nothing that's mine without a fight.

I've never lost a fight yet.

Well, only to that fecker Ryodan. And there's no way he's behind WeCare. He's like, the antithesis of WeCare. He's, like, We-Don't-Fucking-Care all wrapped up with We'll-Eat-You-for-Lunch, too.

There goes my mood again. That's all it takes. One little thought about him. I have to go to "work" again tonight like some fecking slow-mo Joe, trudging along with the masses, and the unfairness of it all is now that the world has melted down, *nobody* has to go to work anymore.

Except me.

I bristle, realizing I can't go sleep like the dead once I get my rag up because I have to set an alarm. Me. I have to get up at a certain time!

I've never paid any attention to time. Dancer says I've enjoyed a luxury most people never have. He hates clocks and watches and everything that has to do with time. He says people already have too many lost days and that most folks live in the past or the future but never the present, always saying stuff like "I'm unhappy because 'X' happened to me yesterday," or "I'll be happy again when 'Y' happens to me tomorrow." He says time is the ultimate villain. I don't really get that but that's probably because until this very frigging moment I never had to look at a clock for anything. I woke up when I felt like it. I went to sleep when I felt like it.

If I'm lucky, I'll be able to squeeze in five whole hours of sleep before I have to go back to "work."

I'm aghast at the horrificness of it all. Clock hands are ticking away my life at someone else's direction.

It's so wrong.

I wake up slow and careful, don't even stretch. I lay still, feeling the boat rock gentle on the waves. I love sleeping on my ship. Got it booby-trapped to the nines. *I* got caught by one of them today, they're so good! I don't open my eyes because it takes me a while to get moving. Sometimes it can take me a half hour. That's why I set my alarm for seven instead of seven-thirty.

My alarm.

Was that what just woke me?

I don't remember turning it off.

I fumble for my cell phone. Signal might be dead but it still plays music and games. And has a stupid alarm clock.

I encounter an obstacle between me and my phone that feels like—

"Aiy-*eeeeeeee*!" I make a sound I didn't know I could make, part gasp, part shriek, and shoot straight up in bed, eyes flying open. What just came out of my mouth is so girly it makes me cringe so I grab my sword and swing it.

He knocks it out of my hand and it clatters across the floor.

I can't even say anything for a sex. I mean sec.

This is like my worst nightmare ever in the whole world! This is worse than all the ZEWs coming after me plus the devil and all the Unseelie princes, too!

Ryodan is in *bed* next to me!

Sitting there, cool as you please! We're in bed together! He's giving me that faint smile and mocking stare. Guess he was watching me sleep. Did I snore? Was I flopped flat on my back with my mouth hanging open? I have no idea how long he's been here! How'd he get in? How the heck did he get past all my booby traps? Obviously I'm going to have to come up with some new ones!

I try to push him off the bed. It's like trying to budge a mountain. I hit him. Like a girl. Not even using my superpowers. Assuming I have them at the moment, the fickle fecking things. What good is it to be a superhero if you only are some of the time and you never get to know when?

He catches my fist and holds it.

I can't get my fist out of his hand. "Dude, give me

some space here! I need room when I wake up! I can't breathe! Move!"

He laughs and I want to crawl under the covers and burrow deep and hide and pretend this is just a really bad nightmare and it'll be over soon.

"Get *off* my bed!"

When he lets me go and stands, the mattress rises four inches on his side. I can't believe I didn't feel him sit down. Yes I can. I sleep hard.

"You're late for work, kid."

"What time is it?" I glance wildly around for my cell phone. I'm so sleep-discombobulated I can barely function. I spot it on the end table next to the bed. It's smashed into a gazillion pieces. "You broke my cell phone!"

"It was smashed when I got here. You must have done it when the alarm went off."

"It's not like it's my fault," I say crossly, shoving my hair out of my face with both hands. "I've never had to use an alarm before."

"Am I giving you shit."

"You're like, here!"

"That's because you're late for work, kid. Get dressed."

Clothes hit me in the chest.

I realize I have on my favorite pjs. They're flannel and have ducks on them. Maybe he didn't notice. I can't stand it. This is my place. It's supposed to be private.

"Captain's quarters. Pretty plush. Get moving. We've got things to do." He walks to the door and heads for the deck. "Nice pjs, kid."

He takes me to a church.

Churches crack me up. They're like money, a conspiracy of faith. Like everyone agreed to believe that not only is there a God, but he comes down and checks on folks, so long as they hang in certain places, put up altars, burn lots of candles and incense, and perform sit-stand-kneel and other wacky rituals that'd make a coven of witches look not OCD. Then to further complicate it, some folks perform rituals, subset A, and other folks perform rituals, subset B, C, or D, and so on into an infinity of denominations, and call themselves different things then deny everyone else's right to heaven if they're not performing the same rituals. Dude. Weird. I figure if there is a God, he or she isn't paying attention to what we build or if we follow some elaborate rules, but copping a ride on our shoulders, watching what we do every day. Seeing if we took this great big adventure called life and did anything interesting with it. I figure the folks that are the most interesting get to go to heaven. I mean, if I was God, that's who I'd want there with me. I also figure being eternally happy would be eternally boring so I try not to be *too* interesting, even though it's hard for me. I'd rather be a superhero in hell, kicking all kinds of demon ass, than an angel in heaven, wafting around with a beatific smile on my face, playing a pansy harp all day. Dude, give me drums and big cymbals! I like the crash and bang.

So, Ryodan takes me to a church and I stand outside looking in, stymied.

I mentally review the places I've seen so far that got iced: Chester's subclub, a warehouse on the outskirts of town, two small underground pubs, a fitness center, the rural Laundromat-family, and now a small congregation in a church.

I linger at the tall, double-door entrance, absorbing details because I'm in no hurry to rush in. The cold emanating from the interior is brutal, worse than any scene yet. My breath burns all the way down into my lungs, even with a good fifty yards between me and the front of the church where the folks are gathered at the altar in a frosty nativity scene. There are eight men, three women, a priest, a dog standing there, and an old man sitting at the organ. I hear more men than women survived Halloween, and in a lot of rural places women have become a wicked hot commodity with men tripping all over themselves to score one. The pipes of the organ behind the altar are covered with icicles, and the ceiling drips enormous stalactites. There's a frozen fog hanging around the entire interior. The priest is standing behind the altar, facing the others, his arms raised, like he was in the middle of a sermon.

"It's colder than any of the rest, which suggests it happened more recently, ambient temperature and all factored in," I say, and when I talk, my breath crystallizes in little clouds that hang in the air. I jerk with a sudden uncontrollable shiver. "Feck, it's cold!"

"Too cold for you."

I look at him. There was nearly a question mark at the end of that one. "Dude, you worried about me? I'm indestructible. When did you find out about this one?"

"Fade found it about forty minutes ago. He'd passed the church ten minutes earlier, and it wasn't iced. On his way back it was."

"So it *is* the freshest one we've seen so far." I notice he's not pressing into the church in slow-mo like he has at prior scenes. Guess it's a little cold even for him.

I breathe in and out, fast and hard, bellowing my lungs, priming my adrenaline pump. "Let's do it."

I mentally pick myself up, shift gears and freeze-frame in.

There's cold and then there's something worse. This cold knifes into me and twists, catching gristle and bone. It slices down through muscle and tendon, razoring my nerves. But this scene is the freshest of them all, and if there's anyplace I'm going to find clues, it's here, before the temperature starts to rise and things change. If things do. I just don't know enough.

I circle the small gathering, shivering. I've stuttered with cold at other scenes but never shivered while freeze-framing. I think shivering is cool because it's the body's way of freeze-framing on a molecular level. Your cells sense the temperature is too cold for you, and your brain makes you vibrate minutely all over to generate heat. So I'm, like, freeze-framing twice right now, on a cellular level and on my feet. The body is a brilliant thing.

I look at their faces first.

They're frozen with their mouths open, faces contorted, screaming, same as the outdoor Laundromat-people. These folks saw it coming, too. All except for the priest who's looking startled at the folks standing there, which tells me whatever it was, it came from behind the priest and it came *fast* because his head isn't even turning. He must have been reacting to the looks on their faces. It must have appeared and iced simultaneously, or he'd have had time to begin to look behind him.

I feel a little better about whatever's happening because twice now people saw it coming. That means I have a chance of getting out of its way if it comes in my direction.

"Save your. Observations and breath," Ryodan says at my ear. "Gather. Info and. Get out."

I look at him because of how he just spoke. Soon as I do I understand why he kept stopping and starting. His face is iced solid. It cracks when he adds, "Hurry the. Fuck. Up."

My face isn't iced. Why is his? I reach out without thinking, like I'm going to touch him or something, and he knocks my hand away. "Don't. Fucking touch. Anything. Not. Even me." Ice shatters and re-forms on his face four times before he completes the sentence.

Embarrassed, I whiz away, snap my mind up tight and focus on the details. I have no clue why I almost touched him. There's no explanation for my behavior. I think he put some kind of spell on me with his application.

What's happening at these iced places? Why is it happening? Is some inhumanly cold part of Faery really bleeding through? I understand why Ryodan thinks it is. At each scene, nothing appears to have been taken. I see no common denominators. Nothing was eaten. No one was harmed. Then why did it happen? I consider each of these iced scenes a crime. People are dead. Crimes require motive. I whiz back and forth, trying to discern some inkling of a motive, a hint of a sentient mind behind this. Looking close, for tiny injuries, say from something like needle-thin teeth. Are they drained of bodily fluids certain sick Fae consider tasty? The thought makes me think of a few Fae I should have killed. If I had, everything would be fine between me and Mac. She'd never have known. Still don't know why I didn't. Wasn't like I *wanted* to get caught.

I see no signs of harm or foul play of any kind.

Then I see her and it's an instant heart punch.

"Aw, bugger!" I say.

I don't mind so much when adults get killed because I know they had a life. They lived. They had their chance. And hopefully they died fighting. But kids . . . well, kids just slay me. They didn't even get to know what a crazy, wonderful, amazing place the world is! They didn't even get to have hardly any adventures.

This one didn't get any adventures at all. She never even got past the "Gee, I'm glad I got milk" stage.

One of the women is holding a baby girl with a halo of curly red hair just like mine, nestled in the crook of her arm. She has a tiny fist wrapped around her mom's finger and is frozen staring up at her mom like she's the most beautiful, magical angel in the world, which is exactly how I felt about mine before everything got so . . . yeah, well. So.

And something nuts happens to me that I don't understand, but I'm going to start doing what the rest of the world does and blame everything on my hormones because I used to be the coolest of the cool until I started having periods.

I get all mushy inside like some kind of wimp that buys into those greeting card commercials, and I think about Mom, and even though she did things to me that other people would think were awful, I understand why she kept me in a cage. There weren't many choices and she didn't have much money and she wasn't *always* mean to me. She did it to keep me safe. I never blamed her for keeping me in a cage with a collar.

I just wished she'd stop forgetting me.

Like she didn't want to remember me.

Or maybe she wished she'd never had me.

But it wasn't always like that with us. I remember feeling crazy-loved. I remember when it was different. I just never could get it back.

And all the sudden there's like this stupid fecking thing so cold at the corner of my eyes on the insides like I tried to *cry* or something and I don't fecking cry, and it froze the second it started and my head hurts and I reach out and I touch the tiny fist wrapped around her mommy's finger and my heart squinches and then I have this horrible pressure in my ears and then something inside me gives with a soft squishing sound, and all the sudden I can't breathe and I'm so cold I guess it must be like getting dumped naked in space.

The cold knifes into me, flays me, slays me, glacierizes me.

Cold takes on new meanings and just about when I think I understand it, like it's some complex state of being that I could exist inside of, it flips all around on me, and I burn everywhere and I'm hot, and I'm hot, and I'm so fecking unbelievably hot that I start tearing off my clothes and I can't do it fast enough because I feel thick and slow and stupid and I realize somehow I've dropped back down into slow-mo!

Was it when I touched her? Was that why he told me not to touch anything? Does touching something so cold knock you down from fast-mo? How does he know that, if it's true? Did it knock him down once somewhere, is that how he knew? Then why didn't it kill him?

It's too cold down in slow-mo, seriously like outer space.

I try to freeze-frame back up.

I stumble to my knees. I must have waited too long. Maybe the instant I dropped down was too long.

God, the floor is cold! It hurts, it hurts, it hurts! I just thought "God." I don't use that word. Do I believe? Have I found faith here, on my knees, now, at the end? That seems kind of hypocritical-like to me. Ain't dying a hypocrite. I start to snicker. I'm not shivering. I'm hot. I'm so hot.

Even now I try to absorb more details. Curiosity. Cat dying. May as well. It's a vacuum here. Something's wrong, something's missing that I couldn't feel missing in fast-mo but I don't understand what. The stuff around me, the people and everything feel . . . somehow flat, void of an essential ingredient that would give it multi-dimensionality.

"Ry—" I can't get his name out.

I hear him yelling, but I can't understand the words and it sounds weird. Like he's talking muffled into a pillow.

I try to skinny off my jeans. Need them off. They're cold, so cold. Have to get everything off. It's so cold it's burning my skin. He's fighting me, trying to keep them on me. *Get out of my way,* I try to say but nothing comes out. I need them *off.* If I can get them *off* I might be okay.

And all I can think is—

Help me! I scream inside my head.

My heart is going. It summons up the energy for one last violent feck-you pump but only manages a soft squish.

I can't die like this. I have things to do. My adventure has hardly begun. Everything goes black. I see Death. Ain't so fascinating. It's a sledgehammer.

Aw, shit. I know what rigor mortis is. I know my face is going to stick. I'm choosing how.

I belly up a laugh from way down deep where I'm always half laughing anyway because being alive— dude!—it's the greatest adventure in the world. What a ride it's been. Short but stupendous. Ain't nobody can say Dani Mega O'Malley didn't live while she was here.

No regrets!

Dani out.

FIFTEEN

"Hot child in the city"

I lose track of them for one minute, distracted by a female Unseelie down in the streets that has what the Highlander in me considers revolting parts but the prince in me thinks are all the right ones. Sex has become bloody weird. Incredible. But weird. She's a few blocks south of the church, and she's throwing off pheromones that make my dick go flat to my stomach, and by the time I realize what's happened to Dani, I have one more reason to hate Ryodan and the whole fucking world, as if I needed one.

"No!" I roar as I rush for the edge of the roof. That's the bad thing about being a half-breed. The Highlander in me wants to take the stairs. The Unseelie in me wants to use wings.

Too bad I don't have any yet.

My heart makes the decision without me and tries to get to her the fastest way possible.

I jump.

I curse as I plummet four stories and brace for impact. Contrary to what she thinks, I can't sift yet so I can't cut out of this fall. What kind of idiot breaks all his bones at the precise moment his damsel needs him the most? Up to now I've been glad I can't sift yet. I think it's the

168 · KAREN MARIE MONING

point of no return. The day I can blink out of existence and back in at a mere thought, I'm no longer human.

I twist in midair, trying to land on my feet.

I'm astonished when it works. I discover new things about myself every day, most of which disgust me, but this is a welcome change. My center of balance has shifted. I pivot and realign flawlessly. My bones seem to have developed an incredible rubbery resilience. My knees bend slightly, bowing in a distinctly inhuman way to absorb the impact. I land like a graceful cat. I stare down at my feet, which are intact and functioning perfectly, and all I can think is bloody hell, I just fell four—

"Bring her OUT here! NOW, you buggering idiot!"

My head whips up.

Some teenage guy wearing glasses is standing outside the church, looking in, screaming at Ryodan. I have no idea who he is or where he came from. But he just said *my* line, although I'd've done it minus the buggering part and with a lot more "fucks."

The kid's hands are fists and he's plastered up against the doorjamb of the church. His face and hair are frosted and he's shivering violently.

I push past him, shouldering him aside. "She doesn't need you. Worthless human. Get lost."

He snarls at me.

I laugh. Looking me in the face and snarling takes major balls. "Kudos to you, kid. Now take yourself off somewhere and die before I decide to cram those big balls you think you have down your throat." I shove into the church, so I can rescue Dani and kill Ryodan for taking a hothouse flower into the arctic zone.

The cold hits me like a brick wall and stops me in my tracks. A solid shell of ice forms on my skin. When I flex my muscles, the ice cracks and falls in a tinkle of crystals to the floor. I take another step and ice, mid-step this time, while I'm still moving.

I spent a small eternity in the Unseelie prison and never had this problem, and it was inhumanly cold there. I'm half Unseelie prince. I didn't think there *was* anyplace too cold for me. How can that dickhead Ryodan tolerate it, if I can't?

I take another step, ice again, crack it and step back. It won't do me any good to freeze up like the Tin Man and become useless to her. I don't understand how this is happening. The cold in the Unseelie King's kingdom iced my soul and made me hate being alive. This is worse. I wouldn't have believed there was anything worse. There's something familiar about this place, this scene, this cold. Déjà vu. I despise this cold. It makes me feel bad in the center of my bones. Empty, hollow, some-how . . . flawed. I narrow my eyes, looking around.

Dani!

She's on the floor and it's not the cold that takes my breath away. Her jeans are tangled around her knees. She has on a black bra and underwear with little white skulls and crossbones all over them. She's thrashing her arms and legs and crying incoherently.

And I can't get to her. My girl is half naked and dying and I can't get to her!

I push forward.

I ice solid.

I crack it and pull back.

Fuck!

She's trying to kick off her jeans the rest of the way and he's fighting her, trying to keep them on. He needs to get her out of there. Why is he wasting time trying to keep her clothes on?

"Bring her to me!" I demand.

"Don't freeze-frame with her!" the kid on the steps bellows. He's got some lungs. "If you move fast, you'll kill her!"

"What the fuck do *you* know," Ryodan says.

"Everything there is to know about hypothermia! And I'm willing to bet neither of you can warm her. Bring her to me if you want her to live! Stop trying to put her clothes back on. It's not going to help!"

"Fuck you, kid," Ryodan says, but he quits trying to dress her and scoops her up. Her jeans fall to the floor. She's mostly naked in his arms. I can't see past the red rage in my eyes.

"Don't move her any more than you have to! It'll force cold blood to her heart and she'll have afterdrop!" the kid yells.

Ryodan walks with her real slow and easy.

She's stopped flailing.

She's not making any noise now either. She's gone limp. Her arms and legs flop like a rag doll with each step he takes. If he killed her I'm going to beat him bloody and eat him piece by piece, slowly, with steak sauce.

It's all I can do to keep my feet rooted where I am and not attack him as he passes. Glorious, beautiful scenes of death and destruction, battlefields and torture chambers, crowd my mind, enticing, sexual, egging me on to smash and crash and raze everything in my path with no care for the consequences because there are no consequences for what I'm becoming.

When he walks past me, my fists drip blood. But I don't fight for her. If I fight for her, I could kill her. That would turn me into something worse than an Unseelie prince.

"You!" The kid stabs a finger at me. "I need sleeping bags, an aluminum blanket, and hot packs. Outdoor store on Ninth and Central. Get me sugar, Jell-O, and water if you can find it. Don't waste time if you can't. Same goes for a generator. Now!"

"I don't fetch for humans!"

But I'd cut the fucking moon out of the sky for her.

* * *

When I return with blankets and hot packs, she's on the sidewalk on the opposite side of the street from the church.

The kid with glasses is in his underwear. Apparently dickhead doesn't wear any.

Rage chokes me. I fight for control. The human part of my brain knows exactly why they took their clothes off. So they could bundle her in them. She needed everything they had. She's curled in a fetal ball, packed in their pants and shirts and jackets. The Unseelie part of my brain comprehends nothing but that two male dicks are way too close to something that's mine.

The kid is on top of her, on his hands and knees, with his face brushing hers like he's kissing her.

Ryodan looks like he's about to rip his head off. As I get closer, I see the kid is breathing just over her nose and mouth, letting his breath drift up her nostrils. I'm shaking with rage. My hands are fists again, bleeding from clenching them so tight.

"She keeps curling up," Ryodan says.

"Burrowing instinct. Freezing people do it when they're about to die."

"You let her die," I say to the kid, "I'll kill you every way a human can get killed, bring you back and do it all over again."

"Did you get what I need?" The kid thrusts a hand behind him, ignoring my threat. "Aluminum blanket. Now. And easy when you move her," he says over his shoulder, like he doesn't even know two homicidal maniacs are watching his every move and want him dead just for being so close to her. "Nothing sudden."

"Why aluminum?" I want to know exactly what he's doing so I can do it myself when there's a next time. I'd say that there's not going to be one, but since the walls fell there's always a next time.

"Superinsulation. Traps in heat. Keeps out everything else."

Ryodan and I place her gently on the blanket, then the kid stretches over her again. She's motionless. I can't even see her chest rising and falling. She's pale and still as death. It's a disturbing turn-on. I've never seen an Unseelie princess but I suspect they're like this: white and cold and beautiful. "Is she breathing?"

"Barely. Her body is using everything it's got just to keep her brain and organs functioning. She needs to urinate."

"You can't fucking know that," Ryodan says.

The kid doesn't turn his head or look at him, just talks straight up her nose. "She eats and drinks constantly. Her bladder is always at least partially full. Her body is wasting precious energy trying to keep the urine in her bladder from freezing. We need that energy directed at her heart. Ergo, she needs to piss. The sooner the better. We need her conscious to do that, unless you have a handy catheter."

"Get her conscious," Ryodan snarls.

"You're not putting a catheter in her," I growl.

"I'll do whatever I need to do to save her life. You. Bloody. Idiots," the kid says.

He pops open heat packs and shoves them in her armpits and groin. Then he stretches out next to her. "Roll us up in sleeping bags."

I look at Ryodan and he looks at me and for a second I think we might both kill the kid. Ryodan's more stone-faced than usual, if that's possible without turning to concrete, and his fangs are out. I look down. Ryodan's dick is as big as mine. "Why the bloody hell don't you wear underwear?" To an Unseelie prince, an exposed male dick is a call to battle.

"They chafe. Too small and confining."

"Fuck you," I say.

"Dudes. Get over yourselves," the kid says. "Roll us up. Do you want her to die?"

"You should never have taken her in there. I'm going to kill you for that," I say to Ryodan as I help roll up a nearly naked kid with my girl.

"I told her not to touch anything," Ryodan says. "I knew it would drop her out of fast-motion. I reminded her at every scene we went to. And bring it on, Highlander. Any time you think you're ready."

"And we all know how well she listens," the kid says dryly.

Ryodan gives him a look that would make grown, armed, psychopathic men shut up. "There was no reason for her to touch anything."

"Obviously she thought otherwise," the kid says, completely unperturbed.

"I was right there with her. I figured I could get her out."

"You figured wrong, dickhead," I say.

"I didn't think it would affect her so quickly if she did. It didn't do that to me when I tried it."

"She's not like you. And shut up, both of you," the kid says, and puts his face on hers again, breathing, cupping his hands around their faces to keep the warm air in.

"Why are you doing that?" I say.

"Warm air. Hypothalamus. Regulates internal temperature and will help raise her consciousness. I need her conscious so she can piss."

"I would have rubbed her down to warm her. Restored her circulation."

"Brilliant. You would have killed her. Her blood is too cold. It would have stopped her heart."

"I don't understand why she stripped," Ryodan says.

I look at him. He's doing the same thing I am. Learning what to do if it happens again. Both of us would have sped off with her, trying to get her somewhere warm. And according to this kid, we both would have killed her.

"Blood vessels widen. She thought she was hot. Hikers get found all the time dead in the mountains, naked with their clothes folded nearby. They get confused. Brain tries to make order out of chaos."

"How do you know all this?" I despise that he knows it and I don't. Makes him the better man for her in this situation. I want to be the better man for her in every situation.

"Mom was a doctor. I nearly died of hypothermia in the Andes once."

"I almost killed you," Ryodan says.

"She can't hear you," the kid tells him.

"I wasn't talking to her."

"Give me more hot packs," the kid says. "Bugger, she's cold!"

"A few weeks back. I almost killed you."

The kid gives him a look. I think, what the fuck gives a kid this young the balls it takes to snarl at me and give dickhead a look like that?

Ryodan says, "I stood in the shadows of an alley you were walking down. You wouldn't have seen me coming. She would have died tonight if I'd killed you."

"Is that, like, an apology?" I mock.

"Does she gasp in horror every time she sees you, Highlander?"

I unfurl wings that aren't there yet and hiss.

"You both talk too much," the kid says. "Shut up. Don't make me tell you again."

We shut up, which I find hysterically funny.

I suddenly see us from above. I do that all the time now. I think it's because I'm losing my humanity and it's my way of marking my descent into hell. I observe that there's only one human male at this scene and it's not me.

I see a radiant woman-child who has more curves under her clothes than I guessed, and from the way Ryodan is looking at her, he didn't guess it either. She's bloodless, blue-tinged, rolled up tight in the arms of a half-naked teenager that could have been, should have been, me. Keeping vigil over her are two monsters of very different breeds but monsters just the same.

Death on her left.

Devil on her right.

The kid looks like I did at his age, except for the glasses and a few inches of height he has on me. Dark hair, great smile, wide shoulders, the kid's going to be good-looking.

If he survives past next week.

At the moment I'd wager strongly against it.

He's in a sleeping bag with her, holding her. She has skulls and crossbones on her underwear. It charms me beyond reason.

The way I see it, if it's not Ryodan in that next dark alley, it's going to be me.

SIXTEEN

I fight authority and ~~authority always wins~~
probably always will

I make a new discovery that totally blows.
   Dying is the easy part.
  It's coming back to life that sucks.
  One second I'm gone. I don't even exist.
  The next second, I'm on fire with pain.
  I hear voices talking but I feel like somebody stacked weights on my eyes and don't even try to open them. I hurt so bad I *want* to lose consciousness again. I groan, miserable.
  "You said we could move her, so let's do it. Now. We'll take her to my place."
  It's Christian. I wonder what he's doing here.
  "She's not going anywhere with you. She's coming with me. If you're wrong and it's not safe now, kid, you're dead."
  That's Ryodan. But who'd he call kid? The only person I know that he calls "kid" is me.
  "I don't take chances with her. It's safe."
  "D-D-D-Dancer?" I chatter.
  "Easy, Mega. You almost died." He closes his hand around mine and I hold on. I like his hand. It's big and holds easy but sure. It's the kind of hold that says, *I got you if you want me, but I'll let go if you feel like running*

for a while. "She's not going anywhere with either of you. She's coming with me," he says.

"The fuck she is!" Christian explodes, and I see flashing lights behind my eyelids from the hugeness of his voice and the pain I'm in.

Ryodan says, "She's weak, and you don't have what it takes to protect her."

"I'm n-not weak," I mutter. "I'm n-never weak." I slit my eyes open and the faint light in the street nearly splits my head. I close them again. Feck, I'm weak.

"The hell I don't."

"I sauntered right into your place and took her from you."

"I wasn't there at the time. Or you wouldn't have."

Ryodan laughs. "Puny human."

"She comes with me," Christian says.

"D-Dudes, I feel really s-sick," I say. "What's closest?"

"My place," Christian says.

"The hell it is," Ryodan says.

"You don't even know where it is," Christian says.

"I know everything."

Dancer says, "Chester's."

To him I say, "Take me there. And h-hurry. I'm starving and f-f-freezing."

When we walk into Chester's the noise just about splits my skull from temple to temple. I'm so sick I'm wobbly. Ryodan tells Lor to get blankets warmed and take them to a room somewhere upstairs. I hope it's soundproofed. Knowing Ryodan, it is. Like Batman, he has all the best toys. I don't care where I go right now. I just need to lie down. I want them to stop making me walk but I insisted that they let me walk, because I hate being carried so I'm faking. Every muscle I've got is burning and cramping. I can't think straight.

"Get the kid out of here," Ryodan says to another of his men.

Two men move in, close their hands on his arms.

"Leave Dancer alone!" I say.

"It's okay, Mega. I've got things to do anyway. You take care, you hear?" He looks at me hard and for a second I want everyone to go away and leave me alone with him. Life is so easy with Dancer. I want to ask him how he ended up in the street with me. I want to know what happened. Someone saved my life tonight. I want to know who and all the details.

But I don't want him here. Not in Chester's. I don't want the stain of it on him. "See you tonight?" I say.

He grins. "Hope so, Mega. Got a movie to watch."

"Get him out of here. Now," Ryodan barks.

Dancer impresses the feck out of me when he shakes their hands off his arms and says real calm, "I can see myself out." He doesn't shake testosterone off his skin like a wet dog. He doesn't turn into a stupid bull, throwing his horns around. He just takes care of himself.

I'd watch him go but Ryodan is suddenly turning me away, steering me like I'm a go-cart. He snaps an order for warm water and Jell-O and tells Christian to get the feck out of his club.

Christian laughs and settles on a bar stool in the sub-club closest to the stairs.

As I hobble up the stairs, I see a funny thing. Ryodan pauses for a sec and I look back. He's looking out over the dance floor, down at the kiddie subclub, and like she can feel him or something, Jo looks up, straight at him. Almost like she's been waiting for this moment. Like there's some kind of rubber band between them and she can feel him if he tugs on it. I think her highlights are even more dramatic than they were a couple days ago, gold in her dark hair. She's sparkly between the boobs again—I wouldn't notice except the sparkly makes you look there!—and wearing pretty bangles on her arms. She never wears jewelry. Even sick as I feel, I think Jo looks *good*. Ryodan gives her an imperceptible nod and she goes real still and wipes her hands on her skirt and swallows so hard I see her throat work from here. They look at each other and neither looks away.

After a long moment Jo nods back.

And I think what the feck? Is she an empath like Kat? How did she know what he was saying? And what *was* he saying anyway? And why is she turning her tray over to somebody else?

Then my legs are going out from under me because I faked as long as I could, and he's got me before I hit the floor, carrying me, and I don't even fight it because I'm too miserable.

They take me to a room a few doors down from Ryodan's office and put me in bed. I burrow deep into the soft mattress, sigh with relief and pass out cold. Ryodan pisses me off what can't be more than three minutes later by waking me back up and forcing me to drink warm Jell-O water.

At first I don't want it but it tastes like heaven.

"What happened?" I say. "Did I, like, die and come back?" What an adventure! I wonder if this'll get put into the legend of me when I do die. I wonder how many times I might kick Death's ass in my life. How wicked cool is that?

"Drink."

"Where'd Dancer come from?" My stomach cramps. "Aw, it's hurting my stomach."

"Stop gulping. Take small sips."

I see another funny thing when he pours a second glass of warm Jell-O water. "Dude, shake much?"

"I got too cold."

Lor laughs and gives him a look. "Or too hot. Get out of here. I've got it."

Ryodan looks at my empty glass. I've drained the pitcher already and I want more.

"I'll get it," Lor says. "Go do what you need to do, boss."

I wonder what he needs to do, why he's shaking. If this is his weakness, I want to know all about it. Too bad I'm about to pass out again.

Ryodan stands up. "Take care of her." He walks out.

Lor says, "Sleep, kid. I'll be back before you know it. With candy bars."

I slump into the pillows, curl up and sigh. Candy bars. Life is sweet. All I have to do is lie here where it's cozy and warm and wait for them. They heated blankets for me. Someone's bringing me candy bars in bed.

I'm going to sleep for days.

I wonder what happened. Dying to talk to Dancer. But it'll have to wait.

I'm drifting, just about to pass out again when I suddenly get wired, struck by a certainty that pisses me all kinds of off.

I know why Ryodan gave Jo that look!

Because they're in his office right now, talking about me! Conspiring, with Jo all worried about me because I almost died.

And they're trying to figure out what to do with me since I don't follow rules and almost got myself killed tonight. I hate it when adults have their stupid pow-wows about me! They always end with me getting read the riot act and handed a whole new list of rules that nobody in their right mind could possibly obey, most of which aren't even logical or smart.

How the feck was I supposed to know if I touched one tiny little thing it would snap me out of freeze-frame?

Why couldn't he have just told me that? I would never have done it!

Thinking about how I didn't almost get myself killed tonight, really *he* did, I start to steam from the inside and warm right up from sheer temper. I crawl out from under my huddle of blankets, get my sword, stumble to the door and wobble out into the hall. I look up and down but don't see anybody. 'Cause, like everybody's probably already in his office, dissing me.

I careen down the hall, stumbling from wall to wall, using them to steady me until I make it to his door, then I slap my palm where I always see him put his, and the door slides open. I don't even wait for it to finish opening before I begin airing my gripes.

"It is *not* my fault I almost got killed, dude. It's *your* fault and here's ho—*ooooww*—Ew!" I shake my head, horrified and . . . and . . . and . . .

Horrified.

My mouth hangs open, with nothing coming out.

Ryodan looks over his shoulder at me.

He's got Jo in there but they're not talking. She's bent over his desk with her skirt up. And he's doing that thing I wish I'd never seen him doing. Holy travel agent! Did I, like, go through a time warp or something? How long did it take me to get here? Don't grown-ups do *other* things before they get to this point? Like maybe hug and kiss, make out for a little while? I move fast and all but, dude! Kind of thinking some things'd be nice, a little slow, like maybe give you a chance to get ready for stuff that's happening!

Jo gasps and turns bright red. "Oh! Dani! Get *out* of here!"

I'm seeing more of Jo than I ever wanted to.

They aren't talking about me.

They weren't even *thinking* about me.

Like I wasn't even lying a few doors down the hall on

my deathbed with obviously nobody worrying about me at all!

"You are such a traitor! Sleeping with the enemy! What's wrong with you? This is just too gross for my eyeballs!"

"Go back to bed, Dani," Ryodan says, looking at me funny.

I hate him and I hate her and I hate his stupid retracting door.

I can't even slam it on the way out.

I wake up feeling amazing. Usually I wake up confused and cross. I'm thinking maybe I should almost get killed more often. I have no clue why I feel so good but I love it so I stretch, milking it for all I can get. My muscles are totally smooth and happy and relaxed, and I don't feel a bruise anywhere, which is impossible. My muscles are always knotted somewhere. Bruises are me. This feels like a brand-new body! I figure I must be in some kind of pre-waking state I never been in before, where the brain's been turned on but the body's still numb. I feel candy bars in bed with me, melty in my warm nest. One's mashed between my cheek and the pillow, I feel another plastered to my butt. I scootch them both out, tear one open and eat it without opening my eyes, blissfully happy. I could get used to this. No pain from assorted bumps and bruises, breakfast in bed.

Then I remember where I am.

Chester's.

And I remember what I saw before I fell asleep.

Ryodan doing the dirty with Jo.

On his desk.

Gah!

Like I'm ever going to be able to look at his desk again! How am I supposed to sit in his office now?

I'm so pissed off I shoot bolt upright in bed and swallow the last half of my candy bar so fast it gets stuck in my throat.

I start choking and all the sudden a fist slams into my back. My mouth pops open and half a mangled candy bar goes flying into the glass wall with a gooey chocolate splat. It's too gross for me so early in the morning. My stomach heaves and I double over trying to keep it down.

Yeah, this is more like how I wake up. All screwed up and confused. When I lived at the abbey, Ro told me I have growing pains and that superheroes have them worse than most people. She said that's why I need to sleep so hard and deep, and wake up so slow, because my body has to do more work to repair me on a cellular level. Makes scientific sense.

"Might help, kid," Lor says behind me, "if you chew more than once before you swallow."

"I never chew more than once. I wouldn't be able to eat fast enough if I did. I'd have to spend my whole day chewing. I'd get jaw muscles the size of Popeye's biceps."

"You're too young to know who Popeye is."

When you spent most of your childhood in a cage in front of a TV, you know who everybody is. I can sing the songs for *Green Acres* and *Gilligan's Island*. I even know who *That Girl* was. I learned everything I know about the world from watching TV. There's a whole lot of psychology in there if you're paying attention, and I was a captive audience. Ro said I got all my melodrama from growing up that way. That I think folks are supposed to be larger than life like they are in shows. Dude, of course I do! But I didn't need TV to tell me that. Life's a choice: you can live in black and white, or you can live in color. I'll take every shade of the rainbow and the gazillion in between! I push up from the bed, grab my sword and head for the door.

Lor's in front of it, arms folded over his chest. "Boss didn't say you could leave."

"I didn't say your boss could boink Jo," I say real calm-like, but inside I'm seething. I don't know why I feel so betrayed. Why do I care? They're grown-ups. Grown-ups never make sense. Jo doesn't even like him. And I know he doesn't give a shit about Jo.

"Honey, boss don't ask nobody who he fucks."

"Well, he ain't going to do Jo again. Get out of my way. Move." I'm going to tell her I'm never talking to her if she has sex with him ever again. I'll make her choose and she'll choose me.

"So you can start some shit?"

"Yep." I don't even try to deny it. I'm ready to knock heads and I'm not going to feel better until I make somebody else as miserable as I am.

He looks down at me. I slant my jaw at a jauntier angle, and I can tell he's trying not to laugh.

"What? You think I'm funny?" I'm so sick of people smiling at me like that. My hand goes to the hilt of my sword. It closes on his hand. They're all faster than me. "I'm not funny. I'm dangerous. You just wait and see. I'm not full grown yet, but when I am, I'm going to kick your ass from one end of Chester's to the other. You just wait and see."

He lets go of my sword and moves out of my way, laughing. "Go ahead, kid. Raise some hell. Been boring around here lately."

On my way out the door I decide maybe I could like Lor. He lives in color, too.

When I blow past Ryodan's office, I think I feel a breeze and spin around real fast, ready to fight him if I have to, but nobody's there. I shake my head and bounce down the stairs, freeze-framing sideways in between steps because I have so much energy this morning, checking out the dance floor as I go. It's packed and the place is rocking. Looks like I either didn't sleep long or I slept a whole day until the next night, because there's Jo, waiting tables in the kiddie subclub, looking all long-legged and . . . Geez! I squint over the railing at her. Happy. She's, like, glowing! What does she think? That this is some kind of fairy tale she's living? It ain't. These fairies maim and kill, and the dude she's having sex with lets them. How can she glow about that? There wasn't even any romance or anything. Just . . . Gah! I don't even want to think about it. I can't scrape that memory off the inside of my skull fast enough!

I freeze-frame through the club, hyperfast, knocking folks out of my way left and right. Hearing grunts all around makes me feel better 'bout stuff.

When I stop in front of her, she looks startled then mad. What the feck does she have to be mad at *me* about?

She removes the last drink from her tray, sits it on a napkin in front of a Rhino-boy then holds the tray to her chest, her arms around it like it's a shield or something.

"Traitor."

"Dani, don't do this. Not here. Not now."

"You did *that* up *there*," I say, flinging my arm up toward Ryodan's office, "without worrying for one tiny little sec about *my* here and now. The whole time I was practically dying, you were having sex two doors down with the dude you came to rescue me from. From his *dungeon*. Like, where he was holding me *prisoner*. Remember?"

"It's not like that."

"What? I wasn't in the dungeon? Or you didn't come to rescue me from him? Don't tell me you weren't having sex. I saw what I saw."

"I didn't believe he'd hurt you and he didn't. He didn't hurt either of us."

"He's got us both working like dogs for him! You're waiting on Fae, and I'm running around on his fecking leash! He feeds people to the Fae, Jo. He kills them!"

"He does not. He runs a club. It's not his fault if people want to die. What is he supposed to do? Talk them out of it? Start a Chester's counseling service? What do you expect of him, Dani?"

I stare at her in disbelief. "You've got to fecking be kidding me! You're going to defend him? Stockholm syndrome much, Jo?" I mock.

She moves to an empty table and begins to clear it, stacking dirty dishes on her tray. It makes me madder that she's cleaning up after these monsters. Doubly mad that she looks so good doing it. Jo's making herself prettier. I don't understand it. She used to be perfectly happy wearing jeans and a T-shirt and no makeup and just hanging with the girls. We had pj parties and watched movies. Now she's all superglam Jo. I hate it.

"I thought you didn't know what that was."

"I looked it up and, dude, you got it bad. You're letting him screw you every which way. How long do you think it's going to last? You think he's going to bring you flowers? You think you're going to, like, go steady with the owner of Chester's?"

She stacks a small tower of glasses on her tray and gives me an exasperated look. "Can we just not do this right now?"

"Sure. If you tell me you'll never have sex with him again, I'll go away. Right now. End of conversation."

Her mouth tightens. As she wipes the table off with a damp cloth, she glances up at his office. It pisses me off how soft her face goes when she looks up. The tension fades and she looks like a woman in love. I hate it. I hate him.

She looks back at me.

"No, Dani. I won't. And stay out of this. It's none of your business. This is grown-up stuff between grown-ups." She turns away and heads for the bar with her cluttered tray. Distantly I hear Fae calling orders, trying to get her attention, but I don't care. *I* want her attention.

I freeze-frame in behind her hard and fast, causing a wicked breeze in the subclub and nearly knocking the tray from her hands. She has to work hard to catch it. Almost doesn't. Ryodan's not the only one that can screw with people and things.

"Don't walk away from me. I'm not done yet."

"Yes, you are."

I hiss in her ear, "Don't you get it? Dude's never going to love you. He's not wired that way. He's just using you and he's going to throw you away, and then there you're going to be like a dirty piece of toilet paper he doesn't want anymore."

She sucks in a breath and gives me a look over her shoulder that just fecking slays me.

I drown in instant self-hate for saying what I just said. And I hate him because I know it's true. Jo will never be able to keep Ryodan's interest. She's too good. Clean and nice inside. She doesn't have an ounce of malice or deceit or unkind feelings or anything bad in her. She's not complicated enough for him. He's twisted like that. I chose the wrong person to chew out. I should have chosen him. He's going to hurt her and I'm never going to forgive him. So, here I am, hurting her first. Dude, stupid much?

"Do you really think I don't know that?" If we weren't in Chester's, I'm pretty sure the wet in her eyes would start to slide down her cheeks.

All the sudden I'm miserable I said anything about any of it. I want to hug her. I want to run away. I don't want Jo to hurt. I should have kept my mouth shut. I can't keep my mouth shut. Grown-ups are so strange. But I don't understand! "Then *why*? Why would you do something that you know is going to end up bad? Why would anyone ever do something they know is going to hurt them?"

"You're too young to be talking about this kind of stuff."

"Aw, c'mon, Jo, it's me. I was never young. Life didn't happen that way in my world. Tell me."

"It's complicated."

"Like everything isn't. Try."

She doesn't say anything so I just stand and wait. A long silence usually makes people fill it up with something.

It stretches. Finally she looks away like she's embarrassed and, so soft it's almost like she's talking to herself, not me at all, she says, "Every morning he comes to the top of the stairs and looks down over the club and he stands there, so big and powerful and beautiful and . . . " She swallows hard like her mouth just went totally dry. "Sexy. God, so unbelievably sexy." Her eyes get a weird, intense look like she's remembering something, then she makes a soft noise and doesn't say anything for a second. "And he's funny. Do you know he's funny? You must know that. You spend a lot of time with him."

I fist my hands. Sure I do. I didn't know she did. What do they do? Crack jokes with each other like Dancer and me?

Her expression is far off, seeing a memory. "Every morning when the night shift ends, he singles out a woman in the crowd and he nods at her. She goes upstairs and when she eventually shows up in the club again she looks like . . . " She shivers like she just got goose bumps. "And you wonder what he did that made her look like that. You watch her walking around, smiling, moving different than she moved before she went to him, and you know something happened up there that made her feel more alive than she ever felt before, that she got to be the way you hope you'll get to be with a man, even if it's just once in your life. A man has to see women a certain way for it to be that way. You try not to think about him, but it doesn't work. I swore if he ever gave me that nod, I wouldn't go."

"Dude, wake-up call. You went."

"I know."

She's glowing again like she won some kind of prize instead of got picked by a class-A sociopath to be his disposable lube.

"Why *him*?" I don't understand and I want to. I don't want to feel like Jo's a traitor. I lost Mac. I don't want to lose Jo, too. "You know what he's like!"

"He's not a bad man, Dani."

"Bullshit."

"Everything isn't black and white like you want it to be."

Some things are, and Ryodan's blacker than black. He's one of the bad guys, period, end of subject. I'm pissed. She needs to wake up and smell the coffee burning before the whole fecking coffeemaker goes up in flames. "And when he comes to those stairs tomorrow and chooses someone else?" I say. "It's only a matter of time, Jo. You know he will. You'll be standing here looking all dreamy like you do right now and it'll be the waitress *next* to you that he chooses and you'll never go upstairs again because a dude like that don't press the replay button. When he's done he's done. How are you going to feel then?"

She turns away.

I go after her, grab her elbow, make her stop. "Well? What do you think, Jo? That you're special? That you'll be the one that changes him? Give me a fecking break!

You think you and him are going to go pick out china patterns together? Register for flatware?"

She inhales like she forgot to breathe, then when she remembered couldn't get air fast enough. "I know what I'm doing, Dani."

"Good, then you can explain it to me! 'Cause it sure looks like every shade of stupid from where I'm standing!"

She's distant again, talking soft, like I'm not even here. Even with my superhearing I lean in to catch it.

"There are men you build a future with, Dani. And then there are men that you know, going in, that you're only making a memory with. I know the difference."

Doesn't look like it to me.

"Some memories are worth the price. I'll deal with it."

But she won't. I know she won't. I know Jo. She's brilliant and kind and has the heart of a warrior but she doesn't have ice and razor blades inside where your soul is supposed to be. She loves. And she doesn't know how to take it back when you have to, because sometimes you sure as feck have to. Got to grab it up with both hands and pull it back before somebody turns it into knives and uses it to cut you to pieces. She's not going to be able to deal with it good at all. And I'm going to have to clean up the mess he made, and kill him. I suck in a breath. "You're too stupid to live and I'm not talking to you anymore. You need to pull your head out."

"You need to quit judging everyone."

"You don't know shit about me. And I'd rather judge people than be a pansy-ass that can't make her mind up about anyone or anything and gets sucked into all kinds of stupid shit."

"Dani, please don't—"

"My ears are full. I can't hear anymore!" I turn away and start to slip into freeze-frame. I have no idea what makes me look up. Kind of like a rubber-band feeling, like it's fused into my gut, and like something at the top of the stairs is pulling at my opposite end.

Ryodan is standing at the top of the stairs looking down at me. And I think what Jo said about him being big and powerful and beautiful.

We lock eyes.

Mine say, "Don't you ever choose her again. You leave her alone."

His say something I don't get at all. Then he does that ocular-shiver thing all over me and I get a real clear: "Go home, kid."

He looks right past me at Jo.

And he nods.

SEVENTEEN

"These girls fall like dominoes"

We're not so different, you and I, Cruce says as he moves inside me. *Both born to lead.*

I try desperately to wake myself. I'm in the Dreaming and he has me in his wings. The moment I fell asleep, he was there, waiting for me at the end of a white marble path in a garden of exquisite blood roses. He lays me on them, with a crush of velvet petals. I brace for the thorns.

You must not rue it, Kat. The sun does not rue that it rises.

He goes deep, filling me completely, making every nerve ending in my body vibrate with erotic ecstasy. I arch my back and hiss with pleasure.

We will rule the world and they will love us. We will save them.

"Dreaming of me, are you now, my sweet Kat?"

Like a dropped snow globe, my dream world shatters and I remember why I asked Sean to stay the night with me at the abbey. Why I slipped him around back and into my suite of rooms. To save me from Cruce. To ground me to the world I know and love.

I roll into Sean's arms and press against him, shuddering with fear that I pretend is desire. We make love quick and hard and fast. He never knows I'm trying to erase someone else.

Someone that makes me come harder. Better. More.

Sean, my love, my childhood friend, teenage sweetheart, mate to my soul. I've never known life without him. We shared a playpen and went to our first day of school together. We got the measles the same week, swapped our first flu snuggled in blankets in front of the TV. We got pimples and got rid of them. He was there the night I started my period, and I was there the day his voice began to change. We know everything about each other. Our history is rich and long. I love his dark eyes, his black hair and fair Irish skin. I love the way he wears a fisherman's sweater with faded jeans and always has a quick smile. I love how strong his arms are from years of pulling fishing nets, and the way his long-limbed body moves, how he looks when he's lost in a good book, the way he feels moving inside me.

"Are you all right, love?" He brushes a tangle of hair from my face.

I lay my head on his chest and listen to his heart beating, solid and sure. Sometimes I think he has a touch of my *sidhe*-seer gift, he reads me so well. He's known about my emotional empathy since we were children. Nothing about me disturbs him, a rare gift from those who fully understand what I do. Few can lie to me. I sense their inner conflict, unless they suffer no guilt or scruple about anything, and I've been blessed to encounter only a handful of those in my life—all of them in or near Chester's, recently. I don't know the truth, only that there is a lie. It takes a scrupulously honest man to love me. That's my Sean. We learned to trust each other completely before we were old enough to have learned suspicion.

"What if I can't do it?" I say. I don't elaborate. With Sean few words are necessary. We've been finishing each other's sentences since we were young. We were virgins when we made love the first time. There's never been anyone else for either of us.

Now I have an invisible lover violating everything I hold dear. Making me want *him* and not my Sean.

He laughs. "Kat, sweetheart, you can do anything."

My heart feels like a rock in my chest. I burn with shame, and deceit. I've made love in my dreams in exquisite detail with another man, and have done so every night for over a week. I've taken him in my mouth, felt him at the entrance of my womb, places that are Sean's alone. "But what if I can't? What if I make mistakes that cost lives?"

He rolls onto his side and pulls me back into him, spooning. I press in. We fit together perfectly. Like we were carved from the same piece of wood, from the same tree.

"Hush, sweet Kat. I'm here. I'll always be here. Together we can do anything. You know that. Remember our vows."

I pull his arms tighter around me. We were young, so young. Everything was simple then. We were fifteen, deliriously and passionately in love, delighted by our developing bodies, growing up together into one. We stole off to Paradise Point out by the lighthouse, dressed up like it was our wedding day, and took vows with each other. We came from broken families, temperamental fighting families, and we learned from watching them. Too much passion burns. Tenderness fuses. We knew what it took to stay together. It was nothing fancy. Common sense, really.

If you weaken, I'll be strong. If you get lost, I'll be your way home. If you despair, I'll bring you joy. I will love you until the end of time.

"I love you, Sean O'Bannion. Never leave me."

"Wild horses, Kat. Couldn't drag me an inch. You're

the only one for me. Always." There's a smile in his voice.

We make love again, and this time, when dark wings try to shadow me, they fail. There's no one else in bed with me but my Sean.

I watch him dress while dawn paints pale white rectangles around the heavy drapes. I have young charges at the abbey and we are not wed. We'd begun making plans to marry before the walls fell but our families interfered. The O'Bannions tried to stop it. When they realized Sean was having none of it, they tried to take over and turn it into the spectacle of the decade.

An O'Bannion marries a McLaughlin!

It would have been a grand step up for my family. We were small-time criminals. His family controlled nearly all Dublin's mob underbelly. I grew up with Sean because my mother was his nanny.

We'd been fighting bitterly with our parents for months before the walls fell and billions died.

Including our families. Where else would they have been than out in the riots, watching the chaos, trying to profit from the lawlessness?

I can't pretend that I'm sorry for their deaths, and I won't feel ashamed that I'm not. The only deaths I rue are those of my two half brothers that survived the fall, only to be killed by Shades. Rowena didn't teach us about eating Unseelie in time for me to save them. My parents and other siblings were corrupt to the core. Sometimes people are born into the wrong family. Sean and I turned our backs on them years ago. But our families never stopped pressuring us and never accepted letting us go. I used to worry so much about what they would do to Sean, how they might try to force him into the family ways, but now such worries are a thing of the past.

It's today and we're free!

As soon as we get a quiet moment, and a priest, we plan to wed. Some of the girls are hoping we'll decide to make a lovely ceremony of it here at the abbey. A wedding in times like these can be an uplifting thing, but I'll not make my wedding into something for another. It's between Sean and God and me.

When he holds my face in his hands and kisses me, I feel his heart, both against my chest and with my gift. He's happy. It's all I need.

He asks if I'll have him again tonight and I smile and kiss him.

"Aye, and every night thereafter and well you know it. If you're fishing for a compliment, my bonny Sean, I've thousands for you."

But as he slips out, my laughter dies and I stare at the bed.

I should tell him what's happening. I would wish it from him. I would fight for him at night against my invisible foe. We would stand together as one. I would know all the secrets of his tormenting succubus, the better to defeat her.

But I can't. I just can't. It happened before I could stop it the first time. I've had intimate carnal knowledge of another man. I've felt things with Cruce I've never felt with Sean. And I hate myself and I can't tell him. I just can't.

So I'm walking home slow-mo Joe style, pissed off but having a hard time focusing on being pissed off because my body feels so good. My mind's grumpy, but my body's saying, "Hey, dude, let's *play*!"

I kick a can down the alley and send it flying into a

wall, and I do mean *into* it. It flattens and gets impacted in the brick, and I crack up. Someday somebody is going to see it and be like, dude, what happened here? I leave clues about me all over the city, bending sculptures and broken streetlamps into twisty D's for Dani and Dude and Dangerous, leaving my calling card for folks to see. It's my Bat Signal, letting the world know somebody is out there, watching, caring.

I got a whole day stretching ahead of me and almost can't believe it! It feels like old times. I think about what to do with myself. Stupid as it is, I resent working on the ice mystery during the day because Ryodan's taking such a big chunk of my time every night. But I don't have the luxury of being stupid when folks' lives are at stake. It sure would be nice if I could get Dancer's super-brain in on it!

Trouble is, I should also head out to the abbey for a checkup. It's been a while since I was out there and *sidhe*-sheep can get in trouble faster than I can waggle my ass and say *baa*. I got a worried feeling about them I ain't been able to shake.

Then there's Inspector Jayne. I'm pretty sure I'm due for a cage-cleaning session.

I mosey through Temple Bar, taking my time, drinking my city in, trying to decide how to prioritize my day. Kind of reveling in the simple fact that the choice is mine for a change! I used to love this part of town before the walls fell, so much cool stuff happening every night with tourists and pubs and new Fae to spy on and kill. I found out what it was like to live in these streets after mom died. No collar, no cage. Just a crazy old witch I learned to keep a little afraid of me all the time.

Then Mac came and the streets got even cooler. There's nothing like having a sidekick superhero to pal around with. Especially one that was part sister, part mom, and all best friend.

Now, like the rest of my city, Temple Bar is a mess. Abandoned cars, wrecked and stripped, are shoved up on the sidewalks, opening a tight lane down the middle of the street for traffic. There's broken glass everywhere from shattered windows and streetlamps; you can hardly take a step that doesn't crunch. Newspapers and trash and husks of what used to be people blow down the streets. On a gray, rainy day it can look real grim, if you don't superimpose a bright future over it. Mac's mom is heading up some kind of Green-up Program, and I hear her dad is working on a Cleanup Program, as well as hearing disputes and stuff, and one day Dublin's going to be rocking and full of *craic* again.

I saunter past the bright red facade of *the* Temple Bar of the district and feel it before I even turn the corner. I stop instantly.

It's like a breeze blowing down on me from a glacier.

I consider not turning the corner. I haven't investigated one of these scenes alone. I could nudge Ryodan this way tonight and pretend we just found it. It's not like they change too much between "recently iced" and "iced for a few days." Besides, if I turn the corner and find kids dead, it'll totally ruin my day.

Almost dying is fresh in my mind. If I'd been alone at the church last night . . . That's a weird thought. I can't imagine me dead. I look around, and up. As far as I can tell, I'm by myself. Christian can't be spying on me all the time. So, like, if I leave, nobody will know I'm not always a superhero. If I stay and something bad happens to me, well, my heart could stop, and there'd be nobody around to save me.

"Wussy girl! Get your cool back!" I just disgusted myself. I don't walk away and I don't need backup. Never have. A superhero isn't something you play at sometimes—it's something you *are*. Full-time, all the time, every day.

I flip back my long coat, liking the crisp leathery sound it makes, draw my sword and turn the corner, ready for action. My sword frosts white and my fingers get stiff with an instant chill.

In the middle of the street is one of those fancy cars Mac likes so much, totally iced, glittering diamond-crusted in the sunlight. An iced arm is sticking out the open window on the driver's side. A dude is hanging half out the passenger side, like he tried to climb out or something, mouth open on a scream, eyes closed, fist up in the air like he was trying to fight something off. No kids. That's a relief. Looks like only two casualties this time. That's another relief.

I study it, absorbing the details.

This scene's not so cold. Brutal, but nothing like the church or the subclub at Chester's. More like the laundry scene. I figure being outside, the frosted vignettes warm up faster. Piece of cake!

I take a couple of deep breaths, locking everything down on my mental grid, psyching myself up to freeze-frame in.

Just as I've nearly got it perfect, right exactly when I've almost got everything snapped into precise place and I'm preparing to shift gears smooth and easy, folks start shouting behind me and guns start going off.

Bullets can hurt me. I'm not *that* superhero. It spooks me and I startle into freeze-frame before I mean to. That's even more dangerous than leading with your head!

I blast off wild, and try to get control of myself, but it's hard to do once I'm moving so fast. I whirl dizzy-ingly like a drunken Tasmanian devil and smash into the side of the iced car.

It knocks me out of freeze-frame but either doesn't catch me so much by surprise this time or the cold isn't as deadly as it was in the church or a little of both, because I manage to shove myself right back up into freeze-frame almost as fast as I dropped down. I can't get my feet under control, though, because I didn't get off on the right foot to begin with, and I slam into the car again and this time the people inside it blow like supercharged grenades into a gazillion shards of ice and I get sprayed by icy pink shrapnel.

Diamond-hard splinters of frozen flesh pierce every inch of my exposed skin. A thick dagger of ice as big around as a hot dog punctures my jeans and sinks into my thigh, and another impales my shoulder.

I get knocked out of freeze-frame again and push myself back up, and when I do, the ice splinters shove deeper into my body from the pressure of how fast I'm moving and it hurts so fecking bad that I drop back down instantly without thinking. Reflexive, just trying to stop the pain.

I start to freeze to death.

I push back up.

Ow! Shit, shit, shit, it *hurts*!

Down, I'll die.

Up, I'll only wish I would.

I stay in freeze-frame, stumble into the stupid car again, bounce back, careen off another car, and give it everything I've got in a violent effort to get out of the cold zone. I can't feel my hands. I can't feel my feet. Feck, I can't believe I did this! Who was yelling and why were they shooting?

I push, push, *push* with all my might!

I collapse facedown in the street. Ice daggers bite deep. But I don't care. I'm out. I'm back around the corner where it's warm enough to live. I made it. At least the hundreds of splinters in me will melt now. Either they're already starting to or I'm bleeding a lot, because something warm and wet is trickling all over my skin.

I'm out of immediate mortal danger. I won't freeze to death. Now I just have to worry about bleeding to death.

It takes me three tries to manage to roll over on my back, and by the time I get there I'm panting worse than I do when I've freeze-framed for an hour, and shaking like a leaf. There's blood in my eyes. I try to blink it away. Dude, that was a grand debacle! How embarrassing! Glad nobody saw it!

I assess my situation without moving. I'm severely cut up. My skin burns where I can feel myself. The biggest threats to my survival are the holes in my thigh and shoulder, or what *will* be holes when the ice finishes melting. I'll need to get them bandaged fast. The problem is, I can't feel my hands. I close my eyes, trying to focus on moving my fingers. Nothing happens.

"Ah, Dani."

I look up to see Inspector Jayne bending over me. I've never been gladder to see him in my whole life.

"You've certainly done it now, haven't you?"

"C-C-Candy b-b-bar," I manage.

He smiles but it doesn't reach his eyes.

"In m-m-m-my p-puh . . . " I trail off. I don't even have the energy to say *pocket*. I give him a longing, starving look and I know he gets the picture.

He looks across me. I realize I'm surrounded by Guardians. Good, they can carry me to Chester's and help me get patched up!

"Have you got it?" Jayne says.

"Got it, Captain."

I go ice cold in a way that has nothing to do with cars or frozen people. I try to lunge to my feet but succeed only in flopping on the pavement like a beached fish. "D-D-Don't you d-d-d-d-dare—"

"It's been six days, Dani."

Six days? How long did I sleep at Chester's?

"You should have come. If you'd kept your word, I

might have continued trying to put up with it. But I won't allow the fate of our city to rest in whimsical hands. The sword is ours now, for the good of Dublin. We take far more of them off the streets than you do. In time you'll understand it always should have been this way."

"Y-Y-You—"

"Don't try to take it back. Your first warning is your final one. I won't treat you like a child if you do."

"K-K-*Kill* y-you!" I explode. I still can't feel my hands or feet but I feel my head. It's about to explode. He has no right. It's *my* sword!

"Don't make it war, Dani. You won't win."

I try to tell him he better kill me right here and now because there's no way they can keep my sword from me. I'll take it back the second I'm on my feet again. There's no place on Earth, feck, there's no place in all of heaven or hell that they'll ever be safe from me again! But I'm too light-headed to talk. Dizzy. My vision's getting weird.

"She's awful bloody, Captain. She gonna live?"

"She's tough," Jayne says.

"Maybe we should do something."

"We can't help her, not even a little, or she'll be able to take it back."

I flop on the pavement, unable to do a thing to stop them. I'm vulnerable, completely at his mercy.

And he's not having any.

I won't have any for him when the time comes.

He's leaving me here, to live or die on my own. I'll never forgive. I'll never forget.

They walk away. Just like that they leave me in the middle of a dirty street like a dog that got hit by a car, bleeding and helpless and alone. Dead if another car comes along. I'll remember that, too, when I see him again. Dude, they could have at least moved me to the sidewalk, balled up a shirt or something for a pillow beneath my head.

Something really bad happens to me then. Worse even than everything that's already happened to me in the past few days.

I feel woozy and strange and all the sudden it's like I'm outside of my body, watching me. But the me lying in the street has long blond hair and is looking up at the redheaded me with tears in her eyes and telling me she can't die yet because she's got people to protect. She's got a sister named Mac back home in Georgia and she just left her a message, and if she dies, Mac will come over to hunt her killer because she's stubborn and ideal-istic, and she'll die, too. But I don't seem to be able to feel anything about what's happening, and none of it seems real, so I walk away just like Jayne did.

My stomach heaves and I puke my guts out right there in the middle of the street. I can't even get on my hands and knees to do it. Lying on my back, I get sick all over myself. Not the blond-haired me that's the ghost of Alina, but the real, red-haired Dani that's really lying in the street wondering if she's going to bite it this time. And if there's something wet on my face that isn't blood or vomit . . . Nah. Ain't.

Eventually I get the feeling back in my hands and feet. I guess they thaw. I fumble for a candy bar. I curl in a ball in the street and eat every candy bar I've got and plot revenge.

Don't make it war, he said, and I won't.

I don't have to.

He already did.

EIGHTEEN

"I can be your hero, baby"

I find her stumbling through the streets, bleeding to death.

If not for all that hair, I might not have recognized her. She's covered with blood, it's on her clothes, matted in her curls, crusted on her face. Her long coat is flayed and hangs in tatters from her shoulders. It looks like she went through a dicer.

I don't see her sword anywhere. I look around, nothing shiny in the streets but her.

I roar and she clamps her arms around her head and falls to her knees, and I remember how much noise I'm capable of making and kick myself. I deafened a human woman I recently had sex with. I broke her arm, too. I didn't mean to. I can't get used to what's happening to me. Try living your whole life one way then abruptly being something else. It's not easy to remember what you are every single bloody fucking second.

Except enraged. That, I'm aware of all the time. It never diminishes, never stops. The blackouts where I lose chunks of time are getting more frequent, lasting longer.

She topples in the street. I throw myself from the roof, land on the balls of my feet, and gather her in my arms.

Where was I when she needed me? Fucking another faceless woman. Trying to defuse the constant lust.

She feels so slight against my chest.

I'm not surprised to feel myself trembling. I'm touching my goddess.

"Och, lass, what've you done to yourself now?" I push hair from her face. There's so much blood that I can't see what's causing it. How is she even walking? It makes me crazy that she's in this city, without a guardian or consort, always getting into trouble. I want to lock her up somewhere I can keep her safe forever. Someplace white and shining and beautiful, where nothing ever goes wrong.

Her brain has more muscles than her body, and less sense. Her passion for life pushes her limbs further than they were meant to go. She's going to burn herself to ash if she doesn't find someone or something that takes her all the way down to ground zero and recharges her. She needs to crash as hard as she lives or she'll die young. I can't stand the thought of her dying. If I knew how, I would make her Fae so she would never die. Doesn't matter that I hate being it myself, or that she would, too. Immortality is immortality.

I run with her, careful to move easy. I take her where I've pictured her a thousand times but knew better. I still know better. I'm doing it anyway.

Just one time before I turn into the villain of this piece, just one time before I become the fourth and final Unseelie prince, I want to be her Highlander. And her hero.

She'll remember, when there's nothing else left of me worth remembering.

I can't wait till I grow up enough that I stop having superhero growing pains. Waking up confused and cross all the time sucks. My hair is in my face and it makes me so mad for a sec that I almost tear it out at the scalp, trying to get it out of my eyes, and it's matted, then my bracelet gets stuck in it and there's something crusty—"Ew," I say irritably, then somebody else has their hands in my hair, trying to gently disentangle my wrist from my hair.

Who? What? Where?

I'm always doing a mental check when I first wake up, trying to remember what happened before I fell asleep so I can connect to where I am and how I got there. When I first got run of the abbey (dude, like a million times bigger than my cage with Mom!) I was constantly knocking myself out because I couldn't get over how far and fast I was able to run and giddiness made me a freeze-framing train wreck. I'm never real sure when I first wake up if I went to sleep or just managed to brain myself unconscious again. Then that fecker Ryodan knocked me out, too, and now I have to add that in to my worries when I wake.

Memory slams me upside the head. I get so mad I yank my bracelet off my head along with a good chunk of hair, and feel frantically for my sword even though I know it's not at my hip or anywhere else.

A man curses. My eardrums vibrate painfully and my head feels like it might split.

I open my eyes. "Christian, mute it!" I shove my hair out of my face and look up. I'm lying in bed and he's sitting next to me, looking down at me. Something's different. He doesn't look quite so scary. I take that back. Yes, he does, but either I'm getting better at reading his expressions or he's getting better at making them, because there's like an ounce of remorse in his iridescent eyes. Dude. His eyes are full Fae now! They weren't last time I saw him.

"Sorry, lass. But I almost had the bracelet free. You

tore some of your hair out. You might have waited a second longer." He picks up the thatch of hair I yanked out at the root and flattens it straight between his fingers. Curl springs back instantly. "Stubborn as the head it came from," he murmurs. Then he does the weirdest thing. He puts it in his pocket. Maybe the dude collects hair. I got bigger worries on my mind.

"He took my sword! The fecker actually took my sword!" I can't believe it. I have no way to kill my enemies. I could hunt them all day long—and do a great big fat nothing with them when I catch them. It makes me so nuts I can't stand it. I try to push up from the bed but my legs aren't a hundred percent.

"Who took your sword?"

"Inspector Jayne. I'm going to kill him."

"HE DID THIS TO YOU?"

I get an instant migraine, flop down, cover my head with my arms and burrow beneath the pillows.

He sighs so loud I still hear it, even with my ears covered.

"Sorry, lass. Did he?"

I'm not taking my hands from my ears. I think about telling him yes so he'll go after Jayne for me, but I don't like to lie unless the payoff is huge. Lies are horny little buggers, they breed like rabbits and bound around just as insanely and then you have to try to keep track of them. "I got cut up myself but it's his fault. He startled me and I freeze-framed too soon." Speaking of cuts, I don't feel as bad as I did and I don't seem to be bleeding anymore.

"You want help killing him?"

He sounds a little too eager. Like homicidal maniac eager. "Don't need no stinking help," I say crossly. My eardrums hurt. "I mean not that your help is stinking or anything. Your help is totally cool. I just want to do it myself."

"Would you come out from under there, lass?"

"Would you, like, never yell again? You're slaying me. I got superhearing." I poke my head out. "Where am I?" I'm in a cloud of down pillows and comforters, in a high bed, in the corner of a huge room.

"My place."

I look around. Cool digs. He's holed up in a rehabbed industrial warehouse, one of those kinds with a giant living area that has no walls except for the ones you make with furniture and stuff. There's lots of brick and wood floors and exposed heating ducts, tons of light spilling in tall windows and a massive flat-screen 3D TV in front of a ginormous comfy-looking couch. There's a pool table and some old video game machines and an awesome bar, a kitchen with stainless steel appliances, and no racks or torture instruments visible anywhere. It's just the kind of place a college guy would die for— too bad he's not one anymore, but hey, we all have the things we need to pretend. No scary-looking knife collections. No red, no black, their favorite colors. The place is totally *not* Unseelie prince.

A shaft of rosy light is shining on me and I look up. The bed is under a skylight, the sun's setting and it's got one of those new, strange Fae hues to it, brilliant orangey pink. I could sprawl in bed and watch the stars at night. I like it being pushed in the corner, giving me wall at my right and back, leaving only two sides to defend. Feels snug. Makes me think about rearranging some of my own rooms. I'm fascinated by the way other folks live, and love to look in other people's houses. "Aw, man, you ever move out, I'm moving in!"

"Like it, do you, lass?" he says, and his voice sounds funny. Thick and weird.

I look down at him and jerk. "Something on my face?" He's staring at me hard, eyes intense, and what's looking out of them doesn't look like it belongs in this place of brick and wood and sunshine at all. It belongs in the dark somewhere, with razor blades, about to do something real nasty.

"No. Your face is lovely, lass. The sunset looks good on you." He reaches a hand out toward my face and I go real still.

"Dude, you're scaring me."

He looks at me but it's like he's not seeing me at all, so I sit there with his hand about an inch from my face and look back and think about wild animals. About how they'll attack if they smell fear, not that I feel it, but when you're staring at an Unseelie prince, even though you know he started out human, it's kind of hard to predict what might happen next. This isn't a scenario I can lock down on my mental grid and freeze-frame through. This obstacle course has too many unknown variables.

He drops his hand without touching me, pushes up from the bed and goes to the kitchen. He braces his fists on the island and leans there with his back to me. He's bigger than he was when I first saw him up on my water tower. The back of his shirt is stained with blood and his spine presses knobby and weird against it. It's creepy.

I scoot to the exit side of the bed, thinking I'll just be moseying along now, when I realize I'm not wearing enough to get up. I only got on a bra and underwear. I sink back down and tuck my knees up. Not that I want to draw attention to the fact, but looking around yields no results. "Where are my clothes?"

"Destroyed."

He undressed me! He must have washed me, too, because I'm not covered with blood. Holy high wire! An Unseelie death-by-sex Fae that's having all kinds of temper problems undressed and cleaned me up. "Do you, like, have any other clothes I could wear?"

"Don't use that tone with me."

"What tone?"

"The one that thinks I'm some kind of freak predator that molests children. I'm not a freak and you're not a child. I undressed you, lass. I cleaned you up. I healed you. I will never hurt you."

"*How* did you heal me?"

"Fed you my blood."

My gag reflex is instant and uncontrollable. I retch dry and noisy. Unlike a lot of other folks I know, drinking blood doesn't sound cool to me at all. It grosses me out. Same with eating Unseelie flesh; I've never done it and never will. I'm staying an Unseelie-flesh virgin all my life. I'm not even tempted by the possibility that it could make me stronger and faster than I already am. Dude, you got to draw your lines in the sand somewhere and hold them. It's especially important when the sand keeps shifting beneath your feet.

"It's potent. Works better than Unseelie flesh. A few drops in your mouth and . . . " He turns around and smiles at me. I think. Tattoos rush beneath the skin of his face, shadowing the planes and valleys, making it hard to decide just what that twist of his lips means. "There's really only one question: would you rather have died?"

That's an easy one for me. I'd never rather that. Not under any circumstances. I'll take survival at any price. Always. "No. Thanks for the blood, dude. Means a lot." I hate admitting this next part but I'm pretty sure it's true. "You saved my life. I won't forget it." I smile back at him, then I just sit there trying not to gape at his reaction. He totally changes and I see the Highlander he was. His eyes go brown and playful and he looks college-guy hunky again; the tattoos recede from his face. Even his muscles change, smooth, and suddenly his body is more human.

He tosses me a candy bar. I catch it, rip it open and

munch it, and begin making plans to get my sword back. I know Jayne. He knows if I survive I'll come after it, so he'll take it somewhere he thinks I can't get to it. He won't want to waste too many of his men guarding it because he wants them out on the street, fighting. I waste a couple secs trying to figure out where he'd take it, then realize I don't have to. All I have to do is spy on him and follow him back to wherever he takes the Fae he catches to be slaughtered. I can't believe he's so stupid he really thinks he'll be able to keep it!

"Stay there and I'll get you some clothes," Christian says.

He lopes off, moving long-limbed and easy, not gliding in the weird way the princes do. Down the other end of the long room he rummages through an armoire, and comes back with a pair of flannel pj bottoms with a drawstring waist and a huge cream fisherman's sweater.

I suit up under the covers, tying off my waist tight and rolling up the legs and arms about a hundred times. When he tosses me a pair of balled-up socks as he heads off to the kitchen, I'm distracted, still thinking about Jayne, and miss them. They go sailing past me, hit the wall and fall down in the crack. I roll over and reach down, rooting around for them.

It takes me a second to figure out what I close my hand on.

Hair. Attached to a head. There's a head in the narrow space between the bed and the wall. I freeze, totally horrified and massively grossed out.

I jerk my hand back and just sit there, swallowing the creeped-out sound trying to claw its way out of my throat, then look over my shoulder at him. He's humming a weird song under his breath that sounds a lot like the music they play at Chester's and disappearing into a pantry off the kitchen.

I force myself to reach back down and pat around,

never taking my eyes off the pantry door. "I'm hungry, Christian," I call. When he answers, I can make a good guess at how deep the pantry is, how far in it he's gone. How much time I have to figure out what the feck is going on here.

The head has a neck attached to it, and sure enough there's a body, too. It's naked and female and human. She's stiff with rigor mortis and ice cold.

I barely let myself breathe. I hear boxes being moved around on shelves.

"Sorry, lass, I'll have more for you in a second. I thought I had some Snickers in here but so far I'm only finding Almond Joy."

I yank my hand out of the crack and scoot back to the middle of the bed, and when I answer him I sound relaxed, playful. "Aw, dude, keep looking. You know how I love my Snickers."

The boxes stop moving. "Something wrong, lass?"

There's a dead woman wedged between Christian's bed and the wall. Normally I'd say that's a whole lot of wrong and I'd get real vocal about it, but I'm in the killer's apartment, wearing his pjs with no shoes and I got no fecking sword that kills Fae because that fecker Jayne took it, so I'm in no hurry to do that right now.

There's no way I tipped him off. My delivery was perfect. "No, nothing. Just starving out here!" Another flawless lie. I may not do it often but I shine at it like I do most things.

He steps out of the pantry and looks at me. The Highlander is gone. He's full Unseelie prince, iridescent eyes tinged with crimson. "Och, lass, Mac never told you, did she?"

"Told me what?"

"I'm a walking lie detector, Dani, my darling."

"Nobody is."

"It's inherited, like your *sidhe*-seer gifts."

"Which I'm going to use to kick your ass from here to next week."

"And that was one big fat fuck of a lie. You found her, didn't you? I knew I should have put her away. But you were here, and bleeding so much, and I needed her off the bed. Saving you was all that mattered."

"So you shoved her off the side of the bed and thought I wouldn't notice? You stuffed her in a crack!" My hands are fists. The ignominy of it. Dead and disposed of like a used condom. If I hadn't missed the socks, I'd never have known. I'd have left thinking Christian was wicked cool for saving me and not been one ounce the wiser that I'd been in bed next to a dead woman, eaten and dressed without even seeing her two feet away. "Dude, you are one sick feck."

"Och, Dani, my love," he says, gliding toward the bed, "you've really no idea."

NINETEEN

"I stand alone"

I kick up into freeze-frame without even thinking. I don't lock one thing down on my mental grid. I hope I do a lot of damage, break everything I hit and just don't knock myself out, because I have a feeling if I do, I'll wake up strapped down to a rack with an insane ex-Highlander about to do seriously fecked-up things to me.

If he can sift, I'm dead meat.

I make it to the door but he's there in front of me, arms spread, crouched low, looking like he's about to bum-rush me and take me off my feet. His face is contorted with anger, kaleidoscopic tattoos rush beneath his skin. His eyes are full black. Only thing that's missing to complete the Unseelie prince picture is a radioactive torque and huge black wings spreading, getting ready to crush me in a deadly embrace. I backpedal frantically and he lunges.

Then I'm on the floor and he's on top of me, and I know the second he hits me that Christian is so much stronger than me that I don't stand a chance of taking him. I can't believe the strength I feel in his body! The Unseelie part of him has kicked in with a vengeance. It's not just power oozing off him. He's turning into pure sex just like the rest of them. I shake my head, trying to keep it clear. I think about horrible things like the dead woman stuffed into the space between his bed and the wall, and how I don't want to end up like her.

I'm flat on my back and he's got my wrists and he's stretching my hands above my head. I curse and struggle and kick but it's like fighting a concrete wall. Nothing, and dude, I do mean *nothing,* seems to have any impact on him. I head-butt him. He laughs and drops his face into my shoulder, and sniffs me!

I bite his ear, try to tear it off his head. Blood fills my mouth, gagging me, and I let go.

"Dani, Dani, Dani," he says like he doesn't even feel it. "Don't fight me. You don't need to fight me. I'll never hurt you. Not you. You're my brightest shining star."

I ain't nobody's bright shiny nothing! He's a certifiable lunatic! "Get off me!" Up close the death-by-sex Fae part of him is doing wicked bad things to me. Things I don't like feeling. My mouth is dry and I'm seeing those graphic images plastered inside my skull. Christian. Naked. Doing the things I seen Ryodan doing. And I want to watch and I don't want to watch and I have to get the feck out of here now! "Can you even feel? Or are you as dead inside as that woman? Why did you even bother saving me? So you could kill me slower?"

"It's not like that. Would you hold still and listen to me for a second?"

"There's nothing you can say that matters!"

"It's hard to talk to you when I'm touching you."

"Dude, quit sniffing me! That's just rude. Get off me!"

"I can't. You'll run."

"If you really didn't kill her, you'll let me go. You'll trust me to come around. Give me room to breathe."

"If I let you go, will you sit down and hear me out, lass?"

He's relaxed since we're kind of negotiating but he's a

lie detector and I know I can't answer that last question, so I take my best shot and knee him in the balls with everything I've got. There's no such thing as a dirty fight when you're fighting to win.

He roars so loud my head just about blows apart. Then he's off me and curled in a ball, howling. I've kneed a few dudes before. Got to out there on the streets sometimes. Never seen one react so bad. I wonder if it's because he was hard as a rock when I hit him, so I had to twist really hard to get to his balls and I came up on them from underneath and probably mashed his . . . uh, yeah, Mega, now's a good time to run.

I blow out the door so hard I blast it off the hinges.

This morning when I left Chester's after almost dying and coming back to life—I think it was this morning, I spend so much time unconscious lately that I'm never sure if I've been out for a few hours or a couple of days—I was trying to decide what to do with the rarity of a whole day of free time. But then I nearly got killed again, this time by exploding frozen people, then Jayne took my sword, then I passed out from blood loss, got cleaned up by an Unseelie prince and drank his blood, found a dead woman practically in bed with me, and now I'm out on the streets again and feck if it's not time for me to report to work again!

I can't decide which of those things is the worst.

Dude, sucky day. Free time, my ass. I barely survived it.

I bounce from bare foot to bare foot, freeze-framing with all I've got, skinning up my heels something fierce, waiting for Christian to sift into the spot in front of me. Knowing if he does, I'm going so fast I'll knock myself out cold on him and probably wake up dead. Knowing

I don't have the one weapon that would protect me from him because Jayne took it.

Mac has one, though.

Bet I could take her.

Way I see things, I got three options.

Go to Chester's, use Ryodan as a shield against Christian while making him help me get my sword back.

Go straight after Jayne myself, knowing Christian is hot on my heels.

Go after Mac and take the spear. Barrons might be in the way. Who am I kidding? Barrons would definitely be in the way, and even if he wasn't and I took her spear, he'd come after me. Then I'd have Christian hunting me, Ryodan pissed at me for missing work, and Barrons breathing down my neck.

A day in the life of me. The stuff I have to put up with.

I'm always thinking things are as bad as they can get and they get worse. I nearly crash into something in the street, one of those fecking variables that move off my predicted grid, like people, animals, and Fae.

"Stay out of my way, human!" it hisses.

I want to drop out of freeze-frame and kick this monster's ass all the way to dead. I haven't seen her since the night Mac saved me from her, and forced her to give me back my good looks. I almost died that night, too. I almost die a lot. Superheroes do.

"You stay out of mine, you ugly old bitch!" I hiss back at the Gray Woman.

Then she's gone on her way and me on mine. She's off to hunt and kill and I've got an itch I can't scratch. My hand closes on nothing at my waist.

I need my sword like I need to breathe.

I detour into a sporting goods store, jam shoes on my feet, grab an oversized fleece pullover to pull on over my sweater because its fecking cold for May, and dash off again, heading for my best shot at success. Trying to take on Jayne and his men with Christian trying to kill me is a weak shot. I don't have any idea where he's taken my sword. There are times, like Ryodan said, when Batman needs Robin. Well, I don't *need* Ryodan, but he sure will make it easier. He can watch my back like Mac used to. I've got no time for pride. I want results and I know how to get them. He's always telling me to ask. Tonight I'm asking.

I feel naked without my sword.

I feel exposed. It's throwing me all kinds of off balance like I don't even know who I am anymore without it.

When I blast into Ryodan's office, I'm going a million miles a minute, feet and mouth. Every one of his dudes scowls at me on the way in, even Lor, and I have no idea why. Guess Ryodan told them to be pissy to me or something. You never know what's coming next with him.

I blurt out what happened with the frozen car and Jayne and tell him how we have to go get my sword back like right now, like this very instant.

"Drop down, kid," he says without raising his head from his stupid paperwork. "You're messing up my office." Papers are flying around his head.

I drop down from hypermode and he looks up. He's looking at me weird. Takes me a sec to figure it out. It's like he's looking at a stranger. One he doesn't like and is thinking about killing. Why the feck is he mad at *me*?

"You reek of Highlander. The whole club can smell him on you. You're wearing his clothes."

I don't think I've ever heard him talk so soft. "Dude, who cares? Didn't you hear anything I said? Inspector Jayne took my sword!"

"Explain why you're wearing his clothes."

Softer still. If I wasn't so hot with temper I'd get a chill. I don't understand him. What does what I'm wearing have to do with anything that's actually, like, relevant? How could it possibly matter? I don't even understand why it registers! But I can tell by the look on his face he's not budging until I explain, and if I don't get my sword back soon, I'm going to go crazy. I also know if I tell him Christian killed some woman and I was next, he won't pay any attention to the problem of my sword, he'll go after Christian, when I need him to go after Jayne. I'm not sure he can take Christian. Not with what he's turning into. But with my sword, I know I can.

"The explosion cut up my clothes. He gave me some of his."

"You were together at the explosion."

"He found me after."

"And you changed in the street."

"Huh?" Stymied is me. This isn't where I expect the conversation to go at all.

"Elucidate upon where you changed."

"What the feck docs that have to do with anything?"

"Answer me."

"I ducked into a convenience store. That's why they call them that. So they can be, like, convenient."

His gaze shivers up and down me. "If ice splinters tore up your clothes so badly that you needed to change, I'd think your injuries would be greater."

I gape at him, baffled. Somebody took my sword and he wants to talk about what I'm wearing and where I got dressed, and that he doesn't think I look hurt bad enough!

"He healed me. I was bleeding a lot. Holy hurrying hurricane, how'd you get next to me so fast?" Ryodan isn't behind his desk anymore. He's standing practically on my toes. I didn't even see him move. Or feel a breeze or anything! "Give me some personal space!"

He drops his head forward and smells me. "Healed you how?"

What is the deal with everyone sniffing me? If Dancer starts doing it, too, I'm so out of here. "I drank his blood. Got a problem with that?"

"Three."

"Huh?"

"I have three problems with that."

"That was a rhetorical question. Maybe you can't hear me talking or something so I'll say it again: Jayne has my fecking sword. I'm in deep shit without it and need it back. You going to do something or not?"

Just like that he's back behind his desk, head bent over his paperwork, all but ignoring me. "No."

I'm incredulous. "What? Why? You know I'll go after it myself! Is that what you want?"

"Jayne stopped by a few hours ago."

"That took a fecking lot of nerve! He left me for dead. In the middle of a street. Wouldn't even give me a fecking candy bar. Did he tell you how bad off I was? Why didn't you come help me?"

"You look fine to me."

"Whose side are you on?"

"He told me why he took the sword, and agreed not to kill any Fae within five blocks of my club. That's more than you do."

"Why would he agree to that? Jayne hates all the Fae!"

"He knew you'd come to me and ask me to help you get it back."

"And you're on *his* side?" How dare Jayne predict my moves and avert them while I'm busy dying and then being chased by a homicidal maniac! All of which was his fault to begin with!

"Truth is, kid, I prefer you without it."

"Why?"

"You can't kill my patrons. And now maybe you'll start exercising caution. Or at least learn how to spell it."

I glare at his bent head. "I'm asking for your help here, boss. You keep telling me to, and I'm asking."

"I also said how you treat me is how I'll treat you."

"What am I doing wrong?"

"The answer is no."

"You've got to be kidding me!" I tap my foot hyper-fast, hoping maybe I'll crack his stupid floor.

He doesn't say anything. Just keeps working on whatever it is he works on.

"You know what, dude? If you don't help me get my sword back, you and me are through! You solve the ice mystery yourself," I bluff, not about to give it up. "I'm not working for you. You don't help me, I don't help you."

"Jo." He doesn't even raise his head. Just murmurs her name.

"I don't care if you keep boinking her! Just get me my sword back! And don't be making any more deals with folks about me behind my back!"

"That's not our arrangement. You signed a contract. Jo's life is only one of many prices should you renege. There are repercussions for your actions. You can't walk away from me, Dani. Not tonight. Not ever. You're not the one calling the shots. Sit down." He's standing again, and again I didn't see him move. He kicks a chair at me. "Now."

Sometimes I think everybody else in the world knows something I don't know. Like they're all in on some kind of conspiracy and if I just knew that one secret thing, too, the things adults do that baffle me would make perfect sense.

Other times I think I know something extra that the whole rest of the world doesn't know and that's why nothing they do makes sense. 'Cause they don't know it and all their actions stem from flawed logic. Unlike mine.

I told Mac that once and she said it wasn't something everyone else knew; the missing ingredient was that I didn't yet understand my own emotions. They were new and I was just learning them for the first time. She said I was never factoring other people's feelings into things, so of course everything grown-ups did seemed mysterious and weird.

I said, dude, you just said I don't understand them, so how can I factor them in?

She said you can't, so just accept that teenage years are a great big clusterfuck of insecurity and confusion and hunger. Try to survive them without getting yourself killed.

A-fecking-men to that. Except for the insecurity part. Well, without my sword, plus the insecurity part.

As soon as I sit down, Ryodan says, "Get out of here."

"Bipolar much?"

"Go take a shower and change your clothes."

"I don't smell that bad," I say crossly.

He writes something, then turns the page in whatever-the-heck-stupid-thing he's reading.

"Dude, where do you want me to go? I can't go anywhere without my sword. I can't outrun the sifters. Every Fae in your club has a hard-on for killing me. You want me dead? Just do it yourself and get it over with."

He stabs a button on his desk. "Lor, get in here."

Lor blows in like he was plastered to the other side of the door.

"Escort the kid to clean the fuck up and get that stench off her."

"Sure thing, boss." He scowls at me.

I scowl right back.

Lor points through the glass floor. "See that blonde down there with the big tits? I was about to get laid."

"One, I'm too young to hear that kind of stuff, and two, I don't see you carrying a club to knock her over the head with, so how were you going to accomplish that?"

Behind me, Ryodan laughs.

"You're ruining my night, kid."

"Ditto. Ain't life at Chester's grand."

TWENTY

"I've got soul but I'm not a soldier"

I am not the Sinsar Dubh, Kat. He has tricked all of you. You will need me to save you.

Each night Cruce has taken me into the Dreaming, he has made the same claim. His lies hold the polish and consistency of truth. If my emotional empathy works on Fae—a test I've not yet had the opportunity to perform to my satisfaction—I get such conflicting signals from him that my gift is of no avail.

Now, wide-awake after another night of diabolical dreams, I pass through double doors a hundred feet tall, several feet thick, with unfathomable tonnage, but do not afford them a second glance. My eyes are only for him. It does not seem odd to me we cannot close such doors. The oddity is that we were ever able to open them: tiny mortals tampering with chariots of the gods.

I find myself in the position the Meehan twins recently occupied, hands fisted on the glowing bars of Cruce's cage, staring in at the iced vision.

He is War. Divisiveness. Brutality. Heinous crimes against humanity. As an event on the battlefield, and the personification of it in a cage, he is all that and more. How many humans fell before the murderous hooves of this sly horseman of the apocalypse?

Nearly half the world's population, by last count.

Cruce brought down the walls between our races. If not for him, it would never have happened. He arranged the players, nudged them where and when necessary, set the game in motion, then galloped about the board in the guise of an avenging angel, agitating here and stirring up there, until World War III began.

I should not be here with him.

Yet I am.

I told myself white lies as I made my way beneath the abbey, deep into our hidden city, picking through a misleading maze of corridors and crypts and dead-end and pigtailing tunnels. I told myself I must ascertain the cage is secure and he is still in it. That I will see him and realize he is but a pale imitation of my dreams; that I will gaze upon him and scoff at the thrall in which his dreamself holds me. That somehow coming down to check on him might set not him—but me—free.

My knees tremble. Desire parches my mouth and thickens my tongue.

There is no freedom for me here.

This close to him, I long to strip where I stand, dance wildly around his cage and keen the notes of an inhuman melody I do not even know how I know. This close to him I must bite my tongue to prevent myself from moaning with need.

This close to him I feel like an animal.

I stare at my hands on the bars, pale and white, with slender fingers clutching the glowing columns, and in my mind's eye I can only see them wrapped around that part of Cruce that has made of me an adulteress. Curled as they were last night and the night before and the night before. I see the curve of my lips as I smile. I see the soft roundness of my mouth as I take him inside it.

I find my fingers dancing lightly over the pearl buttons of my blouse and snatch them away. I see a shameful vision of my girls discovering their new Grand Mistress cavorting naked around Cruce's cage. It is erotic. It is horrific.

Freedom terrifies you because you never permit yourself any, Cruce said last night in my dreams. *I am not the only one in a cage. The shame you feel is not about me but that you know you stand in a cage, too, and it is of your own making. You have felt the darkest emotions of others since you were a child, you know what monsters crouch inside them, and you confuse your passions with their monsters. They are not the same, my beloved Kat. Not the same at all.*

He says I repress passion. That I do not permit myself to feel any of it. He says my love for Sean is a lie. That I seek comfort and safety and do not know what love is. He says I choose Sean because he, too, feels no passion. He says we are not running toward each other in love, but away from things in fear. *Set yourself free,* he says. *Come to me. Choose me.*

God help me. I walk in a valley of darkness and I need your light to guide me.

I unwrap my hands and back away. I must never come here again.

I will build a blockade of mental tricks in my mind, as I did when I was young and needed to protect myself from the wild, hurtful emotions of my family.

As I turn away I hear a noise so small I nearly overlook it. I don't want to turn back. It is nearly impossible for me to force myself to leave this place.

Yet I turn. I am the Grand Mistress here. The cavernous chamber, lit by a skein of torches on the walls, appears empty. There is nothing in it but a stone slab, Cruce's cage, and me. If I share this chamber with another, they are either behind the slab or on the far side of his cage. Hiding. Quiet. Waiting for me to leave.

Cognizant of my position at the abbey, I avert my gaze

from the iced prince and sedately walk the circumference of his cage, head straight, shoulders squared.

I turn the corner. "Margery," I say. She is directly opposite where, moments ago, I stood. Had she made no sound, I would have left none the wiser.

"Kat."

Hostility buffets me in hot waves. The emotions of others have temperature and color, and when intense, texture as well.

Margery is red, fevered, and complexly crafted as a honeycomb, with hundreds of tiny deceits and angers and resentments tucked into each small nook. I know a thing about resentment: it is a poison you drink yourself, expecting others to die.

I've been classifying emotions into categories all my life. Navigating the hearts of those around me is a minefield. There are people I stand near a single time and skirt forevermore. Margery's emotions are deeply conflicted, dangerous.

I wonder if I could feel my own, I would also be hot, red, a honeycomb of lies and resentments. *But I do not want to lead!* my soul is crying.

"I was wondering if we overlooked something about the grid," she says. "I fear he is not securely contained."

"As was I. As do I."

"Great minds." She offers a tight smile. Her hands clench the bars, white-knuckled.

I do not add the cued "think alike" because she and I do not. She hungers for power. I long for simplicity. I would have made a fine fisherman's wife, in a cottage by the sea, with five children, cats and dogs. She would make a grand Napoleon.

We assess each other warily.

Does he visit her?

Does he make love to her?

I cannot ask if she is dreaming of him and if that is

what has brought her down here on this rainy, cold morning. Whether she is or not, she will claim she is not then tell the entire abbey that I am, that I am being corrupted and must be replaced.

She will use anything against me to take control of the abbey. At the very core of my first cousin Margery Annabelle Bean-McLaughlin is a great, sucking need. It was there when we were children, playing together, and she broke the knees of my dolls and stole small treasures from me. I have never understood it. I observe her white knuckles. She clenches the bars of his cage as if she is squeezing the life from something. "Your thoughts?"

She moistens her lower lip, looks as if she's about to speak, then stops. I wait and after a moment she says, "What if the king took the book? I mean, took it from Cruce before he iced him."

"Do you think that's possible?" I say, as if it's a perfectly reasonable question. As if I don't know in that instant we are both being fed the same lies.

She looks at Cruce then back at me. Her eyes are billboards, advertising her emotions. She regards Cruce with tender, private communion. She looks at me as if I could not possibly begin to understand the first thing about her, him, or the world we live in. "You are not gifted," she hissed at me when we were nine and she heard her parents praising me for saving the family from a traitor in the endless plots and plans and betrayals that were our life. My parents used to take me to "business" meetings with Dublin's seediest, and watch me carefully to see who made me most uncomfortable. "You are cursed and flawed and no one is ever going to love you!"

All these years later I see the same taunt in her eyes. Oh, yes, he is attending her nightly, too.

I am not only an adulteress, I am a cheap one. I shape that realization into a brick around my heart and slather it with mortar so it is ready for the next brick I can use.

It will be in his way when he comes tonight. My Sean will be in bed beside me.

She shrugs. "Perhaps we don't know what really happened down here that night. What if the king tricked us?"

"Why would he do that?" I say.

"How could I presume to divine his motives?"

I need to know how deep her corruption goes. "Are you thinking perhaps we should free Cruce?"

A hand floats to her chest as if in alarm. "Do you think we should?" A crafty gleam enters her eye. "Do you know how?"

She has always been weaker than me. He is merely a blacker stain in her already corrupt blood.

"I think we need to figure out how to get the grid the Unseelie King created back up and functioning. I think the chamber should be filled with concrete, the grid reactivated, the doors closed, and the entire city beneath our abbey filled with lead."

I nearly stagger from the crippling fury of her emotional reply, although her lips shape sweetly the lie, "You are right, Katarina. As always, as everyone knows, you are right."

I offer my hand and she takes it as she did when we were children, lacing our fingers together. When we jumped rope, she would always pull it short. She had strong conflicting emotions about me when she was young that made her hard to read. I chipped four teeth before I stopped thinking the next time she would be different.

We walk from the chamber hand in hand, as if strengthening one another with love instead of keeping the enemy close.

TWENTY-ONE

*"I'm a cowboy, on a steel horse I ride.
I'm wanted . . ."*

I ain't afraid of nothing. Never have been.

But there are some things that would be plain stupid to do. Got nothing to do with fear. It's all about logic and practicality. You look at the world, assess your odds of survival in light of current circumstances, and choose the course that offers the best chance for whatever it is you want.

Like, say, continuing to breathe.

I stand outside Chester's, staring up at a streetlamp in the scant light of dawn. The sky is one big bank of thunderclouds. It's going to be a dismal, wet day. Happy fecking May in Dublin. Cold, too. I'm starting to wonder if summer's ever going to get here.

Hanging on the side of the streetlamp is a poster. At first when I walked out of the club, I thought We-the-feck-Care had posted another paper in the few hours I spent cleaning up then sitting in Ryodan's office doing a great big fat nothing but glaring at the top of his head while he worked, trying not to think about what stupid purpose his stupid desk served so recently—like, did he disinfect it or what? Whole time I was there he wouldn't even look at me. Not even when he finally told me I could leave. I know I look bizarre in the clothes Lor gave me after my shower, but c'mon, get over it already. He didn't have to not look at me the whole time and make me feel even more stupid than I already do.

Back to the poster . . . despite what I'm wearing and despite not having my sword, I was going to freeze-frame around the city and tear them all down.

Except WTFC didn't post this paper.

Something worse did.

The flyer tacked on the lamppost is poster quality. Staring out from it, my face looks back at me in living color, full frontal and profile.

And I think: when did they take pictures of me? I study it, trying to remember the last time I wore that shirt. I think it was four or five days ago. There's no mistaking who it is. Anybody would recognize me in a heartbeat. They were either really close to me and I somehow didn't know it, which is inconceivable, or someone else took the pictures for them, or they had one heck of a good lens. I look pretty good. Well, except for the black eye and cut-up lip, but I hardly see those kinds of things on my face anymore. I'm used to the terrain, who notices trees in the forest? I squint. "Bugger. You kidding me?" There were guts in my hair whenever it was. I sigh. One day I'm going to have clean hair and no bruises. Right. And one day Ryodan will apologize for being such a total dickhead all the time.

The message is direct and to the point.

WANTED

Alive
If you are human immortality
is the reward
If you are fae you will rule
beside us
she no longer has the sword
she is _defenseless_

There's info on where to bring me when I'm found.

To the Unseelie princes. The fecking feckers have taken out a hit on me. I always wanted everybody to know my face, but not this way!

"Defenseless, my ass." Oh, yeah, they're pissed at me. And they aren't too busy fighting each other to hunt me. Or to be keeping constant tabs on me.

I look down the street.

A poster flaps on every single lamppost left standing, as far as I can see. I imagine they wallpapered the city with them.

"Aw, feck it."

Then I brighten. Dude, I'm worth immortality and co-rule! They put a wicked high price on my head! 'Cause I'm, like, wicked dangerous!

I want to go hang with Dancer, enlist his help getting my sword back. It took me nearly an hour to shake Lor. Ryodan's got him trailing me, making like my protective shadow. If I had my sword, Lor and me wouldn't have to put up with each other. I finally managed to get him distracted with what he likes best: blonde with boobs.

I tear down the poster and ball it up. If these hadn't been up, I would have already sped off into the morning, sword or no sword, taking my chances. This was a rude and unwanted wake-up call.

She no longer has the sword.

Gah, feckers! They just had to broadcast that, didn't they? I guess Jayne is already using it, and word got back to the princes.

She is _defenseless._

Did they have to underline that word, make it bigger than all the rest *and* red, too? I mean, what part of defenseless needs emphasizing? The word is bad enough! The whole bloody city is going to be gunning for me soon. Every big bad out there I ever beat up on, everyone I threatened or just irritated is about to learn I can no longer kill them. They already know I can't outrun the sifters. But having the sword always tipped the balance in my favor. Kept them all from trying.

I feel exposed, standing in the street. Anything could sift in behind me, grab me, and the fight would be on. Would I win? What if there were a dozen of them? What if humans come for me in a small army? What if the princes themselves come?

Gah, I'm what-iffing! I don't what-if! What-iffing is for grown-ups. They what-if themselves right into doing nothing, and die without ever living.

I turn around and look back at Chester's.

Then I turn back around and look down the street.

In front of me, high odds of death. Behind me, a cage.

I hate cages. For most folks, they're built from fear and they do it to themselves. Not me. Mine were forged of helplessness. Most kids' are.

So this is what it comes down to: death or a cage.

I grin. Dude, I'm a superhero. No contest.

I flip the street both birds and slide sideways into freeze-framing, ripping down the posters as I go.

I go hunting for Dancer and find him hunting for me in, like, no time at all. It cracks me up because what are the odds we could go looking for each other in the hugeness that's Dublin and actually find each other? But we always do. Like magnets.

When I see him, I grin. He's walking down the street in the gray dawn, glowing like a star going supernova. I can't look straight at him. I have to take quick looks at him from the corner of my eye. There's a bubble of light around him so bright it's blinding. He's wearing sunglasses over his glasses and looks like some kind of glowing Mutant X guy with a superpower of his own, like say Super Brain.

"Dude!" I say.

"Like it? Hold on, let me turn it down." He fiddles with something near his waist and the light dims to something closer to what my MacHalo throws off.

I check him out. His clothes are shiny. Shiny jeans, shiny shirt, even shiny ball cap. Clothes hang on his tall, lanky frame like something out of one of those glossy magazines, casual perfection. His hair's getting long again. He's going to ask me to cut it soon. I like those times. We take care of each other like two monkeys picking each other's nits. Folks underestimate a good nit-pick. "New fashion statement?" I tease.

"Thinking about your wardrobe, Mega," he says. "I was working on the spray for Papa Roach when all the sudden I got this idea for Shade protection. I need to spray your clothes with a reflective base, then I designed a harness of lights for you that runs off a battery system, and get this: it self-charges with motion!" He fiddles with a gizmo at his waist, wearing the rapt expression of a boy genius playing with electronics. All the sudden his head whips up and he grins and I just grin back because when Dancer grins like that all my worries disappear.

"Because of the way you move, it'll never go out. I've been testing it and it stays charged off even my movements for days. I figure one good freeze-frame will juice it up for a week. That means when you go to Shadetown, you can sleep easy, wearing it."

I'm speechless. Dancer was thinking about me, pondering the ins and outs of my life, so he could make it better. He spent his time working on something, not to save Dublin, like the Papa Roach spray, but just me. I fiddle with the bracelet on my wrist. He gave me that, too. It weirded me out when he did because I was afraid he was going to get mushy on me but that was way back in the beginning of us hanging together when I didn't know that Dancer never gets mushy. We don't let that kind of stupid stuff get between us. Using some of your own time to make someone else's life better is, like, the nicest thing you can do for anybody. I almost can't stand it, it makes me so happy.

"You're the Shit," I tell him.

And this time he doesn't say it right back at me, he says, "You think so?" like he wants to hear it again, so I say it again and his grin gets even bigger.

After a sec he notices the wad of posters I forgot I was holding.

He makes a sound of disgust. "Mega, I been tearing those things down for hours. I stumbled on one of the crews putting them up and followed them around, ripping them down. They've got a bunch of Rhino-boys hanging them. Is it true? Did somebody take your sword?" He looks me up and down, searching for it. He blinks like he just noticed me for the first time and I get so embarrassed it's all I can do to not freeze-frame right out of there. I feel so stupid!

I forgot what I was wearing!

My jaw juts and I say, stiff-like, "It's all they had that fit me. Ryodan made me change. I didn't have nothing to do with this getup. I wouldn'ta picked it in a million years!"

Dancer's looking at me like I'm an alien from outer space. I could just sink into the street, yank the concrete and trash over my head and hide. I hug my arms over my chest, cross my feet at the ankles and turn sideways a little, trying to make myself narrower so there won't be so much of me to see.

"I know I look stupid, okay? It's been a real sucky day for me and I got bigger problems on my mind than what I'm wearing so quit looking at me like I'm some kind of geek dressed up for Halloween, because I didn't have a choice since Christian gave me his stupid pajamas and Ryodan said they smelled—"

"Christian gave you his pajamas and they smelled? Wait a minute, Christian *wears* pajamas?"

"I only needed his pjs because I woke up in his bed with only my bra and underwear on and all my clothes destroyed, otherwise I never would have worn them," I clarify when I realize how weird the first part sounded.

"Well. That explains things."

I love that about Dancer. He always gets me without me having to go on and on telling how point A got to point B. "All I'm saying is this ain't my fashion statement, so don't hold it against me."

"S'cool, Mega. You look cool."

"I look stupid." I'm so mortified I could expire of mortification.

"You look older. Sixteen or seventeen. If you had on makeup you'd probably look eighteen."

I think I'm nonplussed. I've never been nonplussed before but I know the definition and I imagine this must be what it feels like. It's not quite flummoxed, or bewildered. Words have subtle nuances. A year or two ago I might have been flabbergasted. This is a slightly different kind of stymied. Yes. I think it's nonplussed. "Well," I say, and smooth my skirt.

Gah! Feck! What are my hands doing to me? I actually just smoothed my skirt! Am I turning into some kind of sissy? I don't even wear skirts! But when Ryodan made me change the only thing they could find that fit me was the waitress uniform from the kiddie subclub and I was so pissed off about the posters, then so glad to see Dancer, that I totally forgot I was wearing a short skirt, snug blouse, and baby doll heels that suck to freeze-frame in, but I had more important things to do than dash into a store and switch shoes, like tear my face off every fecking lamppost in the city. Feet are feet sometimes; if they're working that's good enough.

"Who took your sword, Mega? And how did any-body even get it from you?"

My mood darkens instantly. I get so mad I get lockjaw and I can't talk for a sec. "Jayne," I finally grind out through my teeth. I rub my jaw muscles a sec and loosen my mouth back up. Superstrength sucks sometimes when it's in every single muscle in your body. When you get a muscle cramp, it's a big deal. It can go on for a good long while. "That fecker Jayne took it and left me for dead. I got hurt by one of those . . . " All Dancer knows about the iced scenes is what he saw the other night and it still hadn't exploded by the time they got me out of there. At least I don't think it had. It occurs to me I'm not sure. I need to ask somebody later. "I got hurt and Jayne took it while I couldn't do anything to stop him. I went to Ryodan and told him we needed to go get my sword back and he refused. Said he liked me better without it."

"Dude!"

In a single word Dancer just gave me all the righteous indignation and pissed-offedness that the situation deserves. "I know, right?"

"What is he thinking? You're the Mega. You don't take Wolverine's claws!"

"I know, right?"

"Dude," he says again.

We look at each other commiserating, because grown-ups are so fecked up and we're never going to turn out like them.

Then he grins. "What are we waiting for? Let's go take it back."

Since the walls fell, Dublin feels a lot like a movie set to me.

It's the quiet. The city is a ghost town with squatters

hiding in the wreckage, rifles cocked. Sometimes I see whites of eyes gleaming at me through boarded-up windows. If they're human, I try to talk to them. Not all of them are receptive. There are some real nuts out there, as creepy as some of the Unseelie.

Before the walls crashed, back when I used to pedal around the districts on my courier bike, back when the *sidhe*-seers were masquerading as an international messenger service run by Ro, the city was filled with a constant white noise. It was hard, even with my superhearing, to distinguish between the congestion of cars and buses, folks' heels on pavers and cement, planes landing and taking off, boats docking in the bay. Cell phones drove me crazy. There were days when all I heard was a blur of text message alerts, e-mail alerts, rings, songs, games.

Still, as annoying as it could be, it was music to my ears, the complex chords of the city I love. Now there are only the flat notes of soldiers marching, monsters hunting, and the occasional plaintive trill of something dying.

Dancer and I race through the streets, telling each other jokes, laughing our heads off. Hanging with him is the only time I can totally forget myself.

We round a corner and belly up to a contingent of Rhino-boys.

When they see us, one of them grunts into a radio, "Got her, boss, she's at Dame and Trinity."

I glance over my shoulder, lock everything down on my grid, grab Dancer, slide sideways and freeze-frame us out of there.

A short time later we're skulking around outside Dublin Castle, quiet as two mice sneaking around the kitchen looking for cheese.

Dancer's eyes are bright with excitement. I'd never

freeze-framed him before. He said it was the coolest thing he'd ever done and wants to do it again. It used to make Mac almost puke when I did it to her.

After I hit a department store and changed into a cooler outfit of jeans, tennis shoes, and a new leather coat, we stopped in one of his digs I didn't even know he had and got some explosives. Some of the best plans are the simplest, less room for error. He's going to make me a distraction by blowing something up while I go in after my sword. I'll grab it, grab him, and we're gone. Then I'll swagger into Chester's tonight at eight and everybody will see you don't mess with the Mega. Ryodan'll see I don't need him for nothing.

"You were right," Dancer says, "the cages are crammed full of Unseelie waiting to be killed."

I snicker. "Jayne didn't know what he was getting into when he took my sword. I knew he didn't have enough time to kill six days' worth. Only way I can is I do it in hyperspeed."

Covered trucks are parked near the training green. We circle behind them. Fresh Unseelie bodies are piled in the back of one, still dripping. That means somebody is currently using my sword, and it's nearby. My fingers curl, aching for it. I don't know where Jayne disposes of the bodies. He has them trucked somewhere. I know his routine. I've been a part of it for a long time. His men patrol the streets, capture every Unseelie they can get their hands on and imprison them in iron holding cells in buildings behind Dublin Castle. The facilities are guarded, because several times in the past one Fae faction or another has hired humans to try to break somebody—or all of them—out.

Whenever the cages started getting full and I had free time I zoomed in, sliced and diced Unseelie, then loaded the bodies and trucked them out. It ran fast and efficient.

But only because I kill in superspeed. No slow-mo Joe can walk into a cage filled with Unseelie armed only with a single weapon, whether it's the Sword of Light or not. He'd be torn to pieces while he was still stabbing his first Fae.

Now, Jayne is being forced to separate out each Unseelie, take it out of the cage, kill it, separate the next, kill it, and so on for days. He'll need a full-time contingent to run it. It will take dozens of his men to replace me. And he was already shorthanded.

"Mega, I know where the sword is," Dancer says.

"Me, too."

When I slay Unseelie, I do it so fast that there's not much time for the Unseelie standing nearby to react. They die quickly. Most of them before they even know what's happening.

But the way Jayne's doing it, they have to be standing around, watching the others get slaughtered for hours, watching Death inch closer.

I hate Fae. But there's something about knowing that they're just standing there, locked up, watching their buddies die a few feet away, waiting to be killed, that makes me feel . . . queasy. It's not like we owe them mercy—they don't show us any—but I figure if you're going to kill something you should do it quick and painless or you're just as sick as whatever you're killing.

I don't need my sword back just for me. I need it back because I'm the best person to do this job. Jayne needs to pull his head out and see that. This is fecked up, this drawn-out protracted slaughter.

Dancer's eyes aren't shining anymore. He looks as somber as I feel. I decide I'll make a show of good faith when I get my sword back.

I'll stay and slay, and put everything out of its misery fast and clean.

Then me and Jayne are going to sit ourselves down and have a serious talk.

I look at Dancer and he nods.

We head for the screaming.

The corrugated steel dock doors are wide open on the warehouse, making room enough for two semis to back in and unload if they wanted to. Seeing into the building where Jayne is killing all the Unseelie isn't the hard part.

It's not being seen if someone looks out that's tricky.

The concrete dock is five feet high, and I've crept along it until I'm standing real close to the entrance, with just my eyes and hair sticking up above the side while I assess the scene and start building my mental grid. Even that small slice of me showing makes me feel too exposed. Having red hair is like wearing a neon sign sometimes. Dirty blond would blend with the background, mouse brown would merge nicely with the murky dawn, but my hair never fades into obscurity unless I'm backdropped by a crimson sky.

Dancer's off somewhere up high, laying explosives. Times like these I wish I had a clone so I could do the cool stuff I'm doing plus hang with him. I love blowing up things. But my part of the job is to whiz in, grab my sword and blast us out of here.

I was right about it taking a contingent to handle the slaying, although Jayne would probably keep that many around the sword at all times just to protect it from me.

As if that's enough to protect it from me!

Jayne's got two dozen men with him, toting automatic weapons, draped in ammo. They're standing inside the entrance at full alert, watching every move being made. I hate guns. Automatic weapons can dump a spray of bullets that's nearly impossible for me to avoid.

That's why I need the distraction. I need most of them

gone before I'm willing to freeze-frame in, smash into Jayne and weave a zigzag path out of there, making it as hard as possible for anyone to shoot me.

I look up, scanning the rooftops around me. No snipers up there. If I were Jayne, I would have had at least six men up on the rooftops, watching for me. But that's why I'm the Mega and he's not.

I glance back inside and see my sword. Used to be, Ro took it from me sometimes, when I was younger. But when all the shit started hitting the fan with Mac, I took it back and never let anyone touch it again. Once, in battle, I saw Mac toss her spear to Kat to use. Dude, she's a bigger man than me. Ain't never sharing my weapon. It's my second skin. I can't stand seeing someone else touching it, holding it, using it. It's mine and he took it and he had no right to. I won't feel like me again until I have it back.

The screaming isn't so bad right now because Jayne isn't currently killing a Fae. But as I watch, his men bring a Rhino-boy up to the front of the warehouse near the dock and shove it to its stumpy knees on the floor in front of him.

Jayne draws back his arm, swings my sword and neatly decapitates it.

Not. I snicker.

Like maybe in his dreams. I see what's going to go wrong before it even does. "Holy webbed feet, it's going to duck," I mutter.

The Rhino-boy twists and ducks at the last second and my sword gets lodged in one of its yellow tusks.

I sigh. What does Jayne think their tusks are for besides blocking blows to their heads? Well, they use them for impaling, too, but mostly to protect their skulls and necks.

The Rhino-boy is enraged. Squealing and grunting, it

nearly breaks free. Somebody shoots it, then Jayne's men wrestle it back down to the floor.

He yanks the sword from its tusk and when it comes out he stumbles. Somewhere an Unseelie guffaws.

Jayne regains his balance, raises his arm and swings again.

I wince.

Jayne is strong. But Unseelie are made of sinew and gristle and weird bony structure where you least expect to find it, and cutting their head off isn't as easy as it looks like it should be.

Now the sword is halfway through its thick neck and the Rhino-boy is gushing green goo, squealing like a stuck pig, flopping stumpy arms and legs, and hundreds of caged Unseelie start screaming again.

Jayne saws at the thing's head with the sword and I almost puke. His men don't look any happier. The noise is deafening. Rhino-boys are emitting one continuous high-pitched squeal, tiny winged Fae (the ones that make you laugh yourself to death!) are chiming with fury and making dazzling light displays as they try to escape their iron pens, slithering multilegged Unseeliepedes writhe between their pen-mates, and the sound they make is like several tons of gravel dumped onto metal sheets, getting dragged across it. Gaunt, slender wraiths flicker in and out of solidity, emitting a high-pitched whine. The sound is so huge I feel the vibration of it in the concrete dock beneath my palms.

Jayne finally manages to kill the Rhino-boy he's hacking away at, and turns to one of his men for a towel to wipe away the goo and blood. He looks back at the cages, his expression bleak. I snicker mirthlessly. No doubt he's got a new appreciation for the speedy services of *moi*! It isn't easy walking into a warehouse full of condemned monsters and killing them all. But each one that gets back out on the streets will ultimately kill doz-

ens, maybe hundreds or thousands of humans, in its immortal existence. It's what they do. It's us or them.

I check my cell phone. My timer's counting down. I
got seven minutes before Dancer sets off the charges. I
would have gone for a single explosion but Dancer
wanted multiple sites, the better to divide Jayne's men
and increase our odds of getting in and out smooth and
easy.

I stare at my sword. I'm fixated. I know it. I don't
care. There are worse things to be fixated with. Like,
say, Jo with Ryodan. Duh. How fecked up is that?

Jayne's men have emptied a cage of all but the tiny,
death-by-laughter Fae. Now they net the brilliant little
harpies and toss the nets on the floor in front of Jayne.
Dainty, pretty Fae scream and shake their fists as Jayne
swings again and again. Making the scene even more
macabre, the men in the immediate area, including the
good inspector, laugh helplessly, many of them doubled
over with mirth, until the last one is dead.

The caged Unseelie roar and howl.

Because I'm a *sidhe*-seer, I can sense Fae in my bones,
in my marrow, in that strange hot/cold center of my
brain other folks don't have.

Before the walls fell, when there were fewer of them in
our world, my "spidey-sense" was a crystal clear beacon, warning me if one of them got too close to me long
before it was close enough to be a threat. But ever since
the walls fell, there are so many of them around me that
my Fae-alarm is constantly going off, 24/7. Like every
other *sidhe*-seer that wants to remain sane—or just get
some much-needed sleep—I've learned to mute it. If you
don't figure out how to turn the volume down, you'll go
crazy. It's not just an inner alarm saying, "Warning, a
Fae is near." It rides tandem with a flash of pure rage, of
prime directive to kill, kill, kill, and do it right now this
very instant even if you have to use your bare hands to

tear it apart. It's not something you can suppress. It's too strong. The older women at the abbey say it's like having the worst, most bloodthirsty hot flash imaginable, a hormone surge of pure homicidal fury. I don't want to live long enough to get hot flashes. Puberty is bad enough.

My Fae-sensor is on full mute right now. And even with it completely shut down, I feel it: a very powerful Unseelie is close to me, too close for comfort.

In order for it to be penetrating the barricade of silence I've erected around myself, its power has to be enormous. I nudge my volume up a hair, trying to figure out the who, what, and where. With so many Unseelie in the warehouse it takes me a few seconds to isolate the new arrival.

There it is!

I expand my awareness, taking its measure.

Ancient. Deadly.

Sex. Hunger. Rage. Hunger. Sex. Hunger. Rage. Hunger.

I feel it but I can't see it.

The short hairs on the back of my neck are tiny needles in my skin.

Suddenly a shadow moves in the gloomy, humid dawn and it's there, on the other side of the dock, hair and eyes barely visible. We're directly across from each other, no more than thirty feet of concrete between us.

It's not Christian this time. It's one of the full-blood Unseelie princes. Then again, after finding the dead naked woman stuffed between his bed and the wall, I'm not sure that's a meaningful distinction.

I go as still as Christian's dead woman.

It's not looking at me. It's watching Jayne. It appears to be completely unaware of me. I consider slinking down out of sight and cowering on my knees, focus hard on trying not to see all those graphic sex pictures on the inside walls of my skull like I'm seeing now.

Hunger. Need. Sex.

But I can't slink down because I don't dare take my eyes off it. I'm too dangerous to let a prince capture me, turn me Pri-ya and control me! *That's* the argument I should have made to Ryodan! Without my sword the princes can take me hostage, turn me into one of their mindless sex-crazed slaves and use me as a weapon against him. I bet he'd have listened if I'd said that, but I didn't think of it because I was too pissed off.

I scan the edge of the dock but I see just the one prince. Where is the other? Holding my head perfectly still, slanting only my eyes, I peer down at my timer. I've got over four minutes before our first explosion goes off.

How did it find me so fast? Well, it hasn't found me yet, but apparently it knew where to look. Did we pass more Rhino-boys without realizing it, and they phoned my whereabouts in?

I stare, holding my breath, trying to decide if I should drop to my knees now or just try to continue not breathing or moving. I watch it while it watches Jayne, who's killing another Unseelie, and all the sudden I get this total epiphany: it didn't come here looking for me!

It came for my sword.

Now that I'm no longer the sword's guardian, the princes actually have a chance to take it and destroy it. It can't resist the opportunity to eliminate one of only two weapons that can kill Fae. It couldn't take it from me because I'm the Mega, but it thinks it can steal it from Jayne because he doesn't have any special powers. He's just a man.

Worst part is, it's probably right. It probably *can* sift in and grab it before Jayne even knows what happened. It's an Unseelie, which means it won't actually be able to touch it because the Dark Fae can't touch the Light Hallows and vice versa, but I'm willing to bet it's got some kind of plan for that.

I'm fast but I can't beat a sifter. That's the whole reason I need my sword back so bad. With all the sifters I've pissed off, I'm a walking dead girl without it.

I envision the possible scenarios, starting with the worst first. I like to do it that way so I can end on the happy thought and aim for it.

One: the Unseelie prince sifts in, and kills everyone. He has one of his Pri-ya chick groupies with him whose head is currently not visible because it's somewhere lower doing something totally disgusting, and she picks up the sword, and he sifts out with her holding the booty.

Two: the Unseelie prince spots me, sifts over and kills me.

Three: the Unseelie prince spots me, sifts over, captures me and turns me Pri-ya. I refuse to follow that thought further. Bottom line: any version with the Unseelie prince spotting me ends badly.

Four: I drop to my knees and hide. It never knows I'm here. Dancer's bombs go off in quick succession. I freeze-frame in and take my sword while everyone is discombobulated. I kill the Unseelie prince in a dazzlingly display of dexterity and grace. Sonnets are composed about me.

I grin. I like that one.

I return my attention to the situation at hand and realize Reality—the impatient bitch—has made my decision for me. She does that a lot. You get busy planning your life, then it has the nerve to just go ahead and happen to you before you're ready. Before you even get the chance to aim yourself right!

It's one of the bad scenarios.

The Unseelie prince spotted me.

TWENTY-TWO

"Your mind's in disturbia, it's like the darkness is light"

The most scared I get is the most alive I ever feel.

I should collapse into a puddle of terror but adrenaline shoves a broomstick up my spine.

If the Unseelie prince gets within a few feet of me, I'll collapse anyway whether I've got a supercharged backbone or not. Nobody's immune to Fae royalty. Nobody's got any protection against them. The Seelie royalty keep their deadly eroticism mostly muted around humans as a courtesy. The Unseelie revel in using it on us full force. The princes have already turned hundreds of women Pri-ya. Nobody knows what to do with them. Folks can't decide whether to lock them up or mercy-kill them. Last I heard, they were keeping them locked up in what used to be a psych ward.

My superpowers are useless against the princes. All that sex and need and hunger wipes your mind clean of everything but lust that you're willing to die for. I saw Mac at her worst, when she was Pri-ya. She's the only person anybody knows of that's ever been brought back from the mentally shattered condition. It's one thing to have your body caged. I can't think of anything worse than losing your mind. I glance in at Jayne, desperate for my sword. He's currently using it to hack another

Unseelie to death in front of a screaming, snarling, roaring audience. Without Dancer's diversion there's no way I'll make it past all those Guardians and guns. I glance at my watch. Still three and a half minutes to go!

"Hey, dude, what's up?" I say all nonchalant-like to the Unseelie prince, while I pull the pin out of one of the grenades Dancer altered, months ago, to cause a blinding, delayed explosion. I use them as Shade-grenades, tucked into a ball of immortal flesh. While we were at his digs earlier, I stuffed my pockets with all kinds of things. I cram a candy bar in my mouth with my other hand and say, "Check this out. It came off the sword before Jayne took it. What do you think it is?"

I lob it high, straight over the dock. The prince does exactly what I was pretty sure it would do: catches it. A human would recognize what I threw, but I'm betting it won't. Whether or not it does, its reaction isn't at all what I expected. I figured worst-case scenario, it would pitch it over its shoulder.

The fecker tosses it right back at me!

Like an idiot, I catch it, too. I think there are two kinds of people in life: those you can throw something at that will instinctively duck and bat it away and those that will instinctively grab it. I've always been a grabber. I'll take offense over defense any day. I rubberneck in freeze-frame and assess my situation: Jayne is clueless that we're here because he can't hear us over the racket the caged monsters are making. The grenade in my hand is going to explode in five, four, three—

"No, *you* take it," I say, and lob it high, right back at the prince.

He catches it, closes a hand around it, and I see a flash of light in his fist. Then he opens his hand and black dust falls to the ground. If I could make out its expression, it might have just given me a total smirk.

Well, feck me. What is it made of? Galvanized steel?

250 · KAREN MARIE MONING

Suddenly I know where the second prince is because the temperature in the space behind me just dropped forty or so degrees. The hairs on the back of my neck frost and I shiver.

I lunge into reverse freeze-frame but it blocks me and I slam back into its icy, powerful body.

Feck feck feck! I slam it into forward. It's there before me. I twist and duck but crash into it sideways. We do this whiz/block thing about ten more times, with me cramming candy bars in my mouth. We're moving like an orchestrated dance. It seems to read my body's smallest cues, anticipate my moves. The thing is wicked fast! All I can make out is a tangle of long black hair and the brilliant flash of kaleidoscopic tattoos rushing beneath its dark skin.

I drop low and roll past it, then spring up to flee, but it grabs me from behind and yanks me back into it. I can't stop shivering. I have to get away. It makes a sound against my ear that I heard a lot of Ryodan's men making on level four when they were all having sex, low and rough and strained. I hear myself making a noise I didn't even know I knew how to make.

I turn into a Dani-grenade, fighting with all I've got. It ain't happening to me like this!

I punch, I kick, I bite. It doesn't fight back. It bands its arms around me from behind and keeps me pulled back hard against its body, waiting for my fury to turn into something else.

And it does.

I'm losing myself!

I can feel my mind slipping away!

I'm changing into something I don't want to be and I can't stop it! Is this what Mac went through? How did she stand it? Three princes at once, then Cruce, too!

I don't want this! It isn't supposed to be like this! I'm

supposed to lose my virginity in some awesome, super-spectacular, sensational way. Not like this!

But everything inside me is going gooey like rich, warm, velvety chocolate fondue that's so thick and sweet and scrumptious that I want to swim in it, let it cover my head, take me down deep into a place where I don't have to think anymore and I don't have to fight anymore and I can just be without always having to struggle to stay on top and protect myself and win all the time.

I want to get naked here in the street. I want to do it every which way, standing up and lying down, doggy style and reverse cowgirl. Long black hair is tangling around my neck, sliding like hot silk. Its arms around me feel like the best slow dance I ever imagined, not that I imagine wussy things like slow dancing with Dancer or anything but I'm having a hard time breathing right, it's getting all shallow and caught in my throat.

It makes a sound like dark wind chimes caught in a storm, beautiful and brittle. The haunting melody scrapes across my nerve endings, turning each one into a tiny mass of orgasmic tissue.

I'm lost. I press back against it. It's hard where I'm soft and pretty much perfect in every way.

"Och, Dani my darling, you're not giving me a single reason to wait for you to grow up. You're giving me a thousand reasons not to."

It's Christian! I'm so glad it's him, not one of the other princes! I turn around in his arms and tip my head back. "Hi, Christian!" I beam at him. He's hotter than the other princes. I'm glad I got him. I'll take the others, too, but I want him first. "I *want* to grow up. Now. Hurry."

"Not. Like. This."

I reach up and pull Christian's head down for kisses but he knocks my hands away. It makes me mad. I grab him again. He shoves me and I stumble.

He slaps me then. Hard, across the face. My ears ring from the violence of his blow. I wet my lips and give him a look. Pain isn't what I need. I need him to *ease* my pain. I might be a virgin but my body knows how to move, what to do. It's kind of embarrassing, but at the same time I like it. Sex is powerful. It makes all your cells feel hyperalive. How didn't I know that? I want to explore it. I want to learn it inside and out like everything else I do. I feel amazing! Like I'm about to learn stuff I got no idea about and it's going to change me forever. When this is done, I'll be a woman. Not a child anymore. I'm fascinated by the idea.

I'm not ready for it!

I'm racing toward it, can't get there fast enough.

He slaps me again. "Stop looking at me like that. Get mad at me. Hate me for what I would do to you. I'll kill you if you keep looking at me like that! I'll fuck you until you die!" he hisses.

Suddenly the Unseelie prince who was across the dock from me is standing shoulder-to-shoulder with him. They begin to argue in Unseelie and I can't understand a word they're saying but I get the tone. The other prince is pissed.

A third prince sifts in. Or a second, if you're counting Christian as an almost-prince. They look so much alike, I wonder if maybe he's already gone through the final change in the short time since I saw him last. Yesterday, being so close to him didn't mess me up this badly. Did something happen to him overnight? Is it because there's more than one prince here and they amp each other up? Did he really just say something weird about waiting for me? My brain is a mess. None of my circuits are working.

I can't stand up to the princes. For all my superhero powers, here I'm nothing. I'm as weak and helpless and doomed as any other person. I'm a willing victim, ready, waiting, eager to be destroyed. I know with one part of my mind how horrifying that is, but with another part of my mind—a much larger one—I don't care. Being a victim to eternal pleasure sounds like the most perfect state of existence I could ever imagine.

I stare at them. My cheeks are wet. I want to look away but I can't. I wipe my face and my hands come away bloody from my tears. I try to back up but there's superglue on the bottom of my boots. The spell Christian had begun to shatter is weaving itself around me again and I can't do anything to stop it. I'm standing ten feet away from three death-by-sex Fae and I don't see any way to get out of this one. Could Christian actually protect me from them if I don't want him to? Because if they move even one inch closer, I'm not going to want him to.

"Get behind me, kid," Lor growls from somewhere behind me. It seems mere thoughts of Ryodan conjured his men. If I could move, I'd go limp with relief. I can't. I stand there.

Lor grabs me and shoves me behind him. He's got half a dozen of his dudes flanking him and they circle in around me.

They face off with the princes, and just when all hell is about to break loose between them, one of Jayne's men barks a sharp command because they spotted us, and the Guardians swing their guns our way.

Then the Unseelie trapped in the cages must see their princes standing outside because they start roaring and howling at the top of their lungs, I guess trying to get them to set them free.

That's when the first of Dancer's bombs goes off.

TWENTY-THREE

"My pretty pretty thing. Do you want to freeze?...
The Iceman cometh"

Dancer planted the bombs up on the top floors be-cause we try not to destroy whole buildings unless they're nests and need to be demolished.

When the charges start going off, the roofs blow sky high, one after the next, and rubble rains down on us.

Glass and bricks and chunks of drywall spray the street. The air is so full of dust that I can't see for a couple seconds.

We all start scrambling and ducking, covering our heads, even the Unseelie princes. I guess being immortal doesn't make you like getting slammed by a slab of con-crete any more than the next guy. So we all start looking for cover, except Jayne and his men, who are already standing inside the warehouse and don't need it.

The bombs detonating didn't work as I'd planned. The Guardians were supposed to look outside when they went off, and see no one because I'd be hiding. Then they were supposed to go hunting for whoever was setting the bombs in the surrounding buildings, and I was going to take on Jayne and whoever was left.

Instead, they look out and see all of us because we're dodging falling debris and we're all doing it in slow-mo because you can't fast-mo through an unpredictable, un-mappable rain of bomb shrapnel.

The Guardians start trying to line us up in their sights and bark orders for us to freeze and drop our weapons, which is ridiculous, like anybody's actually going to listen, but I guess old habits die hard. Nobody freezes or drops anything. And I wonder, doesn't Jayne get that me and the Unseelie princes want what's in his hand and we'll kill for it? Dude, if I was him, I'd drop it and run.

Once I'm pretty sure the biggest chunks of roof have hit the ground, I freeze-frame past Lor to take back my sword from Jayne. Only I slam into Lor on the way there because the fecker's faster than me.

Then we both crash into two Unseelie princes that weren't there two seconds ago and my head starts getting screwed up with sex thoughts again. Lor grabs me and we freeze-frame away. The princes take one look at Lor and vanish, too, leaving Jayne a sitting duck for me. I try to freeze-frame around Lor again, and again I slam right back up into his chest. Then we're all scrambling for cover, because a chimney just crashed to the ground and exploded in a spray of bricks.

"Why does everything leave you alone?" I say pissily as we crouch behind the dock. "You got some kind of Fae-repellent spray? Ever hear of sharing, dude?"

He gives me a look. His face is gray with grime. I taste mortar dust on my tongue. Stuff is still falling but the shower of debris is slowing. Dancer makes killer awesome bombs!

"Why don't you just let me get my fecking sword?" I make the argument with him I should have made with Ryodan. "If the princes turn me Pri-ya they can use me against you guys."

"All the more reason he should have killed you. But no, he bloody 'hires' you."

"I didn't ask to be hired. Fact is, I asked *not* to."

"Then he makes me fucking babysit you."

"I didn't ask to be babysat either." I poke my head up over the dock. The princes are trying to get to Jayne! I try to freeze-frame around Lor again but I don't even make it two feet. I slam into him. Dude's a wall. No holes anywhere. This is getting old. "Get. Out. Of. My. Way."

"I'll get it for you."

"Why would you do that?" I say suspiciously. More like it he'll take it to Ryodan, who will use it as leverage to boss me around.

"Boss says I've got to keep you safe. He's had me shadowing you constantly."

"Nuh-uh. I would have noticed."

"You never see him when he's shadowing you either. And he's been doing it a lot longer than you think."

"Bull-crikey."

"I'll never get laid trying to keep you safe. You're a train wreck on steroids."

"Am not." Usually I'm cooler than cool. It's been a rough couple of days. "So, like, if you get it, you're going to give it back to me right now this very instant?"

"Didn't I just say so? Go hide somewhere and shut up, kid."

The Mega doesn't hide. "My ass."

"Can't possibly be worth what he thinks."

I have no idea what he's talking about but it doesn't have anything to do with me so I dismiss it.

I freeze-frame back toward Jayne the second he lets go of my arm. This time he's not expecting it because he thinks I'll just wait around like a wuss for somebody else to get my sword. Not. I snicker when I hear him cursing behind me.

Then I slam into Christian halfway up the stairs to the warehouse, blocking my way to Jayne.

Then Lor has me again and I kind of melt over his

shoulder because the death-by-sex Fae punch Christian's packing is doing funny things to me, but it fades as soon as we get away from him, so I bite Lor because I hate being carried around like a sack of potatoes. If he feels it, he has no reaction.

"Stay the fuck away from the Unseelie princes."

"I'm just trying to get my sword. He got in the way."

"I said I'll get it for you."

"I want to get it myself!" I want to look Jayne in the eyes when I take it from him. He left me to die like a dog in the street. No mercy. Not one drop.

Lor dumps me and shoves me up against a wall. "Fade, Kasteo, get over here and keep her out of my fucking hair."

Then I've got two of his dudes on me, one on each arm, and I freeze-frame or try to but they weigh so much I end up buzzing around in drunken circles like a bug dying on its back because I can't get all four of their feet off the ground at the same time. One or the other keeps digging a heel in. We slam into the wall then stumble all over each other and the whole time I'm trying to watch what's going on with Jayne and the sword. "Let go of me!"

They don't. In fact, they don't even acknowledge that I'm speaking, much less breathing. They hang on my arms like deadweights and eventually I wise up enough to stop trying. Exercises in futility aren't me. They could hold me till I run my gas tank out and there I'd be. A noodle, and somebody would no doubt fecking toss me over his shoulder again and tote me around rather than give me a candy bar.

After a few minutes I end up standing there, pissed as all get-out, just watching.

And that's how I have a front row seat when the real circus begins.

The two original Unseelie princes keep sifting in, trying to get close to Jayne. Each time they do, Lor or one of his men is there, blocking their way.

Christian keeps trying to get to Jayne, too, and I realize he can't sift yet. He's moving at just under full sift mode. Still, he's faster than me. Fecker. Lately, seems everybody is.

Jayne is spinning in a circle with my sword out in front of him, trying to keep everyone from taking it.

The Guardians are spinning in circles, pointing their guns, trying to get a fix on something. Good luck with that. They can't even see anything that's happening, just feel the wind of everyone freeze-framing past them.

The hundreds of caged Unseelie are grunting and howling, stomping and rattling bars and making a deafening noise, and there's some kind of Unseelie in there that starts making a sound I've never heard before. It's enormous and dissonant and it sets my teeth on edge, crawls under my skin and makes me want to crawl right out of it. I'm not the only one it bothers.

"What the hell is making that noise?" Fade snarls.

"I know, right?" I want to cover my ears but they've got my arms so I clench my teeth and begin to hum real loud instead.

An Unseelie prince materializes in the middle of the whole shebang, Lor pops in directly in front of him, they smash into each other and careen off, then go slamming into a half-dozen Guardians who slam into Jayne, and all the sudden everyone is stumbling off the edge of the dock.

When Jayne falls, my sword goes flying straight up in the air, end over end, an alabaster column of light. I close my fingers like I'm catching it.

It's there, right there for the taking! I can almost feel the perfect weight of it slapping into my palm.

"Let *go* of me!" I nearly yank my arms out of my sockets but they don't let go. I'm forced to stand there and watch as the princes, Lor, a dozen Guardians, and the latest intended Unseelie victim all try to position themselves to catch my sword when it comes down. One of the princes tries to spread his wings but the quarters are too close and he can't lift off. The other sifts into the air, and Lor lunges in a totally inhuman way and they collide in midair with my sword still going up.

Like I said, a total circus.

And that's when the freak show part of it begins.

I'm standing, wrists manacled by Kasteo and Fade, not going anywhere without somebody losing an arm, and since I don't have anything to cut theirs off with, I'm stuck like a fly in superglue, when all the sudden the air in front of the dock starts to shimmer, and I get this feeling I've never had before in my life. I've been worried on occasion. A time or two, like when the Gray Woman got me, I was actually a smidge scared. She was sucking the life out of me and I could feel it. Nothing wrong with admitting when you know you're in a scary place, so long as you don't let it mess with your head. I stayed cool, even tried to talk Mac out of not making any deals with the fecker, because most of the time deals made under duress come back and bite you in the butt with saber-toothed tiger teeth.

But this is different. I'm feeling panic with a capital P. Crazy, dumb, blind panic. All the sudden, for no reason I can figure, I'm ducking like a rabbit in the middle of a huge, open field with no cover for miles and the sky just went dark with hawks, flying wingtip to wingtip. Death seems that certain. One swoop, a rustle of wings, and I'm gone. All because of some weird spot in the air. What the feck? I'm panicking because of a shimmer in the air? Dude, what's it going to do to me? Give me a Twilight moment, make me all shimmery, too?

I'm torn between fighting to run and staying put so I can see what's happening because I can't conceive of anything that could panic me so bad and I need to see it! I'm tired of these eyeballs missing all the exciting stuff lately!

I realize I'm not the only one freaking out. Everybody that was trying to get my sword is suddenly scrambling away from the dock like they're running for their lives, which I take it to mean we're all in agreement about not liking unexplained shimmery spots in the air. I see my blade is still flying up, but it's moving slow like it's about to come back down. If I could just get Fade and Kasteo off my fecking arms, I'd rush in and catch it . . . well, maybe I would. I'm not real sure about that because my feet aren't obeying a thing I'm telling them about moving forward. Much to my annoyance, they're inching me backward.

The princes vanish.

Jayne and the Guardians are rushing straight for us.

Christian, Lor, and his men freeze-frame out, then Lor's replaced the other two dudes and has my arm, and he's dragging me away from the dock.

Then we're all retreating and I grin when I realize we're backing together, shoulder-to-shoulder, in tight formation. Jayne's next to Kasteo, who's next to Christian, who's next to a Guardian, and way down at the end are the full-blood princes, which totally freaks me because I can't figure anything they'd back away from. There are more balls in twenty feet of street here than there are in all of Dublin, and I'm proud to be swaying in the nut sack. We might fight each other, but in times of danger, we'll fight together. Dude!

A dark slit appears in the center of the shimmering spot. My panic increases exponentially. I'd turn and run but I'm anchored by two dudes that could hold the *Titanic* during a tsunami.

The slit widens and belches thick fog. I shiver. Frozen

fog becomes hard rime. Hard rime coated every person that got iced and died.

The caged Unseelie howl like banshees, and the one making that horrible screeling noise finally nails its hellish crescendo. The windows that didn't shatter when Dancer's bombs went off blow out now—not in slivers and chunks—they're literally pulverized, spraying the streets with glass dust.

The slit widens. More fog puffs out, milky and cold. The temperature plummets.

"Hold!" Jayne shouts, and we stop.

Fade says, "What the—"

Sound ceases.

The world goes silent.

Utterly.

Still.

Did I lose my hearing? Did the Unseelie's crescendo deafen me? I can't even hear my own breath in my ears like when I'm swimming underwater. I look at Lor. He's looking at me and pointing to his ears. I point to my own and nod. Everybody is doing the same thing. Least if I lost my hearing, we all did.

I look back at the widening slit and the oppressive silence grows.

It's worse than a vacuum.

It's. Awful. It's. Messing with my. Head. It's . . .

Void.

Disconnect.

Feels like being dead.

But there's something . . .

I slide into my *sidhe*-seer center and extend curious tentacles . . .

I get a mishmash of impressions but I can't find words for them because what I'm feeling is beyond my ability to comprehend. Like I'm three-dimensional and what I'm feeling is six or seven dimensions. It's . . .

Complicated.

Ancient.

Sentient.

I try to get a read on its . . . well, mind for lack of a better word, and all I get is a weird flash of . . . calculation?

Something missing. Something being searched for.

I look at Lor and see an expression on his face I've never seen before and never thought I'd see.

Fear.

It worries me. A lot.

He looks at Fade and Kasteo and they nod. He tightens his grip on my arm.

The slit widens and it comes.

Holy fecking crikey, it comes!

Part 2

There can be no sound without movement. There can be no movement without sound. There is no stasis in music, only change. It could just as easily have been called the Song of Destruction. Seems someone was feeling optimistic on naming day.

—*The Book of Rain*

TWENTY-FOUR

"And the beat goes on"

Cruce came tonight as he always does, stealing my sleep, parting my lips and thighs, leaving me near dawn in tangled bed linens, soaking with sweat from sex and shame.

In the few moments of rest I snatch before rising, I have a terrifying dream.

I walk to the hidden entry of the catacombs with the shuffling, mindless gait of a woman dead and risen from the grave.

Margery blocks the door of stones that looks like any other wall unless you are privy to its secret. She is voluptuously nude, hair and eyes wild, smelling of him—a scent I know too well. A banshee, she shows sharp teeth in a cackle and tells me he is gone. I am too late.

With violence of which I did not believe myself capable, I shove her aside, and when she slams into the wall, she slumps down it and is still. Blood blossoms behind her head, staining red daisy petals on the wall.

Bemused by the hostility in my heart, I pass through the door and shuffle on.

The tunnels are pitch, forcing me to feel sightless passage along damp stone walls. This is not the Underneath I know: dry and well lit, with everything in its place. In this dark, moist maze, moss grows thickly on walls and bones crunch beneath my feet. The odor of decay couples with some fecund scent on the breeze. There is nothing down here to generate wind unless a thing stirs that cannot possibly be stirring.

I pull my wrapper closer and thrust myself forward on hobbled feet with stunted, stumbling steps, blind in eye but not purpose. I pray, and with the whimsy of dreams the gold cross I wear upon my neck begins to glow. I do not deserve such comfort in this dark night of my soul!

I shuffle for time uncounted through darkness, until finally I reach the chamber wherein the erotic, deadly prince is iced.

There, no darkness preys, no moss grows, no water trickles. There are no bones in this forbidden place. Only flesh. Extraordinary, exquisite flesh.

The walls have been gold-leafed in my absence. The chamber is radiant with brilliant light.

Cruce is still caged!

Nude, towering, wings unfurled, he snarls with animalistic rage.

Iced solid.

I weep with joy. My fears were for naught!

Upon trembling legs I hurry to his cage, celebrating that it holds.

One of the bars is missing.

"Stop. Vibrating." Ryodan plucks a paper out of the air and slaps it back down on his desk.

I wonder if he cleans it. How many tushes have been on that thing? I'm never touching it again. "Can't help it," I say around a mouthful of candy bar. I know what I look like: a smudge of black leather and hair. "It happens when I get really excited. The more excited I get, the more I vibrate."

"Now there's a thought," Lor says.

"If you mean what I think you mean, you want to shut the fuck up and never think it again," Ryodan says.

"Just saying, boss," Lor says. "You can't tell me you didn't think it, too."

Five of Ryodan's dudes are in his office and it's like standing in the middle of heat lightning, closed in with them. Jayne is here, too, but I'm totally ignoring him because, like, if I didn't, I'd have to kill him with my bare hands and that would get messy, then Ryodan would probably make me mop his fecking office.

I never understand half of what these dudes are talking about and don't care. "You can touch me if you want to," I say to Lor magnanimously. I'm so pumped on adrenaline and excitement that I'm feeling downright sociable. I poke one of my shoulders toward him. "Check me out. It feels really cool."

All heads swivel my way, then they look back at Ryodan.

"He doesn't own my fecking shoulder. Why you looking at him?"

Lor guffaws but doesn't reach for my shoulder.

I don't know why. I like touching myself when I'm vibrating like this. It vibrates me twice. If I was really cold and started to shiver, I'd be vibrating three times! "So, what the feck are we going to do to stop this thing?" I beam. We got plans to make and implement. I thrive on times like these! They bring out my best! I'm a riser-to-the-occasion kind of girl. I'm feeling so excited and generous about having such a wicked cool adventure to live that I'm finding it hard to be mad at folks right now. We got an enemy that's bigger and badder than anything I've seen. Fecking-A, it's good to be alive! 'Cause, like, for a sec there by the dock, I wasn't sure I was going to be. I wasn't sure any of us were!

Speaking of back by the dock . . .

My mood shifts and I glower. I still don't have my sword. It got iced. The warehouse is now filled with iced Unseelie, the ceiling covered with stalactites, the floor deep with stalagmites. My sword got frozen in a stalactite way up high, and the place was way too deadly cold for anyone to enter, like freeze-you-to-death-instantly cold. We had to leave it stuck there, in an enormous icicle. Lor ordered Kasteo and Fade to stand guard until the scene thawed enough to retrieve it. Last I saw, the two Unseelie princes were still hanging around, too. If Christian was there, he was staying out of sight. No sign of Dancer. I didn't want to leave but Lor threatened to potato-sack me over his shoulder, and seeing how he can do it as easily as Ryodan, I didn't see any point in making myself miserable.

"It's your fault," I tell Ryodan. "You should never have let Jayne keep my sword. Now who knows what's going to happen to it! If the scene explodes like the others . . . " I trail off because I can't stand the thought of my sword blowing up into alabaster smithereens.

"That's the least of our problems," Ryodan says. "Tell me exactly what happened."

"Lor just told you," I say crossly. "What else do you want to know?"

"I want to hear it from you."

I tear open another candy bar and around mouthfuls repeat most of what Lor said about the fog and the slit widening. The feeling of panic we all experienced. How all the sudden none of us could hear a thing, like we'd gone deaf. "Then this . . . this . . . *thing* that was twice the size of your office sailed out."

"Thing."

"Dude, Lor didn't describe it any better. I mean, come on, 'dark mass about the size of two semis, side by side'?"

"Try."

I frown, thinking, then brighten. "Did you ever see the movie *The Blob*? It was like that. Only it was oblong. And I don't know if it was slimy and it levitated instead of rolled. And I don't know if it was dense. But it didn't look like a Shade. It was nothing like a Shade."

"*The Blob.*"

"Old movie, from way back in silent movie times."

"It's not that old," Jayne says. "I saw it when I was a kid."

"Which was like, way back during silent movie times, right? You shouldn't even be talking to me. Don't talk to me. You shouldn't even be here. I should kill you. You're lucky I'm not killing you right now. You left me for dead." I look at Ryodan. "And you let him. Feckers. All of you."

"I went straight to Chester's and told Ryodan where you were," Jayne says. "I wasn't going to let you die. I didn't like leaving you. I needed the sword. I couldn't afford to pass up the chance."

He told Ryodan where I was? "I said don't talk to me. And that worked out real well for you, didn't it? How many years do you think it might have taken you to kill a few hundred Unseelie?" I glare at Ryodan. "And you didn't say nothing about him telling you where I was. You didn't come neither." Didn't he care that I might've died?

"Boss sent me for you the second Jayne showed up," Lor says. "You were gone by the time I got there. I was following your blood trail but it disappeared."

"Texture," Ryodan says to me.

"You mean did it have any? Not that I could see."

"Then what happened."

"It moved into the warehouse, all ponderous-like, and belched white fog out everywhere and we couldn't see a thing. It iced the whole place, worse than anyplace we've seen yet. I mean, dude, the ceiling sprouted stalactites and the floor is covered with stalagmites so thick you can't even walk in there! We never seen anything like that at the other scenes."

"Postulate on why it got iced worse."

I'd pondered that on the way back. There was only one significant difference I'd been able to isolate. "There were a lot more people and Fae at this scene than any we've investigated. There were hundreds of Unseelie in cages and they all got frosted. It's possible more ice was necessary. Or maybe the thing had more juice today for some reason. We got iced, too, but it was only a thin layer, and once we moved, it cracked. We kept re-icing the second we stopped moving so I started doing jumping jacks and, like sheep can't think for themselves, everybody copied me, then there we were all standing in the street doing jumping jacks. I got worried the commotion might make it turn around and come after us but the thing never even noticed us. It was like we were fish and it wanted chips. Or maybe we weren't even noticeable as food. Then it vanished. Another of those slits opened inside the warehouse, all the white fog got sucked into it and the thing followed. Once it closed, we could hear again. Sort of."

"Clarify."

"There wasn't any noise. Nothing. You'd think the ice on all those Unseelie might have popped or cracked a little like ice does when it settles because they were warm before they got iced but it didn't. When we walked, our shoes didn't sound right on the pavement. When we talked it was . . . flat. It was worse than flat. There was a feeling to the silence. A really bad feeling."

"Elucidate," Ryodan says.

"I just did. I think you mean speculate."

Lor snorts. Ryodan gives me a look. Don't even know why I bother answering him sometimes. Maybe I like to hear myself talk. I've got a lot of interesting things to say. "You know how sound is really movement, and vibration is what makes noise? Which is, like, total contradiction to its effect on things because when the world went dead quiet, it was still moving while making absolutely no noise. But what I'm saying is, after it departed, things never got back to normal. It's like things weren't vibrating all the way. Or maybe the sound waves weren't bouncing off things the way they should. Or maybe the things the waves were bouncing off weren't right."

"Narrow it down."

I shrug. "Got insufficient data to form conclusive deductions."

"How long from the time it appeared to the time it disappeared."

"That was the weird thing. It felt like it was happening in slow-mo but I figure two seconds from start to finish. It came. It iced. It vanished." Sometimes I don't have the most accurate sense of time because I'm in a kind of in-between fast-mo and slow-mo and don't even realize it, which makes things around me seem to be happening more slowly. I'm pretty sure when it came, I was so wound up I was half freeze-framing. I look at Lor, who nods.

"Two to three seconds at most, boss. The fog rushed out, the thing came, the fog sucked back in and it was gone."

"I assume it was Fae," Ryodan says.

"Unequivocally," I say.

"You're a *sidhe*-seer. That means you should be able to get a read on it like Mac did with the *Sinsar Dubh*."

"I could to a degree."

"Intelligence."

"Enormous sentience. Stupefying." I wish I'd felt the Unseelie King. I'd have something to compare it to.

"Emotion."

"None discernible. No malevolence. I got the impression destruction was a by-product, not a goal." I notice everyone's looking at me funny. "Dude," I add and flash my best street-urchin grin at the room in general. "Fecking-A, was it ever cool!" Got to watch my tendency to geek out when I get excited.

"You think it had a goal."

"There was . . . I don't know . . . *purpose* to what it was doing. I could feel it. Some Fae feel simple when I focus on them with my *sidhe*-seer sense. They're dumb, acting on instinct, capable of random destruction. Then there are things like Papa Roach, that Fae that breaks down into little parts," I remind him, in case he missed that especially scintillating edition of my *Dani Daily*. "Papa feels . . . structured. It has plans. So does the Ice Monster. But there's a big difference between Papa and the Ice Monster. Papa has a beady little mind. This thing is . . . vast in construct and purpose."

"Motive."

I sigh. "No clue. Just that it had one."

"No idea why it chose that place, or why it ices things."

"None," I say. "It didn't even touch anything, as far as I could see. It just kind of hovered above it all. Unless the fog is like its fingers or something and it sucks folks' life force up with it and inadvertently ices them in the process. No way around it, I need more time with it. Got to feel it out longer."

Jayne starts cursing and says nobody is going to be spending more time with it because it's too dangerous, and even Lor looks disturbed by the idea of another encounter with the Iceman. Which reminds me . . .

"Why were *you* afraid?" I say. "I didn't think anything scared you dudes."

Lor gives me a cool look, like I didn't see what I saw, and says, "What are you talking about, kid? Only thing

I was worried about was how pissed Boss was going to be if the thing killed you."

Bull. I know these dudes. They don't care about anything but themselves and he was freaked, which means it was a threat to him somehow. I want to know how. I want to know what Ryodan's Kryptonite is. I know a few universals like: he who can destroy a thing controls it. Not that I get off on destroying things but when you get backed against a wall, coming out with both guns blazing is pretty much your only choice. I want enough power to void a contract, enough to quit my job, permanent-like. I'm ready for retirement. I want enough leverage to get Jo out of the kiddie subclub, assuming she ever wants to leave.

She will. The day he chooses someone else.

In my estimation that won't be long at all.

Half an hour later I'm outside Chester's, skidding holes in the rain-slicked pavement, pacing in hyperspeed, munching power bars to keep myself juiced. I'm waiting for Ryodan to get done with whatever the feck business he said he had to take care of that couldn't wait, so we can get on with our investigation. He told me to sit tight inside the club, but me hanging around inside Chester's without my sword ain't real likely and he should know better than to expect it.

Then again, without my sword I'm not straying far either. I hate waiting for backup but I want it. The Unseelie princes freaked me out. I got a major thought brewing about them, an idea I despise but have to consider for its end result. Right now I'm keeping it back-burnered where it can't burn me too much.

I got so many other thoughts exploding inside my head that I expect a few are poking out my ears. One second I'm so excited to be living in these times I almost can't stand it, the next I'm a nervous wreck because my people are out here in these streets and they don't have any clue we got a big scary Ice Monster turning parts of our world into a deep freezer! I got to get the word out fast, but what do I tell them? If you see a shimmery spot in the air—run? That's assuming they even *notice* the shimmery spot before they're iced!

Trouble is, I know folks. You can tell them to run all you want but there aren't a lot of people that will, until they believe they're in major danger—which is usually too late. They gape like cows, and if you don't know it, cows gape a lot. There used to be a big herd out by the abbey where I tested my speed and navigating abilities after Ro took me in and I was drunk on my new freedom. The cow pasture was a great place to practice freeze-framing on a dime because (a) cows move and are unpredictable, therefore hard to map like the real world, and (b) if I hit a cow it usually hurt me more than the cow. I had a riveted bovine audience the entire time. They'd chew their cud and swing their big heads back and forth, watching me like I was cow TV. If all I had to do was chew regurgitated food and watch other cows all day, I'd be riveted by me, too. Heck, that bored, I'd be enraptured by a fly battle on a cow pie.

But back to folks, shimmery spots aren't terrifying enough to make them flee. And there are some folks, like the see-you-in-Faery chicks that hang at Chester's 24/7, sporting new Papa Roach bugged-sized waistlines, trading sex, competing with each other to see who can eat enough Unseelie to turn immortal and get to hang with the Fae first, that would deliberately linger if they saw a shimmery spot, just because it was, like, pretty. Gah, some chicks should be shot. Put out of everyone else's reproduction pool.

I need a couple of pictures to put in my daily, to show peeps the gruesome finality of what the Ice Monster does. I need to get over by Dublin Castle, shoot a few frames. Then I need to get to *TDD* headquarters and fire up the presses! I love printing my dailies. I got double the reason to get one out fast now. After seeing the Unseelie Princes WANTED posters, folks are no doubt worrying their butts off about me! I need to reassure them, let them know I'm still on the job.

"You must be Dani!"

I turn.

And pop up on my heel and keep turning. I'd turn all the way to bum-feck-China if I could. I spin in a full rotation so she's at my back again and stand there, trying to compose myself. I don't want to look at her. I don't want her to see my face. I didn't expect this. Wasn't ready for it. Feck, I'll never be ready for this. It's one thing to know she's out there somewhere, along with Mac. It's another thing to have to face her.

Feck, feck, feck.

I paste on a mask, turn around and begin the pretending game.

"And you're Rainey Lane," I say. Same beautiful blond hair as her daughters, even though they were both adopted. Same pretty demeanor: classy feminine Deep South. She's walking around in chilly, gloomy-ass late afternoon Dublin, dressed like somebody's going to care she's color-coordinated and accessorized. I guess Jack Lane does. Unlike most married folks I've seen—not that I've seen a lot—they seem to be crazy about each other. I saw them in Alina's photo albums. I saw them in Mac's. I've seen pictures of this woman holding her daughters when they were small. I've pored over photos of her beaming at their sides when they were grown.

Like she's beaming at me now.

Like she doesn't know I killed her daughter. I guess she doesn't. I guess the last time Mac talked to her was before she found out it was me that took Alina to that alley to die.

For a second I get this stupid vision of how she'd be looking at me right now if she knew, and it kicks the breath right out of my lungs and leaves me standing there dumb. I have to clamp down all my insides so I don't puke. She'd hate me, despise me, stare at me like I was the most disgusting, horrible thing on the face of the Earth. She'd probably try to claw my face off.

Instead of this . . . this . . . mom-love-bullshit thing glowing in her eyes like I'm her daughter's best friend or something, not her other daughter's murderer. I thought Mac was the worst thing I'd have to face one day on these streets.

I'm smothered in a hug before I can dodge it, which shows how discombobulated I am. On a good day I can dodge raindrops! I forget myself for a sec, because she's got soft mom arms and hair and a neck you want to cling to. Worries melt on mom bosoms. She smells good. I'm enveloped in a cloud that's part perfume, part something she baked lingering on her clothes, and part some indefinable thing I think are mother-hormones that a woman's skin doesn't smell like until she's raised babies. It all combines to make one of the best scents in the world.

After my mom was dead and Ro took me to the abbey, I used to whiz by the house every couple days. I'd go into Mom's bedroom to smell her on her pillow. She had a yellow pillowcase embroidered with little ducks along the edges like my favorite pajamas. One day the smell was just gone. Every vestige of it vanished without a trace. Not one tiny little sniff left for my supersniffer. That's the day I knew she was never coming back.

"Get off me!" I eject myself violently from her embrace and back away, scowling at her.

She beams like one of Ryodan's supercharged flash-lights.

"And stop beaming at me! You don't even know me!"

"Mac told me so much about you that I feel like I do."

"Well that's just stupid on your part."

"I read the latest *Dani Daily*. Jack and I hadn't heard of those bugs. You've been doing a wonderful job keeping everyone informed. I bet that's a lot of work for you."

"So?" I say suspiciously. I hear a "but" coming.

"But you really don't need to anymore, honey. You can relax and let the adults take over."

"Yeah, right. Weren't adults in charge when the walls fell? And haven't they been in charge since? Doing a real bang-up job, aren't you all?"

She laughs, and the sound is music to my ears. Mom laughter. Melts me like nothing else can. Guess because I heard it so rarely from my own. I think I made my mom laugh three times. All before I "transported" for the first time. Maybe it happened once or twice after that. I tried. I'd memorize funny things I saw on TV while she was gone. I'd watch musicals, learn cheery songs. Nothing I did was right. Rainey Lane is looking at me with more approval than my mom ever did.

"Go. Away. No, wait. Don't. You can't be out here alone. I'll find somebody to take you back wherever you go. What are you doing walking around Dublin alone? Don't you know nothing? There's all kinds of monsters in the streets! It's going to be dark soon!" Somebody needs to knock some sense into her.

"Aren't you the sweetest, to worry about me? But you don't need to. Jack's just around the corner, parking, honey. There's too much debris in the streets to park any closer. I keep telling Mr. Ryodan he needs to clean up outside his club but he hasn't gotten around to it yet. I suppose we may have to help him out with that. He's a busy man, you know, a lot on his plate."

"Crime *is* time-consuming, isn't it?"

She laughs and I get my first suspicion she might just be totally clueless. "Aren't you funny? Mr. Ryodan a criminal. That nice man." She shakes her head, smiling like I'm just the funniest thing. Yep, clueless. "Dani, honey, I've been hoping to run into you. Mac has been, too. Why don't you come have dinner with us tomorrow night?"

Yeah, right. Skewered Dani on the menu, served up with a side of veggies. Not. Would all three of them take turns beating me to death, once Mac ratted me out?

"There are some people I'd love for you to meet. There's a wonderful new organization in the city that's been doing fabulous things, bringing about some real changes."

I shoot a big, melodramatic, beleaguered look at the heavens, then back at her. "You can't be talking about WeCare. Please tell me you're not talking about We-Care."

"Why, yes, I am. You've heard of us!" She's beaming again.

"Us? Gah! Please tell me you're not part of them! You can't be part of them! Do you know they hate me?"

"No we don't. WeCare doesn't hate anyone. We're all about rebuilding and helping. Whatever gave you that idea?"

"We." She's slaying me. Is Mac part of them, too? "Dude, like, maybe the way they copied my paper, took over my posts, and printed all kinds of lies about me."

"I happen to know for a fact that top individuals at WeCare are eager to meet you. They think as much of you as Mac does."

Gee, great, so they want me dead, too. Top individuals. Lovely. They can get in line behind Christian. Who's behind the Unseelie princes.

"They think you could be a tremendous asset. I think so, too."

I give her a look. "You might want to recheck your facts. I think you're missing a few. Folks in charge of organizations don't consider me an asset. Never have, never will." I hate organizations. Folks got to be free, able to breathe, and make up their own minds about stuff, not be fed a party line. Ritual numbs the brain. Repetition is grass for sheep.

"Mrs. Lane, so nice to see you again," Ryodan says, and I almost fall over. Not only didn't I hear him approach us, he's being polite. Ryodan is never polite.

I squinch up my face, studying him. "Dude, you feeling okay?"

"Never better."

"Why are you, like, pretending to be nice?"

"Mr. Ryodan is always nice. He was a lovely host while we stayed at Chester's."

"You didn't *stay* at Chester's, you were *hostages*." What is wrong with everyone that they can't see things for what they are?

"He and his men were keeping us safe, Dani. The *Sinsar Dubh* was targeting people Mac loved."

"Was the door to your room locked? Dude, that makes you a hostage," I say.

"Our door was never locked."

Huh? "Yeah, but did you even know how to get out? He's got those tricky panels."

"Mr. Ryodan showed Jack and me both how to operate the doors."

Huh? "Yeah, but there were guards outside. Keeping you in."

"For our protection. We were free to come and go. We chose to stay. The city was dangerous when the Book was loose. Jack and I are very grateful for Mr. Ryodan's help during those difficult times."

I scowl at Ryodan, who's wearing a smug-ass smile. He probably worked some kind of spell on them, like the kind of thing he did to me in the Hummer when he forced me to take the candy bar from him by muttering strange words. He makes people puppets. Empty-headed slaves. Not me.

"Do you know he's forcing me to work for him by holding Jo hostage?" I tell Rainey. She needs to wake up and smell the coffee.

"You mean that lovely young waitress? I've seen the way she looks at him. She's crazy about him," Rainey says.

And that pisses me off even more. Mac's mom can tell Jo's stupid crazy about this psychopath just by looking at her? Gah! Just gah! On top of it all, said psychopath has Rainey so fooled there's no point in even talking to her anymore! Not that lack of a point would shut me up. "Do you know he has private clubs under Chester's where—"

"I just spoke with Barrons," Ryodan cuts me off. "Mac's on her way to meet you, Mrs. Lane. She should be here any second now."

I give him a suspicious look. He's probably lying. And he knows perfectly well I won't risk finding out.

Rainey gives me a warm smile. "Dani, she'll be so glad to see you! She's been looking for you for weeks."

I'm sure she has.

I lock down my mental grid to freeze-frame, make like folks on *Gunsmoke* and get the feck out of Dodge.

TWENTY-FIVE

"I don't know who he is behind that mask"

"What are you doing."

"Why do you care?" I got belligerence stuck in my craw and I don't even know why. Sometimes just standing next to Ryodan makes me feel that way.

"Because if there's no point in what you're doing, you're wasting my time."

"Dude, got eyes? I'm collecting evidence." Finally! I been trying to get out for a second look at the exploded scenes for just about fecking ever but things keep coming up, like me almost getting killed. Oh, and me almost getting killed again. There's never a dull moment in the Mega-verse. The Ice Monster would freak me out a lot more if my world hadn't been jam-packed with monsters of all kinds since pretty much my birth: big, small, human, not.

"In Ziploc bags."

"I think they're Glad."

"They look impartial to me."

I start to snicker then stop myself. This is Ryodan. I hate Ryodan. Lying deceitful dickhead. Tricking folks into thinking he's really nice so I look stupid. "Think my sword's unfrozen yet?"

"No."

I stoop and scoop. I know a thing or two about myself. I see a lot. But sometimes there are small things going on that even I miss. Ergo my impartial ziplocks. I'll fill one at each scene. Go deep into the frigid center of the exploded debris, scoop up handfuls of icy detritus, stuff it in, and label it all neat and tidy-like. Later, me and Dancer will sift through the ziplock bags and look for clues. I pull a Sharpie from my pocket and write on the white strip "Warehouse, North Dublin." Then I tuck it carefully away in a backpack slung over my shoulder. Collecting my ziplocks makes perfect sense to me.

"It doesn't make sense. You could examine the detritus thoroughly right here at the scene."

"Dude, do I ask you to explain yourself?"

"Kid, are you ever not prickly."

I root around in the rubble, making sure I got some of everything, keeping my back to him because sometimes looking at him is more than I can stand. "Sure. Like, when I'm not around a *prick*. We investigating or having a conversation all personal-like? 'Cause I got business to take care of today and you're wasting my time. It's going to be dark soon."

"Observations."

"I got two. The scene blew to smither-fecking-reens and everything's still cold."

"Give me something I can use."

"I wish I could, boss, but this is . . . well, this is a mess." I rock back on my heels, shove hair out of my face and look up at him. The sun's nearly level with the horizon, right behind his head, making this weird halo effect around his face—as if! I'm surprised he doesn't smell like brimstone. He probably has a red pitchfork and hides horns under his hair. Making it weirder, the sun's got a sparkly gold tint to it—thank you, fairies for changing everything in our world—and he looks—oh, who cares how he looks? Why am I even noticing?

I look away, focusing on my investigation. We got a Fae that appears out of a slit and arrives with a lot of fog. It ices everything in its path then disappears back into another slit. Sometime after that the scene explodes. But why? That's the big question. Why is it icing what it ices, and why does the scene explode afterward? And why does it take varying amounts of time for the different places to explode?

I feel the ground with my palm. It's freezing. There's a chill that hasn't dissipated. I wonder if it ever will. Might be kind of cool if it didn't. You could clear the ground, build a house and never need air-conditioning. It'd suck in the winter, though.

I survey the scene. Where the warehouse used to be are piles of crumbled bricks and mortar and splintered framing, with twisted girders from steel racking everywhere, some bent, some poking straight up at the sky. Chunks of Unseelie flesh are plastered to pretty much every—

I smack myself in the forehead. "Holy priceless collection of Etruscan snoods, they're not moving!" I exclaim.

There's a choking noise over my head somewhere. "Etruscan snoods?"

I glow quietly inside. Some accomplishments mean more than others. I am officially the Shit. Now and forever. "Dude, watch your question marks. I just pried one out of you."

"I have no idea what you're talking about."

"Admit it, you lost your eternal fecking composure."

"You have an obsession with a delusion about how I end my sentences. What the fuck are Etruscan snoods?"

"Dunno. It's just another of Robin's sayings. Like, 'Holy strawberries, Batman, we're in a jam!'"

"Strawberries."

"Or, 'Holy Kleenex, Batman, it was right under our nose and we blew it!'"

There's another choking noise above my head. I could go on for hours.

"Check out this one, it's one of my faves! 'Holey rusted metal, Batman! The ground. It's all metal. It's full of holes. You know, holey.'" I snicker. Gotta love the dudes that wrote Batman. They had to sit around cracking themselves up all the time. "Or, 'Holy crystal ball, Batman, how did you see that coming?'" I look up at him.

He's staring at me like I have three heads.

The truth dawns on me. "Holy prostrate rugs, you lied! You've never even *read* Batman, have you? Like not one single issue. You never even watched an episode on TV! That was, like, your only redeeming quality and it wasn't even true. You been pretending we're superhero partners and you don't even know the first thing about Robin!" No wonder Ryodan's no fun to hang with. I'm so disgusted I can't stand it!

I skirt my irritation and get back to the important stuff. "The Unseelie parts are motionless. Dead as the humans. Look at them. Unseelie don't die. Nothing but my sword and Mac's spear kill them that dead. Unseelie are immortal. You can slice and dice them with human weapons, and the pieces will flop around forever. These ain't flopping. This thing is killing them dead. And we never even noticed." Preconceptions. They trip you up every time. When something explodes, you expect to see dead things. Maybe there's something to my idea it's after folks' life force. Kind of like the Shades, sucking them empty but instead of leaving husks, it leaves the whole shell of their bodies iced. "And notice something else: none of the pieces, human or Unseelie, are rotting. Why is that?"

"I'll be damned."

"I know, right?"

"And you didn't notice this before."

I glare at him. "You didn't either. And I tried to re-check scenes twice but you made me sit in your office while you did paperwork. The third time I was thinking about rechecking a scene, I stumbled on a fresh one and almost got exploded myself." I stand up and walk away to get a good bird's-eye view of the destruction. I pull out the new phone I grabbed to replace the one I smashed and snap a couple pictures. "So," I say crossly, "where to next?"

As we head for the church where I almost died, I realize Ryodan's been keeping me so busy asking the questions he wants answered that I never get around to asking any questions I want answered. "So, what happened to me when I got frozen that night? When I came to, Dancer was there with you and Christian. Talk about unexpected. How'd Dancer get there? Who saved me?"

"I got you out of the church or you would have died right there on the floor."

"You're the one who took me into the church to begin with and didn't warn me what would happen if I touched something. You're *why* I almost died, dude. So, who saved me?"

"I had to take you out slow or you would have had afterdrop."

"Yeah, but did Dancer tell you about afterdrop? 'Cause that sounds like something he would know."

"Why did you laugh right before you lost consciousness."

"Death's an adventure. I lived big. Rigor mortis makes your face stick. So, who knew how to thaw me?"

"Death's an insult."

"At least an affront," I agree. "Think my sword's un-frozen yet? Maybe we should go check."

"You're too young to laugh when you're dying. And no. I don't think your sword is unfrozen. Focus."

"Ain't too young for nothing."

"In some societies that would be true. Different places. Different times. You'd be old enough to be a wife and mother."

"That's a horrible thought. So, Dancer saved me."

"I didn't say that."

"That's how I know. Maybe we could use hair dryers to melt the ice around my sword."

"You need to get rid of him. He's a liability. Forget about the fucking sword. I'm taking care of it."

I whirl on him, fists at my waist. "He's an asset! He's my best friend! You don't know nothing about Dancer!"

" 'Nothing' is the key word there. Because that's what he is. Nothing. He's just human."

"Bull-crikey, Dancer's the Shit!"

"He wears glasses. I bet that works out real well for him in battle. No, wait, he doesn't battle. Never will. Too fragile. One poke with a sharp stick and his guts would spill all over the street. Sayonara, human."

"His guts aren't spilling anywhere. He's supersmart and . . . and . . . and he's super, *super*smart—"

"What the fuck kind of name is Dancer, anyway."

"—and he can build anything. He made my Shade-grenades and he made me this net of lights that charges just off me moving, and it totally outperforms the MacHalo! Besides, all Batman had was a cool costume and the best toys and the smartest ideas, and everybody knows he's the greatest superhero of all time! Besides, I'm just human, too."

All the sudden Ryodan's standing one inch away from me, hand under my chin, holding my face up to his.

"You'll never be just anything. A tsunami can never be 'just' a wave."

"Get off my chin."

"I like that about you. Waves are banal. Tsunamis reshape the Earth. Under the right circumstances, even entire civilizations."

I blink.

"You're going to be one hell of a woman one day, Dani."

I never knew my jaw was flexible enough to hit the pavement. My arms aren't even long enough to pick it back up. Catch flies in it, my butt, you could drive a truck in my mouth right now. Did Ryodan just, like, compliment me? Has hell frozen over? Are birds flying backward? It makes me so uncomfortable in my own skin, I feel like skinning myself. A three-quarter moon is behind his head, and his face is all shadows. "Fecking-A, dude, I know that. Everybody knows that. I'm the Mega. As in, short for 'Alpha and O.'" I shrug him off me and push past him.

He laughs. "You might have to fight somebody else for that title."

"Get a move on," I say crossly. I'm so behind on work I can't stand it. "You only got me for a limited time tonight. I need to get a *Daily* out. Folks need to know about the Iceman." I lock down my grid and slip into freeze-frame.

"You're going to get the boy killed one day, Dani," Ryodan says behind me.

"Rot in purgatory, dude. Batman never dies. Dancer won't either."

When we arrive at the church, I roll my eyes.

Five Seelie are standing in front of the demolished cathedral, amid rubble, shredded hymn books with pages everywhere like they rained down from heaven, chunks of organ, and miscellaneous debris. "Think my sword's unfrozen yet?" I say, making a fist around the empty space where my sword hilt should be. I see sifting Fae, and all I can think of is how I don't have my sword. 'Course, I have that thought pretty much every other second anyway.

"Kid, you're a broken record."

"Well, it might be."

The Seelie are talking, and although they know we're here, they completely ignore us. I ignore them, too. Despite them being so beautiful I have to pry my eyeballs off their faces. I'm not making the same mistake I made with V'lane. Getting sucked in by how gorgeous they are. Thinking they're any different than the Unseelie. Just because they're gold and velvet and iridescent-eyed and hunky. Christian's hunky too. He keeps dead women by his bed.

I'm feeling major juice coming from at least one of them but they're muting it. That worries me. Fae don't mute themselves unless they're up to no good, trying to pretend to be something they're not to make us less worried when we should be really, really worried. "Fecking Fae. I wish they'd all just go away."

"Then what would we do for excitement."

I snicker. He's got a point. I pull out my phone and snap a picture of the scene, planning to get my ziplock out next, skirt the fairies and go to work.

All the sudden there's a disturbance in the air in front of me. It takes a sec for the dust to settle in my brain. One of the Fae just tried to sift over to me to do who knows what. Ryodan beat it to its destination and they collided. The Fae looks like a pissed cat, eyes narrowed, spine twitching, iridescent eyes flashing fire. I've seen this one in Chester's. He has a taste for human women and the stupid sheep are nuts about him, with his tight leather pants and open shirts and sleek golden hair and skin.

Ryodan's standing between it and me, legs spread, arms folded. He's a mountain. Nothing's getting past him that he doesn't want past him. It pisses me off I need him there. With my sword, no Fae would dare bum-rush me! I'm used to more respect than this. This bites.

The Fae says all stiff-like, "His highness does not permit his likeness to be captured in small human boxes. The runt will give me the box."

Runt? *Moi?* I'm at least five-foot-three with my tennis shoes on! "I'm not a runt. I'm young and still growing. And we call them cameras, dickhead."

"Whose highness," Ryodan says.

"Ours. Yours. All he suffers to live. Give me the box or the runt dies."

"You just try," I say. "Better fairies than you have. Worse ones, too. They all tasted delicious. With catsup. And mustard. And a side of onion rings."

"Should have left it at catsup," Ryodan says. "Less is more sometimes, kid." To the Fae, he says, "Queen Aoibheal."

"Was never our true queen. She is gone. We have a new leader. Our sacred light, King R'jan."

"The Fae are matriarchal," Ryodan says.

"Were. We have decided it is time for a new rule. If not for the flaws of a woman, so many of our race would not have died, and still be dying. If not for her idiocy, the abominations would not have been freed. She was not even Fae," he sneers. "She began her life as one of you! The indignity of it, to have been ruled by a mortal masquerading—"

"Enough, Velvet," R'jan says. "We do not explain ourselves to humans. Kill the runt and bring me the box."

"I'm not a runt." My hand closes where my sword hilt used to be.

"Missing something, runt?" one of the courtiers standing with the new "king" says and they all laugh. Guess everybody has seen the fecking Wanted posters. I take a mental snapshot of its face and mark it for death. Someday, somewhere, fairy.

Velvet was just getting started airing his grievances. "She forced us to grant humans rights to which they were never entitled. No more. It is a new rule. A new age. We are no longer weakened by a weak queen."

"I said 'enough,'" R'jan says. "If I must tell you again it will be the last thing you hear for ten thousand years. You will not enjoy where you pass them."

I give R'jan a conspiratorial wink. "You going to give him a 'time out,' dude?"

Velvet looks horrified. "If you are fool enough to address King R'jan, you will do it thus and in no other manner! 'My King, Liege, Lord, and Master, your servant begs you grant it leave to speak.'"

"Wow. Totally delusionary there."

"Good luck with that," Ryodan says. "She doesn't beg to speak, or do anything else. You can lock her up, down, and sideways and it's never going to happen."

I beam at him. I had no idea he thought so highly of me.

Then he's gone. So is Velvet.

I stand there a little uncertain because Ryodan didn't telegraph a single intention before he and the Fae disappeared. I'm not even sure who took who. Or if one took off and the other chased. All I know is both of them are gone.

I shift from foot to foot, looking at R'jan and his remaining three cohorts, and he looks at me and I try to think of something to say. Best I come up with is: "So, why are you guys here, anyway?"

"Kill the runt," R'jan says.

I yank out two candy bars and cram them in my mouth, wrapper and all, and give them a superstrength chew that makes the wrapper explode so I can swallow some chocolate and get a rush fast, because I've got no sword and who the feck knows where Ryodan went. I crunch, swallow, spit out the wrappers, and lock down my grid to freeze-frame when all the sudden Ryodan's back.

He's standing right in front of R'jan.

"In these streets," he says so cool-like I almost expire from the sheer coolness of it, "*I'm* King, Liege, Lord, and Master. You are the 'it.'"

Then he dumps Velvet's dead body at his feet.

TWENTY-SIX

"It's the hard-knock life"

"You did me a favor. Velvet was an annoyance," R'jan says. "He spoke too often and too much, saying little of consequence."

Ryodan looks at the king's remaining courtiers and says, "I'll do you three more 'favors.' Just say the word. Wrong one or right one. Doesn't matter to me."

The courtiers sneer at him. Uneasily. We might have postured for hours and never gotten to the position of strength Ryodan established with a single action. I'm learning from him. I'd never tell him that, though.

R'jan opens his mouth then closes it, not entirely sure Ryodan didn't just say that he was going to kill the other three courtiers if he said even one more word. Smart dude. I'm not sure Ryodan didn't mean that, too. How the feck did he kill Velvet? I study the Fae corpse but see no obvious wounds. No cuts or . . . wait a minute, is that a few drops of blood on his shirt? I sidle left for a better view but Ryodan moves like there's a tether between us, conveniently blocking it. I got no doubts he left so I wouldn't know. He's so fecking secretive!

Does he have my sword somewhere? Did Mac loan him the spear? Never! Obviously he's got some other weapon that kills Fae, and I want it. The prick. He's been holding out on me big-time. When I lost my sword he could have given me whatever he just used. I'm so pissed I could spit. He knows how to kill Fae. No wonder he's so fearless. He's faster than me, stronger, and has a Fae-killing weapon. I pine for the days I was the biggest, baddest superhero in town!

Abruptly, I got graphic sex images in my brain! I'm hot and uncomfortable in my jeans. Bugger it all! R'jan is a prince, a death-by-sex Fae. He's the one I sensed muting himself so as not to draw attention to his little entourage, but now that the crap's hitting the fan, he's going to use any weapon at his disposal. I guess he figures to mess me up to get to Ryodan.

But R'jan is staring at Ryodan like he expects it to be working on him. Huh? I thought they were hetero and their killer eroticism only worked on the opposite sex. I realize that was a stupid assumption. It's just that I never saw the Unseelie princes around men and V'lane always kept it muted around humans. There's no reason, whatever the mechanism, that it wouldn't work on both genders.

"On your knees, human." R'jan tosses his golden mane imperiously. "You will crawl before your king."

Ryodan laughs. "Is that all you've got."

I hang back, listening, not about to get closer. It's all I can do to not start stripping. Aw, bugger, I am! My coat's on the ground and I'm pulling up my shirt! I make a sound of protest but it doesn't come out like that at all.

"Turn it off," Ryodan says without even looking at me. "You're distressing Dani. No one distresses Dani but me."

"I said 'kneel,'" R'jan says, like he can't believe Ryodan is still standing there.

"And I said 'fuck you.' Turn it off or die."

R'jan cuts it off so suddenly I'm shivering, cold and

miserable, like I was just sunning by a pool then got an iceberg dropped on me.

"Why are you here," Ryodan says.

R'jan says tightly, "What the fuck are you?"

Darn good question. I wonder it myself.

"If you answer me wrong one more time, your death." He kicks Velvet's lifeless body.

R'jan grimaces. Unlike Unseelie, Seelie expressions make sense to me. They're similar to ours, I guess because they've spent so much time preying on us. "Something is killing our people."

"I didn't know you counted the Unseelie as yours."

"It has visited . . . places other than Dublin. It has killed Seelie, too."

"It's been in Faery."

"Twice. How dare an abomination enter our realm? Never has an Unseelie been suffered in Faery!"

The temperature drops and I tense, searching for a shimmer in the air. It was already colder near the church than in the rest of Dublin, but now the pages of the hymnals scattered around the street glisten with a thin sheen of ice. I see Ryodan looking around, too. Snow starts to fall. I realize R'jan's temper is doing it at the same time Ryodan does. I brush snow off my bare shoulders, then I jerk, embarrassed. I was so riveted by stuff happening that I didn't realize I'm only wearing my bra. I scoop up my clothes and yank my shirt over my head. I hate Fae.

To R'jan, I say, "Cruce lived in Faery for hundreds of thousands of years and you guys never figured it out. There's an Unseelie in Faery for you, sitting right next to your queen. Wait!" I snicker. "I forgot. She wasn't your queen either. She was human. Dudes, stupid much?"

"I will speak with you," R'jan says to Ryodan, "when you make the runt be silent."

I puff myself up, waiting for Ryodan's defense.

"Be quiet, kid."

I deflate.

"You're certain it's Unseelie," Ryodan says to R'jan.

"*I* said it was," I say indignantly.

"Unequivocally."

"Like, I even used that exact word!"

"What is this 'abomination?'" Ryodan says.

"We do not know. We have never needed to know about our foul brethren."

"Yet you're worried enough about it that you're here. In a dark Dublin street. The new king of the Seelie himself."

It seems to mollify R'jan to hear himself called the new king of the Seelie. He looks away and doesn't say anything for a second. Then he shivers. "It brings final death to our kind."

"Like the spear and the sword," I say.

"I told you to shut her up."

"Answer her."

"She cannot understand what it is to be Fae."

Ryodan doesn't say a word. He takes one step forward and R'jan immediately takes one step back all smooth, like they're doing a choreographed dance.

"One day, human—"

"You might want to rethink what you're calling me."

"—I will crush you beneath my heel and—"

"Until that fictitious day, you will answer me when I speak." He steps over Velvet's body, closing the distance between them.

R'jan steps back.

"How does 'final death' differ from what the sword does," Ryodan says.

"Your puny brains were not fashioned to grasp the greatness of being D'Anu."

Ryodan crosses his arms, waiting. Dude's got some

serious presence. I want to be like him when I grow up. "You'll have no brain at all in three seconds. Two."

R'jan says tightly, "The spear and sword end immortal life. They sever the connection that binds our matter together and scatter it to the wind."

"Tell me something I don't know."

"Even if we die, that of which we are fashioned is still out there, blowing. We feel all our kindred through all time, impressions in the fabric of the universe. We are individual yet a skein, vast and glorious. You cannot know what it is to belong to such an enormous, divine entity. This . . . this . . . thing . . . whatever it is, is pruning our tree. It does more than merely unbind our matter. It scatters nothing to the wind. *Nothing*. It is as if those it takes have never been. Its victims are . . . erased. You cannot begin to perceive how painful that is for us. Death, even by the sword and spear, leaves us connected. This abomination is amputating our race, limb by limb!"

The Ice Monster is stripping away Fae existence on the deepest level. There's something to my "life force" theory!

"You have strong incentive to see it stopped."

I interpret R'jan's expression as a royal "Duh."

"Which makes it worth a lot to you."

R'jan gives him an incredulous look. "You could not hope to terminate it nor do I barter with pigs and fools."

"I will terminate it. You will pay me handsomely for services rendered when and how I choose to invoice you. And, one day, you will kneel before me and swear your fealty. At Chester's. Before an audience of Fae."

"We could do fireworks," I say excitedly.

"Never," R'jan says.

"I'm a patient man," Ryodan says.

* * *

I think about that later, as we dig through the rubble, fill my ziplock and tuck it into my backpack. I munch a candy bar to make more room in my bag. "You're not patient. You zero in on something and lock on like a missile. You're the most pushy, manipulative person I know. And I knew Rowena."

"Patience and persistence aren't mutually exclusive. You have no idea how patient I am. When I want something."

"What does somebody like you want? More power? More toys? More sex?"

"All of the above. All the time."

"Greedy bugger."

"Kid, let me tell you something. Most people spend their short time in this world less than half alive. They wander through their days in a haze of responsibility and resentment. Something happens to them not long after they're born. They get conflicted about what they want and start worshipping the wrong gods. Should. Mercy. Equality. Altruism. There's nothing you *should* do. Do what you want. Mercy isn't Nature's way. She's an equal opportunity killer. We aren't born the same. Some are stronger, smarter, faster. Never apologize for it. Altruism is an impossible concept. There's no action you can make that doesn't spring from how you want to feel about yourself. Not greedy, Dani. Alive. And happy about it every single fucking day."

"Are we done here yet? I got a paper to get out." I roll my eyes when I say it so he doesn't see how much what he just said got to me. I think it might be the smartest thing I ever heard anyone say. "Hey, you think my sword's—"

"For fuck's sake *no*."

"Geez, dude. Just asking."

* * *

We stop by two more scenes in Dublin that got iced, first the fitness center, then one of the small underground pubs. It's a gaping hole in the pavement, with chunks of concrete listing in at dangerous angles. There's nobody around to cordon it off and make sure wandering kids don't fall in. Fortunately there aren't as many wandering kids as there were right after Halloween. We've gotten most of them off the streets. Some of them refused to come in, chose to go underground instead. Got to respect that. It sucks being taken pity on by someone else's family, knowing you're not really part of it. I wonder how wild they'll be in a few years. I can't wait to see what they become. I think in a few years they'll make a heck of an army. Growing up alone makes you tough.

Until the walls fell, I never knew there were so many places beneath Dublin. I used to think there were only a few underground rivers, a couple of crypts like the ones at Christ Church and St. Patrick's, and maybe the occasional cellar. Dublin keeps a lot of secrets. Since the walls came down, I've discovered all kinds of places down under. We Irish are a canny lot, we like multiple ways out of a tight spot. And why shouldn't we? Look at how many folks have tried to be the boss of us, and for how long!

I peer into the rubble-filled hole. "Dude, how am I going to get my ziplock?"

"Boss, we got a problem."

I glance over my shoulder. One of Ryodan's men is standing there, looking pissed. It's a dude I don't often see. I've never heard anyone say his name. I think of him as Shadow because he glides into rooms barely disturbing the air. You almost overlook him, which is a feat considering he's a foot and a half taller than me and got to be three hundred pounds. Watches everything like me. Doesn't speak much, unlike me. Tall and muscled like the rest of them, scarred like the rest of them, hair like night and eyes like whiskey in a glass.

"Listening."

"Fucking half-breed Highlander took the sword."

"What?" I explode. "Christian took my sword? I told you and *told* you it was probably unfrozen! I kept saying that we needed to go check! What the feck is wrong with you dudes? Can't you guard a measly little sword from a measly little half-human?"

Shadow gives me a look. "He's damn-near full Unseelie prince and he had a flamethrower, kid." To Ryodan, he adds, "Lor and Kasteo are badly burned."

A fecking flamethrower! Why didn't *I* think of that? Best I came up with was a measly hair dryer. I need to start thinking on grander scales! I return the look. I'm so pissed off my head is mean with pure pissed-offedness. "You don't understand, when I was in his bed, I found a dead woman stuffed between it and the wall! Now he wants *me* dead and you let him get my sword! What am I supposed to do now? Ryodan won't share whatever the feck weapon he has! How am I supposed to protect myself? Can't you guys do anything right? One little sword! That's all you had to watch over! And why didn't *we* think of a flamethrower? Anybody got a brain among you dudes? Flamethrower! Brilliant! Did it hurt my sword?"

"When were you in Christian's bed," Ryodan says softly.

I gape. "Dude, you got a serious case of selective hearing, the kind that bleeps out all the important stuff! Who cares when I was in his stupid bed? How the feck did you kill Velvet? You been holding out on me! You need to learn to share your weapons!"

"When."

There's something in the way he utters that single word that makes me shiver, and I'm hard to rattle. "So,

I didn't change in a convenience store! So, shoot me! I need my sword. What are you going to do to get it back?"

I've never seen Ryodan's face go so smooth. It's like it got iced blank of all expression. I've never heard him talk so soft and silky either. "Take her back to Chester's and lock her down. I'll get the sword."

Shadow looks grim. Like my own personal grim reaper. Not.

I slip a hand into my pocket. Pull the pin on a grenade. Start counting because I got to time it just right. I'm not getting locked down anywhere. No more cages for Dani Mega O'Malley. A split second before it goes off, I lob the bomb to the pavement in front of them. It detonates with the brilliant, Shade-killing flash of light Dancer rigged up for me. "My ass, you will."

I freeze-frame out of there with everything I've got.

TWENTY-SEVEN

*"'Cause I'm one step closer to the edge
and I'm about to break"*

I think I set a personal best.

I had a lot of incentive. The look on Ryodan's face was like nothing I've ever seen. Worse than when I killed all those Fae in Chester's and he locked me in his dungeon. Way worse.

While I'm freeze-framing, I think about how he's been screwing up my life since the sec he stepped foot on my water tower and told me he had a job for me. I think I got him figured out. I think the reason he's so pissy about both Christian and Dancer is because he's worried I'll get a superhero boyfriend who will kick his ass from one end of Dublin to the other and tear up that nasty little contract he made me sign. He doesn't want any other dudes too close to me because it would interfere with his ability to use me for his own purposes. Christian's a physical competitor. Dancer could brainiac him dead.

He doesn't get that I'm not interested in a superhero boyfriend.

I'm going to *be* the superhero that can kick his ass from one end of Dublin to the other.

"Oh, sweet fecking day," I sigh raptly around a mouthful of chocolate, anticipating it. Peanuts and chocolate get stuck in my throat and I almost can't swallow. I been eating too many candy bars lately because I'm on the go so much and it's all I got handy. I'm having a major salt craving. Sometimes when I eat too much sugar I start obsessing about my mom's corned beef and cabbage with her fresh rosemary bread and potatoes and chives and— Holy Ashleagh Falls, my mouth is watering!

I whiz into a grocery store. Empty. I head north three blocks to Paddy's Stop 'n' Go. Empty. I dash ten blocks south to Porter's. Also completely cleaned out. What I wouldn't give for a bag of chips! Useless for an energy punch but a hopping St. Patty's Day Parade on the tongue! I'm practically drooling I'm so hungry for something besides chocolate. A can of beans. Crimeny, even tuna would cheer me up!

I get over it. Wasted energy. There *is* no other food right now, and one thing I learned in a cage is you either pretend you have what you want or you don't think about it. And if you pretend, make it real, milk it for every nuance, every succulent taste, scent, touch. I don't have time for that kind of indulgence right now. I got a crazy Unseelie prince gunning for me with my own sword. I got a nutty nightclub owner out there who thinks he has a point to make with me and wants to lock me up to do it. I got a bloodthirsty ex–best friend who's after my ass. I got an Ice Monster killing all kinds of innocents.

I can deal with the first three. Dublin needs to know about the last one!

I got several places in the city I can print a daily. It won't take Ryodan long to find them all, so I know I don't have much time. If I can print off even just a thousand and get them up, word will spread fast. Then I'll get down to the business of figuring out how to get my sword back from Christian.

I head for the old Bartlett Building on the south side of the river Liffey, whizzing over Ha'Penny Bridge, freeze-framing parallel to the water. Stars are twinkling on it, ice crystals on a silver slide. It's all kissed with the new lavender-metallic shade the Fae brought with them.

A few seconds later I blast in through double doors, dump my backpack on a table, and fire up the presses, blowing on my hands to warm them. I set up my little miniprinter and hook up my phone to print out the photos I been taking all day. My hands are clumsy with cold. I think the Iceman is starting to screw up our weather or something. Usually in May we run a low of forty, high of sixty. And I run hotter because, well, I *run* everywhere. But I been cold all day. Feels like no more than twenty-five or thirty outside right now. I wish this place had a fireplace like Mac has at Barrons Books & Baubles. I been avoiding that part of town for weeks. Can't stand the thought of seeing her coming and going, knowing I'm dead to her. Knowing I'll never step foot inside BB&B again and laugh with her, feel like I fit somewhere. I wish I had a place like Mac has at Barrons Books & Baubles.

"Wishes. Horses. Fecking waste of time." I was alone a lot as a kid, and at night sometimes there was nothing on TV and the silence would get ten times as big as our house. I used to talk to myself to fill it up. I was scintillating, too, always up on the latest news and stuff because I was stuck in a cage watching it all the time. Maybe that's where I got my love of broadcasting it. I had so much to say and nobody to say it to. Now I got the whole city! I keep up a running monologue as I work on my rag, mostly venting my irritation with current circumstances.

I don't have time to write anything real entertaining, something I try hard to do whenever I put a *Dani Daily* out because any writer worth their salt knows you got

304 · KAREN MARIE MONING

to give folks bread and circuses along with the information they need to save their own asses. Otherwise they won't read it. There was this whole series on TV when I was nine about how to write and keep folks reading and I was riveted by it because I knew I'd be writing my memoirs one day.

I had no idea I'd start running a paper when I was still only thirteen and get a book published when I was fourteen!

The Dani Daily

**NEW MONSTER LOOSE
IN DUBLIN!!!!
The ICEMAN slays hundreds!!!
READ ALL ABOUT IT!**

**AND BY THE WAY I'M NOT DEFENSELESS.
DUDES, YOU THINK I'M DEFENSELESS, YOU
JUST TRY. BRING IT ON! I GOT ALL KINDS OF
SECRET WEAPONS UP MY SLEEVE!**

You heard it from me first and nobody else!

There's some kind of big, bad Unseelie loose in Dublin, icing folks to death. You hardly get any warning that it's about to be in your space. It's hit churches, pubs, gyms, warehouses, rural yards, and spots smack in the middle of the street. No place is off its grid! You got to watch for it real careful. At best, if you're paying close attention, you'll see a kind of shimmery spot in the air then a slit opens, fog spills out, and the monster comes. In like, just two seconds it ices everything in its path TO DEATH INSTANTLY then disappears.

Lie low, stay off the streets! I'll keep you posted, Dublin.

Oh, and if you stumble across one of its iced scenes,
steer clear—they explode!

"They're not worth it."

I just about squirt right out of my skin like a dab of toothpaste in a tube squeezed too tight. I expected Ryodan to find me first.

I freeze-frame.

And slam into Christian.

"I'm a full sifter now, lass. You'll never outrun me again. It was driving me bugfuck that you could get away from me. No more." His hands close on my waist and I try to twist free but it's like I got steel vises biting into my body, clamping down on bone. I look up at him. The faint outline of a torque is luminous at his neck. His eyes are iridescent fire. If insanity has a color, it's swirling in there.

"Humans," he says coldly, and his face is like chiseled ice. Pale against midnight hair. Brilliant tattoos rush up his neck, around his jaw, back down his body, a kaleidoscopic storm just beneath his skin. "Puny. Stupid. Frightened of their shadow. Why do you bother with them? Why waste your time? You're worth so much more than that."

"Dude. I *am* one. Give me my fecking sword. It ain't yours."

"No you're not. You're beyond human. You're what the race should aspire to be." He leans in, sniffs my hair and sighs. "Stay the fuck away from Ryodan. I bloody hate it when you smell like him. It turns my stomach."

I search my brain for a way out of this one. With my sword. Is it on him somewhere? I let my lids drift down, peek at his lower body. Don't want to telegraph. I don't see it anywhere. Jeans, hiking boots, cream fisherman's sweater that strains across shoulders way wider than they used to be. To support the wing structure he's developing? Does he miss who he was? Is that why he's dressed like this? No visible sign of any weapons on him anywhere, but then he's so far past needing a weapon. He *is* a weapon. There's blood all over his sweater. I don't even want to know why. "You're human, too, remember?" Obviously with some part of his brain he does. The Unseelie princes rarely wear clothing.

"Not anymore, Dani, my sweet darling. You know how I'm so sure? I'm a lie detector. I said, 'I'm human' and heard my own lie." He laughs, and there's madness in it.

"You are what you choose to be," I say. All the sudden I can't breathe because his hands have slipped up over my ribs and he's squeezing me so tight I think they're going to crack.

"I would NEVER have fucking chosen this!"

"Ow! Volume control, Christian! And you're hurting me!"

He releases his grip instantly. "Are you all right, lass? Are your ears bleeding? I made the last woman's ears bleed. Nose, too. And her . . . well, that's neither here nor there."

"Let me go. I got stuff to do."

"No."

"Look, if you're going to try to kill me, get it over with." I put both of my fists in front of my face. "Put up your dukes!"

He stares at me. "Why would I do that?"

"Hello—Mister I Keep Dead Women Stuffed Down the Side of My Bed!"

"I tried to explain that to you. You wouldn't listen. You ran away from me. Why did you run away from me? Don't I keep telling you I'll never hurt you?"

"Did you kill her?"

"No."

I give him a look. I don't need to be a lie detector to see through that one. It was there in the shifty slide of his eyes. "Try again."

"Fine. Okay. I killed her. But I didn't mean to. And I didn't *kill* her, kill her."

"Oh, I see. As long as you didn't *kill* her, kill her, then that's okay."

"I knew you'd understand," he says, like I'm not being totally facetious. I'm not sure he gets human nuances anymore. I think he's too far gone.

"All ears here."

He shrugs. "There's not much to tell. We were having sex and all the sudden she was dead."

"Just like that?"

"Just like. It was the bloody weirdest thing. I don't even know what I did."

"Your hands weren't, like, around her throat or holding a knife or anything?"

"No. That's why I kept her. I wanted to examine her to figure out what I did so I don't do it again. It's not like I can go without sex for the rest of my life. I can barely make it a few bloody hours. One second she was having a great time and so was I, and she was making this really hot noise while I was—sorry, you probably don't want to hear about that. I'm not trying to make you jealous, lass. Then she just wasn't moving and you have no idea how disturbing that was. Well, mostly. But not entirely. I think the Unseelie I'm becoming was aroused because once she stopped moving it was like—"

"Too much information! I can't hear you!" I start humming to tune him out. Jealous? What is he talking about?

"I got distracted and left her on the bed to look at later, then I found you bleeding to death and brought you back to my place. I didn't want you to see her and get upset. I was going to figure out what I did to her after you were gone."

"Did you?"

"Still no clue. There wasn't a mark on her anywhere. I thought I must have been too rough and bruised her from the inside, but if I did, you'd think there'd be external bruises somewhere, and there aren't any. Maybe you'd take a look at her. I've been considering an autopsy but I don't know any morticians. Do you?"

He asks it like it's a normal question. Like he's the person investigating a murder, not the one who committed it. "Nope." I wonder how crazy he is. "Does it bother you that you killed her?"

He looks aghast. "Of course it does! I don't want to kill anything. Well . . . actually that's not entirely true. I do want to kill things. Lots of things. Especially Ryodan lately. I can lose myself for hours in a soothing haze of murderous intent about that dickhead."

"Won't argue with you there," I commiserate.

"But I don't. At least I didn't until now. And if I can't figure out what I did this time, I can't stop myself from doing it in the future."

"Where's my sword." I say it like Ryodan, with no question mark at the end. I'm beginning to understand why he does it. It's a subtle demand instead of a question. Folks answer instinctively, against their better judgment. That's Ryodan, always playing the odds, stacking them in his favor.

Christian smiles and for a second I see a hint of who he was. Now that his face has completed most of the transition to Unseelie prince, his expressions are more readable. I guess the muscles aren't always at war, trying to shape a look. He has a dazzling smile, almost a killer smile, but not quite. It's the smile of a man who could get any woman he wanted into bed, but might just kill her while she's there.

"You have to admit, the flamethrower was bloody brilliant, wasn't it? I blasted the thing right out of the stalagmite and fried Ryodan's men. They didn't even think of it. Fucking idiots. You want something, take it."

"Did you hurt my sword? Wait a minute!" I realize something I can't believe it took me so long to realize. "You're not making me feel like I'm turning Pri-ya!"

"I figured out how to mute it. It's just as easy to turn back on. All I have to do is this."

Horniness slams into me, and I hear myself making

such an embarrassing sound I could die of embarrassment.

He keeps me from sinking to the pavement, physically holding me up, hands around my waist. "Lass, doona be looking up at me like that. On the other hand, do. Yes. Yes. Exactly like that. Princess, you're slaying me."

"Turn it off, Christian! I want to choose my first time!"

I collapse on the floor, blinking, dazed.

Christian is gone.

Without his hands holding me, I slumped in on myself like a wet cardboard box. I sit there, looking around but seeing nothing, trying to clear my head. Either he's completely gone or he's muting himself again. But the aftereffects linger.

His voice floats down from somewhere in the rafters above my head. "First time, is it now? I was fair certain, lass, but I like hearing it from you. I'll wait. I want you to choose your first time, too. It'll be chocolate and roses. Music and sweet kisses. Everything a lass dreams of. I want it to be perfect for you."

I turn beet red. Nobody, but *nobody* talks about my virginity but me! "Butt out of my virginity-losing plans! They're none of your business."

"They're my business and mine alone. But we don't have to talk about them. Yet."

I feel like I just got brained upside the head with a frying pan. Is he kidding me? Has Christian decided in his half-mad Unseelie prince mind that he's going to be, like, my boyfriend and be, like, my first? Dude, I'm fourteen and he's an Unseelie prince! And he's like ten years older than me! I open my mouth to read him the fecking riot act and set things straight between us when I think about how an Unseelie prince with a crush on me might not be an entirely bad thing to have, and close my mouth again. He might be tricky to handle but all weapons are good weapons, and Christian on a leash would be like, the ultimate weapon. Especially against Ryodan.

The question is: can I leash him? And if I manage to, will I be able to hang on to his collar when it counts?

I choose my words carefully. Prince and a lie detector to boot. If I can collar this dude, I can do anything! It'll be like dancing on a minefield. I'm fascinated by the prospect. What a way to test myself. "Thanks for understanding, Christian," I say.

"No problem. Well, it is. But I'll deal with it. For now."

"The other Unseelie princes scare me."

"They should. They're walking nightmares! You wouldn't believe some of the sick shit they do."

The irony that's lost on him isn't on me. One second he's aware of himself as Unseelie prince, the next he acts like he's the furthest thing from it. I don't say *Yes I would because, dude, you do sick stuff, too.* Casting aspersions won't win me any points. "I feel so unsafe without my sword." I squint up toward the ceiling. The Bartlett Building used to be an old warehouse before it was converted. They left the steel beams and girders exposed when they moved in. I don't see him up there anywhere.

Then he's in front of me, sweeping low in a formal bow.

"Your sword, my lady. I would have razed heaven and earth to get it back for you." He's holding it across both hands, presenting it to me. He looks at me and I look straight back, measuring the madness in his eyes. I feel moisture pressing at the corners of mine, like they're going to start bleeding. I pinch the bridge of my nose, hard. I can't stop staring at him. It's like his eyes are made of liquid silver on top of rainbows, like the kaleidoscopic tattoos beneath his skin run like a river at the bottom of them, like I could tumble in and dive down deep. I feel woozy.

"Don't look me straight in the eyes, lass. Stop it!" He chucks me under the chin, jarring me into breaking eye contact. He trails his fingers across my cheek and when his hand comes away bloody, he licks it. "Never look in my eyes too long. It hurts people." Then he smiles. "You'll notice I can touch the hallow. I worried I wouldn't be able to."

I look down at the Seelie hallow across his hands, one of four Fae talismans that only humans and those of the Light Court can touch. I could take it, drive the blade through his heart and be free of him forever.

I reach for my sword.

He pulls it back. "A little thanks might be nice."

"Christian, you're the Shit," I say. "First, you saved my life and now you're giving me back my sword when nobody else would even help me."

"Dickhead sure didn't."

"He sure didn't," I agree and reach for my sword again. "Nobody cares about me like you do."

"Och, lass, you've no bloody idea," he says in a near-whisper. "I see you from the inside."

"Can I have it now?" I want it so bad my palms itch.

He cocks his head and looks at me then swivels his head just like an Unseelie prince, like his head and neck aren't put together quite right. It gives me chills. "You wouldn't be thinking of killing me with it, now would you, lass?"

"Of course I would. But I'm not going to." Not right now, anyway.

His smile is blinding. "Good, because I have another gift for you tonight. I know you like to save humans, so I'm going to help you. You may consider it one of many early wedding gifts."

I blink. Huh? Either I manage to mask my astonishment or he doesn't even notice the look on my face, because he just keeps talking.

"The Unseelie princes know the thing that came through the slit at the warehouse. They called it Gh'luk-ra d'J'hai."

"What the heck does that mean?" Also, wedding gifts? Has he completely lost his marbles?

"It's hard to translate. Unseelie have forty-nine words for ice, and there's a nuance to d'J'hai I'm not sure I understand. Loosely, I'd call it the Hoar Frost King."

"The Hoar Frost King," I echo. "What is it? How do you kill it? Will the sword work?" Assuming anyone could even get close enough without freezing to death.

"I don't know. But I know a place where we might find out. If there are answers anywhere, they'll be there. Take the sword, lass. I don't like you being unprotected. And I know you don't want me hanging around all the time. Not that I blame you with the monster I'm becoming."

I reach for it with both hands. I almost can't contain myself. I'm trembling with excitement.

He leans in and lays the sword across my palms.

I close my eyes and sigh with ecstasy. The heft of cool steel in my hands is . . . well, better than I think sex must be! It's like having both arms amputated and thinking you'll have to learn to live without them, then getting them put back on completely fine again. I love my sword. I'm invincible with it. I don't know one fecking ounce of fear with this thing in my hands. Deep inside where my blood runs a little stranger than other folks', gears shift and slide back into perfect alignment. I am one with my blade. I'm complete.

"Och, and there's the woman you'll be one day," Christian murmurs. "Passion enough to rule an army. Not that I have one. Yet."

I might want an Unseelie prince on a leash but we

need to get one thing straight. "I ain't ever getting married."

"Who said anything about getting married?"

"Dude, early wedding gifts."

He looks at me like *I'm* nuts. "Who said anything about wedding gifts?"

"And I don't want an Unseelie army to rule."

"Army? Dani, my bonny will o' the wisp, what are you talking about? I was telling you about the Hoar Frost King. Are you coming or not? It's a fine night to be alive. We've a monster to catch." He winks at me. "And tonight it's not me."

Dude. Sometimes that's all you can say.

TWENTY-EIGHT

*"I walk up on high and I step to the edge
to see my world below"*

A good leader knows her world.
   I know nothing of my world.
   Well, that's not entirely true.

I know that 152 paces beyond where I stand looking out of Rowena's dressing room window there is a serene arbor of shaped topiary with a tiled pavilion, stone benches, and a reflecting pool that centuries-dead Grand Mistress Deborah Siobhan O'Connor built for meditation in times of turmoil. Far enough from the abbey to grant privacy, near enough to be used often, the silvery pool was long ago usurped by fat frogs on lily pads, and on a gentle summer night, in my old room three floors above Rowena's and two to the south, they charmed me to sleep with their lazy baritone *ah-uuups* for many years.

I know also that there are 437 rooms in the abbey, in common-knowledge use. I know of an additional twenty-three on the main floor alone, with more on the other three, and undoubtedly countless more of which I know nothing at all. The rambling fortress is a hive of concealed passageways and hidden panels, stones and floorboards and fireplaces that move, if you've the secret to their operation. Then there is the Underneath. That is how I have always seen the abbey: the Upstairs proper where sunshine glitters on windowpanes and we bake and clean and are normal women, and the Underneath where a dark city twists and turns, with passageways and catacombs and vaults, and the sweet Lord only knows what all. There, those of us in the Haven become something else sometimes, something ancient in our blood.

I know that a quarter of a mile behind the abbey is a barn with 282 stalls where cows and horses and pigs were once penned. I know a brisk walk beyond it is a dairy that housed forty-odd milk cows, with a chilled larder where we made butter and cream. I know that there are seventeen rows of five beds making eighty-five tiered vegetable garden beds behind the dairy that once grew enough to sustain the abbey's thousands of occupants plus more to sell in the village for a tidy sum.

All these things I know belonged to a different world.

The world I live in is no longer a world I know.

It is four-thirty in the morning. I pull my wrapper more closely around me and stare out the window at gnarled oaks casting long shadows, and moonbeams crisscrossing the lawn through latticed branches. My comforting view of the familiar shaped topiary is blocked by one of those dangerous aberrations of physics Mac calls Interdimensional Fairy Potholes; IFPs for short, an expedient abbreviation. This one has the funnel shape of a crystalline tornado and shines milky-lilac, its dull, faceted exterior reflecting the moonlight. In the light of day those pellucid facets are difficult to distinguish from the surrounding countryside, compounded by their extreme variations in shape, texture, and size. I have seen IFPs larger than our back field and smaller than my hand. This one is taller than a four-story building and as wide.

When first she told me her name for them, I laughed.

That was back when my family had recently been killed and I was drunk on freedom. For the first time in my life, when everyone around me felt anxious about the many new monsters on the loose, I felt gloriously, deliriously safe. My monsters were gone. They'd been trying to pry me from the abbey again, my mother evidencing a triumphant gleam in her eye at Sunday-supper-last, and I was certain she and Father had finally struck upon something Rowena wanted badly enough to give me up. For years, the diminutive Grand Mistress had commanded my blind devotion merely for standing bulwark between them and me.

IFPs are no longer a laughing matter. They never were. This one was discovered a week ago, heading straight for our abbey. We wasted days tracking its progress, trying to devise ways to divert it. Nothing worked. It is not as if an IFP can be blown off course with a giant fan. I am the leader of this enclave, yet I'm unable to do something so simple as protect it from being swallowed up by a fractured piece of Faery! The IFP is not even a sentient enemy. It is merely an accident of circumstance.

Then there are the sentient enemies I have to worry about. The thinking, coveting ones whose Upstairs never matches their Underneath, who are no doubt even now talking about the repository of endless knowledge and power the world now knows we have locked beneath our fortress, guarded by a snortingly inept 289 women ranging in age from seven all the way up to Tanty Anna, at one hundred and two.

These are my charges. Trusted to my care.

I see no end for them that does not involve their hapless slaughter!

I need more *sidhe*-seers. I need to strengthen our numbers.

Last night I gathered my girls around the IFP when it was a mere mile from the abbey. We'd plotted its course with ninety-nine percent certainty: it would enter our home. The only questions were how much of the south chapel next to Rowena's chambers would it instantly engulf, and would it raze every square inch of our abbey or leave the occasional pile of rubble, perhaps a glowing, red-hot wall standing here and there?

Given its rate of locomotion, it would take nearly an hour for it to complete its passage from end to end. We were able to plot the time and trajectory of its destruction so accurately because it had already left hundreds of miles of fine, sooty ash in its wake. Dirt fields were emblazoned with deep ruts of scorched earth. Large buildings were reduced to small mountains of post-apocalyptic embers.

A drifting crematorium, the IFP on a crash course with our abbey contained a fire-world fragment, a roaring inferno capable of instantly reducing concrete to cinders. Were it to enter our walls, it would leave us homeless. To say nothing of what such heat might do to a certain ice cube beneath our fortress.

We tried to spell it, divert it, destroy it, bind it into place. I'd spent the entire day scouring old books Rowena kept in her bedchamber library, although I was fairly certain it was useless. I have yet to find her real "library." This is another thing I know, because I saw her carrying books at times of crisis that are nowhere to be found. Yet.

My girls wept at the end. We were hot and tired and soon to be homeless. We'd tried everything we knew.

Then a black Humvee drove up and three of Ryodan's men got out.

With Margery.

The men bade us retreat to a safe perimeter. Using dark magic that mystified us, they tethered the IFP to the earth a mere twenty yards from our walls, where it has remained stationary since. Where, they assured me, it shall continue to remain stationary for all time.

"But I don't want it there," I told them. "What am I to do with it? Can we not move it?"

They looked at me as if I had five heads. "Woman, we saved you from certain destruction and you want to critique how we did it? Use the bloody thing as a trash compactor. Incinerate your dead and enemies. Boss'd love to have something like this near Chester's. It's a fire that will never go out."

"Take it there, then!"

"Only way to get it there is cut the tether. Do that and it goes straight through your abbey. Be glad he hasn't decided he wants it or this place would be forfeit. Dublin is on the other side of your walls. Keep your door open. Ryodan will be by in a few days to tell you what you owe him."

After they left, Margery pumped her fist in the air and called for celebration that the danger was averted and we lived to fight another day. My girls rallied around her, jubilant, cheering. I stood jostled and forgotten in the melee.

Ryodan will be by in a few days.

To tell me what I owe him.

For years I have hidden behind these walls, trying to be as unimportant as possible. Unassuming. Overlooked. I was happy to walk the fields, daydreaming of Sean and the future we would have, studying *sidhe*-seer magic and occasionally guiding the girls with gentle wisdom, praising God for my blessings.

I love this abbey. I love these girls.

I turn and walk past the transparent vision of Cruce, who has been sitting on the divan in my dressing room watching me ever since the bells chimed the witching hour, four and a half hours ago, winged and naked as only he could be. I dab my brow with a handkerchief, blotting the sheen of perspiration that is constant of late. As Sean was unable to come last night, I have not slept in two days. Not to be deterred, Cruce found a waking way to torment me. Fortunately all he is capable of at the moment is a weak transmission of his appearance. He cannot speak or touch me. Or he surely would have. I slide my gaze over him with only the smallest hitch.

I begin to dress.

Last night my first cousin was a better leader than me.

Because I don't know my world.

The time has come to change that.

The drive to Dublin is long and silent. There are no longer any radio stations to listen to and I don't carry a phone or iPod.

The day was arduous, with Margery presiding over the abbey as if she were in charge, riding the wave of adulation for her last-minute save, peppering her salted commentary on my many failings with inflammatory phrases calculated to incite the girls and make them feel as if I am restricting them as Rowena did. I watch her and think: Am I to take less than three hundred children, young girls, and aging women to war? Later, I tell her. We must fight smart and hard, not fearlessly.

Smart and hard would have left us homeless, she retorted. Fearless is why the abbey stands today.

On that score she is correct, but here, between us and for the fate of my girls, is a deeper problem. She does not *care*. In order to gain control, Margery would lead the *sidhe*-seers to their deaths, because for her, leadership is not about their well-being, only hers. Ironically, her very self-engrossment makes her charismatic where I am not. On my way into the city I ponder the need for charm in my management of the girls. It is clear that a decision looms: I must either abdicate leadership or change in more ways than I am certain I can survive.

I arrive at Chester's just after ten, stunned to find a line spanning three demolished city blocks. I had no idea so many young people were alive in Dublin or that I might find them lined up as if it were a common Tuesday night, as if this were the new Temple Bar. Do they not know the world is infected and dying? Do they not feel the pounding hooves of the Horsemen of the Apocalypse riding? One has been unhorsed for now, although he smiled seductively at me from my divan before I left. Another is being remade. Soon there will be four again.

I leave my car in an alley and walk to the end of the line, resigned to turning what will inevitably be an all-night wait into a lesson about my new world.

I have barely begun to say hellos to my new companions when a hand closes on my upper arm from behind.

"Ryodan will see you now."

It is one of his men, tall, muscled, scarred as the rest. He escorts me to the front of the line, over protests and promises, from the flirtatious to the grotesque. As we descend into the club, I raise barriers to shield my empath heart.

Music hammers me, pounding, visceral. Emotions bite deep despite my efforts to deflect them. Such naked hunger, such anguished desire for connection and relevance! But they are going about it the wrong way. I see here the very definition of insanity: attending Chester's, looking for love. Why not go to the desert, expecting to find water?

They would fare better to loot a hardware store and hope to meet another looter in the process; at least they'd know he was a responsible, capable man intent on rebuilding something. Or pilfer a library! Any man who reads is a fine one. Find a prayer group; they've sprung up all over the city.

On the surface, each person we pass seems happier than the next, but I feel it all: pain, insecurity, isolation, and fear. Most of them have no idea how they will survive past this night. Some have lost so many loved ones they no longer care. They live in isolated pockets of abandoned houses and buildings with no televisions and no way to keep up on the threats in the world, which are constantly evolving. Their prime directive is simple: to not sleep alone tonight. These are people who only recently could find out anything they wanted to know at the mere touch of a screen. Now, stripped of their outer hulls, defenses breached, they are adrift and listing badly.

And I cannot help but wonder . . .

Could I reach them? Could I somehow gather them into a single place and shape them for a purpose? I feel light-headed at the thought. They are not *sidhe-seers* . . . but they are young and strong, and impressionable.

A woman dances, her head back in mock ecstasy, smiling, surrounded by men and Unseelie. I get a flash of her heart as we pass and know that she believes a man will never love her unless she always makes him feel good. She has relinquished her right to be a person with needs and desires, and become a receptacle for filling the needs of a lover. If she is bright as a butterfly and sexual as a lioness in mating season, she will be cherished.

"That is not love," I say as we pass. "That is a bargain. You should charge for it. You should get something in return."

When I was young, I began ranking people by a number system: one to ten—how broken are they? She is a seven. Her heart could be healed but it would take an intensely committed man and much time. Few are so lucky. Fewer still are soul mates like me and my Sean.

As we ascend to the second floor, I look out over the

subclubs and see Jo, dressed as a Catholic, school-age child. I dislike the mockery of my faith and am still uneasy with her decision to work here, but she argued passionately for it, strongly committed to her mission to gather intelligence at the richest source. She has yet to tell me anything that makes me feel subjecting her to this cesspool is worthwhile. I know a thing about people: who and what we surround ourselves with is who and what we become. In the midst of good people, it is easy to be good. In the midst of bad people, it is easy to be bad.

As we top the stairs, I find my eyes drawn back to the subclub where the waiters wear only tight black leather pants and a bow tie, revealing vast expanses of tanned, muscled skin, or in other cases generous bare bosoms. Only the stunning are employed there. I catch my breath. One of the male waiters has a beautiful back, a lovely long-limbed way of moving. I could watch him walk away for hours. I am a woman and I appreciate a fine-backed man. I am relieved because it is not Cruce. He has not so thoroughly perverted me that I no longer find human men attractive.

My escort guides me down a hallway of smooth glass walls to my left and my right, unbroken but by nearly nonexistent seams. The rooms up here are all made of two-way glass. Depending on how the lighting is adjusted in each room, you can either see into it from the outside but not out or out from the inside but not in. I had heard from Dani a description of the upper levels of Chester's so I knew to expect a see-through glass floor, but expecting it and walking on it are two very different things. People do not like to see what lies beneath. Yet here at Chester's the owner forces you to view it with every step you take in his demesne. He is a calculating man, and a dangerous one. And so I have come here tonight to determine my debt, pay it, and get it over with.

My escort stops before a seemingly seamless glass wall and places his palm against it. A glass panel whisks aside with a hydraulic hiss. The weight of his palm on my neck guides me into the darkened room.

"Boss'll be with you in a minute."

I can see out on all sides, up and down. From Ryodan's glass aerie, he studies his world by naked eye and camera. The perimeter of the room, at the ceiling, is lined with hundreds of small monitors, three rows deep. I scan them. There are cameras focused on every room, from nearly every angle. There are rooms that are sordid beyond my awareness of such activities. This is the world I must learn if I am to lead my girls.

The door hisses open behind me and I say nothing, wait for him to speak. When he does not, I expand my empath gift to get a feel for him. There is no one in the room with me. I realize someone must have opened the door, seen me, not him, and walked on. I continue with my observations of the screens, turning slowly as I absorb the faces, the actions, the offerings. I must learn people as I have never learned them before.

The hand on my shoulder draws from me a small, involuntary scream.

I whirl, frightened, and I'm against Ryodan's chest, with his arms gently around me. I would speak but I know I would only stammer. There was no one in this room with me. I did not hear the door open again. How, then, is he in the room?

"Easy, Katarina. I did not save you from harm last night to harm you tonight."

I look into a face that is unreadable. It is said of this man that he wears three expressions and three alone: amused mockery, urbane aloofness, or anger. It is said if you see anger, you are dead.

I open my empath gift.

I am in this room alone.

I can find no words to say. I decide to use the ones I have. "I am in this room alone."

"Not quite."

"You don't exist."

"Touch me, Katarina. Tell me I don't exist." He brushes my cheek with a kiss and I shiver. "Turn your head for me and I'll kiss you as a woman should be kissed." He waits, his mouth brushing my cheek, for me to turn ever-so-slightly, part my lips and take his tongue. I shiver again. This man would not kiss me as I like to be kissed but as *he* does. His way is too hard, demanding, dangerous. His way is not love. It is passion and it burns. Incinerates. It leaves only embers as surely as the IFP his men tethered at my abbey last eve.

When I pull back, he laughs and drops his loose embrace. I give him a level look. "Thank you for sending your men to tether the fragment of Faery. They spoke of payment. We do not have much. What can our abbey offer in return for such generous aid?"

He smiles faintly. "Ah, so that is how we are to be. You speak eloquently for one who spoke no words at all until she was nearly five."

I will not be rattled. So, he knows I was without voice for years after I was born. Many know the story. The pain of the world's emotions overwhelmed me upon birth. I was a terrible baby, an awful infant. I cried incessantly. I never spoke. I curled into a ball and tried to escape the pain of the world. They called me autistic. "Thank you."

"Until Rowena came and offered your family a deal."

"I did not come to speak of myself, but of how I may repay you."

"She would draw you from your autistic shell, but at eighteen years of age you were hers. You would come live at the abbey. Your parents leapt at the opportunity. They despaired of ever silencing your weeping."

Sometimes, even then, Sean had been there. Sometimes in the delirium of my pain he had curled beside me and said, "Girl, why do you cry?" I remember moments of silence then. He would put his chubby arms around me, and for a short time the pain would go away.

"How would they make a grand alliance with larger and nastier criminals if their only marriageable daughter was defective?" I say dryly.

He laughs. "There you are, behind that eternal serenity. The woman that feels. Funny thing is, I, too, thought I was in this room alone. Until you said that. The dearth of emotion here is not mine alone." His smile fades and he looks straight into my eyes with a stare so penetrating, direct, and uncomfortable that I feel I am an insect pinned to a board, prepared for dissection. "You owe me nothing further."

I blink. "But I haven't paid you yet."

"You have."

"No, I haven't. I've given nothing."

"The price was not required of you."

I get a chill and almost can't get my breath. This man is dangerous. Clever. Terrifying to me. "Of whom was it required? I am the one responsible. I am the one who failed. I am the one who should have led them to safety, therefore it should be me and me alone who pays a price!"

"Funny thing about payment is that it isn't the buyer of the goods or services that gets to set it. It's the seller. That's me." His face is hard and cold now.

"What price did you set?" I school my breath slow and even, waiting for his reply,

He moves to my side, guides me to the glass and directs my attention below. "I have had difficulty staffing lately. My servers keep dying on me."

The skin of my spine begins to crawl.

"One club in particular is hard to keep staffed. The Tuxedo Club is constantly requiring replacements."

It is the subclub where the servers dress in tight black leather pants and bow ties, and serve topless.

"Your Sean was good enough to fill in for a time."

Bile rises in the back of my throat. "My Sean does not belong here."

"Perhaps. But even you have to admit he looks good in the uniform."

I look where he's pointing. The back I admired on my way up the stairs has known my hands on its shoulder blades as he moved inside me. I have tickled it many nights as he drifted to sleep. I have massaged it when he worked the nets overlong. I have kissed each and every muscle and curve. It is, indeed, a beautiful back.

"How long?"

"I haven't decided."

"Don't do this to me."

"Why."

"He is . . . " I stop and sigh. This man would understand nothing of what I would say.

"Go on."

"Sean is my soul mate."

"Soul mate."

He mocks me. He mocks God. "Such things are sacred."

"To who? Your god may love soul mates but man does not. Such a couple is vulnerable, particularly if they are fool enough to let the world see how shiny and happy they are. Their risk rises tenfold during times of war. There are two courses a couple in such circumstances can chart: go deep into the country and hide as far from humanity as possible, hoping like hell nobody finds them. Because the world *will* tear them apart."

He is wrong. He knows nothing of soul mates. Still I cannot help but ask, "The other?"

"Sink up to their necks in the stench and filth and corruption of their war-torn existence—"

"You mean behave like common criminals. Would you prefer us ruthless animals? Why are you doing this?"

"I mean look at it, Katarina. See things for what they are. Drop your blinders and raise the sewer to eye level; admit you're swimming in shit. If you don't acknowledge the turd hurtling down the drain toward you, you can't dodge it. You have to face every challenge together. Because the world *will* tear you apart."

"You are manipulative, cynical, and base."

"Guilty as charged."

"Life is not as you see it. You don't know anything about love."

"I am intimately acquainted with the vagaries of fate in times of war. They've been my worst and best centuries."

"That is not love."

"I didn't say it was." He flashes a smile, white teeth gleaming in shadow. "I prefer war. The colors run more brilliant; food and drink are more rare, and the sweeter for it. People are so much more interesting. More alive."

"And more dead," I say sharply. "We lost nearly half the world and you find it 'interesting'? You are a pig. Barbaric and cruel." I turn away. I have had enough. If this is his price then I am free to go. There is nothing more I owe him. He has already taken it all.

I move for the door.

"You must tell him, Katarina. If you are to have any hope at all."

I stop. He cannot know. There is no way that he could know. "Tell who, what?"

"Sean. About Cruce. You must tell him."

I whirl, hand fluttering to my throat. "What in God's name are you talking about?"

I search his eyes and I see there that somehow he knows my deepest shame. They hold a secret smile and a certain amused resignation. As if he has watched humanity's idiocies play out in front of him so many times that they have begun to . . . not pain but perhaps perturb him. As if he wearies of watching the rats in the maze run into the same walls over and over. I expand my empath gift, I push with all I've got, and still I can't even sense that he is in the room with me. There is *nothing* where he stands.

"If you don't tell Sean that Cruce is fucking you while you sleep, it will destroy what you have with him more certainly than any job in my club could. That, down there"—he points to Sean serving a drink to a pretty, nearly naked Seelie—"is a bump in the road, a test of temptation and fidelity. If your Sean loves you, he will pass it with flying colors. Cruce is a test of your fucking soul."

I don't bother arguing with him. He knows. Somehow he knows. Perhaps he can read thoughts like I read emotions. It is a terrifying idea. "Why can't I feel you?"

"Perhaps the lack is not mine. Perhaps it is within you."

"No." Of this I am certain. "There's something wrong with you."

Again he flashes that smile. "Or something right."

Perhaps I take the coward's way. Perhaps I take the honorable path. I cannot decide. My head is a muddle. But I give the Tuxedo Club wide berth and pull up the hood of my cloak. I do not confront my Sean as I leave. If he tells me, we will discuss it. If he does not, we will not. I tell myself I am respecting his boundaries, preserving his dignity. This is where he will be instead of in my bed in coming nights.

The price of saving my abbey is a piece of my heart and the lion's share of my spine. That is what Ryodan called due.

My Sean will face temptation alone every night at Chester's, and I will face it alone at the abbey, in my bed.

This is not a world I ever wanted to know.

TWENTY-NINE

"In the white room"

One night when Mac and me were killing Unseelie back-to-back, she had a kind of meltdown and started crying and yelling while she sliced and diced. She said that she was going to send them all straight back to hell because they stole everything from her that mattered. She said she used to know her sister, everything about her, and that was where love was, in the knowing and sharing, but it turned out Alina had a boyfriend she'd never mentioned and a whole other life she knew nothing about, and not only didn't Alina love her, her entire existence to date had been one great big fat lie. Her parents weren't her parents, her sister probably wasn't her sister, nobody was what they seemed, not even her.

In Rowena's stash of journals chronicling her nasty, evil reign, I found Mac's sister's diary. I have over four hundred journals locked away with the Grand Mistresses emblem emblazoned on dark green kidskin leather. She was eighty-eight when she died, though she didn't look a day over sixty. She had a Fae she'd been nibbling on for decades locked in a vault beneath the abbey. I killed it when I found out about it.

When I discovered Alina's diary, I tore out pages and

got them to Mac on the sly, trying to make up for silencing her sister's voice and show her she'd meant everything in the world to Alina.

"Why the feck are we here?" I say crossly. I wouldn't even be thinking about Mac if we weren't. Christian's been sifting me around the city, helping me plaster my *Dailies* on lampposts. I been letting him touch my pinky finger to do it. He keeps trying to put his arms around me. His last sift deposited us catty-corner to Barrons Books & Baubles, with the street between us.

I feel like puking.

I ain't been here since the night Mac found out the truth about me. The night she baked me a cake and painted my fingernails and saved me from the Gray Woman, only to end up ready to kill me herself a few minutes later.

In the middle of a ruined city, Barrons Books & Baubles stands untouched. I think a silent benediction: May it always. There's something about this place. As if its mere existence means the world will always have hope. I can't explain why I feel that way but all the folks I know that have ever visited it, all the other *sidhe*-seers, feel the same. There's something different, something extraordinary on this island, in this city, on this street, in this precise spot. It feels almost like once, a very long time ago, something terrible nearly happened here at this longitude and latitude, and somebody put BB&B on the gash to keep the possibility from ever occurring again. As long as the walls stand and the place is manned, we're okay. I snicker, picturing it looking just like it does right here and now, in prehistoric times. It doesn't seem so improbable.

To the left and right the cobbled street is swept clean. There's no riot-detritus outside Barrons's establishment. No husks left from Shades gorging. No trash. Planters line the cobbled street, and there are small plants trying to grow in them, valiantly fighting the uncommon chill. The entry to the tall, deep brick building is drenched in dark cherry and brass and polished to a high gloss. The place is Old World and urbane as the dude himself, with pillars and wrought-iron latticework and a great big heavy door with fancy sidelights and a transom that I used to bang through, and sometimes I'd go in and out, in and out, just to hear the bell above the door tinkle. It sounded really cool in fast-mo, used to crack me up.

A hand-painted shingle hangs perpendicular to the sidewalk, suspended by an elaborate brass pole bolted into the brick above the door alcove, swaying in a light breeze.

Amber lights glow behind glass panes tinged with a hint of green.

It's all I can do not to go banging in that door, say, "Dude, what's up?"

I'm never going to bang in that door again.

"Get us out of here," I say crossly.

"Can't. This is where we need to be. And what the bloody hell is up with that?"

I look at him. He's looking up at the roof of BB&B, where dozens of enormous floodlights shine down into the street. I have to back up a few steps to see past them and see what he's seeing because I'm so much shorter. I gape. "What the feck are ZEWs doing here?" The entire roof of BB&B is covered with Zombie Eating Wraiths. Hulking anorexic vultures, with creepily hunched bodies and a gaunt grimness that defies description, they huddle in their voluminous black robes, dusted with dirt and cobwebs, unmoving. Carrion-eaters, packed shoulder-to-shoulder, they're as fixedly still as a death-watch. I'm not sure I would have even noticed them if Christian hadn't pointed them out. They're not chittering and it's somehow worse that they're silent. "Why they hanging out on Mac's roof like that?"

"How the fuck would I know? Sorry, lass. I mean, how would I know?"

"You can say 'fuck' around me. Everybody does. And you'd know because you're Unseelie."

"Not completely, not yet and not originally. That's a lot of nots. And just because the rest of the men in this city are pigs doesn't mean I am. There's another 'not' for you. I'm bloody well made of nots tonight. I'm not the monster being hunted either."

I give him a look. His eyes are wild. This is a dude on serious edge, teetering, arms pinwheeling. "So, what are we doing here?" I try to bring some focus back to the conversation.

He doesn't answer me. Just stalks off, straight toward the bookstore, and right when I'm about to freeze-frame it out of there because there's no way I'm going inside, even if nobody's home, he turns sharp and heads down the alley between BB&B and the neighboring Dark Zone.

"If you want to stop the Hoar Frost King, you'll have to come with me, lass. I'm taking you to the Unseelie King's library. If there are answers to be had, they'll be found there."

The Unseelie King's library! "Holy borrowing bibliophile, let's book!" I take one last look up at the ZEWs and freeze-frame to catch up. If Mac's in the bookstore, she won't notice the blur that just passed her door. I shiver as I chase after him. It's fecking cold tonight. I more than *want* to stop the Hoar Frost King. I've got to. It's getting downright frigid in Dublin and I got a terrible feeling it's going to get a lot worse.

When Christian pushes into the brick wall of the building catty-corner to the rear of BB&B—first left on the Dark Zone side—and disappears, I melt down in a fit of the giggles. I toss a rock at the spot where he vanished. It bounces off the brick and clatters to the cobblestone. I'm feeling twenty shades of Harry Potter's train station, especially when he pokes his head back out of the wall and says impatiently, "Come on, lass. This is hardly my favorite place to be."

I approach the wall and study it, trying to decide if I'd be able to find the spot again without knowing exactly where it was. His head disappears. I wouldn't. I want to chalk a big X on it, in case I need it again, but that would betray its location to everyone else, too, being as "X marks the spot" and all, so I back up partway down the alley and lock the scene down on my mental grid, permanent-like. I got that kind of memory. If I deliberately file something, I can always find it again. Hard part is remembering to deliberately file it. I'm usually so excited by the life I'm living I forget to take pictures.

Then I follow him in. Dude! I step *into* a brick wall! It's the freakiest thing I've ever felt. Like it's a sponge and I'm a sponge and for a second there all our sponge parts are one and I don't just have square pants, everything about me is squarish because I'm part of a wall, then I'm me again and the wall kind of squirts me out on the other side in a completely white room.

White floor, white ceiling, white walls. Inside the white room are ten mirrors. Just like that. Standing there, in thin air. You can circle all the way around them. Nothing is holding them up that I can see. They're all different sizes and shapes, in different frames. Some of the glass surfaces are dark as pitch and you can't see a thing. Others swirl with silver fog but the things that move in their cloudy shadows are too fast and strange to define.

"Good," he says. "They're where I left them."

"Where else would they be?"

"They used to hang on the wall. I shuffled them

around so if anyone else knew where they went, they'd lose track. Used to be the one we're taking was fourth from the left. Now it's second from the right."

I take one last look around, I don't know, maybe looking for tired starlings, but there aren't any, and push into the mirror behind him. I get all spongy again and this time it's like I pass through a lot of things and just when I'm starting to get a little tense about it, wondering if all my parts are definitely going to come back together, I squirt out into Christian's back. "Ooof! What are you doing, standing there blocking the mirror?"

"Hush, I thought I heard something."

I perk up my superhearing. "I don't hear nothing and I can hear everything."

"There are things in here," he says. "You never know what you might find."

"Bad things?"

"Depends on your definition. And who you are. Being a prince has its advantages."

I look around. "Where are we?"

"The White Mansion."

"Duh, like I might never have figured that out," I say, because we're in yet another white room. "Is the whole place this boring? Don't the Fae ever use paint, maybe a little wallpaper?"

He chimes softly.

"Dude, you're ringing like a bell."

He stops abruptly and I realize he was laughing. I'm beginning to understand how to interact social-like with an Unseelie prince.

"The White Mansion isn't boring, lass. Never boring. It's the grand demesne the Unseelie King built for his concubine. It's a living, breathing love story, testament to the brightest passion that ever burned between our races. You can follow the scenes through if you've time enough and are willing to risk getting lost for a few centuries."

I heard of the White Mansion from eavesdropping but never paid much attention to the talk. I was always more interested in the *Sinsar Dubh*. "What do you mean, you can follow the scenes through?"

"Their residue is still here. They loved so intensely that moments of their life have been etched into the very fabric of the mansion. Some say the king designed it that way, so if one day he lost her he could come live with her residue. Some say the mansion was built of memory-tissue and is a living creature, with a great brain and heart hidden somewhere in the house. I've no wish to believe it's true because that would mean the White Mansion can be killed, and she must never die. The record of the greatest love in the history of History would be lost, along with countless artifacts from myriad universes that could never be collected together again. This place is home, love story, and museum all in one."

"So, where's the library?"

"You see, lass," he says tenderly, like I never even just opened my mouth, like I'm looking for a lesson in love, and I ain't, "the Unseelie King fell in love with a mortal woman. She was his reason for being. His every defining moment occurred because of her, and only in her presence did he know peace. She was his brightest shining star. She made him a better man, and to men who know how fundamentally and deeply they're flawed, such a woman is irresistible. The idea that she would live less than a single century was more than he could bear, so he resolved to make her Fae like himself that they might live forever together. While he worked in his laboratory, trying to perfect the Song of Making, he needed to keep her safe and alive. He knew it might take him eons to learn to wield the power of creation."

If he was human I might call that funny glint in Christian's iridescent eyes speculative as it rests on me. I can't look too long trying to decide because one short lock with his gaze and my eyes are already leaking blood. Dude's getting more potent by the minute. And weirder. Like he's thinking him and me are like the Unseelie King and his concubine, some kind of star-crossed lovers. "And where did you say the library was?"

"He built his beloved a playground of infinite proportions, tucked away in a safe pocket of reality where she could stay for all time, unchanging. Unaging. She would be safe. Nothing and no one could ever hurt her. He would never have to worry that he might lose her." His voice sinks to a whisper, as if he's forgotten I'm even here. "They would be together always. Soul mates. He would never be alone. Never get lost in madness, for she would never fail to find him and bring him back."

"Dude, your story's fascinating and all, but where's the library? Time's wasting. We got the Hoar Frost King to stop."

"If you stayed here, Dani, my light o' love, you'd never die. I'd never have to worry about anyone hurting you. Ever."

"Yeah, and I'd, like, be fourteen forever. I'd kind of like to grow a few more inches," I say irritably. In more than a few places. He tries to keep me here out of some lunatic thought that I'm his queen, we'll be staining this place with a whole new residue: it'll be war in the White Mansion.

"I'd forgotten that." He sighs. "Come, lass. Shall we go find the library?"

"Dude, thought you'd never ask."

We exit the white room on white marble floors and enter a sparkling white hallway with floor-to-ceiling windows that stretch to domed ceilings forty feet high. There I see my first residue. Beyond tall windows is a beautiful woman in a snowy garden, silken folds of a bloodred gown spilling over a white marble bench. Face pressed into her hands, she weeps.

"It's the king's concubine," he says.

"I thought you said they were crazy in love. Why is she crying?"

"She wearied of being alone while the king labored at his experiments. She waited hundreds of thousands of years for him, alone except for those few creatures he trusted with her, and his occasional visits."

Christian tells me the rest of the story while we twist and turn down hallways and corridors. I'm riveted in spite of myself. Who'd have ever thought such fantastical places existed side by side with our world, accessible through hidden portals and mirrors? My life is so fecking interesting I almost can't stand it!

We pass over lemon marble floors in sunny wings with tall windows that frame brilliant summer days, down rose quartz floors that reflect violet hues of the sunset beyond, across bronze tiles that wind through rooms that have no windows, only stately, enormous, kingly chairs and couches and beds. There are fireplaces here as tall as a small house, with ceilings higher than the spires on cathedrals.

"How big is this place?"

"Some say it goes on forever, that the king created a house that constantly grows itself."

"How do you find anything?"

"Och, and there's the rub, lass. It's difficult. Things move. It doesn't help that the king created decoys. To better protect his dangerous journals, he seeded multiple libraries within the house. Barrons thinks he found the true repository. He didn't. I saw the books he pilfered. They came from the king's Green Study."

"How do *you* know where the true library is?"

He hesitates. "Something in it calls to me," he says finally. "I was trapped for a while in the king's boudoir, and I could feel the pull of the house beyond it. The residue in his chambers was so strong that reality and illusion blurred for a time. Sometimes I would hear whispers as I fell asleep, and those times I would dream I was the king, walking my halls. I knew where everything was, as if it was I who'd fashioned this house. I even understood how things shifted. A few of those memories remain. Others aren't so trustworthy. Still, I know that down a crimson hall that will always be found off a bronze corridor is a music room with thousands of instruments that play themselves when you twist a key inside the door, like a giant music box. I know there is a vast arena in the cobalt wing with no gravity, and stars painted all around where sometimes he took his beloved and created universes in the air for her amusement. And I know that because he feared other Fae would find the journals he kept, filled with notes about his experiments, he brought them into the White Mansion. It is said that he locked away the recipe for every Unseelie he ever created, and countless more unborn, that he chiseled a warning above the entry when he left. It is by that inscription you can know it's the true library."

"What does it say?"

He stops. "See for yourself, lass."

I look up, and up some more. We're standing outside doors that are nearly identical to those in our abbey, at the entrance to the chamber where Cruce is trapped. Alien symbols glow with eerie blue-black fire, chiseled into the stone all around the doors, with much larger symbols carved across the arch.

"I can't read it. It's not in English."

Christian moves from side to side of the archway, pressing various symbols, and after a moment the doors

swing open silently. "It says, 'Read them and weep.'
Come, lass. We've a needle in a haystack to find."

The king's library is the craziest place I've ever seen.

Christian disappears the second we're in the door. Me,
I stand in the doorway, catching flies in my open mouth.
The view seems to go on forever, between jagged, zig-
zagging bookcases, dwindling to a tiny black point that
seems miles away. I step inside, fascinated.

Despite how ginormous the doors are, I can spread
my arms wide as they go and my fingertips brush the
walls of books on both sides. Lined with shelves and
cubbyholes and built-in desktops that drop down on invisible hinges and are covered with more books and jars
and knickknacks, every horizontal surface perches at
skewed, absurd angles that defy physics. The things on
those shelves shouldn't be staying on them. The bookcases lean in, and close over me in places, which means
the books should be falling on my head. The walls soar
to a ceiling beyond my line of vision. It's like being at the
bottom of a jagged chasm of books, and there are millions of them in all colors, shapes, and sizes.

Here, the passage between the shelves widens to
twenty feet, there it narrows barely wide enough for me
to turn sideways and force myself through. I munch
candy bar after candy bar as I move deeper into the
nutty place.

There are bookshelves that branch off, perpendicular
to the main passageway with only an inch of space between them. "Nobody could even get a book off some
of these!" I say irritably. "How are we supposed to
search?"

"A Fae could." His voice floats down from somewhere above me. I guess he's sifting up and down the
shelves.

I pass through a low-hanging doorway, the top of which is a shelf of upside-down books. They should be dropping on my head as I walk under them. There's a bronze plaque on the ceiling near them, I suppose saying what that section is, but I can't read the language. I reach up and pluck one from the shelf. I have to tug, like the book is set in glue or something, and it comes off with a wet *pop*. The pale green cover is soft and mossy, and the book smells like the woods after a spring rain. I open it and realize it was pointless to bring me here. I can't read a word. It's all in some other language and I have no idea what it is. I don't think even Jo could translate this stuff.

I'm about to close it when the sentence at the top of the page gets up and starts crawling across the page like a centipede. I snicker until it pauses at the edge of the page like it's psyching itself up for something then flings itself off the book with a mighty leap and starts wriggling up my arm. I jerk back my hand to shake it off, but it digs in by pointy letters and holds on. I pinch the sentence's butt with my other hand and tug it from my skin like a leech, smack it back on the page and clamp the book shut. Part of it's hanging out, and it waves jerkily at me with what appears to be blatant hostility. I stick the book back on the upside-down shelf over my head, pissed-off sentence first, counting on the gluey base to hold it in. All I need is a badly mangled, irate sentence stalking me.

I open the next one I pull down more cautiously. Same thing happens, only this time a whole paragraph leaps off the page the sec I open it and lands on my stomach. I swipe at it but the words are sticky like cobwebs and I only succeed in smearing them around on my shirt. Then they all start to separate and I spend the next few minutes trying to catch them all and put them back in the book, but every time I open it, something else gets out.

"You aren't messing with the Boora-Boora books, are you, Dani?" Christian says from somewhere far away. "You're awfully quiet down there."

"What are the Boora-Boora books?"

"The ones where the words crawl off the pages. They're named after their home world. Nothing works like it's supposed to there." He makes a sound that is suspiciously like a choked laugh. "You have to watch out, they sting like fire ants if they get pissed."

"Ow! You could have told me that sooner!" No sooner did he say the word "sting" than they started doing it. I swat at them with the book they're supposed to be in. They scurry under a pile of teetering manuscripts and disappear. I sigh, hoping they weren't a critical part that someone comes looking for in a few hundred years, and stick the tome back up on its upsidedown shelf. "So, not all of the words are self-propelled like that?"

"Some of the books are just books. Bloody few, though."

"Found anything up there?"

"Not yet."

"Dude, I can't read a thing. I'm useless here."

I wait but there's no reply. I squint up at the ceiling. He could be anywhere, sifting from shelf to shelf. When he said he was taking me to the Unseelie King's library, I expected something like the one we got at the abbey. Even if I could read whatever languages the Unseelie King's books are written in, it would take an eternity to search this place, not to mention a couple of gazillion-foot ladders. It was stupid to come here. I don't regret it, though, because now I know how to get in the White Mansion. Dude! What a perfect place to hide out for a while if I need to. And there's so much to explore. Who knows what kinds of useful things I might find in here!

I wander the passage between shelves, periodically calling for Christian. He doesn't answer. Books are piled in haphazard stacks along the sides and I have to be careful not to bump into them. I get the feeling that if I knock over a stack and half a dozen come open at once, not even my speedy freeze-framing will be able to keep up with all that comes out. I open a few more books along the way, curiosity and me being best buds and all. One puffs out acrid smoke the sec I lift the cover, making me sneeze, and I slam it shut again. Another has fat brown spiders with hairy legs that spring from the pages! I squash the ones that make it out. Yet another has videos instead of words but the images are so alien I can't make sense of them.

I find a little mini-laboratory amid the stacks, covered with petri-like dishes and stoppered bottles and jars. "Christian!" I call again as I study the contents visible through thick wavy glass.

I get a reply this time but it's so far away I can't make it out.

"Dude, unless you're finding something, this is a total waste of time! I'd rather be back in Dublin, investigating."

"Hang on, lass," comes his faraway reply. "I think I'm on to something."

One of the stoppered bottles has a dab of crimson at the bottom. I pick it up and turn it in my hand, watching the crimson liquid ripple. Rainbow colors skitter across the surface in kaleidoscopic designs. It's so beautiful I almost can't take my eyes off it. I turn the bottle upside down and study the label on the bottom. No clue what the glyphlike symbols mean. As I turn the bottle back upright, I must have nudged the stopper a little because I get a whiff of the scent of its contents and it's like sticking your nose right up into heaven. It's night jasmine and fresh-baked bread, homemade fish and chips and salt air, it's the smell of my mom's neck, fresh-washed pjs, and sunshine on Dancer's skin. It's the scent of all my favorite things rolled up into one. I swear my hair lifts on the breeze of it. I groan and pull out a candy bar, abruptly ravenous.

There's curiosity and there's cats.

You'd think I'd learn.

I unplug the bottle while I chew.

THIRTY

In the court of the crimson king hag

"What the hell is that smell?" Christian says.

"Fecking awesome, isn't it?" I say dreamily. Crimson smoke swirls in the glass bottle, poking tentative tendrils at the rim. The amazing aroma fills the library, making me giddy. I want to stretch out, fold my arms behind my head, be lazy and bask in the fragrance. I want to share it with Dancer. I've never smelled anything so scrumptious.

"Bloody fucking noxious," he says from much nearer than he's been in a while.

"How can you say that?"

"Because it is."

Crimson strands puff from the bottle and swirl above it. After a moment they begin to dart toward each other, circle around and dart back, slender red strands knitting themselves into a smoky shape.

"Dude, it smells like heaven! There's something wrong with your nose. Maybe you only like Unseelie smells now." I can't wait to see what awesome thing comes out of this!

"It smells," he says from directly above me, "like rotting intestines. What did you open? A book?" He drops down beside me, carrying a stack of books beneath his arm. I'm glad to see he found something. "A bottle? Christ, lass, you can't be randomly unplugging bottles in this place! Give me that. Let's see what you've done."

The hint of a face is forming in the crimson smoke; delicate, pointy chin, enormous eyes slanted up at the corners. I try to turn my head to look at Christian but my head isn't taking orders. It's stuck, still staring at the materializing face. I can't force myself to look away no matter how hard I try. It's got me mesmerized. I've never seen a face so beautiful, smelled a smell so good. I want to stand in the middle of it and breathe it deep into my lungs.

When he plucks the bottle from my hand, the spell is broken. When he turns it on its side to read the label on the bottom, a cloud of crimson smoke gushes out, obscuring the passageway between the shelves. Tendrils lick at me, rough as tiny cat tongues.

Suddenly, everything changes.

Now that I'm no longer holding the bottle, I can smell what he smelled. Saliva floods my mouth, my stomach heaves, and I just about puke the candy bars I just ate. The face in the smoke isn't so beautiful anymore. It's morphing into something monstrous before my eyes. Long fangs slide from thin lips, bloody hair writhes like snakes. "Dude, what the feck did I open?" I say, aghast.

The bottle clatters to the floor.

My blood goes cold when Christian utters a single word.

"RUN."

There are a few absolute no-brainer rules in my world. Real close to the top of this list is: if an Unseelie prince runs from it, I'm going to run from it, too. I'm not even going to ask any questions. I'm just going to vamoose with all my might.

Still . . . I can't help but try to steal a peek over my shoulder. I'm the one that let it out. I have to know what it is so I can hunt it down and kill it.

"DON'T LOOK BACK!" Christian roars.

I cradle my head with my arms, trying to hold my skull together until the instant headache subsides. "Stop yelling at me and sift us, dude!" I'm freeze-framing, trying to keep up with him, but I don't know these halls. They're a maze that isn't on any of my maps. I have to keep dropping down, lock my grid into place and kick back up again. The stench of rotting meat behind me is getting stronger. The skin on the back of my neck is crawling. I keep waiting for whatever is chasing us to close icy talons on my nape, rip my head off my shoulders, and kill me. All those scary movies I watched with Dancer aren't making me laugh now. They're filling my head with a million gruesome deaths, each more horrible than the last. It'd help if I knew what was chasing us. The unknown is always scarier than the known. I got a Mega-sized imagination, and it can do a real number on me.

"Sifting doesn't work inside the White Mansion. Take my hand. I know these halls."

I grab his hand, ignoring the groaning sound he makes. He laces his fingers with mine and I'm blasted by a wave of horniness. "Mute it, Christian. This ain't the time to go death-by-sex Fae on me."

"Sorry, lass. It's just that it's your hand and there's danger, and danger always—"

"Off it now!"

I can breathe again. Not that I want to. The stench is suffocating and closing in on us fast.

"What's chasing us?"

"Loosely translated, the Crimson Hag."

"How does it kill?"

"Hope you never find out."

"Could it kill even you, an Unseelie prince?"

"She prefers us alive. She once held two princes captive for nearly a hundred thousand years before the king stopped her. Among other foul things, she tried to breed with us. I had no idea he'd stored her in his library. Everybody figured he'd destroyed the bitch."

"Why would she take you captive?"

"Because we're immortal, and once she takes what she wants from us, our bodies grow it back. Then she takes it again. We're a never-ending supply. She can just keep us chained up, sit and knit."

Knit? The idea of an Unseelie monster knitting is more than I can wrap my brain around. "What does she want from you?" A cloud of red smoke slithers over my shoulder. "Hurry, Christian! We've got to go faster! Get us out of here!"

We barrel down bronze halls, twist and turn through lemon wings, until finally we skid onto white marble. I swear I can feel the Hag breathing down my neck.

Then we're in the white room, rushing into the mirror, and I can't help myself, I look back as I turn all spongy.

The Crimson Hag is the most revolting creature I've ever seen. Worse than the Gray Woman, worse than the Unseelie princes, worse even than Papa Roach, and I have a special hatred for roaches. Roaches hang out on floors. My cage was on the floor.

Bloody, matted hair frames an ice-white face with black holes for eyes. She licks crimson fangs when she sees me looking. But the truly disturbing thing about her is what she's wearing. Her upper body is voluptuous and encased in a corset of bone and sinew. She has no lower body that I can see. A tattered, incomplete crimson gown streams behind her.

And now I know why she smells of rotting meat.

Her unfinished gown is made of guts.

My stomach heaves again. "It collects Unseelie prince guts?"

"Among others. She'd take yours, too. Though yours would rot sooner."

"Can't you go any *faster*?" I like my guts. I want to keep them for a long time.

We explode from the mirror into the second white room and leap headfirst into the next mirror. We pass through multiple mirrors, chased by the scent of rotting meat. "Uh, Christian, she's going to get out."

"Good. More prey in Dublin. She'll go after someone else."

"We can't have her loose in my city!"

"You're the one that opened the bottle."

I screwed up. Big-time. But I'll figure it out. I'll trap and kill her and make my city safe again. *Before* she hurts anyone. I can't stand the thought of innocent folks getting killed because of my stupid curiosity. "You should have warned me not to open stuff!"

"I did. Then there was the whole 'read them and weep' thing chiseled over the door. Which warning didn't you get?"

"That was about the books, not bottles!"

"Some warnings are unilateral."

Then we're out and the cold slams into me like the brick wall we just exploded from. It takes my breath away, and when I get it back, it comes out in frosty puffs on the air. I go skidding across the alley on snow and ice and crash into the building opposite. Christian slams into me. We steady each other and I look around disbelievingly. The ground's covered with six inches of snow!

Did the Hoar Frost King ice something in this alley in the few hours we were gone? It can't be more than ten degrees and the windchill is killer. It *never* gets cold like this at night! And never over the space of a few hours. I look around for an ice sculpture nearby.

"Aw, crap," I say, because it's about to hit the fan. Snow's not the only thing in the alley.

Ryodan and Barrons are behind BB&B, getting out of Barrons's Bugatti Veyron. They both stare at me a sec, like they can't believe their eyes, then Ryodan's gaze fixes on where I'm holding Christian's hand. I drop it like a hot potato, but the look on his face doesn't improve. "It's not what you think! He's not going to be my superhero boyfriend and kick your—"

"Yes, I am," Christian says.

"No, you're not," Ryodan says. "And where the fuck have you been. Do you know the problems you've caused me."

"Dude, I only been gone, like, two hours. And we got bigger problems right now," I say.

"No shit. This whole city is turning to ice."

"What the bloody hell were you doing in the White Mansion?" Barrons demands. "Who told you how to get in there?"

"You will never go anywhere without me again," Ryodan says to me. "If you do, I'll lock you in my dungeon until you rot."

"Speaking of rotting, I think—"

"No more. From this moment forward, I'm going to be doing all your thinking for you."

I bristle. "My ass, you will."

"Seal the wall," he says to Barrons. "And get her the fuck out of here. It's time for the Highlander to die."

"You just try," Christian says.

"I ain't going nowhere. Well," I amend, "actually I am and you need to, too. We all have to get out of here." I start trying to freeze-frame but I crash into Barrons and bounce off. What happens next happens so fast I almost can't process it.

The stench of rotten meat fills the air, and Christian and me duck and split off in opposite directions because we know what's coming, then the Crimson Hag explodes from the wall, holding what looks like six-foot-long knitting needles made from bone, like lances at her sides.

She pierces Barrons and Ryodan with them then shoots straight up in the air, trailing their guts behind her.

THIRTY-ONE

"I'm swimming in the smoke of bridges I have burned"

I stand there like an idiot.

I should run before she turns on me, too, but my feet seem to sprout icy roots.

Barrons and Ryodan are lying in the alley on their backs, blood staining the snow in widening circles around them, and I gape, thinking: They can't die! Superheroes don't die!

Misguided beliefs aside, they sure look like they're dying to me. Nothing could get that mutilated and survive.

The Crimson Hag didn't just puncture them, she flayed them from groin to neck, and split them clean through bone. In one quick yank she scrapped all their intestines and internal organs from their bodies. It's a move she's had hundreds of thousands of years to perfect. Puncture, fly, yank. Their chest and abdomen cavities are open and scraped empty. The only way the treacherous bitch could have done this to them was to catch them by surprise.

What the feck was I thinking, standing there saying anything besides "Run"? Bickering as usual, like we had forever and always would!

"I thought you guys would duck at the last minute," I

mutter at their bodies. Or freeze-frame away, faster than me. Or maybe Ryodan would use whatever secret weapon he used against Velvet against her. Never in a gazillion years did I think anything could actually get the jump on them!

But she exploded from the wall and her lances were through them before any of us could even react. Their bodies are still moving but I think it's just the final twitches a body makes when it gets traumatized so abruptly and completely.

I hear a weird clicking sound that affects me the same way the ZEWs' chittering does, terrifies me on a primitive level. Is she coming for me now? I grab my sword and whirl. It takes me a second to spot her. I follow the trail of blood.

Up.

The Crimson Hag is perched on the roof of the building behind BB&B, with ropes of entrails dangling over the side in long glistening strands, dripping on the sidewalk. The bony needles she used to flay Barrons and Ryodan are actually her legs, which bend weirdly, sort of like a praying mantis's front legs, and have curved hooks on the ends.

With insectlike appendages, she's knitting their guts into the hem of her dress. As her bony legs click and clack together, the guts sway over the edge, shortening, inch by inch, smearing blood up the brick.

It's so disturbing that my stomach heaves and my body tries to burst into tears and puke at the same time. I swallow it all and choke.

I hear a guttural sound followed by a weak sigh and look back at the bodies.

"I'm going to kill the kid," Barrons says faintly.

Ryodan makes a burbling sound like a bloody laugh. I don't think he even has the parts left to laugh with. "Get in line."

They both deflate and go still.

I stare dumbly.

They die like superheroes: cracking a joke. Like they're just going to get up tomorrow and fight another day. No fear. Balls to the wall until the bloody end.

I feel like somebody ripped my guts out, too. I can't stand to look at them anymore so I drop my head, and squinch my eyes up tight. My head's a muddle. How did I get here? How did deciding to go to the Unseelie King's library end up with Ryodan and Barrons dead? I can't make sense of it. I mean, I can, because duh, I can follow the chain of events, but who the feck could have foreseen such a bizarre and preposterous outcome? How am I supposed to make small decisions when they can have such large, unforeseeable results?

"Well, that was fortuitous." Christian skirts their bodies and moves toward me, laughing. "Two down, seven to go. I wonder if we can just point the bitch at the rest of them. Mac, too."

My head whips up. He's laughing. They died and he's *laughing*. I start to shake. "Stay. Away. From. Me."

"What did I do, lass?"

"You took me in there, that's what you did! You didn't warn me enough. I'm only fourteen! I don't know everything! I can't know everything! You're older! You're supposed to warn me about stuff! And now you act like it's good that they're dead!"

"I thought you wanted Ryodan out of the picture."

"I just wanted him to leave me alone! And I never wanted Barrons to die! Aw, crap, Mac!" I wail. I look at the back of the bookstore, now even more miserable than before. Mac's in there. How long before she comes out and finds Barrons in the alley, bled out in the snow? How long before she discovers my complicity in this, too? I can see her, finding him, flinging herself over his body, weeping. One more tragic loss in her life.

Because I opened a fecking bottle.

Because I was curious.

The night Alina died, I felt like I wasn't . . . really there. I never been able to shake the feeling there was something wrong with me. I searched Ro's journals from beginning to end but she never wrote a single fecking word about me. Never. Makes me think maybe she had other journals I ain't found yet.

But tonight I'm all here.

I suffer that unpleasant shift I felt once before, the night I got Jo stuck working in the club. The one where I move sideways into a different way of being me, see myself different, and I don't like it. It's the shift where I'm a boat and there are all kinds of people capsized in my wake. No, not a boat. What did Ryodan say I was? A tsunami. That's it. Crashing into things and leveling them. When he said that, he had no idea he'd be one of those things I leveled. Or that he wouldn't live to see the one hell of a woman I'm going to become.

Above my head bony needles clack away. I hear the wet slap of intestines against the wall as they're drawn up the side. I should be terrified. I should be running for my life so she doesn't do to me what she did to them. Should I hide their bodies so Mac won't find them and figure out what I did?

"Come, lass. We have to get out of here while she's busy. The Hag gets obsessed with her knitting but she'll be done soon," Christian says.

My legs are made of cement and I have concrete blocks for feet. I just keep looking from Barrons and Ryodan to the bookstore and back. First Alina. Now Barrons. There isn't going to be any place on the face of this planet Mac won't hunt me down when she finds out what happened here tonight.

I look at Ryodan. How can he be dead? Who's going to run Chester's? Who's going to keep the loser Fae and humans in line? With both Barrons and Ryodan gone, is there any safe place in Dublin? Will BB&B and Chester's get abandoned?

A hand closes on my shoulder and I just about jump out of my skin.

"We've got to get out of here, Dani. She's finishing up."

I shake him off violently. "Don't you ever touch me again, Christian MacKeltar!"

He exhales sharp and sudden like I punched him in the gut. "You don't mean that."

"Try me." I fist my hand around the hilt of my sword.

"I'm the one that gave it back to you, lass. I'm the one that watches out for you."

"You're the one that took me somewhere I didn't know was as dangerous as it was. Folks got killed because of it. Did you at least manage to bring out the books you found?"

"I had other things on my mind. You were in danger."

It was all for nothing. The books got dropped, forgotten. I look at the wall. Sure, I could go back in, but I can't read any of the stuff in the library, so what's the point? And who knows what else I might set free by opening anything else in there?

I look up. Blood drips down the side of the building. As the gruesome Hag knits away, she plucks a small bone from the mess of entrails and organs and tucks it into her corset, taking a moment to rearrange her obscenely human-looking breasts. Then she stops abruptly and looks down at me as if she's suddenly realized there's more prey in the alley and it's watching her. After a moment she dismisses me and returns to her stitching, but I feel . . . marked somehow. Like she filed me away in her Unseelie-insect brain.

"How do I kill her? Will my sword work?"

"Might. But you'd never get close enough. Her nee-

358 · KAREN MARIE MONING

dles are longer than your sword. She'd have your guts in her dress before you even managed to swing it."

"You said she gets obsessed while she's knitting."

"Not that obsessed."

The ambience in the back alley changes abruptly and it takes me a minute to figure out why. A light just came on in the back of BB&B and is spilling out the window, across the bloodstained snow.

I know what that means. Mac's moving around inside, looking for Barrons. I imagine it won't be long before she looks out back to see if his car's out there.

If Mac walked out that door and tried to kill me right now, I'm not sure how well I'd fight.

I take one last look at Barrons and Ryodan. I have to make this right somehow. I have to balance the scales and there's a lot weighing in against me.

"Come near me again and I'll kill you," I say, soft like Ryodan used to talk.

I freeze-frame into the night.

THIRTY-TWO

"If I stay lucky then my tongue will stay tied"

I spend the next two days slapping up terse *Dani Dailies* that describe the Crimson Hag and her M.O., hunting for Dancer, collecting the rest of the ziplocks I need from the other iced scenes (except for the club beneath Chester's, which I'm in no hurry to go near), and packing my backpack full of samples. They're some of the most miserable days of my life. I go up and down like a fecking psychotic elevator being controlled by some fecking psychotic little kid, punching random floor buttons. One second I'm swaggering, the next I'm drooping.

One minute I'm elated because I never have to go to work again. My life is my own. Jo can quit the subclub. She'll stop wearing sparkly stuff between her boobs and boinking Ryodan. The next minute I remember that if Ryodan's remaining men learn that I played even one tiny little part in their boss's death, I'm deader than every doornail in Dublin. On top of that, the Crimson Hag is loose, the Hoar Frost King is still out there, Dublin is slowly turning into Ant-fecking-arctica, Christian and me are on the outs, and now Mac has double the reasons to kill me, assuming she knows.

I can't decide if she knows. One minute I think she does, the next I don't.

The bodies are gone. I went back in the middle of the night to hide them. I should have hidden them right away but I wasn't thinking clear. Aside from blood in the alley and up the brick wall, no trace of them remained.

At first I thought Mac must have found and taken them somewhere for a proper burial, but then I decided she didn't, because yesterday I saw her hurrying down the street toward Chester's, all bundled up and shivering in the cold, and she didn't look sad. I've seen Mac sad. I know what it looks like. She looked a little tense but otherwise normal. She had a trail of ZEWs behind her, chittering away. I wonder if, like crows, the ZEWs are harbingers of death. It worries me they're following Mac. Her tension is probably because of what's happening to Dublin. Everybody I'm seeing is tense. And shivering. It's ten degrees in Dublin during the day, even colder at night. Snow's been falling, piling up. The city isn't set up to handle this kind of weather. Lots of folks don't have power where they're staying. They won't survive these conditions long.

I wonder if the Crimson Hag ate Barrons's and Ryodan's bodies. Stitched up their entrails then dined on the rest. I'd think she'd have spit up a few bones but maybe she needed them all to spruce up her corset. Then I figured Christian probably went back to tidy up and hide the evidence. Trying to get on my good side again or something.

I wonder where the heck Dancer is! I need his superbrain to help me crunch the facts so I can save my city from turning into an iceberg. So then I can save folks from getting knitted up into a dress.

I got two more places to check for him, then I'm out of places to hunt.

I freeze-frame up O'Connell, yanking WeCare posters off streetlamps as I go. Stupid fecking stupid feckers are trying to take advantage of people not having power, encouraging them to come into prayer meetings, to get warm and "take the white." I didn't know what that meant till I saw a couple folks coming out of one of the churches the WeCare people have designated as their own, wearing long white robes over their clothes.

They were carrying bags of canned goods and smiling. In my experience, anybody besides your mom that feeds you is going to want something in exchange for it.

I whiz up to Dancer's penthouse, where we like to stretch out in the sun, disarm his booby traps and poke my head in the door, calling for him. The place is silent and empty. I decide to see if he's got any food in the pantry 'cause I'm starving. When I get there, I crack up. There's a note taped to a stack of cans sitting smack in the middle of the floor. It's a cryptogram. It's how we leave messages for each other.

I pop open can after can of beanie weenies and gorge while I solve the puzzle that tells me where he is.

There's a lot hidden away in Dublin, just like out at the abbey. When I first started hanging out in the city, I got one of those sightseeing books and visited all the hot spots like any tourist. I was embarrassed to be a stranger in my own town, never having been out of my cage much. I wanted to know everything everybody else knew, see it all with my own eyeballs instead of watching it on TV or reading about it in a book.

I went to Trinity College and toured all the cool stuff there. I never got to go to school so it was neat to see the classrooms and labs and libraries and folks being all social instead of being kept by themselves all the time. I couldn't wrap my brain around growing up that way. Mom taught me to read. I taught myself the rest.

I hit up the museums, dropped by the brewery, hung

out in Temple Bar, visited the catacombs beneath Christ Church Cathedral and St. Michan's Church, and eventually hunted down the underground rivers. I listened when college kids raved about their favorite places and went there, too. I paid attention when old folks talked on the streets about things that used to be.

That's how I found Dublin-down. Couple of wrinkly old dudes playing checkers by river Liffey used to work for a mob family and knew some interesting stuff. Beneath a restaurant run by a dude name of Rocky O'Bannion, this big-time mobster that disappeared last year in the craziness of the walls coming down, I found it. A honeycomb of tunnels and hidden crypts beyond a pile of rubble and a series of grated entrances so complex only someone as curious as me or a criminal trying to hide bodies and booty would ever have gone through. Dancer and me mapped out parts but we still got a lot to explore.

That's where I find him now, in one of the underground catacombs, down a collapsed tunnel (unless you knew how to find the hidden detour) beyond bolted steel doors, hinged into stone, all booby-trapped.

The room he's in is long and narrow and made completely of stone, with those old vaulted fornix ceilings, supported by massive columns, like I only ever seen in ancient crypts and the library at the abbey. He's got lights set up that I figure have to be battery-powered 'cause I don't hear a generator, and setting one up to vent down here would take a lot of work. He's standing behind a stone slab that used to hold a corpse but is now covered with notebooks and envelopes, laptops, bottles, beakers, and burners. Yep, this place is Dancer, just missing a TV to watch movies on, a fridge and shower, and knowing him, he probably has a hidey-hole rigged up nearby with all the conveniences. Another slab is crammed with bottled water and food. His head is down and he's working on something, deep in thought.

"Dude, this is fecking awesome!" I say as I step inside.

Dancer looks up and the grin he gives me is blinding. His whole body changes, like he was strung up on wires hanging him from the ceiling and they just got cut. His shoulders ride lower, his limbs slide smoother, the hard planes of his face relax into the Dancer I know. "Mega!" he says. Then he says it again, "Mega!"

"That's my name, dude. Don't wear it out." I swagger into the chamber and see he's been collecting things from the scenes, too. Behind him is the pièce de résistance: a mystery board! He blew up maps and pieced together an enormous topographical survey of Dublin and the outlying areas and has pins and notes plastered all over it. I beam. I couldn't have done better myself. "This place is the Shit," I say.

"Thought you'd like it." He picks his glasses up off the slab, pushes them back on his nose and grins at me. His eyes are red like he's been studying too long. He's tall and lanky and pretty much perfect. I grin back and we just grin at each other for a few seconds, 'cause we're so happy to see each other again. It's a big city. Sometimes I feel alone in it. Then I see Dancer.

I toss my backpack on a nearby folding table and pull out my ziplocks and photos to add to his board. He comes over and we sort through them in happy silence, brushing shoulders and grinning at each other. He keeps looking at me like he can't exactly believe I'm there. Dude's acting like he really missed me. We're always glad to see each other, but something's different today.

I go to start pinning my photos of the scenes on the board, and I look back at him, 'cause something don't make sense to me, besides how strange he's acting. "There ain't this many iced places in Dublin!" I gesture at the pins on the board.

"There weren't a few weeks ago. It's been escalating."

"Dude, there were only ten. You got, like, twenty-five pins on this board! You telling me fifteen more places got iced in the past few days?"

"Mega, the last time I saw you was nearly a month ago. The day we tried to get your sword back from Jayne."

I gape. "That wasn't a month ago. That was a couple days ago!"

"Nope. I haven't seen you for three weeks, four days, and"—he looks at his watch—"seventeen hours."

I let out a low whistle. I knew time moved different in Faery but it didn't occur to me that the White Mansion was part of Faery. No wonder Ryodan was so pissed at me! I missed work for *weeks*. I snicker. It must have been driving him crazy. My snicker dies. I forgot for a sec that he was dead. I feel sick all the sudden so I tear open a candy bar and eat it.

"I was worried."

I look at him. He's looking me right in the eyes, more serious than I ever seen him. It makes me uncomfortable. Like I'm supposed to say something and I don't know what.

I stare back and we just look at each other for a few seconds. I root around in my repertoire and come up with: "Dude, get over yourself. I'm the Mega. You never got to worry about me. I been on my own forever. I like it that way." I flash him my trademark grin.

I get a faint smile in return. "Got the message, Mega. Loud and clear." He turns around, walks back to the slab. He's not moving smooth anymore. Some of those wires are back. I don't like those wires. They look . . . I don't know, grown-up to me.

"Just saying, don't worry about me. Stupid to worry about me. I can take care of myself."

"Now I'm stupid."

"I didn't say *you* were stupid. I say *it* was stupid to worry about me."

"And it—the act of worrying—isn't to be confused with the person doing it."

"Exactly. I'm the Mega, remember? I kick butt all over Dublin!" I don't know what's wrong with him. He's not responding right to anything I'm saying!

"Ability to defend oneself has absolutely no bearing on or relevance to deportment or emotional comportment of others."

"Huh?"

"Don't tell me what I can and can't feel. If I feel like worrying about you, I buggering well will."

"Dude, no need to get snippy."

"I'm not snippy. I'm offended. You were gone nearly a month. Between dodging the psychotic jackass that stalks you day and night, analyzing evidence, and trying to save this city, I've been haunting every iced scene that pops up. Visiting them two and three times a day. Do you know why?"

"To collect more evidence?"

"I've been waiting for them to melt enough that I could see if you were in there. Dead. Never to be talking to me again."

I stare at him. We never talk about stuff like this. It reeks of a cage to me. Like there's one more person I'm supposed to check in with now. Like my life isn't already owned by too many other folks. "I got my sword back now," I say stiffly. "I'm not going to get iced."

"Invalid. Those two statements have no relevance to each other. None. Zip. Zilch. Nada. The sword won't protect you from getting iced. I left notes for you in the pantry of every hideout I've got and all of yours I could find. Do you know what I heard? Nothing. For almost a month."

"Dude, I got the picture. You didn't like not being

able to find me. Too bad you can't put a leash on me, huh? Maybe stick me in a cage somewhere?" He's pissing me off. I think we're having our first ever fight. It makes me feel sick to my stomach.

"Excuse the crap out of me for caring about you."

"Dude, what's wrong with you? This ain't us. Why are you ruining us?"

"Caring about you is ruining us?"

"Caring is one thing. Trying to lock me up is another."

He gives me a look that I just don't get. Like I'm being obtuse when he's the one being obtuse. I thought our way of hanging was clear and well-defined. We're superheroes. He's not sticking to the script. If he keeps deviating, I'm jumping comic books.

"My mistake. I won't make it again." Just like that, he goes back to being Dancer, all business. "That day at the castle was the first time I got a look at what's been freezing things. A lot's happened since then. It freezes a new place just about every day. Ryodan and his men have been tearing this city apart looking for you. He raided half my stoops. I moved down here to get the bloody feck away from him. He's going to kill you when he finds you."

"Not if I kill him first," I mutter around a mouthful of candy bar, pretending I didn't already. When you have a secret that folks would kill you for, you sit mum on it. From everyone. 'Course, if I'm learning from my mistakes, I should kill Christian like I didn't kill those stupid lisping fairies that ate Alina and ratted me out to Mac. I'm a little irked that Dancer's back to talking about stuff like we never even had our first spat, because it's a big deal to me. It's going to take me hours to stop feeling nauseous and confused inside. I eat when I get confused. I stuff another candy bar in my mouth.

"Even Barrons got in on the hunt. So did those abbey girls you sometimes hang with. The city keeps getting colder with each new place that's iced. People are falling apart. Nobody knows what to do, how to stop it, or even where it's safe to be anymore." He steps back and looks at the map. "So far I haven't been able to discern the pattern. We've got to figure out what it's looking for."

"What do you mean 'looking for'?" That was exactly the feeling I picked up with my *sidhe*-seer senses, but Dancer doesn't have those. I start to feel a little less sick. I don't know if it's the candy bars in my stomach or thinking about work.

"Unless it's behaving in a random, illogical manner driven by absolutely no biological imperative—which I postulate is antithetical for any sentient life form—it has purpose."

I beam, our fight forgotten. Got to love a dude that says stuff like "postulate" and "antithetical"! "I love hanging with you!" I tell him.

He gives me a look that's vintage Dancer but a little wary, so I turn up the wattage on my grin till he grins back.

"That purpose may be alien enough," he goes on, "to elude ready detection, but it's there. It's our methods that are lacking. We have to step outside our box and process the facts with no preconceptions. This thing isn't from our world. It doesn't follow our rules or any laws of physics. It appears capable of opening a portal wherever it feels like it. I've seen it do it twice now."

"You saw it *again*?" I'm so fecking jealous I could spit.

"I've been keeping an eye on WeCare, trying to figure who the head honcho is. Nobody seems to know who started the organization up. A few nights ago I went to check out one of their prayer meetings. The church where they were holding it got iced when I was half a block away. One minute they were singing, the next I couldn't hear a thing. Seemed like the whole world went still or I went deaf. I stood in the street and watched. It did exactly the same thing it did at Dublin Castle. Came out of a portal, fogged everything, iced it, opened another portal, and vanished."

I flinch. He was half a block away! What if he'd been, like, one single minute earlier? Then I have a worse thought. What if I hadn't been able to find him for a month? Would I have been freeze-framing from one ice sculpture to the next, waiting for them to melt, wondering if I'd lost my best friend?

I'm suddenly ashamed. "Dude. Sorry I was gone so long."

His head whips up and he gives me a grin that fecking slays me. "Dude. Thanks. Glad you're back."

"I hear you saved my life at the church that night. You're the Shit."

"No, you are."

We grin at each other for what feels like an hour of heaven, and just like that everything is okay between us again.

We start yakking our heads off like nothing was ever wrong. He tells me scoop about new gangs forming in the city. I tell him about the Unseelie King's library. I can't keep that kind of fascinating stuff to myself. I can tell by how bright his eyes get that he's dying to see it.

He tells me a huge fire-world IFP almost burned the abbey to the ground! It evaporated iron and concrete and if it had made it to the abbey, nothing would have been left. But Ryodan's men stopped it by tethering it stationary to the ground somehow. I don't like that it's out there by the abbey, tied up or not. It makes me nervous.

I tell him about the Boora-Boora books and he laughs his butt off about me chasing unruly sentences down. He fills me in on how WeCare started painting buildings white to let folks know it's one of theirs, and if you go in and sign up, and attend meetings, they give you all kinds of food and stuff. I tell him about R'jan trying to take over as king of the Fae and that the ice monster has a name: the Hoar Frost King. I think it's the most we've ever told each other about the daily details of our lives. He tells me food is getting really hard to find. I tell him about the Fae being totally inert at the scenes and about what R'jan said about it killing Seelie and Unseelie deader than dead, wiping them out of all record of existence. "I think it might be after folks' life force," I tell him.

"But why those scenes? How does it select the ones it chooses and why does it ice them? And if it wanted people's life force, why wouldn't it go where the greatest number were gathered? At some of these scenes, there were only a few people."

"You mean like why would it ice the small club beneath Chester's when it could have iced the whole place?"

"It iced part of Chester's?"

"That was the first place it iced that I know of. It's the reason Ryodan dragged me into this mess."

"It can't be after life force. It took out a church spire, too. There wasn't a single person or Fae at that scene."

"Maybe it was just flying over that spire and accidentally iced it. Or maybe there was a tiny life force, like a mouse there, and it was feeling peckish."

He grins. "Maybe."

"I kind of doubt it, though. I think we should label them by order of occurrence. Maybe that'll help us see something."

"What bites," he says, "is we can't even tell people something so simple as: stay in small groups and you'll be okay. People are scared of their own shadows, Mega. The whole city is on edge, tempers are high, and people are getting into fights over nothing. We've got to figure out what's going on because if they don't freeze to death first, they'll kill each other. They've lost too much and been afraid too long. While you were gone, there were no *Dani Dailies* getting out, and in times like these, no news *isn't* good news. People need to believe someone is in the streets watching out for them."

"What about WeCare? Aren't they taking their job seriously? Dude, when I was gone, they should have stepped up to the plate, put out more issues! A newspaper's got a responsibility to the people!"

"The only thing WeCare is telling people is that they need to 'take the white' and everything will be all right. Half the city is rushing in to blindly embrace faith; the other half isn't buying it. Toss in the shortage of food and water, and the brutal cold, and we're going to have riots on our hands any day now."

I push my hair out of my face and stare at the mystery board. I count twenty-four pins. My nine ziplocks are no longer representative of the scenes. "Did you collect debris?"

He gives me a what-kind-of-idiot-do-you-think-I-am look, and a grin, and picks a box up off the floor that's crammed with more yellow envelopes like the ones on the slab. "I've been analyzing samples from the scenes, categorizing and isolating commonalities. I took photos, too."

I grin back because great minds think alike and it's so fecking cool to be peas in the Mega-pod.

While he opens envelopes, I get back to pinning pictures of the scenes where they go on our mystery board. I thought my life force idea was right until he pointed out two glaring flaws. Feck. It's a good thing I got my "impartial" ziplocks of evidence. I start to snicker then remember again that Ryodan's dead. It's hard for me to remember for some reason. Like I thought he was eternal or something. I got no clue why it feels like such a kick in the teeth every time I think about it. Sure, I let the Hag out, but he's the dude that failed to dodge her. I don't move as fast as him, and *I* managed to get away.

Eight hours later I can hardly see straight. Alternately staring at bits of debris then studying the map is making me bug-eyed.

I been awake for three days, juiced on a constant sugar rush from candy bars, sodas, and the pall of something hanging over me that makes me nuts. Guilt. Guilt is for losers. Guilt is for folks who have stupid things like regrets. I contemplate the notion that maybe regrets are a process of accumulation of time, as unavoidable as a closet full of clothes and more bags of them in the attic. Is accumulated baggage what makes people get old? If so, they need to clean out their fecking attics, send the stuff to consignment shops and remember how to walk around naked like kids, little bellies sticking out, always ready for a good laugh. The second I kill the Crimson Hag, I'm sending my guilt straight to hell where it can burn. Problem is, I'm stuck with it till then and it's making me even testier than hormones. I don't like feeling responsible for crap. Like little anchors holding me still on my happy sea that's got an even grander adventure waiting just beyond the next wave.

There's a bit of everything in the plastic bags. Splinters of wood from church pews, stained glass, hair, bits of bone and carpet and leather, dirt, plastic, food, human parts, Unseelie parts. There are chunks of white crystal and shreds of yoga mats, parts of phones, teeth, jewelry, fragments of various electronics, bits of iron bars, a piece of a washboard, metal racking. There's paper and plastic wrappers, part of a fingernail with a finger bone fused to it, a hearing aid, half a driver's license, and so on. We make a list of each scene's contents, tack it to the murder board, and cross off anything that wasn't in every single bag.

We're left with "mystery debris," which is what we decide to call the dirt stuff at the bottom of each ziplock, metal and plastic.

"Does this stuff feel . . . I don't know, weird to you, Mega?"

I scoop a chunk of crystal into my palm and hold it a second. "It's colder than it should be, like it's still partly iced. It doesn't warm up no matter how long you hold it."

"No, there's something else. I can't put my finger on it."

I wait. I didn't go to school and I'm a little in awe of how much stuff Dancer knows. If he says there's something else, there is.

He muses aloud. "If it's not after life forces, how is it selecting its scenes? It might not be metal or plastic that the thing is after, which is at every scene in some form, but an ingredient *in* metal or plastic. The thing could be hunting infinitesimal traces of something."

I push a pile of old bones to the edge of a stone slab, stretch out next to them, fold my arms behind my head and begin mentally rebuilding the scenes to what they were before they blew, thinking it might be easier to find a commonality before they were reduced to rubble. "Like some kind of theoretical vitamin or mineral it needs in order to accomplish something it wants to do?"

"Or a common element at the scenes that makes it think what it wants *might* be at that scene," Dancer says.

"Huh?"

"It could be like a fisherman, going wherever there's salt water, because he's looking for a whale. We wouldn't necessarily ever find a whale. But we would always find saltwater. If we can figure out what draws it, we're half-way to stopping it."

"We still got three scenes we don't have samples from. The two that R'jan said got iced in Faery and the one under Chester's."

"Can you ask Ryodan to help us get samples? From what I hear, pretty much everybody owes that dude something."

All my mental pictures shatter when Dancer says his name, and suddenly I'm seeing two images at the same time: Ryodan on level four laughing, having sex, more alive than anybody I ever met 'cept of course me, and Ryodan, bled out in the alley, guts draping down the side of the building, cracking a joke while he dies, and I'm thinking the most fecked-up thought—I hardly even got to know him! "Yes, I did," I mutter, pushing myself up because if I'm going to puke my candy bar, I'm not going to be on my back while I do it.

"Did what?" Dancer says.

I always fought with him and kept saying I hated him. "He deserved it. He was the most arrogant, irritating fecker I've ever known!"

"Deserved what? Who was?"

Looks like I'll have to start calling Ryodan TP, too. 'Cause he's making my stomach cramp. I don't like him not being in the world. "Does this mean my contract expired, or can one of the other dudes call it in?" You just never know with dudes like them. I don't ever want to go into Chester's again, and I don't want to go into BB&B again, assuming I could, because it's just B&B now and the critical ingredients that made both places so exciting and larger than life had nothing to do with the places themselves.

"What contract?"

Now that those critical ingredients are gone forever I got a bad feeling about Dublin, about the whole world.

Like I might have tilted the planet on its axis into some strange, new, and not nearly as safe a position by eliminating them.

"Mega." Dancer's standing in front of me. "Talk to me."

"We can't ask Ryodan nothing," I tell him.

"Why not?"

I rub my eyes and sigh. "I killed him."

I wake up with my neck all crinked and a ziplock bag stuck to my cheek by drool. I lift my head an inch or two and peek out from under my hair, hoping Dancer isn't looking at me, and when I find him staring at the mystery board, I swallow a sigh of embarrassed relief.

I peel the bag from my face, wipe the drool off with my shirt, and rub at the grooves in my cheek. I can feel part of a ring indent in it plus a couple of those zipper lines. I don't even remember falling asleep. But somewhere along the way I just dropped my head on the stuff I was examining and passed out. A few hours? More? "What time is it?"

"What day, you mean."

"Dude, tell me I didn't sleep that long!"

"You needed it. I'm not sure you're going to be able to move, though. I've never seen anyone sit on a stool, drop her head on a slab and not move for fifteen hours. I thought about getting you to stretch out somewhere more comfortable. You changed my mind." He turns around and grins at me. He's got a busted lip. "You had no intention of being moved. You decked me in your sleep."

"Aw, dude, sorry!" I have no memory of it.

"No worries, Mega."

My stomach growls loud enough to wake the dead, and he says, "I got something I been saving for you." He rummages around in one of his bags on the floor, pulls out a box and tosses it to me.

I light up like a Christmas tree. "Fecking-A! Pop-Tarts! Where did you find Pop-Tarts? I haven't seen any for months!" Even before the walls fell, they could be tough to find. "And they're my favorites—chocolate with frosting!" I rip open a pack and munch happily away. I polish off the first two in a quick inhale then slow down to savor every delicious, preservative-packed, sugar-crammed crumb of the remaining six. When the walls fell, all the good stuff—which is the bad-for-you stuff—got taken off the shelves first. Soda and liquor went real fast. Candy, cake, cookies, pies, things like that were next. Pop-Tarts, all the sugary cereal, flew off the shelves, too. I'm as guilty as the next person. Funny thing is, nowadays I'd just about give my right arm for a hot meal of fresh slow-cooked pot roast, carrots, peas, bread, and gravy.

Still, Pop-Tarts are close to heaven and Dancer got them for me, which makes them taste twice as good. I eat, and he tells me everything he considered and discarded while I was sleeping so I can poke holes in his theories if there are any. When he's done talking, we're no closer to conclusions than we were before I fell asleep.

"So, all we've still got is that every scene has dirt, some kind of plastic, and metal at it."

"Actually it's dirt, plastic, and iron. The metal in every one of the ziplocks is largely iron."

"Iron is what we use to imprison the Fae."

"I know. Remember how much worse the Unseelie at Dublin Castle got iced?"

I nod. "I thought it was because there were so many of them."

"It also happens to be the location with the most iron. Tons of the stuff was used to build those cages."

"Where was the iron at the other scenes?"

"Old railroad tracks run right next to where they were washing clothes out in the country. I checked maps, and discovered railroad tracks run past four other scenes. I found iron bullets in two of the bags. The church steeple had enormous cast-iron bells. The fitness center had part of a cast-iron teapot and iron chime fragments. At another scene there were several older cars that had frames of iron. They don't make them like that anymore. At Dublin Castle there are all those iron cages. The racking in one of the old warehouses was made of iron." He goes on, detailing location after location.

"Why iron? Why not say . . . steel. Isn't steel iron?"

"Iron gets turned into steel. What I'm seeing is a preponderance of *unworked* iron, like the railroad tracks, bells, and bars. Old stuff. You don't see a lot of iron anymore. You see composites. Steel is stronger and iron rusts. You know how old railroad tracks are almost always red with it?"

"You think we need to go back to the scenes and see if it took the iron?"

"No. I'm wondering if iron is in the salt water. If that's what draws it."

"But what is it after?"

He shrugs. "Who knows? Who cares? I only want to know two things: how to lure it to us and how to get rid of it. Its goals are irrelevant."

"But Fae hate iron."

"I know. That's what makes me wonder if it's drawing it somehow. I'm not saying it's coming to iron because it likes it. Maybe it's trying to destroy the iron by icing it. Maybe one of the Fae summoned it to destroy the only means we have of imprisoning them. Maybe trying to understand something that can open a multidimensional portal, sail across the sky, open another portal and vanish, is as much an exercise in futility as trying to divine the motives of God."

"You believe in God?"

"Dude. Only God could have created physics."

I snicker. "Or Pop-Tarts."

He grins. "See. There you are. Proof of the divine. All in the chocolate smudge around your mouth."

"I got chocolate on my face?"

"Kind of hard to see with all those ziplock lines but yeah."

I sigh. Someday I'm going to be around Dancer with no guts in my hair, no weird clothes on, no black eyes or blood, and no food on my face. He probably won't recognize me. "But what about those two places in Faery?" I say.

"What about them?"

"There's no way there's iron in Faery."

"Assumption. Potentially erroneous. The walls came down. Everything got fractured and Faery has been bleeding through to our world. Maybe parts of our world are bleeding through to Faery, and there are railroad ties or bells in those parts. We need samples from Faery."

"And how the feck are we going to get those? Why don't we just try to lure it with iron and see what happens?"

"That's plan B. Let's try to get samples first and I'll keep analyzing this stuff. There's something I'm missing. I can feel it in my gut. I need more time with the evidence. Besides, even if we got it to come, what would we do with it then? We need to know what draws it *and* how to stop it. You get the samples. I'll work on the rest. If there's no iron in Faery, we know we're back at square one without having to round up tons of iron and find a place to stack it all up where nobody will get hurt."

I push up and head for the door.

As I'm leaving, he says, "Don't go to Faery yourself, Mega. Make a sifter do it for you. We can't lose another month. I got a bad feeling about these iced places."

"'Cause they keep exploding?"

He takes off his glasses and rubs his eyes. "No. Like there's something worse about them. A lot worse. I can't explain. It's just a hunch."

I know Dancer. When he gets a hunch, what that really means is his subconscious is seeing something he hasn't wrapped his conscious brain around yet. Every time he's ever told me he had a hunch, he's worked his way around an epiphany. I trust him like I never trusted anybody. If he wants samples and more time, he's got it.

I head up and out into the Dublin night. A light snow is falling. The moon has a blood red ring.

There's one sure place to find a sifting Fae. Conveniently, it's also the third place we need a sample from. With luck, I'll be back here in a few hours with the final three ziplocks to complete our evidence chain.

My luck ain't been so good lately.

THIRTY-THREE

"Who's your daddy?"

Chester's. Feckin-A, I hate this place even more than I used to. The line outside tonight is nuts. It's zero degrees in Dublin, snow's begun to fall in earnest, there's a killer wind kicking up and still five blocks of folks are shivering outside, bundled in layers of clothing, huddled together waiting to get in.

I blast past them in fast-mo, skidding on an icy spot, whiz around one of Ryodan's human bouncers who's got his hands too full controlling the crowd to stop me, jump the ladder down to the main entrance and explode through tall black doors into the club.

It's rocking tonight same as always: music thumping, lights flashing, folks partying up a storm. We got something icing our city, killing innocents everywhere, turning it into an arctic zone in June, and this is what folks are doing about it. Dancing, laughing, getting drunk, getting laid, acting like the walls didn't fall, the world didn't lose half the human race, and nothing's changed.

I stand on the platform inside the door that overlooks it all for a sec, scowling, blowing on my hands, trying to warm them up. I need gloves. And a scarf and earmuffs. The scowl doesn't last long because I get distracted from being pissed by the song that's playing. It's one of my oldie faves from a few decades back, heavy on bass, and it's so loud it vibrates the soles of my combat boots, all the way up my legs and into my belly. My bones rumble with resonance. I love music because it's so fecking brilliant. Music is math, and math is the structure of everything and pretty much perfect. Before everything got so crazy, Dancer was teaching me stuff about math that dazzled me.

My scowl comes back.

Jo's in the kiddie subclub, dressed all sexy, laughing at something some skanky waitress said, moving sleek and pretty with the music as she goes from table to table, chatting up the customers and occasionally looking around, like she's keeping an eye on things in general, or watching for someone. She's still got those highlights and sparkly boobs. I'll be real glad when that stuff's gone and she's the Jo I know again.

I'm going to make her quit tonight. We don't owe a dead man anything, and if the other dudes think to try to enforce our contracts, well, we're walking out anyway and they can just try.

I groan and roll my eyes, realizing I can't make her quit tonight because I can't tell her he's dead. I can't tell nobody he's dead. Only me, Christian, and whoever moved their bodies—assuming it wasn't Christian—know they got killed. It's only been three days. Folks might not decide he's dead for a while yet. Knowing her, she'll stick around for weeks, hoping he comes back!

I feel a little perturbed. I been gone almost a month and she doesn't look sad at all. Didn't she miss me? Worry about me?

I shove that thought away and look up at the ceiling, eyeing the girders, wondering what kind of metal was used in the construction of Chester's. If this place is as old as it seems, I'd think it'd have to be iron because I don't think the method of making steel was figured out till recent times. Well, recent in terms of how old this place is. Then I wonder how old iron is. Then I wonder if Ryodan and his dudes just spelled the whole mess together. Or maybe they created their own kind of metal or brought it with them from whatever planet they were born on.

I wonder who's in charge now that I killed Barrons and Ryodan. Lor?

As if my thoughts conjured him, I hear him say behind me, real close to my ear: "Aw, honey, you got some nerve coming here."

I turn around to say suspiciously, "What do you mean by that?" but he's not there by the time I complete my rotation. I wonder if I imagined him, a product of my guilty conscience. Then I decide if I really did hear him say what I thought he said, he was only referring to how Ryodan's been looking for me for a month and now I waltz in like I never been gone, and he thinks Ryodan's going to toast my ass for missing work so long. Because, like, he doesn't know Ryodan's dead either.

This is exactly why I hate lies. The second you tell one, you know something everybody else doesn't know and you have to constantly keep reminding yourself to behave like you don't know it, so they don't decide you're acting weird and figure out you know something they don't. If they do, they'll back you against a wall and demand to know why you're acting weird and you'll say something stupid and they'll use it to trip you up with. Then everything comes spilling out and you're in ten kinds of trouble! It's so much easier not to tell any lies to begin with.

This is going to be a tough pretending gig. Reminders of Ryodan are everywhere in here. Heck, Ryodan *is* Chester's! It's, hands-down, the hardest place to pretend he's not dead that I could possibly be. But I need those samples. The HFK is icing something practically every day, and Dancer thinks things are going to get worse.

I spot a sifter down in the Tuxedo Club and grin. The Gray Bitch. This is one I'm going to love laying the flat of my sword against and ordering around. Mac promised not to hunt her but I never took no such stupid oath, and besides, I'm not hunting her, I'm just going to threaten her into doing something for me. Hand hovering over the hilt of my sword, I map out the grid as best I can, considering most things on it are moving—not that I mind jabbing all these idiots with my elbows— and freeze-frame down the stairs. At the last minute I detour from the Tuxedo Club and head for Jo. I want to see her face when she sees me. See how glad she gets to know I'm alive. She must have been as worried about me as Dancer and it's only right to put her mind at ease.

"Dani! What are you doing here?" Jo goes white as a sheet when I whiz to a stop in front of her. "Are you *crazy*?"

Not the reaction I expected. Where's the look of relief, the big hug, the excitement to see me alive and back here again? "What are you talking about?"

"Ryodan's been looking for you for a month! You broke your contract with him!"

"And according to that," I say irritably, "you should be dead. But you're not. Fact is, you look pretty darn good to me. Guess boinking him kept you alive, huh? You been doing it all this time? Didn't he get tired of you?"

She flushes. "He said it wasn't fair to take out his displeasure at you on me. Ryodan's a smart man. He makes good decisions. He's not impulsive like some people." She gives me a pointed stare.

I'm disgusted. "Oh, he was just a . . . uh, *is* a fecking saint, now, huh?"

"He's a fine man. You should give him a chance."

"He's a dead man, is what he is!" I blurt, because I can't fecking stand to hear her defending him.

"Would you quit making threats about him every time you turn around? It's getting old." She lowers her voice. "You need to get out of here before he catches you. I've never seen him like he's been since he hasn't been able to find you."

"I ain't scared of Ryodan." Gah, I wish I could just tell her!

"You should be. You pushed him too far this time, Dani. I don't know what he's going to do when he sees you, and I'm not sure I can stop him. I don't think he'll listen to even me about you."

He's never going to find out because he's dead, but that's not what I fixate on. "What do you mean 'even you,' like you're some kind of special to him?"

She blushes and gets this soft-eyed look on her face like a sap in love. "We're a couple, Dani. It's been over a month and we're exclusive. All the waitresses are talking about it. They never thought anybody would . . . you know, get a man like him to settle down."

I just stare at her, blinking. Ryodan ain't exclusive with nobody. Settle down? Tornadoes *touch* down. They don't settle. They leave destruction in their wake. Not shiny, happy people. I feel sick inside, at the idea of him and Jo setting up house together, making plans for the future. As fecking if. What am I going to be? Their little fetch-it dog? I shake my head, reminding myself again that Ryodan's dead. How does she keep getting me all distracted? Talking like he's alive is confusing me.

"I ain't talking to you anymore. I got things to do. Maybe you noticed Dublin is turning into the North Pole?"

"Of course I have. You're the one that took off for a month and didn't tell anyone that you were going to Faery with Christian."

"Huh?" I gape at her. "How'd you know that?"

"Christian told me."

"Scary-Unseelie-prince-Christian dropped in and told you I was okay?"

"I don't know why he came, but he overheard me talking with Cormac yesterday in the Tux Club about how worried I was about you and he said the two of you had just gotten back and you were fine. I'm not going to breathe a word to Ryodan even though we tell each other everything. But I don't appreciate you putting me in a position where I have to lie to him. Now get out of here before he comes down! Things are calm tonight. I'd like them to stay that way."

Tell each other everything? She's wrong on all counts. Ryodan was the most keep-it-to-yourself dude I ever met. Things aren't calm in here; as usual they're a catastrophe waiting to happen. And he ain't ever coming down again.

So I'm walking away from Jo, heading toward the Tuxedo Club to commandeer the Gray Bitch's services, when somebody crashes into me from behind so hard I go flying into one of the fluted columns at the exit of the kiddie subclub. I end up hugging it, to keep myself from puddling to the floor. I hit it so hard I'm going to have another black eye and the whole left side of my face is already working itself into the mother of all contusions. I think: Who the feck would dare attack me when I'm carrying so blatantly? Mac? 'Cause she hates me so much it made her stupid? I didn't hide my sword when I came in. I peeled my leather coat back so everybody could see it's mine again!

I stumble away from the column and am about to turn when I get slammed into it again. This time I swear I see stars and hear cuckoo birds whistling. My hand falls off the hilt of my sword, I'm so dazed. I hear Jo yelling behind me. "Stop it! Don't hurt her! Stop it!"

I get slammed again as soon as I start to move. This time I bust my lip against the column. It pisses me off so bad that I shift up into fast-mo, grab my sword and yank it out. If it's Mac, I don't want to hurt her. I just want to run. But she's really got to stop pushing me around in front of the whole fecking club. I got a reputation to consider.

It's gone from my hand before I even can turn around. I get slammed again and I bite the fecking column a fourth time.

"You move one more time, I'll rip your fucking heart out."

I go still as the slayed Unseelie chunks at the iced scenes. That was *not* Ryodan that just spoke behind me because he, like, got gutted and died. Apparently I'm having hallucinations. Either that or a ghost is haunting me. It would figure the dude would come back from the dead just to make my life miserable. He was such a pro at it when he was alive.

I'm crushed so tight between the column and whatever's behind me I almost can't breathe.

"You can't be here," I say. "You're dead."

He slams me into the column again and I make an involuntary squeak.

"I first learned of your existence when you were nine years old," he says. "Fade told me he'd seen a human child on the streets that could move like us. He advocated, as did the rest of my men, killing you immediately. I have rarely found it necessary to kill human infants. They don't live long anyway."

That sure sounds like Ryodan. Cold. Void of inflection. Maybe Ryodan had a twin brother I knew nothing about. If not, I've gone completely nuts and being tormented by a guilty conscience in a weird and incredibly real way. He died. I watched it happen. There was no mistaking it. I try to move my hand, thinking to wipe blood from my face. He crushes it in his fist so hard my bones grind together.

"I said don't fucking move. Not a hair on your head. Got it."

Another Ryodan characteristic. No question mark. I hate being cued so I don't say anything. A bone snaps in my little finger. Gently. Precisely. Like he's showing me he could break them all, one at a time, if he felt like it. I grit my teeth. "Got it."

"When you were ten, Kasteo told me you'd somehow gotten the sword. Again my men advocated I take it and kill you. Again, I felt the mewling pup would die soon enough."

"I'm not a pup and I don't mewl. Ow! You said don't move. I didn't. I spoke!"

"Don't. And you *will* mewl before the night is over. In a moment I'm going to step back and let you go. You will turn around and follow me, walking behind me. You will not speak to anyone. You will not look at anyone. If anyone but me speaks to you, you will not answer. You will not move any part of your body that is not absolutely necessary to get you up the stairs and into my office. If you deviate from my orders in any way, I will break your left leg in front of the entire club. If you piss me off while I'm doing it, I will break your right leg. Then I'll carry you up the stairs I'm currently giving you the choice to walk up and break both your arms. I trust I've made myself clear. Answer me."

"Clear as the floor of your office." He can't be alive. I watched the Hag scrape his guts out and sew them up into her dress. Surely he wouldn't really break all my arms and legs. Would he?

The presence behind my back is gone and I'm floored for a second by how cold I am. I hadn't realized how much heat he was throwing off until he was gone.

There's no way he's alive. It can't be Ryodan behind me. Is Barrons alive, then, too? How could they be? I know they're tough to kill and all but folks don't survive being gutted! Where did they get new guts from? Did somebody take them back from the Hag and sew them both up again? Will he look like Frankenstein's monster?

I don't want to turn around. I don't like any of the possibilities confronting me. If it's not Ryodan, I've gone nuts. If it is Ryodan, dude, I'm dead.

"Turn around, kid."

I can't make my feet move. I can't wrap my brain around that he's standing behind me. I'm shaking like a leaf. Me! What the feck is wrong with me? I'm tougher than tough! I ain't scared of nothing.

"Now."

I take a deep breath and turn around. I absorb his face, his body, the way he stands, the look in his eyes, the arrogant, faint smile.

It's either Ryodan or a perfect clone.

I do something I can't believe I do. I hate hormones, I hate Chester's, and I bloody fecking hate Ryodan. I'm never going to be able to live this down!

I burst into tears.

Ryodan turns and stalks off for the stairs.

I trail miserably behind him. The whole fecking club is watching Dani Mega O'Malley cry and walk behind Ryodan without saying a word, like a dog brought to heel. I can't fecking believe it. I hate my life. I hate myself. I hate my stupid face. I want to snap, "He broke my ribs and I'm crying from the pain of one of them punc-

388 · KAREN MARIE MONING

turing my lung but I'm tough and I'll kick his ass and be okay and then I'll kick all of your asses, too!" to save face, but I'm pretty sure if I say a word he really *will* break my leg. I wipe angrily at my eyes. My stupid, pansy, betraying eyes with their stupid, pansy, betraying tear ducts.

The whole club has gone silent. Folks and Fae part a wide path to let us walk through. I've never taken a long walk of shame before and it chafes real bad. Jo's standing there, white-faced, looking from me to Ryodan's back, and back at me again. She might be his flavor of the month but I can tell by the look on her face that she's afraid of pushing him. She mouths, *Apologize! Bend. Or he'll break you!*

Over my dead body. The Mega doesn't bend. I pass Lor at the bottom of the steps to the upper level. I turn my face away because I can't stand him to see me being such a baby. He leans in close and says soft-like against my ear, "Honey, you might just have saved your life with those tears. I thought you had too much ego and too little common sense to know when to turn on the waterworks. He can't stand a woman crying. It fucks him up every time."

I look at him. He winks at me.

I flash fire at him with my eyes because I ain't allowed to use my tongue. They say: *I ain't a woman and I ain't crying and I ain't afraid of nothing.*

"He can deal with not being able to control you as long as you let the world believe he does. He's king here, honey. Kings can't be challenged publicly."

Nobody controls me. Ever, my eyes snarl. *And I challenge whoever the feck I want wherever I fecking feel like doing it!*

He grins. "I hear you, kid. Loud and clear. Just remember what I said."

I jut my jaw and follow Ryodan up the stairs.

* * *

He turns on me the second I close the door.

"Turn it off. You don't cry. I expect you not to cry. Stop it. This fucking instant."

"I'm not crying! I got stuff in my eyes when you slammed me into the column. And I expect dead people to stay dead! So, I guess we both got disappointed, huh?"

"Is that what you are? Disappointed? You watched me get gutted and die and now that I'm standing in front of you alive you feel disappointed?"

"Did I just hear, like, three question marks?"

"Do *not* fuck with me right now!" He slams me back into the wall so hard I feel the pane rumble behind my back.

"You don't care what I feel! You never have. You just order me around and expect me to obey and get pissy if I don't. I'm nothing to you so don't pretend you give a royal rat's ass what I feel!"

"Loyalty stems from what you feel. Or don't. You aren't on thin ice, kid. You're underwater and my hand is on your head, holding you down. So choose well: 'D' is for disappointed to see me. And Death. 'L' is for loyalty. And Life. Convince me I should let you live."

His face is an inch from mine. He's breathing hard and I feel violence in him. Lor said I should use my tears to manipulate him. There's no way I'm stooping to such wussy-girl depths. I'm just as big and bad as he is.

He's alive. He's here. Bullying me. No doubt getting ready to eventually—after he's done killing me—order me to report to work again.

We're back to being us. Robin to his Batman.

He's alive.

Tears stream from my eyes.

"Stop it!" He slams me back into the wall again so

hard my teeth clatter but the idiotic tears just keep coming.

I bounce off and use the ricochet to smash into him as hard as I can. He grabs my wrist when I hit him and when he goes flying back, takes me with him. We crash into his desk. I go flying up on it, roll over it and leap to my feet, tossing my hair from my eyes.

I slam my palms against the desk and snarl across it, "Don't you think I would if I could! Do you think I liked looking all sissified in front of your whole fecking club? In front of you? You stupid fecking stupid fecker! What were you doing outside that wall anyway! Why did you have to be right there in that exact spot when we came out? I mean, who has that kind of crap luck? Ever since I started to hang with you, my life has been a total fecking nightmare! Couldn't you just stay dead?"

He slams his hands down on the desk so hard it cracks down the middle. "Not. Convincing. Me."

I glare through my tears. "Not trying to! I don't convince nobody of nothing. You take me or leave me just the way I am! But I ain't changing for you or nobody else and I ain't faking either, and if you think breaking my bones one by one is going to accomplish a thing besides, like, breaking my bones, good luck with that!"

I'm sobbing now and don't have any clue why. Just that it feels like ever since I came out of the wall with the Crimson Hag and watched it kill Barrons and Ryodan, I've been all trussed up in one great big painful knot, and the second I looked at him and realized he was alive, really, truly alive, and I wasn't going to have to walk around for the rest of my life with his death on my head, never seeing his smug-ass smile again, that knot relaxed, and when it let go, everything in me came apart and my whole self heaved a sigh of relief and somewhere I guess I got a well of tears in me, like maybe everybody has a certain allotment of them and if you never let them

out, the second a single one sneaks out, it opens a flood-
gate and you can't shut it again. Why doesn't anyone
ever tell me the rules of life? If I'd known it worked this
way, I would have taken myself off somewhere private
and cried until I'd use up my quota! This is worse than
getting off on the wrong foot when I'm freeze-framing.
This is emotional careening with no control.

I look at him and I think, Crimeny, if only Alina could
have stood back up from what I did to her. Mac could
have had her sister back. And I wouldn't have to walk
around all the time, every single minute of every single
day, hating myself because even though I'm pretty sure
Ro did something to me that night that made me some
kind of automaton that didn't have a will of her own, I
was there. I was *there*! I led her to the spot where she
died by lying to her and telling her I had something
really important to show her and I'm just a kid so she
trusted me! I stood in that alley and I watched Mac's
sister get killed by Fae that I could have stopped with
one flick of my sword and I can never undo it and I can
never scrape it out from behind my eyes. It's seared into
my soul for the rest of my life, if I've even got one after
all the shit I've done!

I hurt Mac worse than anything in her life ever did
and I can never undo it.

Still . . . there's a silver lining to this cloud: if Ryodan
isn't dead, Barrons isn't either. At least Mac still has Barrons.

"You killed Mac's sister," Ryodan says. "I'll be
damned."

I didn't say that. "Stay the feck out of my head!"

He's across the desk and practically on top of me. He
shoves me back against the wall, clamps my head between his hands and forces me to look up at him. "How
did you feel when you thought you'd killed me."

He's looking in my eyes like he doesn't need me to

answer, just think it. I try to double over so he can't poke around in my thoughts but he won't let me. He's holding me firm, but almost gentle now. I hate gentle from him. I prefer fighting. I know exactly where we stand then.

"Answer me."

I don't answer him. I'm never going to answer him. I hate him. Because when I thought I'd killed him, I felt more alone than I've felt in a long time. Like I couldn't stand walking through this city knowing he wasn't in it. Like somehow, as long as he was out there somewhere, if I was ever really in trouble, I knew where I could go and while maybe he wouldn't do exactly what I wanted him to do, he'd keep me alive. He'd get me through whatever it was to live another day. I think that's the kind of feeling you get from parents when you're a kid, if you're lucky. I didn't get that feeling. I curled in a cage and every time she put on her perfume and makeup and hummed while she got dressed, I worried that she was going to kill me this time by forgetting me. I hoped her new boyfriend would suck so she'd come home sooner. I know that no matter what fecked-up things Ryodan does, he'll never forget me. He's meticulous. There's a lot to be said for detail-oriented. Least in my world there is. Especially when I'm one of the details.

I can't look away. How the heck is he alive? I feel like he's stirring around in my brain. Watching the light go out of his cool, clear eyes in the alley behind BB&B had just about slayed me. I missed him. I bloody fecking missed him.

Ryodan says real soft, "Disappointed or loyal."

I got no intention of dying. "Loyal," I say.

He lets me go and walks away. I slump down the wall, scrubbing tears from my face. I hurt everywhere, face, hands, chest, ribs. "But you're going to have to—"

"Do *not* try to barter with me right now."

"But it's not fair that I—"

"Life isn't."

"But I can't stand working every night!"

"Deal with it."

"You're making me nuts! A person needs some time off!"

"Kid, you just never give up."

"I'm like, alive. How could I?" I stand up and dust myself off. My tears are gone as mysteriously as they came.

He kicks a chair at me. "Sit. There are new house rules. Take notes. Violate one and you're dead. Acknowledge."

I roll my eyes and toss myself into the chair, slinging a leg over the side. Belligerence is me. "I'm listening," I say irritably.

I hate rules. They always screw me up.

THIRTY-FOUR

"Where do you think you're going?
Don't you know it's dark outside?"

I slow-mo Joe it down the corridor cussing Ryodan but keeping it under my breath since he's walking right next to me.

The new house rules are the biggest pile of BS I ever heard. It's going to kill me to follow them. Literally result in my death because there's no way I'll remember to do everything he wants me to do while also keeping track of everything I'm not allowed to do. In addition to "Report to work at eight every night" is the most offensive rule of all: "You will never leave Chester's unaccompanied by one of my people again."

"So, I never get to be alone, like, ever?" I exploded, flabbergasted. "Dude, I need my private time." I been alone most of my life. Too many people in my personal space start to chafe me after a while. I get edgy and weird. And tired, too, like they wear me out just being there. I have to get off by myself, or be with one person like Dancer to recharge.

He didn't answer me.

Another one that really gets me is that I'm supposed to never question or argue with him in public! I'm going to be dead by morning. Only way I have a snowball's chance in hell of succeeding there is if I start wearing a muzzle or cut out my own tongue.

"You can say anything you want to me in private," he said. "Which is way the fuck more than I permit anyone else."

"I don't want no private time with you."

"Too bad," he said. "Plan on a lot of it."

"Why do you dick with me? Why don't you just forget about me and let me live my life." It's weird to think he's been watching me since I was nine. I never even noticed him. He's noticed me probably more than anybody else ever has, including my mom.

Again, he doesn't answer.

I walk with him to the end of a hallway on the third floor. He stops at a glass panel that's smoked black and pulls a cloth hood out of his pocket. When he reaches for me, I duck back and say, "You're kidding, right?"

He just looks at me until I snatch the hood from his hand, put it on myself, and let him guide me by an arm.

I suffer the indignity of being blinded in silence, and focus on absorbing every detail I can. I count steps. I sniff through the heavy fabric. I listen hard. When we get on an elevator and go down, I count seconds so I can figure out what floor he's taking me to when I finally get some time alone, and I will. He can't have someone on me every second of every day. He'll get tired of it. I need to get back to Dancer! I need to talk to Ryodan about getting samples but when I brought up the Ice Monster he told me to stow it.

When we arrive at our destination and he pulls the hood off, I'm floored to see Ryodan's got his own War Room, and of course it's top-of-the-line, technological perfection, and makes ours look stupid! Once again I'm jealous. There are computers everywhere. CPUs and monitors and keyboards and I don't know what half the stuff in the room is, and I know a lot. Dancer would go crazy in here!

He's got a map up, too, but unlike our paper one, his is electronic, on a glass panel suspended from the ceiling, about twenty feet wide and ten feet tall. It's something out of a futuristic movie. It's got lots of lines and dots and triangulated areas marked out in different colors.

"Sit."

I drop down in a chair behind an enormous slab table that faces the map. There are nine chairs at the table. I wonder how long this room has been here, how many centuries these dudes who don't seem to be able to die have sat in this room and plotted things. I wonder what kind of things guys like them plot. Coups? Economic catastrophes? World wars?

"So, Barrons is alive, too," I fish.

"Yes."

"Dude, what the feck? I don't know what your superpower is, but I want whatever you've got."

"You think."

"I know."

"You don't even know what it is. Yet you'd take it sight unseen."

"To, like, never die? Fecking-A I would!"

"And if there's a price."

"Dude, we're talking immortality. There ain't no price too high!"

He gives me a faint smile. "Ask me again when you're older."

"Huh?" I say. "Really? When I'm older I can have whatever you got? Like, how much older? Fifteen?"

"I didn't say you could have it. I said you could ask me. And no, not fifteen."

"Dude, give me a little hope here."

"I just did."

He taps something in on a remote device and all the sudden I'm not looking at Dublin on the grid anymore. He's zoomed out and I'm seeing a map of surrounding countries. There are dots pegged in England, Scotland, France, Germany, Spain, Poland, Romania, and Greece. He zooms out farther and I see two in Morocco and one in Norway.

I let out a low whistle, horrified. Dancer and me were only seeing the little picture. "There's more than one Ice Monster."

"Not necessarily. I think if there was more than one, we'd be hearing reports of it all over the world and we're not. So far, it's confined to this region."

"I need samples from Faery and the first place it iced in Chester's."

"Elaborate."

"Dancer and me went through all the evidence. There's iron in every bag and—"

"No."

"You didn't let me finish."

"I don't have to. Iron has nothing to do with it."

"How can you know that?"

"Because there's not a single drop of iron anywhere in or near Chester's."

"Well, what the feck is this place built from?"

"Irrelevant. Besides," he says, "if it was after iron, it would have taken the cages at Dublin Castle and it didn't. It iced the place and vanished. We've been studying the map and scenes for weeks. There's no pattern, no commonality. I put my best man on it, a linchpin pro. He can't find a tipping point, sees no order in this chaos."

"Who's your linchpin pro?" I want to talk to him. I'm fascinated by linchpin theory. If you know where to make the dominoes start toppling, you own the dominoes! Of course, Ryodan doesn't answer that question either so I tell him Dancer's theory about salt water and whales and that maybe it's drawn by something because it's looking for something else.

"Possible. But not iron."

"You dudes been hosting fairies for, like, millennia, haven't you? That's the only reason for a place like this having no iron!"

"There are other things that don't like iron. Not just Fae. A smart person might find a lot of things missing in Chester's." A faint smile plays at his lips, and I almost get the idea he's challenging me to figure something out.

"Dude, if I'm stuck here long enough, I will." I gesture at the map. "Show me Dublin again." When he resets the map, I say, "I need the remote."

He punches numbers in on it, no doubt locking systems off from me, then hands it over.

"Let me stare at the map a while."

When he leaves, he locks me in.

I'm still staring hours later, no closer to an epiphany, when I start smelling the most fecking awesome smell in the world. I try to concentrate on the map but I can't. I shove a candy bar in my mouth. It tastes like Styrofoam. I haven't smelled fresh-cooked beef in longer than I can remember. I never got it at the abbey! Somewhere in Chester's, some spoiled person is feasting. My mouth fills with saliva. I slide down in my chair, drop my head back and inhale real deep and slow, making lip-smacking noises, pretending I'm the lucky recipient. I smell all kinds of spices! I think whatever the meat is, it's accompanied by mashed potatoes and some kind of greens. I smell garlic, salt and pepper, butter! I smell onion and oregano and rosemary! It's almost enough to make me cry, thinking about that kind of food. I'm beyond sick of candy bars and protein bars and canned stuff. I'm so home-cooked-meal starved that not even my chocolate Pop-Tarts hit the spot like they used to.

When the door slides open and Lor comes in, pushing a cart like you see in hotels for room service, I just sit there and stare, thinking: Is this a new way to torture me? I don't move a muscle. I'm not going to make an idiot of myself. Ryodan's probably on his way to eat in front of me just to make me suffer.

Lor rolls the cart to a stop a few inches from the toes of my shoes. I have to grip the arms of my chair so I don't jump out of it and attack whatever's in those covered dishes.

"Boss says eat."

He takes the lid off the biggest plate and sure enough there's meat sizzling like it just came off a grill with a side of mashed potatoes, plus a mixed veggie medley! There's a bowl with bread, hot from the oven. And butter! I almost expire from the sheer excitement of it. Like, the real stuff and a whole carafe of milk! It's the most beautiful sight I think I've ever seen. I stare, holding my breath.

"You're scrawny," he adds.

"That's for me?" I say wonderingly. I still don't move. It's got to be a trick. The meat is a rib-eye steak, perfectly marbled. It's thick and has grill marks on it and looks like it's cooked to perfection. I've only ever had it twice in my life. Once when Mom got engaged—it didn't work, the dude ditched her, they all did eventually—and another time when she got a new job that she thought would get us out of Ireland for good if she saved everything she made for three years. She got fired after a month and cried herself to sleep every night for weeks. I think she thought if she could just get us out of Ireland, everything would be easier. I know other *sidhe*-seer families ran. Mac's did.

Lor nods.

I'm out of the chair and on the cart in fast-mo.

"Kid, slow down. You might want to taste it."

My hands shake when I pick up the fork. I go straight for the steak, slicing a big chunk off. The first bite explodes in my mouth, full of meaty juices and sheer succulent beefy perfection. I slump back into my chair and close my eyes, chewing slowly, delicately milking it for every single taste. I fork up a pile of fluffy mashed potatoes and they're fecking heaven! The bread is tender and warm inside, crusty outside, and kissed with rosemary just like Mom's. I wonder who cooks around here. I wonder where their kitchen is. I'm going to rob them blind if I find it. I slather butter on the bread then lick it off and slather more. I pour a long cool drink of milk down my gullet. I force myself to count to five between each drink and bite. It occurs to me I've never seen Ryodan eat. He probably pigs out in private. Probably eats steak and milk every day!

"The snow's piling up and the temperature's dropping," Lor says. "People are lined up for five blocks, trying to get inside. Generators and gas have gotten scarce. People are freezing to death. It's June in Dublin. Who'd fucking believe it?"

I chew reverently, listening to him and staring at nothing. "Maybe it's not after an element like iron or something. Maybe it's after a feeling. Maybe someone was having sex at every scene, or . . . eating at every scene, or fighting or praying or . . . something."

"Doesn't hold water. There was no life at the steeple."

I knew that. I just forgot for a sec. "So we're back to the inanimate."

"Looks like."

All too soon my meal is over. I've got the best taste ever on my tongue. I won't eat again until I absolutely have to, and I'm not about to brush my teeth for a while. I want to relish the residue from my taste buds till there's nothing left. I may never get this kind of a meal again. After I sop up every drop of beef juice with the last few bites of bread, Lor takes the cart and leaves.

I could almost pass out from the overload of rich food. Digesting it stupefies me for a while and I stretch out on the floor, staring up at the map.

I can't shake the feeling that I'm still not seeing the big picture. I'm lying here, staring at an enormous map, and I know there's something about these scenes I'm missing or reading wrong. I can feel it. Like Dancer, I get hunches and I listen to them. Used to be, when I was little, I couldn't concentrate because of all the things I could hear around me. When Ro took me in, she taught me to plug my ears, shut out the din and focus. Old witch passed on a few good things but they'll never counter all the evil she did.

I dig earplugs out of my backpack. Dancer made them for me out of some kind of stuff that absorbs noise way better than the standard plugs. I wedge them in, tune out the world, and begin sorting through my facts.

One: It's not after iron. There's none at Chester's. I need to get that info to Dancer ASAP.

Two: It's not after life force because one of the scenes had no life forms and I seriously doubt a mouse would be enough.

Three: Dirt, metal, and plastic are the only physical elements all the scenes had in common.

I start mentally rebuilding every scene I visited, labeling and depositing them in one of the more readily accessible drawers in my brain's filing cabinet, right next to where Dancer and me play chess sometimes without a board. It's an important part of your brain to exercise if you want to stay sharp. Being smart is handy, but if you aren't mentally agile, it doesn't get you anywhere but stuck in your own fact-ruts.

First up is the subclub. There were over a hundred

humans and Fae engaged in various social and sexual activities. I visualize the room in detail, from the torture racks to the sofas, the sexual couplings to the band that was playing in the corner, the food that was on a table, the tapestries and mirrors on the walls. I look for something in the club that I can easily spot at every other scene. Maybe it's hunting for a tapestry or a special mirror. It sounds stupid, but who can say what might draw a creature like that? Maybe it was cursed and it needs some hallowed Fae object to free itself. You never know with the Fae.

Next up is the warehouse that got iced, populated only by Unseelie and filled with crates and boxes of guns. What was in this place that was also in the club? No tapestries or mirrors that I saw, but maybe there was one in a crate somewhere behind all the audio equipment and electronics.

Then there were two underground pubs with the usual stuff: wood bar, bottles, drinks, stools, a huge mirror behind the bar, folks dancing, a few shooting pool in the corner of one place, playing darts in the other. The wood could have come from anywhere: the stools, the bar, the framed pictures on the walls, the floor. The plastic also could have come from anything: bottle toppers, chairs, plates, phones, the list goes on and on.

The fitness center had three people in a building filled with treadmills and ellipticals and all kinds of weight machines and twenty or so of those milky-crystal meditation bowls. I guess the wood at that scene must have come from the framing of the building. I go back and begin mentally breaking down the structure of each scene, too, so I can add all that stuff into the mix.

"This is impossible," I mutter. It's worse than looking for a needle in a haystack. I'm looking for a dozen needles in dozens of different haystacks that are no longer even there because they all exploded. It could be after a red Solo cup for all I know! Do they have red Solo cups in Morocco?

I go through the rest of the scenes and realize I need more info on the ones that happened while I was gone in order to visualize them. Ryodan might have a kick-ass War Room but Dancer's got lists already put together.

Too bad I'm locked in.

I look at the door. I don't remember hearing Lor lock it. Lor likes to stir things up, keep them hopping.

I freeze-frame over to it, test the knob and grin.

"Dani, I don't think this is a good idea," Jo says.

"He said I couldn't leave without one of his people. Listening to you talk, you and him are, like, peas in the Jo-pod. That makes you one of his people. Are you or aren't you? 'Cause the way I figure it, if the dude's banging you every day and doesn't consider you one of his people, you're not just getting screwed, you're stupid." I hate manipulating Jo. When her heart's involved, it's way too easy. And her heart's dangling off her sleeve where Ryodan's concerned. "Dude, you been outside lately?" I push. We have to go *now*. It took me twenty minutes to find my way back to the main part of Chester's from the War Room. I got a bad feeling Ryodan doesn't plan to leave me alone in there too long, with all those computers. I wouldn't. If I really *was* stuck in there, that's what I'd be messing with right now, trying to hack into his systems. "The world is falling apart. Folks are dying! I just want to run a quick errand. That's all. One tiny little errand. It won't hardly take any time at all."

"I'll go ask him if it's okay first."

"You got any idea where he is? 'Cause I ain't seen him in hours. Isn't it morning? Did he come to the top of the stairs yet? Is he still summoning you that way for a quickie over his desk, or have you graduated to, like, getting banged in a bed and everything? What's he got, some kind of progressive ranking system? If you last a whole week, you get to do it in a chair, and if you make it two—"

"Now you're just being mean," she says. "Stop it."

"Just saying. I'd like to see you get some real romance, Jo. You deserve it. You're the prettiest girl in here and everybody'd love to date you. Do you know he has steak and milk and bread and stuff? I had the best meal today. Does he feed you like that?"

She tries to mask her surprise but doesn't succeed. "Isn't he still mad at you?"

"Don't look like it from where I'm sitting."

"Steak?"

I lick my lips, still tasting it. "Rib eye."

"Milk?"

"Dude." I nod. "Look, all I want to do is run by Dancer's and get the lists."

"He really gave you steak and milk today?"

I'd laugh but it's sad. We're all so fecking hungry for a home-cooked meal. When spring started to green things up out at the abbey, the girls started talking about growing veggies again. All the produce was gone within a month of the walls falling. If you want to bake something, you have to run a generator to power the oven. Either that or have whatever the feck kind of setup Ryodan's got here at Chester's, and even then you can only bake stuff that doesn't require butter or milk or eggs. Jo's almost as upset that he gave me good food as she is about him not romancing her.

"I'd call and ask Dancer to courier it over but, dude, no phones and no couriers. Can we just go? We'll be back before anybody knows we're gone. And if you and Ryodan really are a 'thing,' he ain't going to give you any guff. He's going to appreciate a woman with a little spine and independence!" Yeah, right. Ryodan despises spine and independence. He likes good little robots.

"Did he give you anything else?"

If I was having sex with somebody and they gave someone besides me awesome food, I'd be ten kinds of furious. The way I see it, intimacy should entitle you to privileges. If it don't, it's just skintimacy like on TV with folks always swapping partners and hurting each other. "Fresh strawberries and ice cream," I lie.

"Ice cream? Are you kidding me? What kind?"

It's sleeting when we get outside. Abandoned cars are shiny with a layer of ice. Skeletal trees shimmer like they're crusted with diamonds. Snowdrifts are piling up. There's a group of people outside Chester's but it's a somber, quiet crowd and I realize these ain't partiers trying to get inside, these are folks looking to survive what's coming. I guess all the partiers have already been let in. Wrapped in blankets, wearing hats, earmuffs, and gloves, these are folks that got no generators at home, and the weather has turned dangerously cold, sending them out into the streets to look for a source of heat before it's too late.

Jo and me look at the folks as we pass.

"Let us in," they say. "We just want to get warm."

You can tell there's heat in the club—and a lot of it—because the area above Chester's is bare of accumulation. The pavement is an underinsulated roof, and the heat radiating up keeps melting the snow. Even that nominal sign of warmth is enough to keep folks standing around, hoping, waiting.

There's old people here, with nothing to trade for food or drink or the privilege of hanging at Chester's. The big, brawny human bouncers Ryodan uses outside the club turn them back at the door, and a crowd has moved into the snow-free ruin of stone and wood that used to be the club aboveground. They got fires going in cans. They've gathered wood from surrounding buildings and piled it up. They look like they plan to stay a good long while. Like until they get let in. They look too defeated to fight. A cluster has begun to sing "Amazing Grace." Before long fifty voices lift in song.

"Maybe you could talk some sense into your 'boyfriend' and get him to let those folks inside," I say.

"I will," she says. "Or we could bus them to the abbey."

"What about WeCare? Don't they fecking care? Aren't they supposed to be giving away generators left and right?"

"Even if they are," Jo says, "some of these people are too old to get out and hunt down enough gas to keep one running. You've been gone for weeks. A lot changed in that time. The weather is all anybody talks about anymore. Making it through last winter wasn't as hard because the stores were all still stocked and the nights were mild. But supplies have been wiped out. We didn't expect winter in June. All the generators are gone. People are changing. They're fighting each other to survive. We need a long warm summer to give us enough time to grow and stockpile food before winter comes again. We need to get out and hunt for supplies in other towns."

"They're going to die, Jo. If we don't stop the Hoar Frost King, we're going to lose the other half of our world." I look back at the crowd huddled around the fire cans above Chester's. A mom is helping her kids get closer to one of the barrels so they can rub their hands together over the flames. Old folks that look too frail to be hiking through this ice and snow watch the kids with weary eyes that have seen three-quarters of a century of change but never anything like what's been happening since last Halloween. Men that look like they were office workers at desk jobs before the walls fell hold the perimeter, encircling the women, kids, and old folks. They're all displaced now. No jobs. No paychecks. None of the rules they used to live by. They look exhausted. Desperate. It fecking slays me. They've moved on to a new song, another hymn. Folks need faith in times like these. You can't give somebody faith. They either got it or they don't. But you sure can try to give them hope.

She gives me a bleak look. "If there was ever a time for you to dazzle us with your brilliance, it's now."

"I'm working on it. But I need stuff. Let's go. We'll make it back before anybody even knows we're gone."

We turn and begin walking down the street. I'm going to have to leave her aboveground. I'm not about to give away Dublin-down's secrets. But I'll take her as close as I can and leave her someplace sheltered. The snow crunches beneath my boots twice, as I sink through snow then ice, snow then ice. I hear Jo going through three layers because she weighs more than me. The sky is white with thick flakes swirling down in a dizzying display if you look up at them too long. They melt on my face, the only part of me exposed. We raided Chester's coatroom before we left, bundling in layers, tugging on hats and mittens and boots. If this weather keeps up, we could end up with ten feet of ice and drifts in the next day or two and it will totally shut the city down. Folks that didn't think to come out somewhere for warmth will freeze, snowed into their hidey-holes. If the sun doesn't start shining soon, this stuff'll never melt. It'll just keep piling. Time is getting more critical with each passing day. I can't believe I lost almost a whole month in the White Mansion with Christian! Speaking of which, I look around warily, checking all the roof-tops, making sure the Hag isn't sitting on one of them, knitting away, or worse, getting ready to swoop down on us. The crazy blood-and-guts bitch creeps me out. I shiver. "We need to freeze-frame, Jo. Take my hand."

She gives me a look like I'm deranged. "There's no way you're doing that to me! Especially not on ice. Half your face is a bruise and the other half is recovering from one. Have you looked in a mirror lately?"

"That ain't because I'm a sloppy freeze-framer. It's because of stupid jerk-ass Ryodan."

"Stupid jerk-ass Ryodan is going to break both your legs if you take one more step," Ryodan says right behind us.

I whirl on him. "Why are you always stalking me?"

"You're always making me."

"How do you keep finding me?" Do I have a blinking beacon on my forehead that sends a signal straight to him every time I disobey an order? I refuse to believe since he bit me, he can track me wherever I go. That's a suffocating thought. It's wrong and unfair.

"Get back inside. Now."

"You didn't find me in the White Mansion." A light-bulb goes off in my head. I been busy with other worries, or I'd have clued into it sooner. "You can't track me in Faery!" That's why he was so mad. I almost punch air I'm so happy. I have a safety zone. If I ever need to hide from him, Faery's the place to go. "And you're the one who's always making me do stuff that makes me have to do other stuff that ain't what you want me to do. It's not my fault. I'm just reacting to you."

"There's your first mistake. Learn to act, kid."

"I *am* acting. I'm trying to do something about our problems."

"And you, Jo," he says soft, "you should have known better."

"Leave her out of this," I say.

"She helped you disobey me."

"She did not. 'Cause, see, I didn't disobey you. You

said I could leave with one of 'your people.' You're boinking her every day, and if that doesn't make her one of your people then you need to quit boinking her. Either she is or she ain't, and you can't have it both ways. You don't get to have sex with folks then discount them. So. Is Jo one of your people? Or just another piece of booty in your endless lineup?"

"Dani, stop it," Jo warns.

"Feck no, I'm not stopping it." I'm so pissed, I'm vibrating. "He doesn't deserve you and you deserve so much better!" It doesn't help that behind Ryodan the fire-can folks have switched songs again and are now booming out a rousing rendition of "Hail Glorious St. Patrick," clapping their hands and banging on cans with pieces of wood, getting all rambunctious. The louder they sing, the hotter my temper gets. "He's always pushing everybody else around but nobody ever calls him out on the carpet. I say it's way past time. Either you matter to him or you don't, and he needs to say which one it is. I want to know which one it is."

"She matters," Ryodan says.

Jo looks stunned.

It pisses me off even more. She's looking all dreamy-eyed and in love again. Anybody can see she ain't his type. "You liar, she does not!"

"Dani, stow it," Jo says.

I know him. I know how he tricked me. He's splitting verbal hairs. Of course she matters. But he didn't say "to me." She matters to the club, for mercenary reasons, because she's a waitress. "Does she, like, matter to you emotionally? Do you love her?"

"Dani, stop it right now!" Jo says, horrified. To Ryodan she says, "Don't answer her. I'm sorry. Just ignore her. This is so embarrassing."

"Answer me," I say to Ryodan. The hymn folks are really rocking it now, dancing and swaying, and I'm almost having to yell to be heard. But that's okay. I feel like yelling.

"For fuck's sake," Ryodan growls over his shoulder, "can't they go sing somewhere else."

"They want in," I say. "They're going to die on your doorstep because you're too much of a prick to save them."

"The world is not my responsibility."

"Obviously." I put twenty kinds of verbal condemnation in the single word.

"She just wanted to find Dancer," Jo says. "I think it's important. Sometimes you have to trust her."

"Do you love her?" I push.

Jo groans likes she's going to die of embarrassment. "Oh God, Dani, shut *up*!"

I expect him to scoff at me, say something bullying, throw an insult back in my face, but he just says, "Define love."

I stare straight into those clear, cool eyes. There's some kind of challenge there. I don't get this dude. But the definition he wants is easy. I had a lot of time in a cage to think about it. I saw a TV show once that gave the perfect definition, and I say it to him now: "The active caring and concern for the health and well-being of another person's body and heart. Active. Not passive." In a nutshell, you remember that person all the time. You never forget them. You factor their existence into yours every single hour of every single day. No matter what you're doing. And you never leave them locked up somewhere to die.

"Think about what that entails," he says. "Providing food. Shelter. Protection from one's enemies. A place to rest and heal."

"You forgot about the heart part. But I didn't expect anything else. 'Cause you ain't got one. All you got are rules. Oh, and yeah, more rules."

Jo says, "Dani, can we just—"

Ryodan cuts her off. "Those rules keep people alive."

Jo tries again. "Look, guys, I think—"

"Those rules strangle folks who need to breathe," I say, talking right over her. Nobody's listening to her anyway.

All the sudden he has me by the collar, hanging in the air, my feet dangling off the ground, our noses touching.

"By your own definition," he says, "you don't love anyone either. An argument could be made that you only ever do one of three things to the people closest to you: make enemies of them, kill the people they love, or get them killed. Careful. You're on thinner ice than you've ever been with me."

"Because I'm asking if you love Jo?" I say coolly, like I'm not hanging helpless by my shirt. Like he didn't just take a mean shot at me below the belt.

"It's not your business, Dani," Jo says. "I can take care of my—"

"Pull your head out of your ass and see the world," Ryodan says.

"I *do* see the world," I say. "I see it better than most folks and you know it. Put me down."

"—self just fine." Jo is sounding kind of pissed now, too.

"And for that very reason, you're blinder than most," Ryodan says.

"That doesn't make sense. Still dangling here, dude." I try to toe the ground by pointing my foot but I think I'm a few feet above it.

"You don't see the forest for the trees."

"Ain't no forest. Shades ate it. Let me go. You don't get to just dangle folks in the air when you feel like it."

He drops me so abruptly I stumble on the ice and almost fall, but he catches me and puts me back on my feet. I shake his hand off my arm.

"There doesn't need to be love," Jo says. "Sometimes it's not about that."

"Then you shouldn't be boinking him!"

"It's my own business who I boink," Jo says.

"I don't 'boink' anyone. I fuck," Ryodan says.

"Thank you for that much-needed clarification," I say with saccharine pissiness. "Hear that, Jo? You get fucked by him. Not even the decency of a boinking. Screwed. Plain and simple." I'm beyond irate. I'm seeing through a red haze. The fecking fire-can folks are singing so loud they're hampering my ability to think straight. I want Dancer. Ryodan drives me insane. Jo's a hopeless case. Dublin's dying.

I can't stand things anymore so I punch Ryodan in the nose.

We all kind of freeze for a second and even *I* can't believe I just hauled off and decked Ryodan with no warning and no real provocation. At least no more than he's always giving me.

Then Ryodan manacles my arm and starts dragging me back toward Chester's, looking madder than I ever seen him, but Jo gets my other arm, trying to make him stop, yelling at him and yelling at me. I'm slipping and skidding on the ice, trying to get them both off me.

We stumble across snowdrifts, fighting each other, when all the sudden the day gets foggy and I can't hear a sound any of us are making. My mouth's moving and nothing's coming out. I can't hear the fire-can folks either. I can't even hear my breath in my ears. Panic compresses my chest.

Me and Ryodan look at each other and have a moment of perfect communion like me and Dancer do sometimes. No words necessary. We're made of the same stuff. In battle there's nobody else I'd rather be hanging with. Not even Christian or Dancer.

I grab Ryodan and he grabs me and we sandwich Jo between us.

Then we freeze-frame the hell out of there like the devil is on our heels.

Or more precisely, the Hoar Frost King.

THIRTY-FIVE

"She blinded me with science"

Like we're chained together or something, Ryodan and me stop about three-quarters of the way down the block. We go just far enough to escape danger, while staying close enough to get a look back at Chester's.

By the time we glance back, it's too late. The temperature where we're standing just plummeted a good thirty degrees. The Hoar Frost King is vanishing into a slit in the air just above the street about a hundred yards away. The fog sucks in, the dark blob glides into a portal, the slit vanishes and noise returns to the world.

Sort of. Jo's crying but it sounds like she's doing it in a paper bag beneath a pile of blankets.

One day, in the field near the abbey, a cow head-butted me in the stomach because I freeze-framed into her and woke her up, startling her. I feel exactly the same way now: I can't get a breath into my lungs. I keep trying to inflate them but they stay flat as pancakes glued together. When I finally do manage to breathe, it's with a great sucking wheeze that sounds hollow and wrong and it's so cold it burns going down.

I stare bleakly down the street.

They're all dead.

Every last one of them is dead.

Chester's topside is a sculpture of frozen statues shrouded in ice and silence.

"Feck, no!" I explode and wail all at the same time.

Where, moments ago, people were talking and singing, worrying and planning, living, for feck's sake, *living,* not a spark of life remains. Every man, woman, and child we were standing in the middle of is dead.

The human race is down by another few hundred.

Hoar Frost King: 25. Human Race: 0.

Dublin's going to be a fecking ghost town if this keeps up.

I stare. White bumps and knobs and pillars, folks are coated with hoarfrost then glazed with a thick shiny layer of ice. Icicles hang from their hands and elbows. Breaths are frozen plumes of frosted crystals on the air. The cold the scene radiates is painful, even from here, like part of Dublin just got dunked into outer space. Kids are frozen, huddled around the fire cans, warming their hands above them. Adults are frozen, arms around each other, some swaying, some clapping. It's eerily silent, too silent. Like the whole scene is heavily baffled and all noise is being absorbed.

Beside me, Jo is crying soft and pretty. It's the only noise in the night, heck, it sounds like it's the only noise in the whole world! Figures she even cries like a dainty cat. Me, I blubber like a snot-nosed hound with big wet, gulping sounds, not tiny sighs and mews. I stand in silence, shaking, gritting my teeth and fisting my hands, to keep from blubbering.

I retreat like I do when things are too much for me to deal with. I pretend they aren't people under all that milky frost and ice. I refuse to let what happened touch me because grief isn't going to save Dublin. I pretend they're puzzle pieces. Nothing but evidence. They're the way to keep it from happening again, if I can interpret the clues they left. Later, they'll be folks to me again, and I'll make some kind of memorial here.

They just wanted to get warm.

"You should have let them inside," I say.

"Speculate why it came to this spot at this moment," Ryodan says.

"Speculate, my ass. Dude, you're colder than they are! And ain't that the million-dollar question?" I can't look at him. If he'd let them inside, they wouldn't be dead. If I hadn't stood there arguing about stupid stuff and spent more time talking him into letting them inside, they wouldn't be dead. I shiver and button the top button of my coat, right up under my neck, and scrub frost from the tip of my nose. "Do our voices sound wrong to you?"

"Everything sounds wrong. This whole street feels wrong."

"That's because it *is* wrong," Dancer says behind me. "Massively wrong."

I turn. "Dancer!"

He gives me a faint smile but it doesn't light up his face like usual. He looks tired, pale, and there are dark circles under his eyes. "Mega. Good to see you. I thought you were coming back." He looks at Ryodan and me with a quizzical expression.

I slice my head once to the side and shrug. Last thing I want him to do is bring up that I told him Ryodan was dead. He reads me well, like always. Later we'll chew over how the heck Ryodan survived a gutting. "I *was* coming back—"

"No, you weren't," Ryodan says. "You live at Chester's now."

"Do not."

"I had to go to somewhere," Dancer says, "and thought maybe you came looking for me but missed the note I left."

I try to flash him a grin that says how happy I am to see him but it comes out wobbly.

"Me, too, Mega."

I do grin then, because we're always on the same wavelength.

"She lives with me," Christian says from somewhere above us. "I'm the only one that can take care of her."

I look up but don't spot him. "I take care of myself. I ain't living with nobody. Got my own digs. What are you doing up there?"

"Tracking the Hag. Trying to devise a way to trap her. She's fast but she's not a sifter."

I jerk, and look around warily. That's all we need right now. "Is she here?"

"If you brought that crazy bitch near me again." Ryodan doesn't finish his sentence. He doesn't need to.

"I left her south of the city. Knitting. She'll be busy awhile."

There's a sudden, flat whoosh of air and it instinctively makes me duck, hare to a hawk. I think the noise made by the winged fliers of the Wild Hunt is branded into a *sidhe*-seer's subconscious. I'm dusted with black snow. "Christian, you got your wings!" They're huge. They're incredible. He can fly. I'm so jealous I almost can't stand it.

He cocks his head and looks at me. I don't see anything human left in his face at all. "Don't say it like it's a wonderful fucking life. You didn't hear any bells tinkling. What you heard was the sound of a demon, not an angel, recently born. And like any other newborn, it needs colostrum." He gives me a look that I think is supposed to be a smile. "Och, and you, sweet lass, are mother's milk."

All the sudden he looks like the most gorgeous, hunky dude I've ever seen, and I blink. He's standing there, nearly six and a half feet of black-haired, bronze-skinned

Unseelie prince with gigantic wings, terrifying iridescent eyes, and brilliant tattoos moving like a storm beneath his skin, but I'm seeing a good-looking Highlander. Sort of. This is new. This isn't a blast of his death-by-sex Fae nature. This is a controlled . . .

"You're throwing a glamour!" He hits me with a blast of eroticism that almost buckles my knees. He's learning control, fast. Way too fast for my comfort. I reach for my sword. "Off it!"

"For you. Today. Not always. And remember who gave you that back, lass."

"Touch her, I'll cut off your wings and use them to sweep the floor at Chester's," Ryodan says.

"Oh, I'll touch her. And when I do, you won't be able to do a bloody thing to stop me," Christian says.

"Nobody's going to be touching me," I say. "Unless I say so. I'm not public property."

"What is *wrong* with all of you?" Jo says. "People just got murdered in front of us and you're all too busy arguing to—"

"Humans," Christian cuts in. "Waste of space anyway." He looks at Ryodan. "You're alive. Pity. I was hoping the Hag did you in for good."

"Not a chance."

"You should have let them in," Jo says to Ryodan. "Then they wouldn't all be dead."

"Don't tell me what to do," Ryodan says, soft.

"She's right," I say. "You should have let them in." The flash of hurt in Jo's eyes makes me mad. "And don't you snap at her."

"Right, dickhead," Christian says. "You should have let them in." When I give him a look, he shrugs. "Being supportive, lass. Part of a healthy relationship."

I roll my eyes. "We're not having a relationship and I don't need your support."

"If I'd let them in, the thing might have come inside

after whatever it was that drew it to them in the first place, and iced the whole fucking club," Ryodan says.

He has a point but I'm not about to admit it. "Don't you snap at her," I say again. "You be nice to Jo."

"I can take care of myself, Dani," Jo says.

"Difficult though you all might find it to believe," Dancer says, "we've got bigger problems than your egos. Listen up. We need to talk. Let's go inside. It's bloody cold out here."

Ryodan looks at him hard a sec and I can tell by the look on his face he doesn't like what he's seeing with his weird X-ray vision. "Whatever you have to say can be said here. Now."

"You're such an asshole," Dancer says. "Periodically I suffer the brief delusion you might wise up. Brief."

Jo and Christian look at Dancer like they think he must have a death wish. I snicker but keep it under my breath. Ryodan looks majorly pissed and I'm in no mood to be noodled over a shoulder. I want to hear what Dancer has to say because for him to hunt me down, it's important. I look back at the iced scene and sober in a hurry. All those folks dead make me feel sick to my stomach. They died in a second, for no reason. Death is bad enough. Dying for nothing adds insult to injury.

I look at the ice sculpture. This evidence is as fresh as it's ever going to be. The morning all those Unseelie got iced at Dublin Castle, I didn't get to examine the scene. I want to get as close as I can today, without freeze-framing because that night in the church when I got bumped down into slow-mo and almost died, it seemed I could feel things better.

I move down the street, knowing they'll follow: Dancer because he wants to tell me stuff; Jo because she's . . . well, Jo; Ryodan and Christian because they got some kind of ownership issues with me like I'm a supercar they got the title to. They're so deluded it's laughable.

I open my *sidhe*-seer senses. I'm nearly suffocated by a feeling of . . . wrongness. Like the stuff that got iced is missing some essential ingredient, like they're no longer three-dimensional, just cardboard cutouts stood up in the street.

"Talk, kid," Ryodan says to Dancer.

I know Ryodan irritates him because he makes it clear he's talking to me. "After you left, Mega, I sat there for hours, staring. I knew I was missing something. I wasn't looking at things right. I started thinking about how I came to Dublin last fall to check out Trinity and see what I thought of their Physics Department. I wanted to know if I liked their professors and labs, if they had good enough equipment for the kind of research I planned to specialize in. Not that any of that's relevant anymore. It's just a hobby now. I never got around to checking the place out because two days after I arrived, the walls fell and going to college became a moot point."

"For fuck's sake, do you think I care who you are," Ryodan says.

"Dude's as bad as you say, Mega," Dancer says.

I stop about fifty feet from the frozen folks and look around. Jo and Dancer stopped about ten feet back and are shivering miserably. Ryodan and Christian flank me. I'm pretty sure Ryodan could go farther than any of us but he doesn't. When I exhale, my breath frosts in a suspended plume. My bones hurt with cold and my lungs burn. I can't make it another step without freeze-framing. I shiver, taking it all in. What element is present at this scene that was also present at every other scene that got iced? The answer is right here, staring me in the face, if I can peel my preconception-blinders back and see it.

There's wood, plastic, metal, and dirt everywhere. But I know it's not that simple.

There are no mirrors. No tapestries. No walls. No carpet. No real furnishings of any kind. No Unseelie. Pretty simple scene, really. Folks huddled around fire cans to keep warm. Was there fire at the other scenes? Like the ugly Gray Woman that's drawn by the one thing she was created without—beauty—is the Ice Monster drawn to the warmth it can never have? "So you finally went and checked the college out?" I say.

"Yep. I went to their optical analysis lab. Place is a dream. I wanted to know what was happening to the stuff that got iced on a molecular level. Why it was still cold. Why it felt wrong."

I consider and discard the fire theory swiftly. Off the top of my head I can think of five scenes with no fire present. I dredge my memories, find the file where I put the reconstructed images of the scenes and slap them up on an imaginary screen inside my head. I flash through them as I listen, back and forth, breaking them down, analyzing. "What did you find?"

"Trinity was pretty much untouched. Seems people don't pilfer things that don't address immediate needs. I padlocked everything I wanted for myself before I left. They have ultrafast Femtosecond laser systems! The setup is sweet. Pretty much everything I ever wanted to play with is there. Dude, they've got an FT-IR connected to a Nicolet Continuum Infrared Microscope!"

"Dude," I say appreciatively, though I have no idea what he just said. I look beyond my mental screen at the scene in front of me again, wondering if these folks saw it coming, too, like a lot of the others did. They must have. Beneath the ice their mouths are open, faces contorted. They were screaming at the end. Soundlessly but screaming all the same.

"With enough generators running, there's no kind of spectroscopy I couldn't perform," Dancer says happily.

"What the hell is spectroscopy?" Christian says.

"The study of the interaction of matter and radiated energy," Dancer says. "I wanted to excite molecules so I could study them."

"How . . . exciting," Ryodan says.

"I prefer to excite women," Christian says.

"It excites the feck out of me," I say. "Don't make fun of Dancer. He can think circles around you. He could probably figure how to excite *your* molecules and short them out."

"Excitation," Dancer says, "can be accomplished by a number of means. I was specifically interested in temperature and velocity, curious about the kinetic energy of our ziplock detritus. I thought the base state of the atoms might tell me something."

Got to love a dude that says things like "kinetic" and "detritus."

"What's kinetic energy?" Jo says.

"Everything vibrates, all the time. Nothing is motionless. Atoms and ions are constantly deviating from their equilibrium position," Dancer explains. "Kinetic energy is the energy an object possesses due to its motion."

"Sound is a type of kinetic energy," I say. I've often wondered about the properties of my ability to freeze-frame, why I can use energy the way I can, where I get it from, how my body manufactures it but another person's doesn't. I'm fascinated by the different types of energy, what they can do, how everything around us is constantly in motion on some minuscule level. "When a guitar is strummed, molecules are disturbed and vibrate at whatever frequency they'll vibrate at under those circumstances. Their kinetic energy creates sound."

"Exactly," Dancer says. "Another example of kinetic energy is when you crack a whip in one of several specific modes of motion, the sound it makes is because a portion of the whip is moving faster than the speed of sound, and it creates a small sonic boom."

"I didn't know that." Now I'm jealous of a whip. The speed of sound is over seven hundred miles per hour! I don't make sonic booms. I want a whip. I like the idea of walking around making sonic booms everywhere. I can't believe he never told me this before.

"This better be going somewhere," Ryodan says.

"It is," I say. "Dancer doesn't waste time."

"He's wasting mine."

Something's gnawing at the edge of my brain. I'm relieved to realize these folks died quickly and without suffering, because I just calculated the most likely trajectory of the Hoar Frost King's path, from where I saw it disappear, and I was wrong about my first assumption. There's no way these folks saw it coming. None of them were facing the direction it came from. They died instantly, with no awareness of what killed them. I'm relieved. Unlike me, most folks don't seem to want to live their death in slow-mo. Mom always used to say she hoped she'd die in her sleep, easy and without pain. She didn't.

"You're never going to believe what I discovered," Dancer says. "I was staring straight at the results and still refused to accept it. I kept checking, running different tests, testing different objects. I went back and grabbed more ziplocks and tested that stuff, too. The results were the same over and over. You know what absolute zero is, right, Mega?"

"Like, where the feck I'm standing?" I say, but I don't mean it, because if it was, I wouldn't be standing here. I'd be dead. I frown, studying the scene, trying to make sense of something. If they didn't see it coming, why were they screaming? Did they feel the same suffocating panic I felt at Dublin Castle before it arrived?

"Isn't absolute zero theoretical?" Christian says.

"Technically, yes, because all energy can never be removed. Ground state energy still exists, although laser cooling has managed to produce temperatures less than a billionth of a Kelvin."

"Again, what the hell is your point?" Ryodan says. "Are you saying these scenes are being cooled to absolute zero?"

"No. The only reason I brought that up was to illustrate the connection between extreme cold and molecular activity, and the fact that even at the most extreme cold possible, all objects still have energy of some type."

"And?" Jo says.

"On a molecular level, the debris left by the Hoar Frost King has absolutely no energy. None."

"That's impossible!" I say.

"I know. I ran the tests over and over. I tested multiple samples from every scene. I went to Dublin Castle, dug pieces of Unseelie from the snow and tested them, too," he says. "They're inert, Mega. No energy. No vibrations. Nothing. They're motionless. Deader than dead. The things I was testing can't exist, yet there I was holding them in my hands! Physics as I know it is being reinvented. We're standing in the doorway of a new world."

"So, you think it's drawn by energy, and eats it? Like fuel, maybe it uses it so it can move through dimensions?" Jo says.

Dancer shakes his head. "I don't think it's that simple. Most of the scenes it iced didn't have an impressive stockpile of energy. If it was after energy, there are an infinite number of richer places to fuel up. I speculate the absence of energy when it vanishes is a secondary and perhaps a completely unintended effect of whatever it's doing, tangential to its primary purpose."

I got the same impression with my *sidhe*-seer senses at Dublin Castle, that it wasn't malevolent or intentionally destructive. I sensed it was enormously intelligent and hunting for something.

"What *is* its primary purpose?" Ryodan says.

Dancer shrugs. "Wish I knew. I haven't been able to figure that out. Yet. I'm working on it."

"Well, what are we supposed to do?" Jo says, looking around. "There has to be something!"

"Stand around, hoping the bloody thing decides to appear while we're looking, then hit it with whatever we've got handy in the two seconds it's actually here in our world?" Christian says disgustedly. "At least I know what the Crimson Hag wants. Guts, preferably immortal ones." He gives Ryodan a look. "And I know what to use for bait."

"So do I," Ryodan says.

"What are you talking about?" Jo says, looking between Christian and Ryodan. "What's the Crimson Hag?"

I realize she hasn't seen my *Dani Daily*. Nor does she know Ryodan was ever dead. She has no clue her "boyfriend" is immortal. I decide to save that bombshell for the perfect moment. I also decide I'm going to be spending a lot of time with Christian and Ryodan, hoping the Hag comes after them. I let her loose. I'm the one that has to send her back to hell.

Ryodan says to Dancer, "Work faster. Get back in your lab and find me an answer. Dublin's turning into Siberia and the thing just deposited a pile of frozen shit on top of my club."

"At least it didn't ice the door," I say. "'Cause then we couldn't get back in."

Ryodan gives me a look that says he knows I know the back way in.

"Try a flamethrower," Christian says. "Does the trick. Till everything blows."

"Speaking of which, any ideas what makes the scenes blow up?" I ask Dancer.

"I think it creates a kind of energy vacuum where things get unstable. Like I said, physics aren't working right. It's possible objects reduced to no energy are brittle, and when disturbed by vibrations of objects around them, they explode. The lack of energy may also be the lack of 'glue' necessary to hold matter together. Except in these cases, they're shellacked in ice. Once that shell is compromised, everything comes apart. The larger the disturbance of molecules surrounding the scene, the more violent the explosion. You freeze-framing in to study the scene would generate a significant vibrational disturbance."

Sometimes I miss the most obvious things. How many scenes exploded when Ryodan and me were fast-mo-ing through them and I never put two and two together? I ponder what Dancer just told me, crunch it with a few other facts, mix it all up good to see what I get.

The Hoar Frost King leaves no energy behind when he vanishes. It's stripped from everything he ices.

R'jan said that when the HFK iced places in Seelie, the Fae weren't just killed, they were erased like they'd never been.

Both times I saw the HFK appear, all sound vanished. None of us could hear a thing. Dancer confirmed a third case of similar silence and hollow-sounding aftereffects at the WeCare event he witnessed.

Why would sound vanish? Because everything stopped vibrating the instant the HFK appeared? Why would things stop vibrating? Because it was sucking energy? What exactly is the HFK doing? What attracts it to where it's being attracted? What is the fecking commonality? Until we figure it out, we have no hope of stopping it. We're sitting ducks.

I examine the icy tableau before me. I need answers and I need them now. Before I went into the White Mansion I might have had a little time to play with, but since I've been gone, things in my city have gotten critical.

There's too much snow and the cold's getting too extreme, and if the HFK doesn't kill folks, cold alone will.

How many hundreds, even thousands more people will die before we figure out how to stop it? What if it goes to the abbey next? What if it takes Jo from me? What if everybody's generators run out of gas and they all die holed up, alone?

I sigh and close my eyes.

I shiver. What I need to see is right here in front of me. I can feel it. I'm just not looking with the right eyes, the clear eyes that suffer no conflicts. I need a brain like mine and eyes like Ryodan's.

I focus on the backs of my lids, take the grayness of them and cocoon it around me. I make a bland womb where I can begin the process of erasing myself, detaching from the world; the one where I exist and I'm part of reality and everything I see is colored by my thoughts and feelings.

I strip away all that I know about myself, all that I am, and sink into a quiet cavern in my head where there is no corporeality, no pain.

In that shadowy cave, I don't wear a long black leather coat, or skull-and-crossbones panties, or crack jokes. I don't love being a superhero. I don't think Dancer is hot and I'm not a virgin, because I don't really even exist.

In that cave, I was never born. I won't die.

All things are distilled to their essence.

I go inside my head and become that other me, the one I don't tell anybody about.

The observer.

She can't feel hunger in her belly or cramped muscles from being in a cage for days on end. She isn't Dani. *She* can survive anything. Feel nothing. See what's in front of her for exactly and only what it is. Her heart doesn't break a little every time her mom leaves, and she holds no price too high for survival.

I don't let go of myself and seek her often because once I got stuck there and she took over and the things she did . . .

I live in terror that one day I won't get to be Dani again.

But, fecking-A, she's one smart cookie! Tough, too. She sees everything. It's hard to see like she does. Makes me feel like a freak. She thinks I'm a wuss. But she never refuses me when I come.

I open her eyes and study the scene. She's a receiver. Things go in and come out. She processes. No ego or id. Nothing but a puzzle here, and all puzzles can be solved, all codes decoded, all prisons escaped. No price too high for success. There is an end and there are means, and all means are justified.

The facts, void of emotion, look completely different.

Folks bang cans. Fist-pump the air. Some clap. Others warm themselves. I pick and discard. I strip to bare essence.

Their bodies are bent and moving in ways that suggest intended, even relaxed motion, not the instinctual, tense muscular and skeletal flexion of panic. Everyone whose mouth is frozen open appears to be making an elongated *E*. Their eyes are nearly closed and the cords are tight in their necks.

I couldn't see it, but she can.

It's right there, in front of us. It was there the whole time. She thinks it's obvious and I'm stupid. I think she's a sociopathic nut job.

I have my answer but can't rejoice in it because she doesn't feel. I close my eyes to detach but she won't let me. She wants to stay. She thinks she's better equipped than me. I try to leave the cave but she hides all the doors. I visualize brilliant lights in it, like those on top of BB&B. She turns them off.

I open her eyes because I can't stand the darkness.

Ryodan is staring at me, hard. "Dani," he says. "Are you okay?"

He uses a whole, unadulterated question mark, a bona-fecking-fide interrogatory that rises just like a normal person, and that simple thing penetrates. It surprises me the things that rattle her. It loosens her hold on me and I slip free. I guess my sense of humor is more Dani, not her, than anything else about us because when he cracks me up, just like that, she's gone. For a few fleeting seconds I know I'm going to forget her again. I think she makes me forget her and I won't remember until I need her or I get pushed too far.

Then I don't even know that anymore.

I replay all my filed scenes, looking for—and finding— that single commonality it took me so long to see. It was right in front of me all this time but I couldn't drop my preconceptions. I saw what I expected to see and that wasn't what it was at all. "Holy frozen frequencies, Dancer," I say softly. "It's drinking sound Slurpees!"

"What?" Dancer says.

None of them were screaming. All the folks I thought were yelling in fear and horror at the end were *singing*.

The music changes beneath my feet. A heavy metal song just came on in Chester's and the vibrations increase in tempo and intensity. I feel the blood drain from my face.

If I'm right . . .

And I *am* right.

There are thousands of people below us, in Chester's, and although I'm not real impressed with their choice of a lifestyle, the race we're in now needs all the humans we've got left.

"We've got to turn it off!" I say. "We've got to turn everything off right now! Dude, we've got to shut Chester's down!"

THIRTY-SIX

"Oh the weather outside is frightful"

Beyond the frost-etched window of my bedroom, fat snowflakes drift lazily to the ground. Unlike me, they know no urgency. At the abbey, snow obeys a simple prime directive: fall without cease. It began two days after Sean went to work at Chester's, and has not stopped for twenty-three.

My heart suffers a similar accumulation, with chill piling in treacherous drifts and valleys. Despite our efforts to beat it back, winter claims more of our world with each passing day. Ours has dwindled to paths shoveled between waist-high white walls crusted by ice. I do not know how to navigate this new terrain. I fear my nana's snow goblins lurk in these drifts, waiting to carry off those who stray into the blinding wintry white.

Sean has not been able to reach the abbey nor have I been able to leave for fifteen days. We venture into the countryside with hatchets and saws only to procure timber from hard-iced, felled trees so that we may keep our fires burning bright. We have run dry of gasoline; generators squat in silent reminder of auspicious times we no longer enjoy. We have precious few candles and lack ingredients to make more. If not for the batteries Dani spent obsessive weeks stockpiling as protection against the Shades months past, it is possible we would all be dead, unable to protect ourselves from the amorphous apparitions that may yet lurk within our walls, although we've yet to glimpse one since the night Cruce was interred in his subterranean sepulcher. Some say the Unseelie King took them with him when he left. One can hope.

Night sees us gathered in common rooms to conserve supplies. It is impossible to say when this snow will stop. The sky is night-black or storm-leaden but for an occasional shaft of brilliant sunshine-piercing clouds. If we do not soon remove the weight of accumulation from the roof of our chapel, we will lose both roof and interior supports. Ice will crush our altar and drifts will take our pews. Early this morning the rafters creaked and groaned a somber hymn as I prayed: God, grant me serenity, wisdom, strength, courage, and fortitude.

But all is not snow at our abbey. Oh, no.

All is not chill within or without our walls.

My wing of the abbey is a temperate sixty-five degrees, with not one fire burning.

My chambers are nearer eighty, sweltering for one born and raised on the Emerald Isle. I mop my brow and tuck damp tendrils behind my ears. I unfasten the top button of my blouse and dab at my skin.

Beyond the window, the sharp-shaved crystalline fireworld funnel towers over the abbey, glittering bright as diamonds in a capricious ray of sun. Between it and the perimeter wall of my bedchamber, snow is conspicuously absent.

In that narrow boundary, grass grows.

Grass, by the saints, green as St. Patrick's clover! Kelly green as the misshapen shamrock that symbolizes the mission and integrity of our order to See, Serve, and Protect.

Against the crumbling mortar flush to my bedroom

wall, sultry flowers in every shade of boysenberry and orchid, cerise and Byzantium bend and sway with blossoms so heavy on delicate stems they droop and nod, deceptively dulcet on a breeze as conflicted as my soul; temperate one moment, frigid the next.

Were I to crank the window and part the leaded glass, the scent that drifted in would intoxicate me. The blossoms reek of spices that make me think of Persian carpets and far-off lands where hookahs are smoked for breakfast and sultans keep harems, and life is lazy, licentious, and short-lived.

But *well*-lived, Cruce would say.

I blot sweat from my palms and smooth a blueprint on Rowena's stately desk. I must know and I do not want to know if what I have begun to suspect is true.

Although the IFP is tethered to a piece of earth that has been fired to a kiln-smooth, porcelain black gloss, were one to approach it, one would feel no heat. The fire world is contained.

Yet, between the IFP and our abbey grows that loathsome grass despite the snow, that grass upon which Cruce lays me gently back in my dreams, amid fragrant blooms where he makes me feel things for which I despise myself come dawn.

I am not wise in the ways of geography. I know east when the sun rises. I know west when it sets.

Rowena protected many secrets, clanking keys in the bracelet of power that remained on her wrist, held over our heads, until the day she died. I discovered a cache in her bedchamber four nights ago when, desperate to resist another torturous slumber, I occupied myself by studying every inch of the Grand Mistress's apartment, seeking telltale clues of false panels or retractable floorboards. In the faux bottom of a centuries-old armoire I found maps, sketches, and plans, many of places that baffle me, in which I am unable to divine her interest.

Also therein I found blueprints of the abbey on scrolls and bound in large flat volumes, both Upstairs and Underneath. It is the blueprint of the subterranean chamber and adjoining passages wherein the *Sinsar Dubh* was once entombed, over which I now place the transparent sketch I have prepared of my wing.

I smooth them together so they meet, corner-to-corner, and press my tongue to the roof of my mouth in silent protest, a technique I perfected when young to keep from crying out when lambasted by another's intolerable emotion.

Cruce's chamber is beneath my bedroom!

Begging the question: does the false summer that makes grass grow and flowers bloom come from the fire world adjacent or the iced prince below?

I decide maybe I can stand Ryodan, at least today, because when I say shut Chester's down, the dude doesn't even ask me another question!

He skirts the ice sculpture's perimeter and heads straight for the metal door in the ground. The ice ends some fifteen feet from it, about which I'm real glad because the back way in that I'm not supposed to know about is a long way from here. Takes a lot of underground navigating. And knowing him, since he heard I knew of it, he probably shut it down and had his men make him another one. But I'll find that one, too. It's like a game with me. Him trying to hide stuff just makes me more determined to find it.

I follow, happy he takes my word for things. Jo and Christian sure don't. They're behind me, peppering me with questions that Dancer isn't answering either, I think because he's still busy putting together all the ramifications of what we just figured out. Either that or he's as obsessed as I am about getting every single thing in our general vicinity turned off ASAP.

I'm still missing a few facts that I don't think I can gather since the scenes all blew up. Speculation may be all we got to work with. I know the Hoar Frost King likes ice cream but I don't know what flavor. And I'm pretty sure he's picky. Or else we'd all have been iced months ago.

I follow Ryodan to his office, where he cuts the power to the subclubs. With each tap of the computer screen, one more subclub dies and it's all I can do not to hoot and holler, especially when the kiddie subclub goes dark and still.

Lights dim. Music stops.

People—the fecking sheep who should have pulled their heads out of their asses weeks ago and banded together to save our city—protest vociferously. Some just keep dancing like nothing ever happened, like they're hearing music in their heads.

Others shrug and get back to practically doing the dirty on the dance floor, clothes half off, like everybody wants to see their Baby-Roach-slimmed butts!

"Can I talk to all the clubs at once?" I say. "You got some kind of PA system in here?"

He gives me a look that says: nice try, like I'd ever let you address my patrons en masse.

I snicker. He has a point. I could rant at these folks for hours. "You got to explain," I say. "They need to understand what they're up against. You got to tell them about the Hoar Frost King and that they can't go outside and make noise or else they might die. And you got to tell them how the scenes explode, so if anybody leaves they don't do nothing stupid with the frozen folks up there and get all cut up on shrapnel! And don't forget to tell them that even in here they need to stay as quiet as they can and—"

Ryodan presses a button on his desk. "There will be no lights or music until further notice." He releases the button.

"That's it?" I say. Fecking good thing he ain't writing the Ryodan Rag! Through the glass floor I watch folks rustle angrily. Many are drunk and don't like this new development. They want their bread and circuses. That's why they come here. "Boss, what the feck was that? Maybe you could, like, tell them not to leave or they'll die?"

He presses the button again. "Don't leave or you'll die."

There's a pregnant hush then, like they all think he's God or something, and folks and Fae stop everything they're doing and sit down. Only after a long moment do they begin talking again.

"I think you should lock the doors," Jo says. "Don't let them out for their own good."

"I'd prefer they leave. Less to draw it here."

"If you want me to tell you what to do to keep this place safe," I say, "you better keep *them* safe."

"I thought you were disgusted by the people that come to my club."

"They're still people."

He presses the button again. "If you go outside, you will be killed. If you make noise, you will be sent outside. Don't piss me off."

Just like that, Chester's goes completely silent.

Part 3

No lullabies to lay the children to rest,

No hymns to mourn the dying,

No blues to ease the pain,

No rock and roll to live by.

Without music we would all be

Sociopaths or dead.

—The Book of Rain

THIRTY-SEVEN

"The sound of silence"

I call my *sidhe*-seers to gather in the chapel beneath creaking eaves.

Our sanctum could once scarce contain the half of us. Seated now between marching rows of majestic ivory pillars, those who remain are swallowed in voluminous, echoing silence save the groaning of rafters and the hollow resonance of my footfalls as I walk the center aisle that leads to the sanctuary at the liturgical east of the church.

Dull, despairing eyes follow my progress. My girls occupy the front eleven pews in the nave. The ghosts of cherished friends fill the rest. It was a hard winter followed by the tease of stillborn spring.

Now this incessant snow!

I feel stronger in the chapel.

Here, the divine defies the devil at our door. Faith is an unquenchable flame in my heart. Although twice Cruce has followed me here, these hallowed floors remain inviolate. He has not been able to enter.

Reliquaries of polished ivory and gold, adorned with precious gems, attend the altar. More are sheltered at shrines where once candles flickered, until we were obliged to purloin them for other purposes. These urns and boxes hold sacrosanct bones and bits of cloth from saints canonized not by the Holy See but a more ancient church. I suffer no conflict that they reside beside acceptably venerated bones. Bones are bones and good people are good people. I beseech them all to watch over us in our time of need.

I enter the raised chancel in the sanctuary and approach the lectern. We have no power for the microphone but it is no longer necessary, as my voice will carry clearly to the few occupied front rows.

Two hundred eighty-nine of us remain.

I would weep if I had tears but they are drained dry each dawn when I awaken, exhausted, stained by semen that is not mine by right and guilt that is. Semen from one who has just dipped his fingers in the stoup of holy water and now traces a cross at his forehead, his lips, his heart!

He violates my sanctum. He mocks my rituals.

His fingers do not burst into flame nor is he struck by bolts of celestial retribution and banished to hell as Satan should be. I believed him barred at the door. Was he amused to deceive me or has he gained strength to project himself?

He winks at me as he walks the center aisle. Near the rood screen he pauses and unfurls his wings.

Dark angel. Black-winged and black-souled.

In my church.

In my church!

The girls rustle. I become aware my gaze is fixed on Cruce, exquisite, naked Cruce, standing in the center of my chapel, wings spanning the aisle, stretching half to heaven, and my first emotion is panic. I must not let them know I see him or Margery will stand in my stead!

I sweep my gaze over the pews and lower my barriers so that I may know the state of their hearts. I've been muffling their emotions for months, for they have known such anger, grief, and fear of late that I cannot tender the daily inundation.

Anxiety slams into me. Shame steals my breath. I press shaking fingertips to the hollow of my throat as if to release a catch hidden there that controls my inhalations.

I see clearly for the first time in more than a month.

If I am the only one who sees Cruce, I *should* be deposed.

If I am not, if others see him, too, and I have kept my silence this long, I should be damned.

For what is war renowned?

He divides. He carves down the middle and makes enemies of even brothers and sisters, parents and offspring. War has been dividing my family since birth. Perhaps, indeed, he has been paying me uncommon attention.

How best to divide?

Sean's cousin Rocky kept a watch of gold and diamonds etched with his credo. He vowed, despite education, pedigree, or wealth, all prey fell indiscriminate to this simple strategy: isolate the mark.

Silence is the ultimate isolator.

Have I played into his hands?

He stands smugly certain of me, assured of our private complicity. How pleased he must be when each morning I remain an isolated berg in this winter that has claimed our world!

I turn back to the women in my care. "Who among you sees Cruce standing in the aisle?"

Ryodan calls a meeting in one of the rooms on the second floor. I never seen such quiet in the club. Folks sit alone, not talking. The lights are dim and all music is off. I can't feel the tiniest vibration in my feet. A soft glow radiates at ceiling and floor level. He's got some kind of illuminated tubing behind the moldings. I always assumed he had giant generators somewhere and I just couldn't feel the vibration over the pounding, incessant music. If not generators, what's keeping the lights on?

"Dude, I thought you were turning everything off."

"Everything is off."

"What's powering the lights that are still on?"

"The bulk of Chester's runs on geothermal power."

I smack myself in the forehead with the butt of my palm. Of course. He's got all the best toys. Why wouldn't he dig all the way to the center of the Earth and harness planetary power? The dude, like, lives forever!

Me, Jo, Dancer, and Christian are joined by six of Ryodan's dudes. Every time Jericho Barrons doesn't walk into the room with me, I heave a sigh of relief. One of these days it's going to happen. It's inevitable. And one of these days it will probably be with Mac at his side. S'cool. I've lived most of my life under threat of "one of these days" for one reason or another. Superheroes do.

Ryodan sends three of his men down to the club to keep order, and sends the other three into the icy day to track what noise they find and shut it down. Jo tempers his orders with: "And bring any people you discover back to Chester's so we can keep them alive."

I watch him real careful when she adds to his commands like she has the right. Like she's his girlfriend and they're a team, out to save the world together or something. We'll see if his dudes obey her. If they come back with a band of ragtag survivors, I might just be impressed. I can't read his face. It's like he's got it totally closed to me.

He refuses to let me fire up a press and get a *Dani Daily* out. I argue but Jo makes a point: nobody is venturing out unless they absolutely have to anyway, so the time wasted printing and posting would be better used bringing everyone up to speed so we can make a plan. When did she become Ms. Voice of Reason? Oh, and Glam Girl! When she slips off her coat and unwinds her scarf, her boobs aren't sparkly but she's sure got a push-up bra on!

"Sound Slurpees? Dani, what's going on?" Jo says.

"It's being drawn by music," I say. "At first I thought it was attracted to singing, but it's not. It's a component of music it's after. Sound waves. Frequencies. Who knows, maybe a single note. And the sound doesn't need to be made by a person. It can come from a stereo, a musical instrument, church bells, a car radio, even an Unseelie screaming a note high enough to shatter glass."

"Like at Dublin Castle, the night it iced the cages," Christian says. He's been quiet but I can feel temper rolling off the dude. He's barely keeping his cool.

"Exactly. Or it could be drawn by the chiming of crystal bowls."

"The fitness center," Ryodan says.

"Right. Or playing a washboard, banging on a pot and singing."

"The Laundromat folks," Dancer says.

"And the weird wire contraption around the dude's head wasn't a medical device for an injured neck. It was a harmonica holder," I say. "With their primitive band, the small family managed to make whatever noise draws the Hoar Frost King."

"The band in my subclub must have made it, too."

"So why didn't it ice the entire club?" Christian says.

"I'm guessing it's drawn to a specific sound. The same way I like Life cereal but not Chex. They're both little squares of crunchy goodness but they sure as feck ain't equal to my taste buds. And all the audio equipment in your warehouse must have been hooked up and turned on. At the church where I almost died, they were singing and playing the organ. At all the underground pubs there was a band or a stereo playing."

"The WeCare folks were singing and playing the organ, too," Dancer says.

"So how do we figure out what noise it likes?" Jo says. "All the scenes got blown up, didn't they?"

"I don't think we need to," Dancer says. "We just need to set up somewhere and make an enormous variety of sounds. Wait for it to come."

"Great idea, kid," Christian says. "Then we all bloody get iced!"

"Not necessarily," Ryodan says.

"What do you mean? What are you thinking?" Jo's sloe-eyed puppy-dog expression says she thinks he's the smartest person she's ever met. Gag me! Dancer's the smartest person she ever met, and I'm second.

When he tells us I just shake my head. "It won't work," I say.

"Actually, Mega," Dancer says, "it might."

"Bull-fecking-crikey. He's assuming a lot of things."

"I think it's worth a try," Dancer says.

"Are you defending him?" I say.

"Only the idea, Mega."

"Are you sure you can pull this off?" I ask Ryodan. "You know how many things could go wrong?"

Ryodan gives me a look.

Jo's gone white. "You're crazy. You're talking about setting one monster free to destroy another."

"The world is turning to ice," Ryodan says to Jo. "If this continues, the Hoar Frost King will finish what Cruce started: the destruction of the world. Sometimes you plug the hole any way you can, and worry about fixing the boat later. If the choices are sinking today or tomorrow, I'll take tomorrow."

Him and me think alike a lot of times. I'd never tell him that.

To me, he says, "You and the kid get what we need. I want to be ready by nightfall."

I am blasted by the crimson complexity of Margery's rage.

She surges to her feet to demand my immediate resignation as Grand Mistress, but before she can incite the hue and cry upon which she so thrives, one by one heads bow and hands rise. White flags of surrender are hoisted until each woman has her arm above her head save one. My cousin reclaims her seat in the pew, fists clenched in white-knuckled balls on her lap.

I open myself with a tight, narrow focus. Her fury is bottomless, directed in its entirety at me. She believed she was his only one. She castigates *me* for the wanton ways of our enemy. She is a fool in too many ways to number: in affairs of infidelity, if a man strays, it is not the fault of the woman with whom he lays. A worthy heart eschews temptation, despite the magnitude. Clearly my heart is not worthy.

I dismiss her and regard my girls with regret and resolve.

In my silence, I failed my charges. It was not merely myself I isolated. I cut them off from one another.

"Did any of you tell someone else?"

I hear no replies and need none. I can tell from their faces that not one of them spoke of it. We became a group of close-huddled islands in our shame, eating and working and living side by side, in complete disconnect. For more than a month each of us waged the same hellish battle, and rather than sharing that burden, suffered it alone.

"We permitted him to separate us," I say. "It was exactly what he wanted. But it is over. We have called his bluff and are now united against him."

Cruce's enormous wings rustle. It is the only sound I have ever heard the projected image of him make. Oh, yes, our enemy is gaining strength with each passing day!

Again I wonder if it is Cruce or the presence of the IFP that causes the grass to grow. If it is the IFP, might its location above Cruce's cage also be weakening the integrity of those icy bars? I have not permitted myself to visit his chamber since last Sean and I made love. Failing my soul mate to anchor me, I risk nothing.

Did this clever, clever prince devise a way to summon a fire-world fragment to set him free? Were I to make the long descent into the bowels of this abbey today, what would I find?

Darkness, moss, and bones?

No bar where once one was?

"Must we leave the abbey?" Tanty Anna exclaims. "Is it the only way to escape him?"

"It's our home! We can't leave!" Josie protests.

"Where would we go? How would we get there? Dog sleds?" Margery says.

"There aren't any dogs left. The Shades ate them all," Lorena says.

"That was a joke. The point is we can't leave," Margery says. "Under any circumstances. This is our home. I will let no one drive me from it!"

Again I turn a tight focus on her. She wishes we would vanish, doesn't care the how or why of it, so long as she gets him to herself. She has been in no way dissuaded by the fickleness of his affection.

I dab at my neck, my brow. The temperature in the chapel is rising. I smell blossoms, spicy and sweet.

I cannot move Cruce. But I can and will do something about the IFP.

I must find a way to contact Ryodan and his men. He already has my Sean. What more can he thieve from me?

We will move the fire world, send it back the way it came, and I will have my answer, if the grass dies. Fire world or ice prince; which is overheating our home? Did the Fates cackle when they stitched together the tapestry that froze our greatest enemy in our basement then parked a heater above it?

I do not believe fragments of Faery are one-way.

If it can be tethered, surely it can be towed.

THIRTY-EIGHT

"Burning down the house"

Our exodus from Dublin is a somber one.

It isn't easy to leave the city. It takes a small army of us to battle our way out.

Before we go, we set up sound decoys at the north, south, and west edges of the city, in abandoned neighborhoods where nobody hangs anymore. Dancer hooks them up, broadcasting from a central radio source. Even Ryodan is impressed, making me über-proud Dancer is my best friend! Hopefully it'll be enough to keep the Hoar Frost King from being drawn to all the noise we have to make in order to escape the snowy prison Dublin has become.

I make a quick pit stop in the Cock and Bull tavern and take something off the wall I been dying to have ever since Dancer mentioned it. It's the only place I could remember seeing a whip, mounted like art next to a set of giant bullhorns. I got no doubt it'll come in handy somehow. And if not, so what? I can't resist making something move faster than the speed of sound. Sonic booms are *so* going to be me!

Truck engines roar, scraping a path so Humvees and buses can lumber between snowdrifts piled in enormous banks, iced solid as rock. Streets are impassable with the stuff, and still it falls, landing thick on our windshields. We got dudes up front driving snowplows and trucks that scatter chunks of salt. I got no clue where they found the equipment. We don't get this kind of snow. Knowing Ryodan, he's got all of it tucked away in a warehouse somewhere, prepared for any and every eventuality, even the seemingly impossible.

Got to admit, I like that about him. I'm used to feeling like I'm the only one sees the hard things coming, and I'm always angling to skew the odds in my favor. It's nice to know somebody else is preparing, too.

He's right. The hole has to be plugged because the boat is sinking. Another few days and I'm not sure our exodus would be possible. We'd be iced in. I hate the plan we're about to put in motion but we got to do it. Sometimes when all hell's breaking loose the only thing to do is to break more hell loose.

Before it's too late.

When we get to the abbey and tell her what we're going to do, Kat's going to have a total meltdown.

Night brings a violet aurora borealis to our home. Aubergine and gentian flames flicker on shiny ice-capped snow as if on the swells of an alabaster ocean.

We gather at the windows of the common room to watch the dance of violet vapors. I am appalled to realize how much time I've spent in my chambers the past month, so as not to betray Cruce's visitations. I did not see we were all going off alone for similar reasons. Our abbey had become hauntingly quiet and lonely with me, their leader, unaware. I will never again permit myself to forget that isolation is the first step to defeat.

Tonight our unwanted visitor is conspicuously absent. It is the first evening in weeks he has not dogged my step. He knows we are angry and his appearance would only further rile us. Margery, too, is absent. I will confront the wasp in our nest come morning. She and I will reach terms or she will leave.

Tonight we break into our precious stash of corn sealed airtight in jars late last summer, popping it with oil over flame. We make the evening a celebration, warmed by the last of the cider scalded over a fire, spiced with cinnamon and clove. Communion, warmth, good scents in the air, contribute to a feeling of thanksgiving and hope, and we reconnect into the family we once were with new appreciation. Now that we all know Cruce was plying his seduction upon each of us, we are no longer divided by guilt.

When I hear the roar of engines approaching the abbey, I fear for the safety of my girls and bid them retreat to the cafeteria while I see to the door. Three of those who served in the Haven, Rowena's inner circle, refuse to leave, and another three step forward to join them, Tanty Nana at the forefront, her eyes wise in twin nests of wrinkles. They infuse me with courage. I begin to understand the purpose of the chosen inner circle.

The seven of us bundle into cloaks, scarves, and mittens, and step out into the snow. Lavender lights wisp across a twilight terrain, evoking a surreal, dreamy ambience. We watch as trucks with enormous blades carve their way up our white-capped drive followed by four Humvees and two buses.

When Ryodan steps down from the driver's seat of one of the trucks, for the briefest of startled moments I think: But how serendipitous, I can ask him to tow the IFP away!

Common sense asserts itself and my heart grows chill.

Yes, I wanted to see him. But for this man to come here tonight, for him to use machines to bulldoze a path through mountains of ice to reach our home, means we have something he wants.

Badly.

Through narrowed eyes, I regard him. Lack of visible cloven hoof, tail, or horns does not disguise the devil at my door. He glides, long-limbed and sure-footed, through the snow. He is a beautiful man but unlike my Sean the impression is of animal grace, something not human. Coupled, of course, with the fact that he is not really here! No man stands where he walks. I sense nothing. It is shocking. It is sensational in that it is the very antithesis of sensation. Loath though I am to admit it, it is such a relief! I get nothing from him. Never have I been around anyone that affords me such blissful emotional silence.

He takes both my hands in greeting and leans in to kiss my cheek. I turn my face, press my lips to his ear and say softly, "You can't have it. Whatever it is, you're not taking it. The answer is no."

His breath is warm on my ear. "I have come for something of which you'd like to be quit."

I wonder if he always speaks in the manner he is spoken to. The devil is the master of assimilation. It is how he gains entry: he makes himself appear a friend.

"Again, no." I think perhaps we have something to trade. Perhaps I will give him whatever it is he wants for moving the IFP. But best to deny from the onset.

He slides his hands up my arms to my elbows and cups them lightly, drawing us closer. "We could barter."

Does he read thoughts or merely expressions so well? "Give me my Sean back," I whisper. The stubble on his cheek abrades my skin.

"Your beloved Sean has been free to leave for weeks," he murmurs against my ear.

I mask a tiny jerk and swallow a cry of protest. I do

not know whether he speaks the truth. If it is a lie, it is a bitter and hurtful one.

"It is not a lie." He lets his hands fall from my arms and steps back. I am colder where he was touching me.

I see Dani exiting one of the buses. The clouds part on my troubled heart and I am suddenly buoyant. Her fiery hair is a halo of sunshine around her glowing, delicate, eternally battered face. Her smile of greeting is infectious. How I have missed her!

I open my arms, knowing she will never run into them as I wish. Knowing any hug I steal from the child will be just that—stolen. Beneath her hardy, bruised exterior shines pure gold. She is filled with light as no one I have encountered before. It makes me both harder and gentler on her. Though she is cross and grumpy and irritable as any teen, there is not one ounce of ill will in her and she has had reason to feel it. Indeed, reasons enough to fill a book, but she radiates only excitement and happiness to be alive. I realize Ryodan is watching me watch her, intently. I wonder again if he can pick up my thoughts, and if so, how clearly?

"Why have you come?" I demand.

Dani skids to a stop on the ice in front of me and blurts in a rush of breath, "Hey, Kat, what's up? Long time, no see, huh? Everything okay out here? You got enough to eat and stuff? Sorry I haven't been around to check on things but I got stuck in Faery. Dude! You're never going to believe all the stuff that's been happening! *Brrr,* it's cold out here! Oh, and we think we know how to stop the Unseelie responsible for turning our world into an arctic zone! Hey, I'm freezing, you going to let us in?"

We are again in the common room watching out the window as the most peculiar confederacy I have ever seen collaborate upon a shared goal prepares to destroy us.

I cannot see it any other way. They are wrong. It won't work. It's far too dangerous.

Five men who do not exist, one violent, immensely powerful, sex-obsessed Unseelie prince who believes himself in love with Dani, an exceedingly radiant and happy Jo, and a young, good-looking boy with glasses for whom Dani is the sun, moon, and stars and reminds me of my Sean but harbors secrets so dark and deep that even my gifts cannot reach them, work together to unload equipment from the buses and carry it across mounds of snow and ice to the chosen location.

While Dani told me their plan to trap the Hoar Frost King with the IFP, Ryodan remained silent, and with good reason. He knew each of my objections and that there was no valid rebuttal for any of them. At the end, when permission should have been given or withheld by me—and it most certainly would have been withheld— he informed me that if I failed to cooperate in any way, he would destroy the abbey and continue with his plan.

"You're going to destroy it anyway," I said.

"No we're not. It's going to work, Kat!" Dani exclaimed.

"You don't know that. You don't even know if the Hoar Frost King *can* be killed."

Ryodan's gaze reflected the same odds of success I perceive. He said simply, "How much longer do you think you and your charges will survive if this snow continues."

He has the most jarring way of never punctuating his questions.

They plan to free a monster.

I said, "Assuming it works and the Hoar Frost King is destroyed, how do you plan to tether the IFP again?"

Even Dani had the good grace to look away.

I cannot read Ryodan. I will never be able to. But I can read the rest of them.

Deep down, they do not believe they can.

THIRTY-NINE

*"Crystal world with winter flowers turn my day
to frozen hours"*

I ain't never been to a heavy metal concert though I seen
some on TV. Dancer's been to all kinds of shows.
Growing up in a cage had serious disadvantages. By the
time I got out, there were so many things I wanted to do
that I couldn't get to them all. Now all the good bands
are dead, and tonight is probably as close as I'm going
to ever get. The violet lights flickering in the sky are
perfect for a rock concert, like having our own laser
show! I seen some on TV and they were über-cool.

It's crazy how many speakers and cables and stuff
Dancer and me picked up. We might have gotten a little
carried away. But the music store we looted was untouched and crammed full of equipment, with no windows broken, and a full cash register. I guess in times of
war nobody's thinking, Gee, I want to go steal a stereo.
In the end we filled both buses, figuring the louder the
better.

We set up the sound stage close to the abbey, between
the wall and the IFP.

It's freaky working close to it, knowing if anybody
jostles you into it, you're instantly dead. Creeps me all
kinds of out but I got a job to do hooking up speakers
while Dancer gets everything else up and running. The

long, wide, scorched black trail behind it is a constant reminder that it would char me to cinders if I so much as touched it. Although the IFP emits no actual heat, no snow accumulates on the barren soil, as if where it passed it has left the earth antithetical to cold.

The faceted funnel is taller than the abbey, at least a hundred feet wide at the top, and tapers to forty or so at the base—more than big enough to swallow one Hoar Frost King. The earth beneath it is baked to a slick, shiny black finish, though the fire-world fragment doesn't throw off heat. A ribbon of glowing wards twist around the base, securely tethered to a black loop on a black box etched with symbols about twenty feet away. I skirt the IFP, eyeing the black box suspiciously, thinking how the feck is that tiny thing that is roughly the size of a Rubik's cube keeping an IFP from drifting? It can't weigh more than half a pound. I kick it gently to see how far it moves and just about break my toe! I can't resist trying to pick it up.

I can't even budge it on the snow!

"What? You got some kind of ultradense metal I ain't never heard of?" I say grumpily, but if he hears me he doesn't respond. How does Ryodan always have the coolest stuff? Where the heck does he get it?

I look back up at the funnel. It's eerily beautiful, crystalline planes and angles reflecting the dazzling purples of the aurora borealis. I will a silent thought to the universe: Let this work. We've all had a tough gig lately. Let there be no casualties tonight.

Kat's outside again, watching us. Ryodan told her she has to move the *sidhe*-seers out into the snow once we begin. It almost made her nuts! She took it as the equivalent of him saying the abbey was an accepted casualty, but I know him. He wasn't saying that. He just takes the possibles into consideration and knows that trying to move nearly three hundred women in the middle of a crisis is a nightmare. I've tried to move them during times of peace and quiet and had the luck of a broken mirror nailed beneath an upside-down horseshoe with a ladder nearby that a black cat just walked under. Like sheep, *sidhe*-seers herd by nature, until you *want* them to go somewhere. Then they're all fluffy bottoms and broken legs.

Since we're just about to start, I guess they're all inside bundling up. Freeze-framing the equipment into place is the only thing keeping me from shivering. Well, that and nervousness about overshooting my mark and ending up a crispy critter might be heating me up, too. Some of Ryodan's dudes are getting fires going, and a few *sidhe*-seers begin to straggle out and gather around.

I look at Kat walking toward me from the abbey. She looks so slight with her hair blowing back from her face and her body like a reed that could be too easily broken. I worry about Kat. I know she didn't want to run the abbey but everybody insisted. Kat exudes something peaceful and strong that makes you feel at ease even when you probably shouldn't. She says faith is a rock and as long as you have your feet planted firmly on it you can't falter.

"Dani."

"Hey, Kat."

"It's too close to the abbey. Set it up closer to the IFP."

"Can't. When the Hoar Frost King comes, if the IFP is too close to the speakers, the funnel could get iced before we can cut the tether and use it."

"If it's not closer, the Hoar Frost King could appear, ice, and vanish before the IFP even gets to it."

I don't say nothing. I already took that into consideration when Dancer and me did our time calculations.

"Do you really believe this has any chance of working?"

I plug two speakers into a generator and begin piggy-backing the connections. "Which part of it?"

"Any."

"Well, I'm pretty sure we're going to end up drawing it here. I don't know the exact sound it'll come for, but we'll make it eventually. By the time Dancer's done, the music is going to vie with arena-rock for sheer decibels. We shut everything down in and around the city and Dancer dropped the signal to our decoys once we got here. If sound *is* the Hoar Frost King's Scooby-snacks—and I'm not wrong about this—it's going to be starving and we're leaving it only one source of food. I give attracting it ninety-nine percent odds."

"And destroying it?"

I ponder that. I been pondering that all the way out. "I hear the IFP incinerated everything in its path, even boulders and concrete buildings and stuff, right?"

She nods.

"The IFP is part of Faery so it's not like we're trying to incinerate a Fae monster with human fire. We're trying to burn it in fire from its own world. I think that increases the odds substantially."

"But who says fire will win over ice? You said it's not even made of ice. What if it's made of something fire has no effect on? What if you summon the Hoar Frost King here and it ices the IFP?"

I been trying not to consider that possibility. "Then we're all in a world of shit and probably dead, Kat."

She gives me a look.

I flash her a gamine grin. "But then at least we got rid of the IFP!"

She gives me another look.

I spread my hands, palms up. "What do you want me to say? I'm not going to lie to you. You're like Christian. You know anyway."

"You do realize it will require impeccable timing. You

have to draw it to a precise location, cut the tether holding the IFP, and hope the Ice Monster gets trapped in the few seconds it's in our dimension. And whoever cuts that tether might get iced."

"Dude, a few secs are all we need! Most of us can freeze-frame and Christian can sift. We're darned fast! We're setting up practically on top of the IFP. The instant the Hoar Frost King appears, we cut the tether, and both sound stage *and* Ice Monster get swallowed."

Her gaze spans the fifteen yards between the sound stage and the perimeter wall of what used to be Ro's chambers but are now hers. "And so does the abbey."

"We're going to retether it before that happens!"

"Again, that's going to require impeccable timing."

"Again, dude, we all freeze-frame. 'Sides, I heard the IFP wasn't moving all that fast. Ryodan says as long as he's got thirty seconds and gets it done before it enters the abbey, it's a no-brainer."

"And if it reaches the abbey?"

"It won't."

"If it does?" she presses.

"Look, we got at least a minute before it hits the abbey wall. We ain't going to let it take the abbey." I'm not about to tell her that Ryodan said if it entered the abbey he'd be unable to ward it off until it came out the other side. Something about a containment spell only working if you completely enclose on all four sides the object you want contained.

"One minute," Kat says quietly. "Do you realize if it destroys this place, we will lose everything our order has spent millennia gathering? All our books and sacred objects, our history, our home. Do you see the grass and flowers growing up against the wall? Do you realize if the IFP breaches the abbey, it may very well melt Cruce's prison and set him free? The *Sinsar Dubh* will be loose in our world, walking around in the body of an Unseelie prince!"

"Look, Kat, I ain't saying it's a perfect plan. But if you don't have any better ideas, get out of the way and let us do our job." I look around at the swells of snow, the iced trees, the piles of crusted drifts. "How much longer do you think we'll survive like this?"

She sighs and says, "That's the only reason I haven't stopped you."

"You haven't stopped us because you can't!" I say heatedly. "You're just one person and we're all super-heroes!"

"I won't let it take my abbey, Dani. I won't let these women be ripped from the only home they've ever known. Like you, I'm willing to risk a great deal for those things in which I believe."

I watch her as she walks away and think she's starting to worry me a little.

It's nearly eight when our concert begins. We laid out sheets of plywood on the snow to hold the audio equipment and made a second platform a short distance away for the generators we're using to power it all, then a third platform for the music source and so our tushes don't get cold. We put that one far enough away that we don't get iced when it shows up. We build a couple fires and stack wood nearby. My hair and clothes smell like outdoors and wood smoke, and for a sec it makes me feel like I'm on a family vacation or something. All these folks, including six that are fast enough—and I still don't get to have a decent snowball fight!

Me and Ryodan, Christian, and Jo gather on the plat-form, ready to dart in and cut the tether when it comes.

"Jo shouldn't be here," I say. "She can't freeze-frame."

"I'm not leaving," she says.

"Make her leave," I say to Ryodan. "Unless you want to be responsible for getting her killed."

"Ryodan won't let anything happen to me," she says.

I roll my eyes. "Dude," I say to Ryodan. "Get her out of here."

"She's her own woman," he says. "She can make up her own mind."

Jo glows.

I just about puke. "Fine. It's on your head." Bugger it all. Now I'm going to have to watch out for Jo *and* worry about everything else, too.

Kat, the *sidhe*-seers, and a couple of Ryodan's dudes are at the opposite end of the abbey, down by the lake, with fires burning, sitting in total silence. Conversation is forbidden. They're to make no noise whatsoever.

I get a bad feeling looking at them. "You sure they should be so far away?" I ask Ryodan.

"We need to be split up so, worst-case scenario, we don't all get iced."

"Are we ready?" Dancer walks up and joins us on the platform.

"Get out of here, kid. You got no fucking superpower," Ryodan says.

"Sure I do," Dancer says easily. "I'm the one who saves her life when you guys would have killed her. Remember?"

"If Jo stays," I say, cutting off my nose to spite my face, "Dancer stays." Great. Now I got two people who can't freeze-frame that I have to watch out for.

Dancer and me settle back against a couple of extra speakers we stacked up for something to lean against. "Crank it up," I say. "Let's get this party started." I hand Dancer my iPod, loaded especially for tonight's show. I got almost ten thousand songs on it! Motorhead to Mozart, Linkin Park and Liszt, Velvet Revolver to

Wagner, Puscifer and Pavarotti and everything in between. I even got show tunes and cartoon soundtracks!

Ten minutes later Lor says, "What *is* this crap? Who let her load the iPod?"

"Nobody else brought one," I say. "I chose *awesome* music."

"Where the hell is Hendrix on this thing?" Lor takes it out of the sound dock and scrolls through it, looking pissed. "By whose definition is this music?"

Jo says, "Did you get any Muse? I love Muse."

"If I'd known you all had such crappy taste in songs, I would have brought more earplugs," I say. "Dissing my taste. Like Hendrix is even listenable. And Muse is something you do."

"Well, Disturbed," Jo says, "is something you are."

"And Godsmacked is something you get," Dancer says. "But hopefully not tonight."

"Don't you have any Mötley Crüe or Van Halen?" Lor says. "Maybe 'Girls, Girls, Girls'?"

"How about some Flogging Molly," Christian says. "Dani, my darling, how could you not like the 'Devil's Dance Floor'? And what about Zombie?"

"I got 'Dragula' and 'Living Dead Girl,' " I say defensively.

"Bloody hell, 'Living Dead Girl' is one of my favorites!" Christian says, and grabs the iPod from Lor and starts scrolling to it.

I snatch it and hold it behind my back. "Don't mess with my lineup. Nobody else thought to bring an iPod. That means I'm in charge."

Ryodan takes the iPod from me so fast it's there one sec, gone the next.

"Hey, give it back!"

He scrolls through the playlist. "What's the deal with all the Linkin Park, for fuck's sake."

"Dudes, we need noise. Quit taking the iPod off the

dock." Dancer snatches the iPod from Ryodan and puts it back on the dock. "And Mega has a crush on Chester."

"I do not!"

"Do too, Mega."

"He's like, old!"

"How old?" Christian says.

"Like at least thirty or something!"

Lor laughs. "Fucking ancient, ain't it, kid?"

"Dude," I agree. I like Lor.

"You got any Adele?" Jo says hopefully.

"Not a single song," I say happily. "Got some Nicki Minaj, though."

"Somebody kill me now," Ryodan says and closes his eyes.

Four hours later I'm getting a headache.

Six hours later I *am* a headache, my butt hurts, and I'm low on candy bars.

Eight hours later I'm sick of Nicki Minaj.

Nine hours later I'd give darn near anything for five fecking minutes of silence.

Me, Christian, and Dancer been passing around a bottle of aspirin and it's empty. I got earplugs in my pack but we can't use them because we might miss something and screw up.

Across the drive, way down at the other end of the abbey, the *sidhe*-seers are wrapped in blankets. Dozing. Because, like, the music down there isn't rattling the bone plates in their skull! I'm so jealous I could spit. Dejected, I eat another fecking candy bar. I hate candy bars.

"You said you were sure this would work," Jo says testily.

I'm beat. I haven't slept in days. I rub my eyes and say irritably, "We may have to stick with it for a while."

"Like, how long?" Christian says, and his voice is weirdly guttural. I look at him. He's staring down past the abbey at the *sidhe*-seers and the look on his face is pure, sex-starved Unseelie prince. Kaleidoscopic tattoos rush under his skin. His jeans are . . . wow. Okay. Don't look there.

I realize nine hours is probably the longest he's gone without sex in months. "Don't you be looking at my friends like that," I say. "They're off-limits to Unseelie princes, dude!"

He looks at me and I have to shift my gaze away fast. He's throwing off power like a volcano about to blow. I feel the wetness of blood on my cheeks from a bare glimpse at his eyes.

"How *long*?" he says hoarsely.

"Well, it only ever iced one of the clubs in Chester's. That must mean most music doesn't make whatever sound it's after. If you need to leave and find somebody to . . . you know, go. But try not to kill anybody, okay?"

He gives me a look. I'm not even *looking* at him and I can feel it.

"How is that even possible? We've been listening to some of the weirdest shit I've ever heard," Lor says pissily. "How can this thing *not* want to kill it? It should have been here hours ago! My head hurts. I don't get headaches."

"I'm not going anywhere until you're safe," Christian says to me, real quiet.

"Isn't that quaint. The chivalrous Unseelie prince with the dick of death," Ryodan mocks.

"I'll take that as a compliment," Christian says.

"I'm getting fecking sick of everybody picking on my music!" I say.

"Fine, then I'll just change it," Lor says.

"You touch my iPod, I'll break every one of your fingers!"

"Knock yourself out trying, honey." He scrolls to a new song.

I stick my fingers in my ears. "Gah, I hate Hendrix!"

"Then why do you have it on here?"

"I don't know! I just thought 'Purple Haze' was a cool title, then I listened to it and ain't had time to delete it. Who writes such stupid lyrics? ''Scuse me while I kiss this guy'?"

"Sky," Jo corrects.

"Huh? That don't make no sense either. What the feck is purple haze anyway?"

"She's going to delete Jimi," Lor says disbelievingly. "Sacrilege."

Dancer nudges the volume. Up.

"Traitor!"

"Sorry, Mega, but I have to agree with him on this one."

I look at Ryodan like I'm expecting him to help me out or something but he's just sitting there and I see that Jo's sort of snuggled into him under one of his big shoulders and his cuff is gleaming silver at her throat 'cause his arm is around her neck and it almost makes my head pop off and I don't even know why. Like he's a real person or something, with a girlfriend, instead of some savage beast that would pick his teeth with her bones if he felt like it, and she's falling for it and . . . Oh! I just can't even stand looking at them no more! "This ain't no fecking campfire and cuddle!" I say.

Ryodan gives me his vintage permanently amused look.

I'm so mad I stand up and turn away.

"Don't worry, Mega," Dancer says. "We baited the trap right. The monster *will* come."

He's right.

Just then it does.

Too bad it's not the one we wanted.

FORTY

"Is it the end, my friend?
Satan's coming 'round the bend"

The Crimson Hag explodes from the night, slicing through lavender lights on a cloud of putrefaction, tattered hem of her gut-gown snaking out behind her, to the bizarre accompaniment of "Purple Haze." She swoops us then shoots straight up to the highest dormer on the abbey roof and perches there.

We're all on our feet. "How did she find us?" I say. "You think noise draws *her*, too?"

She sways from side to side, moving only from the waist, creepily reptilian, surveying us with black empty holes where eyes should be.

"I think the bitch is after me," Christian says. "I'm the weakest Unseelie prince with immortal guts. At least for a while yet."

"She's like a bat, isn't she? It's not like we weren't making enough noise. She can't see so she uses echo-location!" I exclaim.

"Don't know, don't care. Let's bag the bitch," Christian says.

"How the fuck do we get past her legs," Ryodan says, and I look at him. I can see he's got a personal itch on to kill her.

I look at Jo when I say, "What? You don't feel like dying again today?"

Then Ryodan isn't standing next to Jo anymore. He's got me and he freeze-framed me twenty feet away before I could even blink. "If the Highlander says something to Jo about that, she'll think he's lying. She might believe you. My men will kill her if she knows. And I won't be able to stop them."

I look at him hard and realize for maybe the first time ever he's telling me a simple truth. "She's not allowed to know you can't be killed?"

"Never."

"Why am I?"

He's gone. Back to Jo. Got his arm around her, protecting her.

The Hag swoops!

It's like some weird rock-opera battle that gets even weirder when the next song Lor cued up comes on and Black Sabbath starts playing "Black Sabbath" at about a gazillion decibels. As if the Crimson Hag ain't disturbing enough, we need that freaky song in the background. Don't get me wrong, I put it on my playlist because sometimes I like to listen to it. But I got to be in a real mood, because, dude, the song makes me feel unsettled and disturbed and pretty much everybody I ever talked to feels the same way about it.

First thing on my mind is Dancer! I grab him and yell at him to hold on to me no matter what. When the Hag swoops us, we duck like we're one big wave then freeze-frame in different directions.

She veers at the last second toward Christian and I see he was right. It's him she wants. But when she just about nabs Lor with one of her bony lances, I realize she'll take anyone she can get those terrible knitting needles on.

We're all freeze-framing or sifting, ducking, and dodging. I'm trying to hold on to Dancer and keep an eye on Ryodan, who's got Jo, and it's making me nuts that she's even here, in the middle of this fight. She ain't got nothing special to protect her except Ryodan and that ain't enough for me.

I can't move fast enough, watch out for her, *and* hold on to Dancer, so I freeze-frame him to the far side of the abbey and dump him with the *sidhe*-seers.

"Mega, what are you *doing*?"

"You got no chance against her. I hardly do. Don't get me killed because I get stupid worrying about you!"

He snaps real cool, "Didn't mean to be a liability."

"Well you are, so don't be," I snap back. I'd die if something happened to him.

He shakes his head, disgusted, like he can't believe I'm such a traitor when I'm just trying to keep him safe.

"Take me back. Buy me time to rewire things. We can electrocute her with some of the stuff we brought, snake a live cable around her!"

"We don't even know if electrocution would work! Maybe she'd just suck it up and use it for fuel!"

"We don't know it won't!"

Me and him are nose-to-nose, yelling at each other.

Jo explodes from a blur and stumbles into us. "Hey!" she shouts at what I think is Ryodan's vanishing backside. "You can't just dump me here!"

"Don't you two fecking move!" I say.

Then I'm back down by the tower of sound equipment, where we're all whizzing around, trying to evade the bitch and figure out how to get past her bony lances!

Ozzy wails away. I ain't never heard this song through a hundred speakers and Black Sabbath this loud makes the hair on my arms stand up on end. I feel like I really am at a Black Mass and Aleister Crowley himself might spontaneously manifest. It's funny how songs can make you feel different ways. I wonder if whatever sound it is that the Hoar Frost King collects makes *him* feel something and that's why he goes after it.

As I zig and zag, I think about how the things that the Unseelie King created turned out so ugly and incomplete when the Seelie are so beautiful and whole.

And I start thinking how all the Unseelie are after *something*, and it seems to be whatever they don't have. Why would the Hoar Frost King be after sound? Things go totally silent when he appears. Because he takes the sound, or because his mere existence eradicates sounds?

Or is it more complex than that? What if the Hoar Frost King is after what *all* the Unseelie lack on the basest, most profound level? What if he's the only Unseelie smart enough to go straight for the root of the problem and, unlike the simpleminded Gray Woman who spends her life trying to collect beauty that can never be hers, or the Hag who's trying to finish a gown that can never be completed, the Hoar Frost King is trying to collect the song they were created without? Is it after the Song of Making? Eating chunks of it, bit by bit?

"Duck, you fucking idiot!" Lor roars, and I roll and freeze-frame. Then folks slam into me from opposite sides and just about squish me flat. I hear a couple of my ribs make protesting noises.

"Dudes, get off me!" Christian and Ryodan are both trying to get me out of there. "I lost focus for a couple secs 'cause I was thinking hard! It won't happen again!"

"You bet your ass it won't," Ryodan says.

Then I'm over a shoulder and wind is whizzing through my hair, then I'm being dumped in the sheep pen!

Me! The Mega! Put out to pasture!

"You can't stick me down here!" I say, indignant as all

get-out. I freeze-frame back toward the action the second I hit my feet but slam into Christian, who noodles me over a shoulder and tosses me back to Ryodan, who dumps me in the middle of the sheep pen again!

"Stop it!" My ribs hurt. They need to quit noodling me.

"Don't be a liability," Ryodan says, and is gone.

I blink.

"Feels real good, doesn't it, Mega?" Dancer gives me a chilly look.

"I ain't no liability!" I wait until they're all back down the other end then freeze-frame back to the action. I'm a fecking superhero. Superheroes don't sit on sidelines.

The Hag is trying to take out Christian.

And Lor and Ryodan ain't doing nothing to help him! In fact, I can't figure out what they *are* trying to do. They're working hard to stay on opposite sides of her, one front, one back, and they keep whizzing in, only to get blocked by one of those deadly legs lancing out. They retreat, whiz back in, get blocked, retreat, whiz back in, get blocked. It's a cool, methodical attack, and if they had all the time in the world, it might eventually work.

Might. Eventually.

And so what if it does? How do they plan to kill her? Doesn't look like the best-thought-out plan to me. I don't see no weapons on them.

The Hag shoots straight up and dive-bombs Christian. He stumbles on ice and goes down.

He sifts out then all the sudden he's right back where he was. Looking startled, like his sift didn't work the way it was supposed to.

That split-second screwup was all she needed.

The Hag's going to get him this time!

And nobody even cares. Nobody's trying to save him. Black Sabbath sounds more evil with each second, and it's all getting on my last nerve. I yank out my sword and throw it straight at the bitch's head. She hears it slicing through the air, veers sharply to the side and blasts into Lor, who goes flying backward.

Then suddenly she's gone!

My sword lodges in a snowbank. Already my hand hurts from the absence of it.

Christian looks from it to me, his alien, iridescent eyes bright. "You threw your sword for me." He looks stupefied.

I *feel* stupefied. I never let my sword go. Unlike Mac, I won't share in battle. Ever.

Ryodan has his head down, looking up at me from under his brows in a way I only ever seen him do once before, and Lor looks major pissed.

"Dude," I say, because I got no other clue what to say, "would you, like, toss it back now?"

Christian slides long black hair over his shoulder and flashes me a killer smile. "Princess, I'd build you a fucking White Mansion." My sword slices through the night, alabaster steel flashing violet fire.

"Where the fuck did the bloody bitch go?" Lor snarls. "I want a piece of her."

"No clue," I say, and we all look around warily.

That's when the *sidhe*-seers start screaming.

FORTY-ONE

"You must whip it, whip it good"

The Hag couldn't get anywhere with us so she went after weaker prey.

We all freeze-frame or sift. I'm the last one there.

When the feck did *I* become the slowpoke?

Two *sidhe*-seers die instantly, guts trailing up into the sky.

After a moment their entrails are dropped back to the snow in a wet glistening tangle.

My jaw locks and I get a muscle cramp in it the size of a walnut. My teeth clamp so hard they hurt.

The Hag isn't even knitting with them. She didn't even want them. She just killed and threw them away like trash!

She wants Christian. And it looks like she's ready to kill every last one of us to get him.

"Get inside!" I shout at the women, trying to herd them back toward the abbey.

Sidhe-seers duck and scatter like a herd of gazelles running from cheetahs. Stupid sheep are supposed to be pack animals and that means, duh, run in a pack!

The Hag swoops and takes two more of my sisters! Blood sprays everywhere and folks are screaming like crazy.

I'm so mad I'm shaking. It's total chaos. Before, it was just us we had to watch out for. Now the Hag is dive-bombing hundreds of helpless humans and I don't know who to help first.

Ryodan's covering Jo, Kat, and a dozen others.

Lor's protecting a bunch of pretty blondes—figures!

Christian has like fifty women around him. I realize he's turned on his death-by-sex Fae lure and it's working like magnet-to-magnets. He's got a second skin of pretty *sidhe*-seers. I wonder if he did it on purpose for a shield or if it's just taking everything he's got to stay out of her reach and he can't suppress it. If he did it for a shield, I'll kill him myself.

How are we going to kill the Hag? None of us can get close enough, past her lethal legs. Not even my sword is any good. I can throw it, but the bitch is faster than a witch on a quidditch broom! Dancer's idea of trying to snake a cable around her and electrocute her is starting to look like a good one. Too bad we don't have any cables handy down this end.

"Holy sonic booms!" I exclaim. I may not have a cable but I do have something that's long and thin, and Indiana Jones sure made good use of it in desperate times.

I yank out my whip, freeze-frame to the outer edge of the crowd for a good shot, and crack it straight up at the Hag!

It flails limply, puddles back down on my head and I get tangled up in it. I can't even get the stupid thing off me. I swear those black holes in her face regard me with amused contempt. Apparently there's some skill to cracking a whip and I don't have time to learn it. It never looked hard on TV.

"Mega!" Dancer yells. I see him in the crowd, jumping up, waving both hands in the air.

I ball it up, knot the cord around the handle for

weight, and toss it to him. He catches it, unties it and snaps it at the swooping Hag.

It explodes within a foot of her lethal left leg and sets off a small sonic boom.

She inhales, a horrific, wet, screeching sound, and rockets straight up into the sky. I don't know if it's because she can't believe something got so close to her leg or if her hearing is so sensitive that the sonar explosion gave her a migraine. Whatever—she doesn't like it one bit.

When she dives again, Dancer goes for her head this time and sets off a sonic boom right next to her ear.

She reels backward and vanishes upward into purple lights.

Me and Dancer beam at each other.

He cracks the whip triumphantly.

But this time it doesn't crack. It makes no sound at all. Not even a tiny little hiss as it slices through the air.

Because, like, all sound just disappeared.

Figures that when the fog finally rolls in, every last one of us is on the wrong end of the playing field.

FORTY-TWO

"Try to set the night on fire"

I think the reason I didn't feel panic preceding the Hoar Frost King's arrival this time is because I was already feeling too much panic for more panic to penetrate. The Crimson Hag butchering *sidhe*-seers had me so frantic, I forgot why we were even out in the snow to begin with.

Like, to summon the Hoar Frost King.

And he's here.

And somebody's got to cut that fecking tether because if we don't turn the IFP loose, the Hoar Frost King is going to ice the speakers and vanish and it'll all have been for nothing! Worse still, if it's as smart as I think, it won't fall for the same trick twice. The sentience I feel rolling off it is gigantic. This is no simpleminded Unseelie. I don't know 'cause I haven't seen them all yet but it could be the most complex one the king ever made. I wonder if he maybe swirled a dash of himself into its beaker.

What happens next feels like it happens in slow-mo though I know it doesn't take any time at all.

Ryodan and Lor vanish, fast-mo-ing it to the other end of the field. I look from the *sidhe*-seers to the slit that's opening, stymied, trying to figure out how to protect the *sidhe*-seers *and* cut the tether at the same time.

Do I save the women I care about who are standing right next to me or do I save the world? I may be a superhero but I got everyday-Joe feelings.

I see Christian and he's looking at me hard. He says without making any sound at all, *You can't do both, Dani, my love.*

I know that, I mouth pissily.

It's me she's after.

Your point?

He vanishes.

I can't find him anywhere for a sec.

Next thing I see is him standing, just standing there in the middle of the field between me and the other end, with his arms spread wide, head tossed back, wearing a "come and get me" expression.

What are you doing? I scream, but not a peep comes out.

The Crimson Hag swoops.

I jerk violently, like I'm the one that got stuck when she guts him.

She doesn't flay him, though. She pierces him with one leg like he's a shish kebab and draws him up toward her skirt. As she folds him into her dripping embrace he gives me a look. I can't make sense of it. I don't get it. Why did he do that? I don't get it! Why would anybody *do* such a stupid thing!

As he vanishes up into the sky, clutched in her hideous legs, I shut it out. Refuse to process what he did. I can leave the *sidhe*-seers behind now in relative safety. I'll think about what he did later.

Assuming there is a later.

I freeze-frame toward the Hoar Frost King. It's major weird not being able to hear a sound. I'm not feeling any vibrations either. At least deaf people can feel vibrations.

This is worse than a sound deprivation chamber, it's a sensory deprivation world with the HFK in it.

As I get close, I see Lor and Ryodan are pushing toward the black box in what looks like slow-mo. Both of them are covered with thick white ice that keeps cracking when they move. It's cold like the night I died at the church.

The Hoar Frost King is hovering silently over the mountain of speakers, icing them one by one. It's lingering longer than usual, I guess all those decibels make the food source richer, and I think maybe it's licking chocolate off its fingers.

When I freeze-frame in behind Ryodan he turns and roars silently: *Get the fuck out of here!*

Icy needles spear my lungs with each breath, my heart labors to pump. My head feels heavy and I realize it's 'cause my hair has iced. I toss it, and the stuff shatters, white crystals rain from my head.

You're not going to make it in time! I yell back, eyeing the distance between ice monster and IFP. When it opened its slit and glided into our dimension, it appeared in the worst possible place—between the IFP and speakers, not between the speakers and the abbey. Although it didn't ice the IFP, it's too fecking cold in the vicinity of the box for us to get there to cut the tether.

I look at Ryodan. He can survive this cold like I can't. I don't know why. Guess it's something to do with him surviving a gutting, too. He's always been able to get closer to the iced scenes than me.

But I can freeze-frame in faster for some reason. He gets bogged down when he gets closer to the center of the cold. Like he's trudging through concrete.

I don't pause to think. It's possible, it's the only plan I got, and there ain't no time for second guesses.

I blast into Ryodan's back and force him forward. As we go fast-mo-ing toward the black box, he totally gets my wavelength: I'm his locomotive and he's my shield. I can push us, but he's got to steer and slice.

I feel him yanking my sword from my coat and drive us forward. He ices, and cracks a half-dozen times, shaking off the crystals like a dog shaking water. I die a thousand icy deaths and come to life again. My lungs feel bloody and raw with each breath so I hold it. My bones hurt. I swear my eyeballs have iced in my head. My vision is getting all fractal-like.

Still I push us into the pain because this is *my* world and no fecking Fae is taking it from me. My mouth is open on a silent howl. Ryodan shakes violently as I force us to the icy epicenter.

He slices down with the sword and cuts the tether.

We're expecting the IFP to move real slow.

Based on the rate of movement Kat documented when the *sidhe*-seers had been tracking its progress toward our home, it takes about a minute between cutting it loose and the fire-world fragment hitting the far wall of the abbey. Giving us plenty of time to retether it, because according to her figures, we really had at least *two* minutes.

Her figures were wrong. Way the feck wrong.

Like a redlined supercar with stockpiled torque, the IFP explodes free and smashes into the Hoar Frost King.

I fast-up as fast as I can go so things transpire in the slowest motion possible.

The fire-world fragment swallows the Hoar Frost King.

It engulfs it.

Sound returns.

I hear ragged breaths. Gasping. Somewhere, folks are crying.

It's gone.

The Hoar Frost King is gone.

Just like that.

It worked so well I almost can't believe it. I stand there stunned, feeling wary. I'm not the only one out of sorts. Ryodan's got his eyes narrowed suspiciously. Lor is kind of hunched like he thinks the sky is going to fall on him. I'd snicker—because, dude, it's pretty sad when you can't just take a happy ending for what it is—but we still got major trubs. The IFP is devouring the mountain of iced speakers and heading straight for the abbey.

Kat, Dancer, and the other *sidhe*-seers are running toward us. "Cruce is below the abbey!" Kat screams. "You've got to stop it!"

Ryodan and Lor begin chanting but I can tell from the look on Ryodan's face he's got no expectation of finishing in time. The ten or twelve seconds we got before it hits the wall isn't the thirty he needs to do the job.

Kat starts screaming at Ryodan because he's not going fast enough, and Jo starts screaming at Kat for screaming at Ryodan because he's doing everything he can. Then all the *sidhe*-seers get in on it, and since Ryodan and Lor are looking down at the totem cord they're trying to ward, nobody's looking at the IFP and I'm the first one to see what's happening.

I *knew* it died too easily!

Ice is forming at the base of the fire-world fragment.

The bottom of the funnel is turning blue, crusted with white hoarfrost.

The IFP sure swallowed the Ice Monster, but now the Ice Monster is icing the fecking IFP!

As I watch, frost spreads rapidly upward.

"Uh, guys," I say.

"Are you bloody kidding me?" Dancer explodes. "It's coming back *out*?"

Lor looks up. "Aw, shit."

"Motherfucker," Ryodan agrees.

* * *

The Hoar Frost King freezes the IFP from the inside out.

I don't know if the fire world is a roaring inferno that makes the sound the HFK likes to eat or if they just had a big battle of fire and ice, and ice won.

But the IFP cracks and hisses, steams and pops, as superfire gets supercooled.

Ice weighs it down and it slows to a stop. As the giant funnel gains substance, it becomes too heavy to drift and crashes thunderously to the ground like an icicle dropping from a gutter, lodging in the snow.

We all just stare at the giant ice funnel rooted in the ground, trying to process the sudden reversal of events. First, the Ice Monster was dead but the abbey was in danger. Now the abbey is safe but the Ice Monster isn't dead.

We didn't succeed in killing it, and virtually everyone standing here that can't freeze-frame is going to die the instant it comes back out.

The walls of the IFP begin to shiver and shake like the Hoar Frost King is trying to find the weakest point to hatch from its icy eggshell.

I narrow my eyes.

Eggshells are delicate. Fragile. But it's not a shell. In fact, the entire interior of the fire world must be *solid ice* right now.

Which means, at the moment, the Hoar Frost King is completely encased in one of its own ice sculptures.

Trapped in a moment of perfect vulnerability.

Perhaps the only moment of vulnerability it has ever known.

I know what happens when an iced scene gets vibrated.

It explodes.

"Dancer," I shout, "use the whip! Make sonic booms!"

To Ryodan and Lor I say, "Freeze-frame around it!" To the *sidhe*-seers, "Dudes, get the feck out of here now!"

Then I freeze-frame in myself, moving as fast as I can on a nearly empty gas tank.

Dancer cracks his whip and we freeze-frame like maniacs.

The frozen IFP trembles and the surface suddenly blossoms a million tiny fissures.

The ground shudders, then there's this rumble like galaxywide thunder rolling inside the IFP.

All the sudden I hear the most awful noise ever, like maybe all the sounds the Hoar Frost King ever collected erupt in one huge dissonant, fingernails-on-a-chalkboard belch and then—fecking-A, I love being a superhero!— just like I thought they would, the fused monsters explode!

FORTY-THREE

"Celebrate good times, come on!"

I'm glowing. There's no denying it. Beaming from every pore. I never had such an amazing adventure in my whole entire life, and I've had some whoppers.

We're hanging in the great room at the abbey, warming up in front of fires blazing on three sides. There's a kettle of instant cocoa (mixed with water, not milk) being warmed in the main hearth, smelling up the room like a chocolate factory, and Kat broke out a hidden stash of—stale, but who cares?—marshmallows and a tin of hard-as-a-rock biscuits she's been saving for a special occasion, and some scrumptious, weirdly gelatinous honey. It all tastes like heaven. Every time I eat, I'm acutely aware we might not have any more of this stuff soon.

We won! We engaged in battle against the biggest bad I ever seen and we won. Unlike the last big battle fought around these parts, I was there to see it all go down with my very own eyeballs. I didn't have to hear about it the next day secondhand from folks that were lucky enough to be there. And no all-powerful Unseelie King swooped in and bailed us out at the last sec either. We did it ourselves!

When the IFP holding the Hoar Frost King exploded,

splinters of ice went sky-high, ground-low, and every place in between. We all ducked and dodged and grabbed someone slower, freeze-framing for the shelter of the abbey. Still, we're a pretty ragtag lot, all beat up with scrapes and cuts and bruises. There was no avoiding the fallout.

We waited inside until it was quiet for a few secs and it seemed the debris had settled, then headed back out to poke around in the chunks and convince ourselves the threats were really gone. Dancer studied the stuff for a good five minutes before flashing me a grin and pronouncing the debris inert. He plans to take samples back to Trinity's labs but he said he was ninety-eight percent certain nothing was going to rise up from the remains.

"How did you know it would work?" Jo says to me.

"I didn't," I say around a mouthful of sticky honey-slathered biscuit. I lick crumbs off my fingers. "But once I saw the Hoar Frost King was icing the fire world from the inside, I realized it was stuck in one of its own frozen scenes, like a bug in amber. And every time Ryodan and me ever freeze-framed near a frozen scene, it exploded into shrapnel-sized slivers." I shrug. "Who knows? Maybe it would have stayed stuck in there and exploded all by itself in time. But I sure thought it looked like it was coming back out."

"I thought so, too," Lor says, and everybody agrees with him.

"Bloody brilliant about the whip, Mega," Dancer says.

I preen.

"It was close. We got lucky," Kat says.

"Lucky, my ass! You got superheroes on the job!" Part of superheroness is precision timing and delicate maneuvering, and if she wants to pretend it's luck, I'm not going to waste breath I could be using to eat arguing.

"Today, Lady Luck had a name." Ryodan looks at me.

"No shit," Lor says. "Nice work, honey."

I just about lose my biscuits then. I glow so hard it almost hurts. I think my skin is leaking light.

I swagger over to the hearth and gulp three marshmallows in quick succession.

"Can you believe what that Unseelie prince did?" goth-chick Josie says.

I choke on the last marshmallow I'm trying to swallow whole. I kick up into fast-mo and try to fast-cough it out but it doesn't work. Belatedly it occurs to me fast-mo might not have been the brightest move. Friction and mucus expand the confection like a waterlogged tampon. It swells in my throat and shuts down my airway.

I thump myself on the chest with a fist. Doesn't help. I'm about to give myself the Heimlich over the back of a chair when Lor pounds the center of my back and the marshmallow splats out onto the coat of arms above the fireplace.

"Dude, no need to shove," Dancer says. "I give her the Heimlich all the time. She doesn't chew when she eats."

I turn around and Dancer's picking himself off the floor, looking irked. And tired. I wonder when he last slept. I forget he's not superpowered like the rest of us just because he's got a superbrain.

"Clean it up, Dani," Kat says. "It'll bake onto the medallion."

I grab a napkin off the biscuit tray, not feeling so cocky anymore. There were casualties. I'd managed to let myself forget that for a sec. "Christian sacrificed himself because I couldn't make up my mind."

"An Unseelie prince sacrificed himself," Kat echoes, like she has no clue what to make of it.

I don't either. Why did he give himself up just to make

my decision easier? I would have made a decision in another sec or two. We would have lost a lot more *sidhe*-seers to the Crimson Hag. Was it his way of proving he wasn't full Unseelie yet? Maybe he was trying to make up for killing the woman he had sex with, or it was his idea of another wedding present.

"It's pretty clear he's obsessed with you, honey," Lor says.

"*Was* obsessed," Ryodan says. "The Hag took him out. Saved me the trouble and good fucking riddance."

Now I have double the reason to track down the bitch and kill her. I have to free Christian so we can be even and call it quits between us. "We lost *sidhe*-seers," I say. "One of them was Tanty Nana. She was too old. She should never have been out there to begin with."

We're all quiet a sec, thinking about her and the others that died.

Then Ryodan stands up and says to me, "Come on, kid. Let's go."

"Huh? Where?"

"You live with me now."

"Bull-fecking-crikey!"

"She's moving back into the abbey," Kat says.

"Bull-fecking-crikey!"

"The Mega can take care of herself," Dancer says. "If you bloody idiots didn't just see that, you're blind. Give her room to breathe."

"Fecking crikey!" I agree totally. I adore Dancer. I shoot him a look that doesn't bother trying to pretend otherwise.

Ryodan says, "She needs rules."

Lor says, "Boss, all she needs is somebody to train with, vent some of that boundless fucking energy."

Kat says, "What she *needs* is—"

While they're all busy discussing my needs that they don't know the first fecking thing about, I make like the wind and blow out, sure to bang the door loud on the way.

I steal Ryodan's Humvee and head for the city.

He'll never catch me in one of the buses or big trucks that are the only other vehicles at the abbey.

I wish I could have brought Dancer with me but I never would have escaped if I'd slowed myself down.

Ain't nobody knows what I need better than me. They're probably all back there, still bickering, trying to decide how to control me and run my life.

I snicker. "Dudes. Never. Going. To. Happen."

FORTY-FOUR

---

*"This is not the end,
this is not the beginning"*

So I'm blowing through the streets of Dublin after ditching the Humvee on the main road where Ryodan or one of his dudes is sure to spot it on their way back to Chester's because no matter how bugfuck he makes me, I got no desire to take something of his permanent-like. He'd probably hunt me for-fecking-ever, instead of just trying to boss me around for-fecking-ever. That dude's radar is something I don't want to be any bigger on.

Live at Chester's, my fecking petunia!

"Ass," I mutter with a scowl. Petunia is one of Mac's words. Her and Alina grew up so stupid and sweet they never even said "feck" until their early twenties when they started seeing Fae. Up till then they had their own cute little vocabulary for things. I hate cute. I hate thinking about Mac. I remember seeing her for the first time, sitting on a bench at Trinity looking all soft and pretty and useless, then finding out she was really made of steel like me and my sword. I remember feeling like my world was finally going to change and bygones might somehow miraculously turn into never-fecking-have-beens.

I miss her. I hate knowing she's in this city somewhere, walking up and down streets just like me, thinking thoughts about killing Fae and saving the world and killing me, and she's on one street and I'm on another and those streets can never meet or one of us is dead.

After how great my day was I can't believe I'm thinking broody thoughts. I hurry through Temple Bar, dodging cars and streetlamps and all kinds of stuff half buried in piles of ice-crusted snow. Now that the Hoar Frost King is gone, the snow should start melting. I couldn't be more ready for summer! I don't tan. I freckle. Dancer likes freckles.

"Summer," I say, grinning. It can't come fast enough! They'll plant gardens at the abbey, grow a mixed veggie medley like the one I had at Chester's. I'll definitely be dropping by more once stuff starts growing! I can load myself down with bars and take a few long freeze-framing trips around Ireland, looking for cows or goats or sheep. Maybe even pigs. "Fecking-A, bacon!" My mouth waters just thinking about it.

Right now I got a ton of stuff to do, and getting around in all this snow is tedious. I can't freeze-frame for long because I have to keep dropping down and re-plot my mental grid. There are too many drifts and piles of ice that weren't there yesterday. Every time I drop down I just about freeze my fingers and toes off. It's night, a wicked breeze is blowing in off the ocean, and I swear it's twenty below with the windchill.

I snap my grid into place, whiz a quarter of a block, stop, replan. Freeze-frame forty feet, turn the corner on a slide, smash into a drift, roll, and remap while sliding some more. I slam into the side of a building and my breath frosts the air in a sharp white gasp. I curse and rub my side. I'm going to be one big bruise tomorrow.

First up on my list of things to do is get a new *Dani Daily* out there *before* We-don't-really-fecking-Care does and totally skews the news. Folks need to know all the scoop: that the villain icing peeps is dead, they can start making noise again, the snow *is* going to melt, and even though it don't look like it right now, summer *is* going to come. They need to know I got my sword back and ain't defenseless anymore. I'm back on my beat 24/7, watching over things and hunting the Crimson Hag, who's going to bite the dust as soon as I can figure how to kill her and get Christian back.

Tomorrow I'll cruise around Dublin slow-mo Joe style, listening for survivors over the crunch of snow and taking them in for food and shelter, which means Ryodan is about to get a lot more folks at Chester's. Our city just keeps getting hammered with walls falling and riots happening, food getting stolen and stockpiled, and now this killing winter in spring. I'm thinking we better get used to things never being predictable again. I suspect we'll lose a lot more folks before the tide starts to turn. Change is hard for most people. Not me. I love re-creating myself. Change means you get to choose again. Become something new. Unless you're dead like Alina. Then you never get to choose again. That's why I'm going to make Ryodan give me whatever secret he's got so I can live forever.

I ease back down into slow-mo to skirt a mound of ice-crusted snow. I'm standing there, starting to get all broody again thinking about all the ghosts I see in these streets sometimes, when I feel the tip of something sharp and pointy in my back.

"Drop your sword, Dani," Mac says, real soft-like behind me.

"Yeah, right. Like I'm actually falling for this." I snicker. Me and my overactive imagination. Like Mac would actually be able to sneak up behind me without my superhearing tipping me off. Like she would ever walk around at night with no MacHalo on. I got mine on and I know exactly how bright it is. If she was standing behind me, we'd be making double the light I'm throwing.

I freeze-frame.

Or try to.

Nothing happens. Just like those two times with Ryodan when all the sudden I just didn't have any juice. No gas in the tank, no engine in the train.

I squeeze my eyes shut hard and try again.

Still standing there.

Still feeling the tip of a spear in my back.

"I said 'drop your fucking sword,'" Mac says.

Mac and Barrons are back with a vengeance
in the seventh novel in the blockbuster Fever series
from #1 *New York Times* bestselling sensation
Karen Marie Moning

BURNED

Coming in 2014

Read on for a sneak peek

"Ms. Lane."

Barrons's voice is deep, touched with that strange Old World accent and mildly pissed off. Jericho Barrons is often mildly pissed off. I think he crawled from the swamp that way, chafed either by some condition in it, out of it, or maybe just by the general mass incompetence he encountered in both places. He's the most controlled, capable man I've ever known.

After all we've been through together, he still calls me Ms. Lane, with one exception: When I'm in his bed. Or on the floor, or some other place where I've temporarily lost my mind and become convinced I can't breathe without him inside me that very instant. Then the things he calls me are varied and nobody's business but mine.

I reply: "Barrons," without inflection. I've learned a few things in our time together. Distance is frequently the only intimacy he'll tolerate. Suits me. I've got my own demons. Besides, I don't believe good relationships come from living inside each other's pockets. I believe divorce comes from that.

I admire the animal grace with which he enters the room and moves toward me. He prefers dark colors, the better to slide in and out of the night, or a room, unnoticed except for whatever he's left behind that you may or may not discover for some time, like, say a tattoo on the back of one's skull.

"What are you doing?"

"Reading," I say nonchalantly, rubbing the tattoo on the back of my skull. I angle the volume so he can't see the cover. If he sees what I'm reading, he'll know I'm looking for something. If he realizes how bad it's gotten, and what I'm thinking about doing, he'll try to stop me.

He circles behind me, looks over my shoulder at the thick vellum of the ancient manuscript. "In the first tongue?"

"Is that what it is?" I feign innocence.

He knows precisely which cells in my body are innocent and which are thoroughly corrupted. He's responsible for most of the corrupted ones. One corner of his mouth ticks up and I see the glint of beast behind his eyes, a feral crimson backlight, bloodstaining the whites.

It turns me on. Barrons makes me feel violently, electrically sexual and alive. I'd march into hell beside him.

But I will not let him march into hell beside me. And there's no doubt that's where I'm going.

I thought I was strong, a heroine. I thought I was the victor. The enemy got inside my head and tried to seduce me with lies.

It's easy to walk away from lies.

Power is another thing.

Temptation isn't a sin that you triumph over once, completely, and then you're free. Temptation slips into bed with you each night and helps you say your prayers.

It wakes you in the morning with a friendly cup of coffee, and knows exactly how you take it.

He skirts the Chesterfield sofa and stands over me. "Looking for something, Ms. Lane?"

I'm eye level with his belt but that's not where my gaze gets stuck and suddenly my mouth is so dry I can hardly swallow and I know I'm going to want to. I'm Pri-ya for this man. I hate it. I love it. I can't escape it.

I reach for his belt buckle. The manuscript slides from my lap, forgotten. Along with everything else but this moment, this man. "I just found it," I tell him.